SUNA & ZAYN :

AF435204

SUNA & ZAYN :

First Pillar

—

Creation

Max DUBRET

Copyright © 2025 Max DUBRET

All rights reserved.

ISBN : 979-10-976871-1-3

Legal deposit: 05/2025

N° : 10000001158536

INPI Protection

National number: DSO2025004133

« The beauty of the world lies in the magic of what we do not yet understand. »

Edmond Rostand

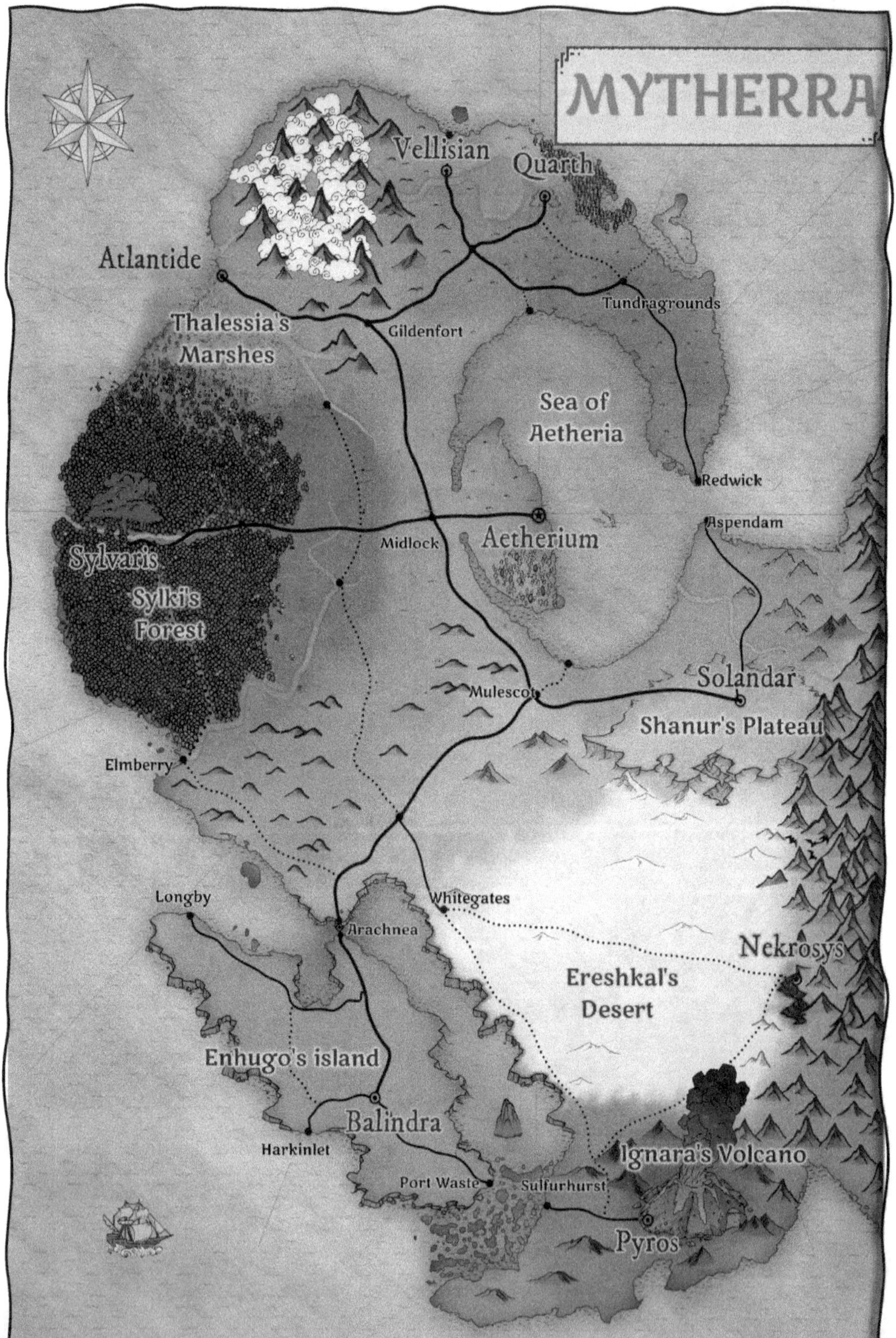

MYTHERRA
Vellisian
Quarth
Atlantide
Thalessia's Marshes
Gildenfort
Tundragrounds
Sea of Aetheria
Redwick
Aspendam
Sylvaris
Sylki's Forest
Midlock
Aetherium
Elmberry
Mulescot
Solandar
Shanur's Plateau
Longby
Whitegates
Arachnea
Nekrosys
Ereshkal's Desert
Enhugo's island
Balindra
Harkinlet
Port Waste
Sulfurhurst
Ignara's Volcano
Pyros

Contents :

Prologue

Ætheris is the entity from which all magic originates.

To protect magical beings from humans and their destructive nature, Ætheris shaped an entirely new world resembling Earth, which she named Mytherra. This world evolved far from human conflicts and untouched by technological advancement. Mytherra thus became a sanctuary, where magic and nature could flourish freely, away from human greed.

But this creation came at a cost: the colossal effort required to create Mytherra deeply exhausted Ætheris, draining much of her energy. Since then, Ætheris has gradually weakened, and with her, magic itself has begun to decline. As Mytherra edges toward disappearance, some see an opportunity emerging…

On Mytherra: In the solemn silence of a Roman temple, a black silhouette slips among the shadows of the columns. The woman, Ereshkal, pauses in front of a majestic statue. The artwork depicts an androgynous figure made of pure energy—a blend of light and shadow: Ætheris.

Ereshkal lingers before the statue, an unreadable glint passing through her eyes. She circles around it and halts, listening carefully for the slightest sound.

No one.

She closes her eyes briefly, focusing. A whisper rises: ancient, forgotten words. Luminous fragments, like stardust, surge between her hands. They trace symbols forming a circle before her.

Gradually, the symbols begin to spin, faster and faster, until they shape a ring larger than the woman herself. At its center, a crack emerges, resembling fractured glass threaded with thin lines.

The light intensifies; the center shatters into a shower of fragments, revealing an entirely different landscape. It's a gateway to Earth that Ereshkal has just opened. She regards the portal with satisfaction. After a brief glance around, she steps forward and crosses through it.

On Earth: Ereshkal emerges in a cemetery.

The air is heavy; the cold glow of a modern city envelops the tombstones. With measured steps, she advances along the pathway, quickly spotting what she came for.

A bit further away, a young man crouches before a grave. She approaches him.

The boy, Zayn, remains motionless, his arms wrapped tightly around himself as if to contain a pain too sharp to bear. Tears stream down his cheeks.

"Have you lost someone?" she asks gently.

The boy startles, pulled from his thoughts, and lifts his head toward the stranger. His reddened eyes betray sadness, fear, and suspicion. He struggles to speak, his throat tight.

"My mother…" he murmurs, indicating the grave before him. "She was all I had."

Zayn immediately lowers his gaze, embarrassed to have exposed his vulnerability to a stranger. He feels as if his whole world is collapsing around him. Without his mother, he's utterly lost—robbed of his anchor, robbed of his life.

The woman kneels gently beside him. She is beautiful, appearing compassionate, with a faint smile illuminating her face.

"My name is Ereshkal," she introduces herself, "and I can bring your mother back to you."

Zayn raises his eyes, startled, as if he hadn't heard properly. He quickly wipes his cheeks, uncomfortable at being caught crying.

"What?!" he chokes out. "That's impossible…"

"I come from a place very far away," she calmly explains, "where magic still exists. Things like this are possible there. If you agree to help me, I promise you'll see her again."

Zayn's face hardens, his jaw clenching. Anger rises within him, fueled by his raw pain. *Why should I believe something like that?* he wonders, annoyed at having briefly felt a hope he considers absurd.

"Magic. You're messing with me, right?" he retorts irritably.

Without answering, Ereshkal scans their surroundings. She notices a small, lifeless bird on the ground and carefully picks it up.

"Watch," she says, "I'll show you."

She brings the bird to her lips and softly blows on its fragile body. The creature trembles slightly, then its eyes open. Under Zayn's astonished gaze, it rises, spreads its wings, and launches into the air.

Zayn remains frozen, breathless. Fascination and confusion cross his face. *Impossible…* he thinks, unable to tear his eyes from the bird.

The animal lands on a nearby branch and calmly observes them.

"How… how did you do that…?" Zayn stammers.

"My magic," Ereshkal replies simply. "But for your mother, I'm not yet strong enough. With your help, I could be."

The promise echoes in Zayn's mind, stirring both hope and suspicion.

"Help me," Ereshkal continues, "and I'll bring your mother back."

The boy's hands start to tremble. Part of him desperately wants to believe in this miracle, but the fear of disappointment is powerful. He hesitates, searching Ereshkal's calm gaze for a sign that might dispel his doubts.

"If I help you… you'll bring my mother back?" he eventually murmurs, cautious yet drawn to her promise.

Ereshkal gently nods. Zayn remains silent for a long moment, lost in thought. A part of him still refuses to believe it, but how could he turn away from such an offer after what he just witnessed?

Finally, he nods.

"All right," he says after a slight hesitation. "My name's Zayn, by the way."

She smiles warmly.

"Nice to meet you, Zayn. Come with me."

Ereshkal leads him toward another alley, where the portal still glows. Instinctively, Zayn steps back from the dazzling passageway. She turns to him, smiling.

"It's a doorway to my world," she says reassuringly. "Come, you have nothing to fear."

She then steps beneath the radiant arch and patiently holds out her hand. Zayn hesitates, awestruck. He casts one last glance toward his mother's grave, feeling a painful tightness in his chest.

Yet, what truly remains for him here? Without her, he has no anchor, no reason to stay. He has nothing left to lose.

And this promise… too tempting to ignore.

He takes a deep breath and grasps her outstretched hand.

Together, they pass through the portal.

Behind them, in the silence of the cemetery, the bird—like a puppet whose strings have suddenly been cut—falls lifelessly from its branch.

5

1 — Suna — An arrival unforeseen

The end-of-day bell rang out, drawing a sigh of relief from Suna. She quickly gathered her things. The day was finally over.

She found high school suffocating, a heavy mix of responsibilities and teenage drama she struggled to escape from.

"See you tomorrow!" she called to her classmates as she walked away.

Her footsteps echoed softly on the pavement as she moved along familiar streets.

The coolness of late afternoon brushed against her skin.

She crossed her arms over her oversized sweater.

Her usual route took her past an old cemetery—a place she found soothing. Century-old trees cast comforting shadows there.

As she entered the main path, she noticed a familiar figure: Zayn.

He was a boy from her class, recently struck by the loss of his only parent.

"Zayn?" she whispered to herself, intrigued by the tension radiating from him.

He was speaking to a woman whose features were hard to distinguish against the light. She wore long, dark clothing with peculiar lines.

Suna slowed her pace, uncertain. The stranger spoke to him quietly. He nodded, shoulders tense, before they moved away together. Curious, Suna followed them with her eyes. They took a parallel row lined with tombstones and statues worn by time.

She saw them pass behind a tomb, then nothing.

Intrigued, she approached to investigate. When she reached the spot, they had completely vanished.

That's when she saw it: a circle of light floating in the air, etched with shifting patterns. Its edges glowed gently, as if breathing. Fascinated, she cautiously stepped closer. A gentle breeze escaped from it, brushing her face. On the other side, she saw the interior of a large room. Like an open door to another world.

She hesitated. Her instinct told her to turn back, but her classmate must have gone through there. Curiosity, stronger than fear, won out. Suna reached out a trembling hand and touched the circle. It felt strange, like plunging her hand into warm water. Taking a deep breath, she closed her eyes and stepped through.

When she opened her eyes again, Suna found herself in the room she had glimpsed through the portal, just behind a colossal statue. She stepped around it and discovered an immense hall resembling the interior of a Roman temple. Marble walls reflected the glow from a few braziers lined up on either side of the chamber.

"Zayn?" she called hesitantly.

No answer.

Suna approached the sculpture, her footsteps echoing through what seemed to be a sanctuary.

The very substance of the statue was astonishing. Its surface shifted and moved. At times, it radiated brightness, evoking golden and silver reflections on its skin, while at other moments, profound darkness flowed across it. This subtle interplay of light and shadow gave the sculpture a living quality.

The statue depicted someone seated cross-legged with immutable grace. Its eyes were closed, its hands gently cupped and resting together in front. Its figure was androgynous and strikingly beautiful.

Directly in front of the statue, on a pedestal, stood a pyramidal stand and a finely engraved stele. The symbols adorning the latter vibrated with subtle energy, pulsing faintly like a heartbeat. Their glow responded to her presence, quickening as she drew nearer. Suna felt each pulse of the stone resonate within her. Their gentle, rhythmic illumination ignited a burning curiosity inside her.

Suna touched her fingers to the surprisingly warm surface of the stele. An intense light flooded the room. Words appeared, floating at eye level.

"The Four Pillars of Creation must be reunited here. Only a magician without magic can find them and restore balance."

The words glowed briefly before vanishing. Suna stepped back, breathless. The temple plunged once more into semi-darkness. She wrapped her arms around herself, seeking nonexistent comfort in this strange and unknown place.

A sound snapped her out of her thoughts. Slow, heavy footsteps echoed in the distance. Her heart raced. Someone was approaching.

Without thinking, she turned and ran back toward the place she had entered.

But the portal had vanished. Nothing remained. She spun around frantically, searching for an exit, a hiding place, but the chamber was empty, devoid of any visible opening.

The footsteps drew closer. Suna felt panic rising within her. Drawing a deep breath, she pressed herself against the base of the statue, trying to steady her breathing. If someone found her here, she had no idea what they might do.

"Who's there?" boomed a deep voice, echoing through the hall like thunder.

Suna swallowed hard, her legs trembling. She held her breath, hoping the darkness would be enough to conceal her.

"We heard you running! Show yourself!" another voice insisted, closer this time.

The footsteps now resonated very near. Each strike against the ground felt like a drumbeat in her chest. Panic gripped her. Hastily, she slipped around the statue, hoping to skirt the men and find an escape route. But in her hurry, she collided headlong into an imposing figure.

The impact sent her staggering back several steps. She stumbled, dazed, her breath knocked out of her. When she finally raised her eyes, her heart nearly stopped. The man before her had an impressive build and wore gleaming Roman armor. But what shocked her most were the two immense golden wings on his back. They fluttered slightly.

"What…" she stammered, the words caught in her throat.

Before she could retreat further, a strong grip seized her arm, causing sharp pain. A second man, wingless but just as imposing in his armor, now stood at her side.

"You don't belong here," he said sharply.

Panicking, Suna tried to pull away, but the man's grip remained firm. His severe gaze paralyzed her.

"I… I'm sorry, I don't know where I am… I got lost," she stuttered, terrified.

"Lost? How could anyone get 'lost' here? This place is inaccessible to outsiders."

He shook her, as if to force an answer.

"I... I saw a portal... and... and I went through it. I didn't know where it led," she tried to explain, her voice trembling.

The two men exchanged a glance, confusion and suspicion mixing on their faces. The man with golden wings narrowed his eyes.

"A portal? Here?" he muttered.

"I don't know! I swear!" Suna protested desperately. "It was just... there, in the cemetery."

The guard holding her raised an eyebrow, visibly puzzled.

"A... cemetery? What is she talking about?"

Suna opened her mouth in surprise. She hadn't anticipated this word causing trouble.

"A place where... where people bury their dead," she explained clumsily, searching for words. "With graves, engraved stones."

The guard exchanged a bewildered look with his companion, while the winged man appeared more attentive. He squinted, intrigued.

"No matter what she claims. It's not up to us to decide her fate," he concluded. "I'll inform the advisor; he'll know what to do."

He nodded to the guard, who immediately tightened his grip on her arm.

"Stay here. Don't move," he ordered before turning away.

Suna watched him go, his armor gleaming in the chamber's dim light.

"What are you going to do with me?" she pleaded.

He stared down at her briefly before responding.

"That will depend on your answers."

Silence fell again, heavy and oppressive. Suna felt her heart racing uncontrollably. She desperately sought an escape, but her guardian's grip left no room for hope.

Moments later, footsteps echoed once more. Another figure appeared behind the winged soldier. A man of average height, in his prime, with an angular face highlighted by prominent cheekbones. His fluid movements accentuated the charismatic aura emanating from him. His piercing blue-green eyes, however, betrayed a cold, calculating intelligence. Unlike the guards in imposing armor, he wore simple yet elegant clothing, complemented by a dark cloak trimmed with a delicate silver edging.

"Here is the intruder," said the guard, stepping forward.

The advisor approached, scrutinizing Suna with unsettling intensity. He examined every detail, from her unusual clothing to her terrified expression.

"You passed the guards and entered Ætheris's chamber," he murmured, almost to himself. "Fascinating."

He gestured, and the guard released her. Suna rubbed her aching arm and stepped back. She took a deep breath, using the brief moment to steady herself.

"I beg your pardon," she pleaded. "I didn't mean to disturb—"

"Silence," the advisor interrupted. "Tell me, girl, who are you and what are you doing here?"

Suna hesitated; facing this charismatic stranger, she felt vulnerable and defenseless.

"My name is Suna and I don't know… I got lost when I stepped through a circle of light and ended up here."

"She's been talking about strange things like that since we found her," one of the guards confirmed.

"I saw the stele in front of the statue glow," she finally replied, indicating the pedestal. "It reacted when I touched it. There was something written. But I didn't mean any harm, I swear!"

The advisor arched an eyebrow, the interest in his gaze intensifying.

"It glowed, you say? And what exactly did it say?"

Suna opened her mouth, but no sound came out. The words she sought slipped completely away, vanishing before she could speak them. For a moment, she stood silent, helpless.

"I... I don't know. It was... something about Pillars. Four Pillars of Creation. But I don't understand what it means," she added. "I won't tell anyone, I promise."

"Show me," the man commanded.

Suna, still accompanied by the guard, approached the stele. Once again, she brushed it lightly, and the words burst forth.

The advisor stared deeply into Suna's eyes. Then, he straightened and turned to the guards.

"Alert Raenos immediately. He must see this with his own eyes."

Suna felt her legs weaken. Who was Raenos? And what would happen to her now? The name, charged with authority, echoed threateningly in her mind. The guards departed to relay the message, leaving Suna alone with the advisor. She swallowed nervously, searching desperately for some way to grasp what was happening.

"I... I won't say anything," she stammered. "I just want to go home."

The advisor narrowed his eyes, carefully examining every nuance of her expression.

"I fear it's more complicated than that," he murmured. "If you are here, it is not by chance."

2 — Zayn — Into the shadows

Ereshkal cast one final glance toward Ætheris's chamber. Her dark eyes searched the shadows. Zayn, standing at her side, stared at the statue in fascination. He felt his heart beating faster. Where was he?

Ereshkal still held his hand—a gesture both protective and calculated.

"Come," she murmured softly. "We mustn't linger. If the guards find us, we'll be thrown straight into the dungeon—or worse."

She slipped out of the chamber, her steps silent upon the marble. Zayn followed. He scanned each shadow anxiously, his fear heightened by the tension he sensed in Ereshkal's movements. He wondered what awaited him.

In the temple corridors, Ereshkal avoided illuminated areas, staying close to the darkened walls. She knew it was crucial not to encounter any guards. Their presence might jeopardize her hold on Zayn, and she couldn't afford such a confrontation—not

When they emerged from the temple, the capital stretched before them. Ætheria, a majestic city, glowed under the twilight. It resembled a grand Roman city at the peak of its glory. Marble buildings reflected the last rays of the sun. Paved avenues were lined with elegant homes supported by countless columns. Everywhere, finely carved altars rose toward the sky, crowned by statues with heroic bearing.

Zayn blinked, overwhelmed. He struggled to absorb the city's wealth and vitality. The entire place was a living fresco of activity and color. Markets bustled with life: merchants' voices echoed beneath arcades, advertising delicate fabrics, colorful potion bottles, and intricately crafted jewelry. A vibrant hum, a symphony of sounds and fragrances filled the air, blending incense, spices, and sun-warmed stone.

As they passed through a busy square, his gaze met that of an extraordinary creature. Time seemed to pause. The animal appeared straight out of a dream or ancient legend. It had a dragon's head attached to a deer's body, covered in shimmering scales. Its fine, delicate hooves contrasted with its ox-like tail, swishing gently through the air behind it. Profound wisdom shone from its eyes.

"That's a Qilin," Ereshkal informed him. "You'll see others. Let's not linger."

Zayn wanted to stop and observe the creature longer, but Ereshkal had already quickened her pace.

They passed a bearded merchant waving a small vial under the noses of passersby, promising extraordinary longevity. He produced another, purportedly bringing unfailing luck. A bit farther along, fairies fluttered above market stalls, their translucent wings catching the fading sunlight. And there… a centaur, very real, strode confidently above the crowd.

Zayn opened his mouth but couldn't utter a sound. He no longer knew where to look. Ereshkal, indifferent to his astonishment, guided him along a broad avenue bordered by massive columns.

The passersby—a varied crowd composed of humans and other creatures—were engrossed in their own business. Near a fountain whose waters sparkled, a group of satyrs played a mesmerizing melody.

Their nimble fingers danced across lyres and strange wooden double flutes, the music blending harmoniously with the city's noises.

Further on, unusual children covered in leaves and twigs chased after a baby griffin, squealing with delight and flapping its tiny wings clumsily. At the entrance of a library, mages in brightly colored robes passionately debated, exchanging rolled parchments inscribed with glowing symbols.

As they moved away from the main avenues, the streets grew quieter but no less fascinating. Open forges cast sparks, illuminating the craftsmen's concentrated faces. Blackened by soot, smiths hammered metal with almost ritualistic precision.

Magical beings of every shape and size wandered casually among the humans, and no one seemed surprised. Zayn longed to speak, to question, to understand, but Ereshkal's firm grip on his hand hurried him ever onward.

The city's excitement, richness, and beauty mingled with a dizzying sense of unreality. Everything here exceeded his imagination, as if the dreams of his childhood were taking shape before his eyes.

Ereshkal led them toward another district of the city. Gradually, the atmosphere shifted. The lively shouts and laughter faded away. The streets narrowed; elegant, light-filled buildings gave way to austere structures of rough stone. The air grew colder, tinged with an indefinable metallic scent.

Zayn shivered. The smell reminded him of wet earth after a storm, yet somehow more disturbing, heavier, carrying an unsettling iron aftertaste. He moistened his lips, trying to understand the disquieting flavor that permeated the air.

Around him, the ambiance became oddly hushed. Passersby, dressed in black or drab colors, moved silently or whispered softly. Their quiet voices faded into the shadows of the alleys. Nothing here resembled the lively bustle of the city center.

A movement caught his attention. In the adjacent alleyway, a man was speaking to… something. Suspended a few feet above the ground floated a faceless form. It looked like a specter.

Zayn froze. He blinked once, twice—but the form dissolved into the darkness, extinguished like a blown-out flame. The alleyway was empty, as though nothing had ever been there.

They passed by a small shop nestled in a recess between two massive buildings. Beneath a flickering lantern, a hooded woman examined glass vials. In the flame's trembling light, reflections from the liquids inside danced as if possessing lives of their own.

Every corner of this part of the city exuded a troubling and unsettling atmosphere.

"This place is… strange," Zayn murmured uneasily.

Ereshkal smiled and inclined her head.

"It's different, yes. But you'll see, it has its charm."

Her voice was gentle, but Zayn wasn't sure he wanted to discover the "charm" of this place.

They turned into an even darker street, where only a few torches fixed to stone walls provided pale illumination. At last, they reached a large, smooth, onyx door.

Two colossal guards clad in dull armor straightened at their approach. Upon seeing Ereshkal, they bowed slightly, though their eyes lingered curiously on Zayn.

Ereshkal placed her hand on the door, pushing it open in one fluid motion. A deep rumbling echoed through the walls as the entrance swung open. She turned toward Zayn with a reassuring smile.

"Welcome to my home."

Her tone grew more enthusiastic.

"Don't worry. Here, we're safe."

But Zayn wasn't convinced. Far from comforting him, each step took him further away from everything familiar.

Inside, dim lighting emanated from suspended crystals, casting greenish reflections on the walls. The air here was cooler, infused with a mineral scent mingled with the faint aroma of burning wax. A stone table stood imposingly at the center of the room. Behind it, in the shadows, loomed an imposing figure.

The man was tall, his mere presence filling the space with an oppressive weight. Zayn could have sworn his armor absorbed the light rather than reflected it.

He stepped forward. His impressive stature was due in part to two large, black wings folded behind his back. His gaze glittered with cold intelligence.

"Mistress," he said in a deep voice, bowing slightly. "What can I do for you?"

Ereshkal placed a gentle hand on Zayn's back, a gesture at once protective and calculated to keep him from retreating.

"This is Zayn," she declared. "He comes from Earth."

She paused, her gaze shifting briefly between Thanatos and Zayn, as if measuring the impact of her words.

"I expect you to treat him courteously, Thanatos. As you know, he's here to help us. He is essential to our plans."

Uncomfortable, Zayn averted his eyes. Thanatos's presence was overwhelming, as if every movement he made were guided by relentless discipline.

"You can trust him, Zayn," Ereshkal reassured him. "Thanatos is loyal. He'll help you."

He wasn't certain he found any comfort in her words. Something about Thanatos filled him with deep unease.

A movement caught his attention. A woman had just entered the room, her steps barely audible.

She was of average height, slender, and moved with almost feline grace. Thick black hair framed her delicate, harmonious features before cascading lightly over her shoulders.

Her pale eyes, fringed with long lashes, had a hypnotic sparkle.

"Ah, Nymeris," Ereshkal said.

With a fluid gesture, she indicated Zayn.

"Watch over our guest for a moment. I need to speak with Thanatos."

Nymeris asked no questions. She merely nodded, her gaze sliding toward Zayn. Then, without a word, she extended her hand toward him.

Zayn hesitated for a fraction of a second before following her.

They crossed a narrow corridor, emerging into a more modest room, with smooth walls and a stone-tiled floor. On a stone counter rested a few utensils, metal cups, and a ceramic jug. It was a simple, austere kitchen, matching the rest of the sanctuary.

Nymeris turned toward him. Then, in a voice softer than he had anticipated, she asked:

"Are you hungry?"

Once the door closed behind Zayn, Ereshkal exhaled deeply, leaning against the stone table. Her breathing, normally controlled, was heavier than she would have liked.

Opening the portal had exhausted her far more than she cared to admit.

Briefly, she clenched her fists, concealing her discomfort before raising her eyes to Thanatos, still motionless in the shadows. He watched her impassively, his black wings folded like a bird of prey awaiting orders.

In a voice deeper than usual, she spoke:

"Thanatos, I entrust you with what comes next. We must be prepared for any eventuality."

"What are your orders?" His voice, calm and controlled, betrayed absolute discipline.

Ereshkal straightened her shoulders, regaining her commanding presence.

"As planned," she said, "I managed to open a portal to Earth… and found a human."

A flicker of satisfaction crossed her face.

"They remain as easily corrupted as ever."

She allowed a brief silence.

"But it cost me more energy than I anticipated," the woman continued. "I need to rest. In the meantime, you must continue in my stead."

Thanatos nodded without a word.

"Assemble a team with the other magicians," she instructed. "Retrieve the Pillars and bring them to me."

For the first time, Thanatos displayed an involuntary reaction—a slight tilt of his head, a subtle twitch of his wings.

"The other magicians?" he asked. "Do we not already have enough disciples?"

"No," she said firmly. "We need their support. And if they become troublesome… we will dispose of them."

She could already read Thanatos's mind: no further explanations were necessary.

Ereshkal slowly stood upright, placing her fingertips on the cold surface of the table.

"Start with Nerath," she said calmly. "He dreams only of battles and glory. His hunger for power and obsession with combat will make him an ideal pawn. Promise him what he desires most: a worthy war, a world to conquer, enemies to crush beneath his feet."

Thanatos nodded, allowing the shadow of a cold, satisfied smile to form on his lips.

"Next," she continued, "approach Thalessa."

"She is unstable," the dark angel pointed out.

An amused breath escaped Ereshkal's lips, a dangerous glint passing through her eyes.

"Precisely. Thalessa is impulsive and uncontrollable, like the oceans she commands. She hates being underestimated. Feed her insecurities and her need for recognition. Flatter her thirst for power. Make her believe our alliance will offer her prestige and authority beyond anything she has ever known. She will fall in line."

Thanatos nodded again.

"Lastly," said the woman, "seek Ignara's favor."

"Ignara will not be easily convinced," he murmured. "Her temperament is as unpredictable and fiery as the flames she commands."

"Indeed," Ereshkal agreed, "she is dangerous. But that destructive nature also makes her vulnerable to her own emotions. Offer her a challenge worthy of her talents, a compelling reason to unleash her devastating power. She will not resist the call of battle and the heat of action."

"Then," Thanatos understood, "we shall offer her what she desires—the chance to fully express her power."

"Exactly," Ereshkal confirmed. "Destruction always draws those who live for it. Ignara is formidable, but properly guided, she could become a powerful weapon in our favor. Ensure she sees our cause as an opportunity, and she will join us."

"I understand," Thanatos agreed. "I will handle it. Nothing will slip from our grasp."

Ereshkal stepped away from the table, folding her arms, her gaze momentarily distant.

"I am counting on you. With Ignara, Thalessa, and Nerath by our side, no force will be able to oppose us."

She took a slow breath, then added softly:

"We have much to lose… and even more to gain."

A silence stretched between them. Everything was in motion.

Finally, she indicated the door through which Zayn had departed.

"The boy must understand he has a vital role to play. Set aside whatever he makes you feel."

"I will do what it takes to ensure he follows us… willingly."

"Excellent. Prepare your departure. You leave tomorrow at dawn."

Without waiting for a reply, she left the room.

Ereshkal sat behind an imposing desk, carved from dark, ancient wood. Documents covered its surface, neatly arranged beneath the pale glow of crystals suspended from the ceiling.

She scanned the parchments, absorbed in her thoughts and the intricate plans she was weaving, when hurried footsteps disturbed the silence of the room.

Someone knocked briefly at the door.

"Enter," she commanded sharply, without even raising her eyes.

The door opened noiselessly, revealing a thin, hesitant man. He quickly stepped into the room and bowed respectfully, though his stance betrayed slight nervousness.

"My queen," he said in a hoarse voice, laced with anxiety, "I bring important news."

Ereshkal slowly raised her gaze, clearly irritated by the interruption, her icy stare piercing through him.

"Speak," she said coldly.

The spy swallowed discreetly but continued without hesitation.

"Another human… A young girl. She also passed through the portal."

Ereshkal's eyes widened, blazing with contained yet intense anger, as if a flame had ignited deep within them.

"A human followed us?" she articulated slowly, weighing each word with chilling calm. "And where is she now?"

"With Raenos," the messenger replied cautiously. "It seems… he has already begun preparations for the quest for the Pillars."

Ereshkal stood abruptly, her robes swirling dramatically, scattering several sheets of paper.

"Raenos… Of course," she spat angrily. "They must not awaken Ætheris. If she returns, everything I have worked for will be destroyed."

She fixed the man mercilessly while contemplating her next move.

"Very well. Return to your post," she dismissed him in a tone brooking no argument.

The spy bowed deeply.

"At your service, my queen," he answered submissively, before retreating and closing the door behind him.

As soon as he was gone, Ereshkal clenched her fists tightly, her face reflecting barely restrained fury. Her mind seethed, struggling to process this unexpected complication.

"Another human…" she murmured menacingly, her eyes glinting dangerously. "Very well. If she thinks she can stand against me, she will soon learn the price of defying my will."

Ereshkal slowly straightened, allowing her gaze to sweep one final time across the papers scattered on her desk. She adjusted her gown, then slipped silently toward the door, her footsteps soundless against the floor.

Before leaving, she turned her head toward a shadowed corner of the room.

"Watch that girl," she ordered. "Every move, every word. I want to know absolutely everything."

A man concealed in the darkness bowed. He was dressed in a black cloak that rendered him invisible in the shadows. He stepped backward before disappearing completely into the gloom. Ereshkal, satisfied, closed the door and resumed her path. Zayn was already waiting for her—fragile and malleable, like clay.

She knew exactly what words to use.

"It's time to act," she murmured to herself.

A predatory expression appeared on her face as she moved down the hallway.

3 — Revelations

Suna

The comforting glow of large braziers spread soothing warmth throughout the room.

Suna, still shaken, stared at the statue of Ætheris, unable to tear her eyes away from the radiant figure. The words engraved on the stele echoed repeatedly in her mind:

"The Four Pillars of Creation must be reunited…"

Why did these words resonate so deeply within her?

The sound of footsteps broke the silence, jolting her from her thoughts. She jumped and spun around, heart racing.

Someone was confidently approaching. A tall man, dressed in a long white tunic adorned with delicate golden embroidery. A simple belt emphasized his upright, majestic posture. A purple cloak decorated with ochre patterns draped his shoulders like a royal garment.

But it was his face that caught Suna's attention. His features were marked yet noble; his silver beard and hair gave him an almost electric aura. His deep, kind gaze radiated wisdom.

When he gave her a reassuring smile, some of the tension gripping Suna eased.

Beside him, Theris, as impassive as ever, bowed his head respectfully.

The man stopped a few steps away. He thanked the advisor and turned toward her. His bright blue eyes rested on this stranger without the slightest hint of judgment, animated only by curiosity and infinite patience.

"Welcome, Suna," he said in a deep voice. "That is your name, isn't it?"

Suna nodded, unable to utter a single word.

The man noted her discomfort briefly before continuing, with the same gentleness that lent each word particular weight.

"I am Raenos."

The name, laden with authority, echoed through the hall.

"I know you're disoriented, but I'm here to help you understand."

Zayn

Suspended from the ceiling, glowing crystals cast cold reflections on the stone walls.

Zayn, sitting on a simple wooden chair, kept his eyes lowered, staring at the tiled floor. He hadn't eaten anything. His stomach was tied in knots, and his mind refused to settle. Everything here felt strange and oppressive.

"Zayn?" called a soft, soothing voice.

He lifted his head.

Standing before him, Ereshkal was poised, wrapped in her black gown whose fabric rippled subtly with each movement.

Her intense, penetrating gaze seemed capable of reading his very thoughts, effortlessly flipping through them like pages of a book.

Yet there was nothing frightening about her look—quite the opposite: it was warm, almost protective.

"Welcome to our world," she said in a measured, almost tender tone. "Thank you for your patience."

She took a step toward him, gently, as if approaching a lost child.

"You must have many questions…and I will give you answers."

She paused at a calculated distance, close enough to inspire trust yet far enough not to intimidate him.

Zayn's eyes remained locked onto hers.

She was already beginning to weave her web around him, long before he could realize it.

Suna

"So, my child, first of all, show me this marvel," Raenos said in a calm voice tinged with fatherly gentleness.

Suna hesitated for a moment, then reached out toward the stele. With a cautious gesture, she touched the engraved surface once again.

Immediately, the stone sprang to life, vibrating beneath her fingertips. The symbols glowed, casting golden flashes across the room.

Raenos observed the phenomenon with keen interest, perhaps even hope.

"Incredible…" he murmured.

He slowly crossed his arms, his expression serious.

"You truly are a human from Earth, then."

Suna nodded, slightly intimidated.

"Um… yes."

Raenos approached the monumental statue of Ætheris. With tenderness, he placed his hand upon its base, as if caressing a precious memory, a relic of a distant past. He carefully chose his words before continuing.

"Ætheris... is the entity from which magic originates," he began calmly, as if narrating a story.

He paused, letting his fingers glide gently over the statue's smooth surface.

"Ætheris is neither male nor female, but pure energy. A creative force."

His gaze lingered for a moment upon Ætheris.

"It created me, long ago."

Suna struggled to believe it could be true. Her brow furrowed in doubt.

Raenos noticed her skepticism and smiled gently. He extended his open palm upward. A tiny cloud materialized before Suna's widened eyes, small bolts of lightning crackling within it, striking his palm.

"Magic is real, Suna."

She nodded silently, mesmerized by the astonishing sight.

"Now, where was I?" Raenos asked himself as he closed his hand, dispersing his creation. "Ah, yes! Together, Ætheris and I gave life to eight other magicians. They were like our children. Together, we... guided the world of men."

Suna listened intently now, her attention fully captured. With a slow gesture, Raenos indicated the frescoes adorning the walls.

Under the golden glow of the braziers, the relief paintings came alive. Extraordinary creatures moved within them, vast landscapes stretched beneath vibrant skies. Human figures mingled harmoniously with fantastic beings.

"All of us together," the old magician continued, "breathed life into every magical creature that ever walked the Earth. Every fantastic being humanity has ever worshipped or feared was born of our will."

He lightly moved his hand over a scene depicting a majestic dragon with golden scales, its wings spread over an ancient city.

"The dragons, griffins, phoenixes, mermaids, nymphs, and so many others… We gave them essence, purpose, and a place in the balance of the world."

Suna, eyes wide, followed each gesture, hanging on his every word.

"All of this… thanks to Ætheris."

The history of the world she had known was merely a fragment of a much greater, older story whose outlines she had barely begun to grasp.

Zayn

Ereshkal crossed her arms, her gaze settling on Zayn with carefully calculated gentleness.

"Ætheris…" she began, weighing each word thoughtfully, "is a very ancient entity said to be the source of all magic. You saw its statue when you arrived."

She took a slow step, calm and controlled, before continuing:

"But what they don't say… what no one here dares admit… is that its heart is corrupted."

She paused, observing Zayn's reaction. She did not intend to overwhelm him—only to plant the seed of doubt.

"It created magic and shaped the magicians. It also created Mytherra. But… it used its power not to protect, but to control."

Her voice softened, taking on a sorrowful tone.

"This world, Zayn—the one I brought you to—is a prison."

Zayn narrowed his eyes.

"A prison?" he repeated uncertainly.

Ereshkal watched him for a moment, then nodded gently.

"Yes. A prison… for magicians," she replied with palpable bitterness.

He observed her, intrigued, wary, yet unable to tear his gaze away.

"Ætheris locked us here. We were betrayed."

She did not raise her voice or cast accusations—she merely stated a fact.

"Then it stole our energy to create four artifacts."

She stepped forward, placing a delicate hand on the table.

"The Four Pillars of Creation."

Her voice grew deeper.

"They are not treasures or sacred relics. They are chains."

She traced a square in the air with her fingers.

"Four pillars… to seal the bars of our cage."

She paused again, carefully watching Zayn, seeking a reaction, a crack through which to slip.

"They exist to prevent anyone from challenging Ætheris."

She tilted her head slightly, allowing silence to settle, letting her words seep gradually into the boy's mind.

Suna

Raenos continued his story, his voice still filled with gentleness.

"For centuries, magical beings and humans coexisted. Through ages and civilizations, we guided the peoples, offering them knowledge and prosperity."

He paused, remembering a distant past.

"Magicians were revered as gods. But magic... the power we possessed... often led to abuses. Humanity, fascinated by this power, sought to exploit it. And we, magicians... well, we made mistakes of our own."

His tone grew heavier.

"The conflicts that arose were terrible."

He stopped briefly, placing a hand upon the cold stone of a sculpted fresco, as if touching a fragment of his own history.

Suna examined the scene carved into the rock.

A marching army.

Roman legions advanced in tight ranks, their banners fluttering in the wind.

But that wasn't what drew her attention.

At the center of the fresco, a radiant figure dominated the battlefield. A man crowned with light, surrounded by a silver halo, extended his hands. Lightning burst forth from his fingers, striking down enemies who knelt before him.

At his side, a rider atop a gigantic bull effortlessly lifted two men by their throats.

Suna shivered.

Raenos gently slid his hand over the stone.

"Rome. The Empire became the greatest symbol of our influence. Our magic enabled the conquest of lands, the building of wonders..."

His expression darkened.

"But it also caused unimaginable destruction."

Suna followed his gaze to another scene on the fresco.

She felt a tightening in her chest.

Flames engulfed an entire city.

Humans ran desperately in all directions. The chaos, frozen in stone, still seemed to vibrate under the glow of the braziers.

At the top of the relief, a magician stood upon a volcano, unleashing hell upon them.

Raenos continued, more softly:

"Countless lives lost… shattered."

Suna was captivated by his story.

"We believed we were a blessing," he murmured. "But we abused our power and lost sight of our duty."

His voice hardened.

"We allowed acts of violence and cruelty."

His fingers tightened imperceptibly against the stone.

On the next fresco, a tidal wave with a woman's face swallowed a coastal city.

"Villages wiped out. Peoples enslaved."

Another scene depicted a man, his arm raised, commanding colossal creatures of stone and roots to raze an entire village.

He stepped back, distancing himself slightly from a past that still deeply affected him.

"The Empire became the enemy of what it should have been."

Suna dared not speak. She had grown up in a world where Rome was a mythologized civilization. Here, before her, stood the version history had forgotten.

Raenos inhaled slowly before continuing, his voice lower, almost a whisper.

"Ætheris watched our madness and downfall with great sorrow. It saw the imbalance grow. It watched as its magic became a weapon of destruction."

He paused before adding:

"It knew this couldn't continue. Ætheris convinced me, and we had to make a difficult decision."

Raenos turned toward the final fresco.

Magicians and their disciples, all magical creatures, were pulled through luminous vortexes, leaving Earth behind—ravaged and abandoned.

"We created Mytherra."

Raenos's gaze was distant, as if reliving that distant moment.

"We removed all magical beings from Earth... We brought them here. Not to punish them, but to create a new world, a fair world, respectful of balance."

Suna, deeply troubled, felt her throat tighten.

"You did all this..." she said, swallowing, searching for the right words, "...to protect magical creatures?"

"Yes," Raenos affirmed, his gaze locked with hers, his expression infinitely grave. "Chaos was growing. The great magicians had become uncontrollable. We had to protect them... from themselves."

His voice softened, but the weight of his story did not diminish.

"But it came at a price. Creating a world... required far more energy than we had anticipated. We drew from our own strength, but it wasn't enough. We had to rely on the energy of our children..."

Suna's eyes widened.

"Not merely as punishment for their excesses," Raenos resumed, "but out of necessity. Without their contribution, Mytherra would never have existed. We crafted four pillars to sustain this world—the Pillars of Creation."

His voice remained calm, but betrayed a shadow of regret.

"But at what cost..."

Zayn

Zayn swallowed with difficulty.

"You mean Ætheris forced the magicians to give up their energy?" Zayn asked.

Ereshkal nodded slowly, observing him with apparent distress.

"She stole it from us."

She crossed her arms, her gaze darkening—not with anger, but with feigned sorrow, as if bearing the weight of a painful past.

"Instead of guiding her people, she oppressed them."

She took a subtle step closer to Zayn, reducing the distance between them, as though sharing a secret that only the oppressed could understand.

"She weakened us, diminished us… all to control us better."

She paused, giving him time to absorb her words, to doubt, to reflect.

"And the Pillars…" she murmured, her voice trembling, choked by emotion long repressed. "They contain an essential part of us… our very essence."

Her expression showed a surprising fragility—entirely feigned.

"She hid them," she continued bitterly, each word seemingly an effort, like reopening a wound willingly for Zayn's sake.

"Ætheris deprived us of a piece of ourselves. We are incomplete, weakened, condemned to live in the shadow of what we once were…"

Her fingers slid slowly along the table's surface, as if gently caressing an invisible relic.

"She sealed them away to ensure no one could ever challenge her authority."

Zayn couldn't look away from her.

Each word seeped steadily into his mind, settling into places he didn't know how to deny.

Ereshkal moved another step forward, her eyes now shining with a new intensity.

No longer sadness.

No longer regret.

But a new, fervent resolve.

"But I, Zayn—I wish to restore justice."

She held his gaze, and for the first time, Zayn felt a shiver that wasn't fear, but a strange sense of conviction.

"You can help me return that power to those who rightfully deserve it."

Suna

Raenos continued, hands clasped behind his back.

"The Pillars of Creation are essential. They maintain Mytherra's balance and protect this world."

He turned toward the statue of Ætheris, gazing up at its serene face.

"But Ætheris concealed them, protected by guardians."

"Why?"

Raenos turned his head toward her.

"Because it knew they shouldn't be accessible to everyone. They form the very foundation of this world, but they're also objects of great desire."

He added softly, carefully measuring each word:

"Ætheris intended for a human, devoid of magic, to find them."

"Why a human?" the young girl asked.

"Because magicians possessed considerable power."

He paused.

"And boundless ambition."

Suna watched his expression closely. He spoke without contempt or anger, yet she sensed sadness and bitterness.

"If the Pillars were accessible to them," Raenos explained, "they might exploit them for their own gain."

He took a deep breath before continuing:

"And this world would fall into chaos once again."

Raenos straightened slightly.

"Humans are imperfect, but they also possess greater balance."

He stepped back, allowing her time to absorb this truth.

"By entrusting this responsibility to humans, Ætheris ensured the quest for the Pillars would not be driven by a lust for power… but by nobler intentions."

Zayn

"You," Ereshkal whispered softly, "you are the key."

Zayn lifted his head, unsettled by this declaration.

"Ætheris, in her madness," she continued, "decided that only humans could touch the Pillars. It was her way of ensuring no one would ever challenge her again."

She paused, letting the idea firmly root itself in his mind.

Then, in a lower voice, as if sharing a forbidden secret, she added:

"But she never anticipated I'd find a way to open a portal."

Ereshkal leaned gently toward him, closing the gap between them. Her gaze was hypnotic.

"Together, we can right this injustice."

She held his eyes with absolute certainty, as if her own faith in this cause was unshakable.

"I only ask you… to trust me."

Zayn felt his heart clench. All this was overwhelming.

He wanted to doubt.

He wanted to refuse.

But deep within, a darker, more painful part of him already reached toward her.

Anger.

Pain.

The weight of injustices he had endured.

Ereshkal's words echoed inside him.

If he could save an entire people, how could he look away?

Zayn felt his stomach knot. This thought—simple yet profound—changed everything.

Suna

Suna remained frozen, absorbing Raenos's words.

Part of her was fascinated, captivated by the grandeur of the story. Another part felt overwhelmed by the weight of what he revealed. Mythical creatures, the balance of the world, the Pillars…

One question burned at Suna's lips.

"Then…" she asked, "if the Pillars are the key, why seek to reunite them?"

"Because Ætheris is dying," the magician said quietly.

He paused, letting the significance of his words linger between them.

"Creating Mytherra was beyond our strength. We had not anticipated how draining it would be. Without Ætheris, Mytherra will vanish, and all its inhabitants with it."

Raenos continued, his voice softer, but full of absolute certainty.

"That is why your arrival is so fortuitous. If Ætheris reopened a portal for you, it means there is still hope. You've given us a chance to save this world."

Suna shook her head, her thoughts spinning in indescribable chaos.

"But… I'm nobody. I'm just… an ordinary girl."

"Sometimes it is the most ordinary beings who accomplish the extraordinary."

Suna raised her eyes, captured by the intensity of Raenos's gaze.

"You're here for a reason, Suna. And I believe Ætheris has entrusted you with a mission."

Suna opened her mouth, then hesitated.

"But…"

She made a vague gesture to dismiss the idea, struggling vainly to rationalize what she knew was impossible.

"The portal didn't open for me…"

Raenos did not let her finish. He saw no other explanation; no magician had ever successfully recreated a portal. It required too much energy.

"Ætheris opened the portal. She would not have allowed anyone through without reason."

His voice held neither doubt nor hesitation.

He regarded her calmly, with conviction.

"If you are here, be certain it is her will. And that you are exactly where you're meant to be."

Zayn

Ereshkal's words echoed through his mind, each sentence leaving an impression both unsettling and alluring.

Was this world truly a prison?

Was Ætheris really a fading tyrant?

And he—could he actually be the key to changing everything?

A small voice deep within whispered that he still didn't understand it all.

So, almost defiantly, he whispered:

"And if I refuse?"

Ereshkal didn't answer immediately. She fixed him with infinite patience, as if unsurprised by his reaction.

"Zayn," she said gently, reassuringly, "you're free to make that choice."

She allowed him a moment to absorb these words. She wanted him to feel he had control.

"But think carefully," Ereshkal added. "The Pillars have the power to change this world's destiny. If we don't retrieve them…"

She paused, holding his gaze, a trace of sadness drifting through her eyes.

"Ætheris will vanish. And with her, all of Mytherra."

She lowered her eyes, as though weighed down by the thought.

"All magicians, every creature in this world… annihilated."

Her voice was solemn.

"But if we recover them…"

She took one final step toward him, delicately placing a hand on his cheek.

The gesture was gentle, almost maternal. It shook him deeply.

"Then I will have the power to heal this world."

A whisper. A promise.

"To change your life."

Her thumb softly brushed against his skin.

"To bring back your mother."

Silence again—but this time, not empty. It brimmed with expectation.

Zayn took a deep breath, his thoughts clashing chaotically, beyond his control.

Ereshkal's words sank deeply into him, settling into the cracks of his doubts.

A small part of him still hesitated, searching for reasons not to believe, not to fall into what seemed a perfect trap.

But the other part…

The part clinging to that last fragment of hope, the part refusing to surrender, the part that still saw, deep in his mind, his mother's radiant face…

That part refused to listen.

He saw her again in a distant memory—her crystalline laughter, the tenderness in her eyes.

And if this trial, this path through shadows, was truly the key to finding her again?

What if it was possible?

He sighed, his chest rising with difficulty, compressed by fear and doubt.

Maybe he was trapped. Maybe he was wrong.

But could he truly afford not to try?

So he silenced the voices within himself.

And allowed Ereshkal's voice to carry him forward.

For his mother, he had to try—no matter the cost.

Suna

Raenos, noticing the doubt in Suna's eyes, made a reassuring gesture.

"You don't need to understand everything right away, Suna. You won't be alone; we'll be here to help you."

He gestured toward the frescoes adorning the walls around them—stories engraved in stone, testifying to a past shaped by magic and the choices of its creators.

"This world has survived unimaginable trials."

He turned toward her, his penetrating gaze capturing every nuance of her expression.

"And today, it relies on you. For the first time in a very long time, magicians and humans will once again join forces."

Suna lowered her eyes. She felt her mind racing, torn between confusion and anxiety.

"What if I don't want this role?" she asked softly.

Her voice wasn't harsh or rebellious; it was heavy with distress.

"I... I don't belong here. This isn't my world."

Her gaze drifted over carvings of a past that wasn't hers.

"I just want... to go home."

Raenos stood motionless, measuring the depth of her anguish.

A shadow of sadness crossed his features.

"I understand, Suna. And I'm sorry. If I could, I would open a portal for you right now. But I don't have that power."

He spoke with sincerity.

"Only Ætheris, the very source of magic, is capable of that. I have no idea how she managed to open a portal in her weakened state, even for an instant…"

He let out a sigh.

"It was already a miracle, but one that must have cost her dearly."

Suna felt a crushing weight settle upon her shoulders.

She was truly trapped here. Her heart ached painfully.

Raenos, as if reading her thoughts, softened even further.

"But I promise you this: if we succeed in restoring Ætheris, she will have the strength to send you home. And when that day comes, the choice will be yours."

Suna took a deep breath, but reality crashed upon her brutally.

She clung desperately to the idea of returning home.

This story of magicians, these frescoes, the quest for the Pillars… none of it belonged to her world.

The thought of being trapped here made her dizzy.

She wanted to flee, to wake up, to return to her ordinary life, as mundane as it had seemed.

But what else could she do?

Wander aimlessly, searching for a door that didn't exist? Collapse in helplessness?

No.

She couldn't afford to be passive. If the only path home depended upon Ætheris, then she had no choice.

Even if her heart screamed that she didn't belong here, even if it all felt like a nightmare she desperately wanted to wake up from—she had to move forward.

"All right," she finally sighed.

She lifted her eyes to meet Raenos's gaze.

"If there's something I can do… I'll try."

Raenos breathed deeply, as if relieved of a burden, and then warmly added:

"Thank you, Suna. You've given us hope… something I'd lost long ago."

Then, quickly remembering her situation, he hurriedly continued:

"But what am I thinking?" he apologized. "You must be exhausted."

He turned toward Theris.

"Theris, please find our guest a room."

The advisor gestured for Suna to follow.

"Good night, Suna. Rest well—we'll speak more tomorrow."

"Thank you," Suna replied softly. "Good night."

They left the room, watched over by Raenos's gentle, reassuring gaze.

Zayn

Ereshkal watched him, sensing the turmoil raging within.

She allowed him a moment to grapple with the weight of his own thoughts, to internally wrestle with everything he had just heard. Then she gently took control again.

"I don't need an immediate answer, Zayn. Take your time to see things clearly."

She tilted her head slightly, capturing his attention.

"But remember—this world needs you."

She let those words settle within him, embedding themselves deeply in his mind.

"Your mother needs you."

Zayn gave an almost imperceptible shudder.

His vision blurred; his throat tightened.

Ereshkal said nothing more. She didn't need to.

She had planted the seed, and now she would wait for it to grow.

She stepped away, finally giving him the space he desperately needed.

Her voice regained its usual serenity, as though the exchange had merely been an ordinary conversation, nothing more.

"Nymeris will take you to your room. Rest, reflect. Tomorrow, Thanatos will show you the way."

Zayn nodded mechanically, his mind spinning in a whirlwind of thoughts.

Ereshkal's words repeated endlessly.

This world needs you. Your mother needs you.

He felt an unbearable, crushing pressure.

Suna and Zayn

Each stood alone at the threshold of a destiny that overwhelmed them.

One, thrust unwillingly into a vital mission, burdened with a responsibility she had never asked to bear.

The other, torn between doubt and conviction, drawn into a conflict whose implications he did not yet fully grasp.

Their paths stretched out before them, seemingly opposed.

Yet, within Mytherra's shadows, their footsteps already echoed in unison.

For although everything still separated them, fate had already bound them inexorably together.

4 — Zayn — The departure

Zayn followed Nymeris through the corridors. His mind struggled to process everything he'd experienced, leaving him with a feeling of profound loneliness.

Nymeris walked ahead, her silhouette casting rippling shadows under the glow of lanterns mounted along the walls.

She stopped before a wooden door and opened it.

"Here's your room," she said, stepping aside to let him enter.

The space was small and austere, devoid of warmth.

"It's basic, but the bed is comfortable, you'll see."

He hesitated briefly before stepping inside.

The room was small and bare.

The rough stone walls absorbed the dim light emitted by a solitary lantern hanging from the ceiling.

A simple bed of rough wood stood in a corner, covered with a coarse, gray blanket.

Opposite stood a modest table accompanied by a stool. On it were arranged a jug of water, a clay cup, a plate holding dry bread and cheese, and a bowl of fruit.

No ornament softened the room's stark simplicity.

"Rest," advised Nymeris. "We leave tomorrow at dawn."

She closed the door quietly behind her, leaving Zayn alone.

He sat on the bed, elbows resting on his knees, hands clasped under his chin.

Everything here felt foreign to him. His eyes drifted toward the lamp, watching the shifting shadows it cast upon the walls. They stretched and flickered. His thoughts were an impenetrable chaos.

Finally, though he had no appetite, he mechanically ate a mouthful of bread and a few fruits. Then he lay down, immediately feeling the roughness of the blanket and the hardness of the mattress beneath his back. At that moment, discomfort mattered little—exhaustion outweighed everything else.

Sleep quickly overtook him. He sank into troubled dreams, swept away into a world where everything was whispers and illusions.

A dull knock on the wooden door pulled him from sleep.

Zayn opened his eyes, disoriented.

For a moment, he couldn't recall where he was.

Then memories returned in successive waves: the previous day, the austere room, Nymeris, Thanatos, Ereshkal…

A muffled voice spoke through the door.

"We're waiting for you downstairs. Breakfast is ready," someone—likely Nymeris—called out.

Zayn sighed. Was the night already over? He felt far from rested. He struggled to sit up, his muscles still stiff from a restless night.

He ran a hand over his face and stood up. Pouring a little water into his palm, he splashed it over his face.

The effect was immediate: a shiver ran through him, chasing away the lingering fog of sleep.

He pulled on his clothes and ran a hand through his hair, without really trying to tame it.

Then, taking a deep breath, he opened the door and left the room.

The aroma of warm bread and cheese subtly perfumed the air.

In the main hall, he found Thanatos and Nymeris already seated around a wooden table. The room was simple, without adornment: bare walls, sturdy benches, and a large window allowing pale light to filter in.

Nymeris raised her eyes as he approached.

"Sit down," she instructed, indicating an empty seat.

Zayn complied, pulling out a chair and taking a seat.

The meal was modest, yet surprisingly appetizing. At the center of the table sat a dense loaf of bread next to fresh cheese and a pitcher of water. Thankfully, dried figs and amber honey added a splash of color to the austere arrangement.

Nymeris broke off a piece of bread and handed it to him.

"Eat," she encouraged gently. "You'll need your strength for the journey."

Zayn accepted the bread and took a bite. Its flavor was richer than he'd expected, slightly coarse in texture yet comforting.

Accustomed to sweeter breakfasts, he tasted the cheese. Its creamy consistency blended perfectly with the subtle saltiness spreading over his tongue. The honey, sweet without being overpowering, provided an unexpected touch of softness.

The dried figs were delicious. Their fragrance filled his mouth—a surprisingly comforting taste in such a dark place.

He chewed slowly, then murmured almost to himself, "This, at least, isn't so different."

"The simplest things are often the best," Thanatos remarked.

After the meal, Thanatos rose.

"If you're ready," he announced, "we leave now."

Without a word, Nymeris nodded. It hadn't truly been a question.

When the door opened to the outside, fresh morning air rushed in, accompanied by a golden light—a striking contrast to the austere, dark corridors they left behind.

Zayn, momentarily blinded by the sudden brightness, squinted. He inhaled deeply, filling his lungs with invigorating air.

Everything he had experienced since his arrival felt surreal, as though all of it was merely a vivid dream, a mirage ready to vanish at any moment. But he had no time to dwell on this feeling.

"This journey will be long, Zayn."

Thanatos's voice drew him from his thoughts.

"It's natural to feel lost. Give yourself time. The answers will come on their own."

These words, free of reproach, resonated unexpectedly within him. Perhaps he could trust them, after all.

Zayn relaxed his shoulders, feeling a fraction of his tension dissipate. He wasn't alone.

Without another word, Thanatos led the way.

At his side, Nymeris advanced, her gaze vigilantly scanning the streets.

Zayn followed, trying to match his pace to theirs.

And with each step, the doubts that assailed him retreated… a little more.

As they moved through the bustling streets of the capital, Zayn was again struck by the vibrant life that contrasted sharply with the darkness and stillness of Ereshkal's district.

Around him, buildings of polished marble reflected the first rays of morning in countless dazzling reflections. The city was bathed in a radiant aura. Everything was beautiful, bright, perfectly placed.

At an intersection, he noticed two imposing figures: a griffon with enormous wings, accompanied by a winged man wearing glittering golden armor. Both stood tall, watching the crowd vigilantly.

Zayn stopped abruptly, breathless at the sight. He had never seen creatures like this before.

But there was no time to marvel further. Thanatos reacted instantly, wrapping a deceptively protective arm around Zayn and firmly guiding him onward.

"They must not see us," his guide murmured, his voice low and tense. "Ætheris would not tolerate your presence here. She would have you killed without hesitation."

Zayn nodded nervously and quickened his pace, staring at the ground to avoid drawing attention.

Gradually, the bustling city receded. The streets widened progressively, the buildings becoming less dense, giving way to simpler, more spaced-out houses.

At last, they reached the outskirts of the capital. Before them stretched fields of golden wheat, rippling gently with the breeze, forming a natural boundary between the urban vibrancy they'd just left behind and the wilder lands now opening ahead.

Zayn breathed deeply, as if to dispel the lingering anxiety clinging to him, and stared resolutely toward the horizon.

Nymeris observed Zayn from the corner of her eye. She clearly sensed the tension he carried, aware that their presence could be intimidating for a human. Truthfully, she felt a certain irritation at this task imposed by Ereshkal. Playing guardian to this lost teenager was neither her ambition nor among her immediate interests. Yet she knew Ereshkal's orders left no room for argument, and she had to at least attempt to ease Zayn's apprehension.

She forced herself to adopt a softer tone, smoothing out the habitual coldness from her voice as best she could.

"So, what do you think of the capital?" she asked, relaxing her features to appear more approachable.

Zayn hesitated. The young woman's posture was less rigid than Thanatos's, but her eyes still betrayed a cold intelligence. To Zayn, she resembled a beautiful but poisonous plant.

"It's… different," he answered. "Magnificent, but strange too. I never imagined a place like this could exist. These creatures, this city… It all feels unreal."

Nymeris gave a faint smile, noting the awe on his face.

"It's the world we built after leaving yours," she said.

Zayn paused, internally conflicted, but his curiosity won out. He wanted to compare Ereshkal's words with another perspective.

"Why did you leave Earth?" he finally asked. "Ereshkal told me this place… that Mytherra is a prison. Is that true?"

Nymeris hesitated briefly, seeming to weigh her words carefully before responding.

"Mytherra is exactly as Ereshkal described: a prison—but a prison for us. Ætheris drained the great magicians of their energy to create this world. It wasn't a refuge, Zayn. It was a sentence. Some call it a necessary sacrifice, but at what cost? Magicians lost their power, their freedom. Ætheris locked away their magic to ensure no one could ever challenge her again."

She gently tucked a stray lock of hair behind her ear.

"Ætheris wanted absolute rule," she continued, "to control every fragment of this world. It was her ultimate act of domination. But she overlooked one thing: her own end."

Zayn turned sharply toward her, surprised.

"Her end?"

Nymeris nodded gravely.

"Ætheris is weakening. Creating Mytherra drained her far more than she expected. Now she is slowly fading. If she disappears completely, she'll likely take Mytherra with her. Already, magic is weaker than before."

Thanatos glanced back over his shoulder, noting with satisfaction the impact of Nymeris's words on Zayn. She was playing her role perfectly, and he decided to support her. Reinforcing the seriousness of Nymeris's statement, he added:

"We must recover the Pillars before it's too late. Their energy could not only save Mytherra, but also establish a new balance—one fairer and more stable."

"That," Nymeris continued, "is why you're so important, Zayn. Ætheris may have thought she permanently made the Pillars inaccessible to magicians. But now, because of you, everything could change."

"And that's why you want to gather them?" he asked. "To free Mytherra?"

"Ereshkal wishes to save our world and correct this injustice," Thanatos went on. "The Pillars shouldn't be tools of control. They should be the foundation of true balance, allowing Mytherra to regain its freedom."

Zayn felt his mind spinning, searching for sense amid these conflicting statements.

"Exactly," Nymeris added. "Without their power, this world is incomplete. Ætheris made them inaccessible to everyone—except a human."

"But why a human?" Zayn asked.

Thanatos intervened before Nymeris could answer.

"Because a human is impartial. You have no power to regain here, no personal interests. You can act clearly, untainted by magic."

He paused for a moment, holding Zayn's gaze intently.

"But make no mistake, Zayn. This won't be easy. The Pillars are hidden and protected by trials only the most determined can overcome."

"Trials? What exactly do you mean?" Zayn asked, a note of concern entering his voice.

Until now, the prospect of retrieving the Pillars had remained abstract. He hadn't truly considered the implications of such a quest.

Nymeris glanced briefly at Thanatos before answering.

"Each Pillar, besides being placed in unknown locations, is protected by a trial that tests much more than strength or intelligence. It involves understanding, facing challenges tied to their very essence."

The mention of trials suddenly made the mission feel very real. Zayn wasn't certain he was prepared to risk his life for a cause he still understood so little about. His heart tightened, apprehension growing stronger.

"And if… if I fail? If I'm not good enough?" he murmured.

Thanatos surprised Zayn by adopting a reassuring tone.

"Ereshkal believes in you, Zayn. She sees someone capable of accomplishing what no one else can. If you're here, it's because you were chosen. You must believe it too."

Zayn wasn't entirely convinced. Nymeris stepped in again.

"You're not alone in this quest," she said. "We'll be there, every step of the way, helping and guiding you."

Zayn looked away, staring at the ground in front of him, their words echoing within. He wanted to believe their sincerity, to believe he had truly been chosen.

"And what happens once we gather the Pillars?" he finally asked.

"Their power will return to their rightful owners," Thanatos explained. "With them, we can repair this world and restore justice."

Nymeris added softly:

"But we can't achieve it alone, Zayn. We need you. Together, we can give Mytherra back the greatness it deserves."

Zayn slowly nodded, torn between the hope they offered and the profound uncertainty he couldn't shake. As they continued onward, the young man's thoughts collided, grappling with troubling truths and intertwined promises.

He tried to imagine what those trials might entail. Was he truly ready to risk his life for people he barely knew?

Thanatos slowed his pace, letting Zayn catch up, his tone becoming more direct.

"Think carefully, Zayn. It's not just our world at stake. I heard Ereshkal's promise. Bringing your mother back to life—it's not an illusion. It's a reality within your grasp, if you see it through."

Suddenly, memories of his mother's funeral flooded him—clear, sharp, painful. The past few hours had been so overwhelming that he had nearly forgotten his grief. Clenching his fists, a newfound determination swept away his doubts. If these trials were the price he had to pay for the promise they'd made him… then no matter how difficult, he would face them.

A tear gently rolled down his cheek as he whispered to himself:

"I'll do it for you, Mom."

Thanatos, walking ahead, allowed himself a discreet smile before diverting Zayn's attention in a calm voice.

"Do you know how to ride a horse?" he asked.

Zayn raised his head abruptly, wiping away the tear with the back of his hand.

"No," he admitted. "Where I come from, it's not something we do often."

Beside him, Nymeris pursed her lips in amusement.

"Well, then—you're going to have to learn."

The road continued as a wide avenue lined with cypress trees. Gradually, an imposing building appeared to one side, surrounded by fields where a few horses grazed quietly.

A stable.

They stopped before the entrance, two large wooden doors already wide open, revealing some activity inside. The sound of hooves hitting the ground and the occasional neigh punctuating the morning air lent the place a peaceful atmosphere.

Thanatos led them inside. The stable was impeccably maintained. On either side, rows of perfectly clean stalls housed horses of impressive stature and powerful musculature. Fresh hay overflowed the feeding troughs, filling the space with a pleasant scent.

Upon seeing them approach, the horses turned their heads, their bright, intelligent eyes watching the newcomers with curiosity.

Zayn stopped abruptly, astonished by the exceptional build of the mounts. They were bigger than any horse he had ever seen before, their powerful muscles visible beneath gleaming coats. A black stallion, particularly imposing, blew loudly and shook its thick mane, merely to assert its presence.

"These horses are… big," he murmured to himself.

Nymeris chuckled softly as she approached a horse whose coat shimmered silver. She ran a reassuring hand over its neck.

"They say that when Mytherra was created, some animals crossed through the portal. The magic transformed them somewhat," she explained, gently stroking the animal's muscular chest. "They might look different from what you're used to, but trust me, they're indispensable. Their stamina and speed are unmatched."

Thanatos, a few steps ahead, approached the central area where an elderly man with gray hair carefully combed back welcomed them. His worn apron was muddy and covered with strands of straw.

"Three horses, ready for travel," Thanatos ordered.

The old man nodded and disappeared into a corner of the stable. Meanwhile, Zayn continued observing the imposing horses with fascination and some apprehension, impressed by their strength and presence.

Soon, the stablehand returned, holding the reins of three impeccably saddled mounts. Thanatos grasped the reins of the least imposing one and handed them to Zayn.

"You said you've never ridden, so we'll explain along the way," Thanatos stated. "You'll have to learn quickly—it isn't complicated."

However, mounting the horse proved no easy task. Zayn stood awkwardly near the animal, eyeing it with visible apprehension. The tall, robust mount stared back at him with apparent indifference.

Nymeris approached.

"Don't worry," she said calmly. "I'll help you. Come."

Carefully, she took hold of the horse's reins, steadying the animal. Zayn took a deep breath, placed one foot in the stirrup, and attempted to pull himself up. But just as he pushed himself upward, the horse shifted, causing him to immediately lose his grip. He nearly slipped, clinging desperately to the saddle, hopping around awkwardly with his foot still trapped in the stirrup.

"Hold on tightly, Zayn," she advised. "And push harder with your other leg."

This time, he secured a firmer footing and gripped the saddle tightly, hoisting himself awkwardly. For a moment, he tilted dangerously to the opposite side, struggling to find balance before finally managing to stabilize himself.

Then he made the mistake of looking down. A brief sensation of dizziness overcame him.

Nymeris supported him with gentle encouragement, while Thanatos mounted effortlessly, paying them no attention.

Zayn nervously patted his mount's neck, seeking more reassurance for himself than comfort for the animal.

"Well, you're in the saddle," Nymeris called out. "Now all you have to do is stay there until evening!"

Zayn smiled nervously, his hands tightly gripping the reins. Clearly uncomfortable atop the horse, he had at least managed to get there.

Zayn gripped the reins tightly, doing his best to maintain his balance.

Each stride of the horse painfully emphasized his lack of experience. He felt awkward, jolted with every step. His legs were growing stiff and numb, making every movement increasingly uncomfortable.

Ahead of him, Nymeris rode effortlessly, fluidly, barely seeming to notice the motion of her mount.

"You managing?" she asked, without malice.

"I'll survive," Zayn replied, a grimace of discomfort on his face.

Nymeris let out a brief laugh, delicate and fleeting. At the front of the group, Thanatos occasionally glanced back to ensure Zayn was still following.

The road gently curved through fallow fields dotted with colorful flowers and bordered by irregularly trimmed hedges.

Zayn tried to focus on the beauty of the landscape, hoping it would distract him from the growing pain spreading through his backside.

He shifted awkwardly, trying to find a more comfortable position in the saddle, but each step of the horse reminded him mercilessly that he clearly wasn't accustomed to this type of activity.

Nymeris slowed her pace to ride alongside him. She had to play her part. She turned her finely featured face toward him, her icy-blue eyes shining with curiosity.

"So?"

"So, what?" Zayn asked, struggling not to lose his balance.

"So, how does it feel to be here?"

"Honestly? I still have trouble believing all of this is real."

"You arrived in this world yesterday, and today you're already traveling on horseback. You adapt quickly."

Zayn let out a small, joyless laugh.

"If you can call this adapting…"

"It's not that bad, you know. But you look a bit like a child trying to walk on stilts."

He rolled his eyes, smiling despite himself.

"Thanks for the compliment."

A peaceful silence settled between them, disturbed only by the steady rhythm of hooves striking the packed earth. Then, driven by curiosity, Zayn asked:

"And what about you?"

Nymeris seemed taken aback by the question.

"What about me?"

"I don't know anything about you."

"What exactly do you want to know?"

Zayn shrugged.

"Everything. Where you come from, who you are... what you're doing here."

Nymeris didn't enjoy talking about herself. Yet, faced with Zayn's persistence, she reluctantly gave in. Was it his curiosity or simply Ereshkal's orders forcing her to answer?

"As you've already guessed," she said, "I serve Ereshkal. I've always been trained for combat and carrying out the missions entrusted to me. That's all."

Zayn waited, hoping she would continue, but she stopped there.

"That's it?" he finally asked, slightly disappointed.

"Do you also want a detailed biography?"

He sighed, straightening up in his saddle.

"Look, I've been catapulted into a world I don't understand. And the only thing I'm certain of is that I can't trust anyone. If I have to spend time with someone, I'd at least like to know who I'm dealing with."

Nymeris studied him carefully, as though weighing the necessity of his request. Eventually, she gave in.

"I grew up in shadows," she began. "A place where light doesn't exist."

"In a cave?"

She chuckled softly.

"No. Well, not exactly. A deep chasm, called Nekrosys. My mother was a disciple of Ereshkal, but she died young. My father—I never knew him. So I had to fend for myself from an early age, learn how to defend myself, how to assert myself."

"Were you strong?"

Nymeris hesitated, her expression darkening.

"Just strong enough to survive."

"And Ereshkal?" Zayn asked.

This time, Nymeris's gaze became colder, more distant.

"She offered me a purpose. A reason to exist."

She tugged on her reins, deliberately putting more distance between them. Zayn realized he'd reached the limits of her patience. Yet one final question slipped out:

"If you hadn't followed Ereshkal… what would you have done?"

Nymeris turned toward him. An icy gleam flashed through her eyes.

"I wouldn't have survived long enough to ask myself that question."

With those words, she urged her horse forward, definitively increasing the distance between them, ending their conversation.

Zayn slumped slightly in his saddle. He wondered if he'd just glimpsed a crack in the young woman's cold, distant armor… or perhaps merely brushed against an even deeper darkness he had yet to comprehend.

After several exhausting hours of riding, they finally reached the outskirts of a bustling city. A wide avenue lined with tall white columns already announced the opulence of a prosperous urban center.

As they advanced, a lively clamor rose: enthusiastic shouts of merchants promoting their wares, rhythmic clattering of sandals on cobblestones, and bursts of laughter emanated from the dense crowd. The white buildings with intricately sculpted façades unmistakably spoke of Midlock's wealth.

All around them, vibrant fabrics fluttered in the breeze, hanging from storefront awnings. The intoxicating scent of exotic spices mingled with that of freshly baked bread, suddenly reminding Zayn of his growing hunger. Snippets of conversations punctuated by exclamations and lively negotiations reached him in bursts.

"This is Midlock," Nymeris announced, noticing the boy's awe. "A bustling crossroads city. Major trade routes meet here, and the Merchant's Guild rules supreme."

Zayn observed the activity filling every corner. Around a vast paved square, an impressive corridor of arcades supported by marble columns housed dozens of shops. Finely crafted jewelry, colorful amphoras filled with fragrant oils or wine, sacks overflowing with golden grains… The abundance seemed endless.

Amidst the busy crowd, he spotted armored legionnaires patrolling calmly, as well as various merchants leading mules laden with goods. Each step the horses took echoed off the cobblestones, adding another layer of sound to the surrounding tumult.

At the head of the group, Thanatos, unperturbed, maintained a more moderate pace, guiding his mount carefully through the passersby without acknowledging them. He glanced at the displayed goods, indifferent to the commotion around him.

"We won't linger here," he declared in a neutral yet firm tone. "We still have two full days of travel ahead."

At his side, Nymeris kept a watchful eye on the passersby, ready to ward off anyone who might approach too closely. Zayn had to suppress his urge to stop at every stall. The vibrant fruit stands, the painted amphoras, the sheer variety of exotic objects fascinated him.

The group crossed the square, weaving their way through the crowds as the cries of merchants competed to advertise their prices. Vendors wearing togas carried baskets filled with bread or grapes, moving among the craftsmen. In some side alleys, Zayn glimpsed taverns tucked into narrower streets, as well as public baths whose steam escaped through vents in the walls.

Without slowing, Thanatos turned onto a street leading northward. Zayn cast one final glance at the lively square, almost regretting not being able to wander freely and stretch his legs. As they moved further from the shops, the tumult gradually faded away.

Soon, they reached an inn situated at the northern edge of Midlock: a modest building with a thatched roof overlooking the main road. At the entrance, a carved wooden sign simply read: *The Traveler's Rest.*

Thanatos halted before the doors, quickly scanning their surroundings before dismounting. Nymeris followed suit, while Zayn, considerably less graceful, took longer to leave his saddle.

He drew in a deep breath, staring at the ground, which seemed far below. As he removed one foot from the stirrup, he nearly lost his balance when his horse shifted restlessly. His fingers instinctively tightened on the reins.

The young rider leaned forward, cautiously trying to slide down the animal's side while gripping the saddle. His sore muscles protested vehemently against the new effort, and his leg, numb after hours spent astride, stubbornly refused to obey. Finally, his foot touched the ground, but he stumbled forward, grasping at the saddle at the last moment to avoid an embarrassing fall.

With difficulty, he managed to straighten himself up on stiff, protesting limbs, attempting to maintain some semblance of dignity.

The interior was warm, illuminated by a lively fire crackling in the hearth. A few simple tables were scattered around the room, occupied by merchants and travelers from all walks of life. The comforting aroma of grilled meat and hot soup drifted through the air. Zayn followed his companions toward an isolated table.

A rosy-cheeked innkeeper approached swiftly, wiping her hands on a stained apron.

"Good evening," she said. "I assume you'll be wanting a hot meal?"

"And rooms for the night," Thanatos added.

Zayn observed with curiosity the discreet ballet of inn employees bringing steaming dishes and filling mugs with wine or beer. When a bowl filled with thick soup and a chunk of crusty bread was placed before him, he realized how hungry he truly was.

He tasted a spoonful, surprised by the dish's rich flavor. The meal unfolded quietly, punctuated only by the murmurs of the other guests and the rhythmic crackling of the fire. Thanatos and Nymeris quietly discussed their next stop.

Later, Zayn entered his own room, modest but clean, simply furnished with a narrow bed covered by a thick woolen blanket, and a small table on which a flickering candle cast a gentle glow. He sat on the edge of the mattress, savoring the relief that came with the privacy of his room at last.

Exhausted by the day's events, he allowed himself to fall back onto the bed, staring at the dark wooden ceiling above. This was his first night at an inn in Mytherra, and at least the mattress was comfortable.

He reflected on recent events, trying to unravel the confused flow of his emotions. Deep inside, he already knew that refusing this adventure was no longer an option. Ereshkal's words still echoed in his mind—the promise of bringing his mother back to life. Though doubts and questions continued to trouble him, he had made himself a promise: he would follow Thanatos, face every trial, every danger, to the very end.

Because this was his only chance to recover the one whose absence weighed so heavily upon him.

5 — Suna — First steps

Theris, the advisor, guided Suna toward the immense porch marking the temple's exit.

Stone columns cast their shadows onto the marble floor. As they stepped outside, Suna spotted two majestic creatures positioned on either side of the entrance: griffins standing guard.

As large as horses, their imposing bodies harmoniously combined the powerful frame of a lion with the aerial grace of an eagle. Their golden feathers, elegantly arranged across broad backs and powerful shoulders, caught and reflected the last rays of sunlight.

Their large, folded wings hinted at an impressive wingspan. Adorned with long, silky feathers shimmering gently with golden hues, they quivered lightly in the evening breeze. Their powerful front legs ended in long eagle talons, a deep, onyx black.

Their heads, noble and proud like those of golden eagles, were crowned by massive, curved beaks the color of polished amber. But it was their eyes that particularly captivated Suna: piercing, golden-brown, sparkling with intelligence, following each of her movements closely.

The griffins sat on their lion-like hindquarters, their long feline tails gracefully curled around their paws like resting cats. Their luminous silhouettes embodied strength, wisdom, and majesty.

Before these extraordinary creatures, Suna felt a wave of emotions rise within her: pure awe at their splendor, instinctive fear in the face of their obvious power, but also an irresistible attraction.

As she followed Theris, passing between the two guardians, one of the griffins slowly tilted its head toward her. She froze, seeking the advisor's approval.

A surge of curiosity overwhelmed her, but she didn't dare move forward.

"Can I… approach?" she asked hesitantly.

Theris turned around, his expression softening, as if fully understanding her desire.

"It's for him to decide," the advisor said gently. "They are Ætheris's guardians. Proud beings, but also deeply sensitive. Move toward him," he reassured her, "but do so slowly."

With her heart racing, Suna carefully reduced the distance separating her from the griffin. The creature straightened, watching her intently but without any sign of aggression.

When she was only a few steps away, she stopped again. She extended her hand slowly, as she'd seen others do with animals, waiting for the griffin to make the final move. For a moment that felt suspended in time, the griffin observed her, assessing this newcomer.

Gracefully, the griffin leaned toward her. Slowly, cautiously, it stretched its robust neck and gently brushed Suna's hand with its beak. She felt the warm, steady breath of the creature on her fingertips.

Her heart pounding wildly, Suna let her fingers glide over the griffin's mane, marveling at the silky texture of its feathers.

"You're magnificent," she whispered softly, moved and fascinated by this sudden and unexpected closeness.

The griffin emitted a low, gentle rumble; she felt it vibrate beneath her fingers.

"He likes you. That's rare," remarked the advisor. "Griffins don't allow just anyone to approach them like this."

After this suspended moment, Suna withdrew her hand, stepping back with a deep sense of gratitude. Her heart overflowed with thankfulness and wonder at this unexpected connection.

"Thank you," she murmured, touched.

The griffin inclined its head slightly once more, as if responding, before resuming its position, motionless, an unwavering guardian of the place.

Theris cleared his throat, gently bringing her back to reality.

"We should go, Suna," he said.

Suna nodded, casting a reluctant glance toward the two majestic creatures before stepping through the temple's golden archway.

The surroundings of Ætheris's temple formed an expansive sanctuary. All around her, the fading sunlight set ablaze the contours of every statue, every column, and every marble fountain. It was an enchanting place.

As she followed Theris, she passed men and women dressed in long white tunics embroidered with intricate patterns. Some carried large platters filled with ripe fruits, clay amphorae, and delicately fragrant dishes. Others, engrossed in quiet conversation, strolled leisurely. All respectfully bowed their heads to the advisor whenever they crossed paths.

Suna also noticed several guards of impressive stature. A few of them—rare and striking—displayed magnificent golden wings, gracefully undulating behind them and elegantly highlighting each movement they made.

While following Theris through the gardens, a young qilin approached. Its golden coat shimmered under the glow of the setting sun, and its gentle eyes briefly met Suna's own.

"You will be free to explore this place as much as you wish," Theris informed her. "But for tonight, I will take you to your room."

Suna nodded gently, suddenly feeling the full weight of the day's accumulated fatigue. She yearned to run around and explore this magical place, but she managed to restrain herself. They continued toward the guest quarters, an area where large arched windows allowed soft, soothing light to filter in.

Finally, Theris stopped before a finely carved wooden door. He opened it and stepped aside, allowing the young woman to enter.

The room was sublime, surpassing anything Suna could have imagined. A large bed, covered in soft white sheets as smooth as satin, dominated the center of the space. Beside it stood a small, round table of carved wood, surrounded by two comfortable chairs inviting rest. Upon the table lay a generously filled platter: warm bread with a crisp crust, fresh fruits bursting with vibrant colors, olives, and small dishes delicately scented with exotic spices. A pitcher of clear water and a carafe of light wine with amber hues completed this simple yet exquisite feast.

"Rest now," Theris said softly. "Eat as you wish and sleep well. Someone will come for you tomorrow morning."

Suna thanked him. The advisor bowed slightly and closed the door behind him. She took a moment to contemplate the room, trying to fully grasp what was happening to her.

"If my friends could see this," she mused aloud.

After a while, she sat at the table and slowly savored the meal, relishing each bite, aware of her fatigue but also of the strange, wonderful feeling within her.

As flavors filled her senses, images gently drifted through her mind: the luminous portal, Ætheris's presence, Raenos's reassuring face, the majestic griffins, and all the fascinating creatures she'd seen.

Finally, having finished the meal, she lay down on the inviting bed. Her body relaxed instantly, though her mind remained awake for a long while, replaying over and over the incredible moments she had just experienced. These memories accompanied her into sleep, as she slowly drifted into dreams where reality and magic intertwined.

The following morning, a soft knock at the door pulled Suna from her sleep.

She reluctantly opened her eyes, still groggy, trying to recognize the surroundings. Memories of recent events quickly returned, and she sat up, suddenly fully awake.

"Madam," a gentle female voice called from behind the door, "Master Raenos awaits you for breakfast."

"I'll be right there," replied Suna, her voice still heavy with sleep.

Regretting leaving the comforting warmth of the bed, she quickly dressed herself. Taking a deep breath to gather her courage, she opened the door. Standing before her was a woman with a kind face, dressed in a simple gown, her hair carefully pinned up.

"Take your time to freshen up, Madam," the maid said, dipping into a slight curtsey. "I'll be waiting right here."

Suna smiled gratefully at her and returned to the room. On a small table near the bed, she found an earthenware basin filled with fresh water, a soft cloth, and a small vial of fragrant oil. Curious, she opened the vial and breathed in the delightful floral scent.

She splashed her face with the cool water, shivering slightly at its touch, and cleaned herself gently with the cloth. Then she carefully applied a bit of the scented oil onto her skin, pleasantly surprised by the refreshing sensation.

Once ready, she rejoined the maid, who waited patiently in the hallway. The woman courteously gestured toward the corridor before them.

"Please, follow me," she said simply.

Suna fell into step behind her. Through the arched windows, she glimpsed lush gardens bathed in the early morning sun. Subtle floral fragrances softly permeated the air, creating a serene and soothing atmosphere.

Soon, they arrived in a spacious, lavishly decorated room.

Raenos and Theris were already seated at the table. Upon seeing Suna, Raenos immediately stood, followed by his advisor.

"Good morning, Suna," greeted the master of the house warmly. "I hope you slept well. Please, join us."

Intimidated yet reassured by his kind welcome, Suna approached the table and took a seat in one of the chairs. Before her, dishes were carefully arranged: warm bread, fresh fruits delicately sliced, golden honey, creamy cheese, and other dishes whose enticing aromas filled the air.

She helped herself generously, savoring with pleasure this feast, as unexpected as it was delicious.

A man entered the room, immediately capturing Suna's attention.

"Suna," Raenos announced, "allow me to introduce Vaelen, Captain of the Guard. I believe you two already met yesterday, albeit under somewhat abrupt circumstances, if I'm not mistaken?"

Suna immediately recognized the angel she'd almost collided with the previous day. Instantly, she felt her cheeks flush. Vaelen stood in the doorway, his elegant golden wings neatly folded behind him. His tall stature and athletic build radiated natural power and confidence. A square jaw reinforced his determined expression.

This time, Suna found him distinctly more approachable. Perhaps it was due to the calm radiance that softened his handsome features, or maybe the gentleness of his pale green eyes and the lightly waving locks of his mid-length blond hair.

"Nice to meet you, Vaelen," she stammered, her cheeks still flushed, embarrassed by the memory of their first meeting.

Vaelen acknowledged her greeting with a simple nod.

Raenos, gently but firmly, spoke again:

"Vaelen, please fetch Aldaren. He's already informed. Return with him, as well as two guards ready for the expedition."

"At your command," the angel replied, exiting the room.

Taking this opportunity, Theris also excused himself to finalize his own preparations.

Raenos gently placed his cup on the table and leaned back in his chair.

"Please, eat, Suna," the magician encouraged her warmly. "Gather your strength for the journey. I imagine you have many questions about what awaits you."

"You said I need to leave," Suna pointed out, hesitantly, "but where exactly are we going?"

"You will travel to Balindra, the city of knowledge," he explained. "Enhugo, one of the eight great magicians, resides there. He is the guardian of knowledge and creation. If anyone can help us locate the Pillars and understand the trials protecting them, it's him."

Suna furrowed her brows, concerned.

"Trials... you mean we'll need to pass tests to reach the Pillars?"

"Yes," Raenos confirmed. "Each Pillar has been hidden and rigorously protected within a sacred temple. Only Ætheris knows their exact location and how they are guarded. But knowing her, she surely left clues."

The magician paused briefly, studying the young woman before continuing.

"What I do know is that only a human without magic can touch these Pillars. This precaution was essential to prevent dangerous ambitions among the magicians."

He straightened slightly, emphasizing his seriousness.

"That's precisely why you're here, Suna. I was not exaggerating— you're an incredible hope."

The young woman lowered her eyes, still uneasy with the responsibility placed upon her shoulders.

"Theris and Vaelen will be by your side. I know I'm leaving you in capable hands."

She raised her eyes to him and noticed that, unlike the others, he didn't appear prepared for the journey.

"But… what about you?" she asked softly. "You're not coming with us?"

"I wish I could, truly. But Ætheris's weakening power affects the great magicians profoundly, and I am particularly affected. My energy declines with each passing day. I would only be a burden on this expedition. My advisor and the captain of my guard have traveled extensively already; their experience will prove invaluable."

Raenos's words struck Suna like a dull blow to the chest. From the very beginning, she'd instinctively counted on the magician's reassuring presence, his charisma, and especially his powers to protect her. Without him, the mission felt even more daunting.

She took a deep breath, attempting to conceal her discomfort, but a shadow of doubt had already spread across her face.

"Don't worry," the old man reassured gently. "I've gathered the best people to accompany you. You'll never be alone. They'll care for you far better than I could myself."

Suna nodded, only partly reassured despite his efforts.

Shortly afterward, Vaelen, the Captain of the Guard, returned to the room, followed by an elderly man: Aldaren.

His features, marked by the passage of years, reflected profound kindness and evident wisdom. Despite his slender frame, refined by age, he still stood perfectly straight. Light gray hair framed a benevolent face, illuminated by a pair of gentle hazel eyes. His face bore those lines that only a life filled with happiness and laughter could carve.

Raenos stepped forward warmly, introducing the man:

"Suna, this is Aldaren. Welcome, dear friend. He is a disciple of Shanur and a master of the Healers' Guild. He also teaches at the capital's hospice. He'll explain all this along the way. He will be a valuable ally on this quest."

Aldaren bowed respectfully toward Raenos, then turned his attention to Suna.

"It's an honor to accompany you," he said softly.

Suna gave him a timid smile, already comforted by the evident kindness of this man.

Two guards entered as well, standing with disciplined precision behind Vaelen. The Captain introduced them briefly. The first, named Korvel, had a bull-like build and a square jaw. Everything about him shouted rugged soldier. The second, named Hestian, was younger, with sharply chiseled features and keen, probing eyes. Both wore armor reminiscent of Roman style, their swords neatly secured at their belts.

At that moment, Theris quietly returned to the room.

"Everything is ready," he announced to Raenos.

Raenos took a deep breath and rose, leaning briefly on the table and revealing the fragility of his condition. Yet, he swiftly regained his dignified stance, meeting the gaze of each member of the group.

"My friends," he began firmly, "this mission is of utmost importance. The Pillars must be recovered to save our world. Protect Suna, guard her well, and support one another. Do not let the trials weaken your unity. Each of you bears an immense responsibility, and know that your actions will be forever engraved in history."

He turned then to Suna, his expression softening.

"As for you, Suna, have faith in yourself. You're not here by chance. Your presence among us represents a precious opportunity, a true hope granted by Ætheris."

A deep warmth filled Suna's heart at the magician's encouraging words. She nodded, ready to face whatever awaited her, reassured now that she was surrounded by people she hoped she could trust.

Theris led the group out of the temple.

As they stepped beyond the main porch, the brilliant morning light revealed a spectacular city.

"I present to you Ætherium, our capital," Theris announced, a touch of pride in his voice as he observed Suna's awestruck expression with satisfaction.

They descended a broad staircase, leaving the temple of Ætheris to enter the heart of the capital. At every street corner, Suna gasped in amazement, captivated by the visual richness and vibrant activity surrounding her. Everywhere she looked, she discovered extraordinary creatures whose existence she had previously known only through books or movies. She had never imagined such a place could truly exist, let alone that she might one day wander through it herself.

Suna suddenly stopped, mouth agape in wonder, in front of a group of satyrs performing energetically. Their instruments, made from finely carved wood, were embedded with luminous gems pulsing in rhythm with their melodies, illuminating the area around them.

"They use magic to amplify their music," Theris explained.

"This is incredible," she murmured in wonder. "Everything feels so... alive. Even the buildings and streets... It's like magic animates them."

Theris nodded, sharing her admiration.

"That's because it does. Raenos and Ætheris used magic to breathe life into this world. Every stone, every creature is imbued with an energy that connects them."

They passed a magnificent fountain with crystal-clear reflections. Tiny transparent aquatic beings swam gracefully in the sparkling water. Children laughed, reaching out toward these creatures, which responded playfully by spraying sparkles as they darted away.

Intrigued, Suna approached for a closer look, mesmerized by their ethereal beauty.

"They are naiads," Theris explained. "They can only survive when in contact with water. Ætherium possesses an extensive network of flowing water, and the coastal area is entirely crisscrossed with canals. But this is nothing compared to the realm of Thalessia."

Suna instantly raised her eyes, curious:

"Thalessia?" she repeated inquisitively.

"The magician of water. She is one of the eight great magicians. Her realm is as majestic as it is dangerous, filled with deep canals and bordered by vast marshlands."

"You haven't yet explained the magicians and our world to her?" Aldaren interjected.

"All in good time," Theris calmly replied. "I was actually counting on you to discuss it with her in detail along the way."

Suna nodded silently, eager to learn more about this enchanting world. However, her attention was soon drawn to a majestic figure perched atop a nearby shop. A phoenix of impressive size stood motionless, its crimson feathers seemingly ablaze in the sunlight. It observed the passersby below with regal calm. As she approached, she realized its plumage was indeed burning.

At the next corner, behind a stall displaying glittering weapons, stood an imposing man with a single large, round eye positioned directly in the center of his forehead. He wore a thick leather apron stained with soot, and behind him an enormous forge glowed red-hot. He hammered a blade heated by the fiery breath of a reptile. Intrigued, she instinctively slowed down to better observe this scene.

"That's a cyclops, one of Ignara's blacksmiths," Vaelen explained, noting her interest. "The creature assisting him is a salamander from the volcano Pyros. They're renowned for crafting artifacts of exceptional finesse," the captain added. "However, their true specialty lies in weapon-making. We purchase our equipment from them. Their swords are as delicate and lightweight as they are strong and sharp."

Suna felt both fascination and apprehension in the presence of these creatures and this bustling city permeated by magic. As she looked around, she began to grasp the incredible adventure awaiting her. Despite her lingering fears and doubts, a growing desire took root within her to journey onward, eager to uncover what this fascinating world had yet to offer.

As they approached the outskirts of the city, the bustling liveliness of the streets gradually gave way to a pleasant calm. The grand, imposing buildings were replaced by modest houses with plain facades and slate roofs. The spaces between structures slowly widened, allowing the fresh, soothing scents of the countryside to fill the air, replacing the aromas of spices and exotic fragrances of the marketplaces.

On the horizon, a large stone building gradually appeared beside the road, surrounded by expansive pastures. As they drew closer, Suna could hear the rhythmic sound of hooves striking the ground, mingled with the occasional neighing of horses.

In the distance, three riders moving away drew her attention. At the front rode an imposing man with black wings, sitting upright on his mount. A woman in dark clothing followed him. Bringing up the rear was another rider who clearly had little experience on horseback, displaying considerably less poise. The sight amused Suna, but quickly made her wonder how she herself would fare.

They entered the stable.

Inside, the pleasant scent of fresh hay and wood filled the air. Theris stepped forward confidently, carefully inspecting the horses lined up in their stalls, then selected four mounts with bright, lightly colored coats.

He stopped in front of a robust, cream-colored horse harnessed to a sturdy carriage. The carriage itself was solidly built from wood, reinforced with finely crafted metal fittings.

"This one will suit Aldaren and Suna perfectly," he declared, gently patting the animal's flank.

Suna immediately felt a wave of relief wash over her. The prospect of not having to ride reduced her initial anxiety significantly—especially since these animals were much larger than she had anticipated.

"I'm not sure I could have managed riding a horse…"

Aldaren, busy adjusting his cape near the carriage, overheard and reassured her.

"Then this arrangement is perfect," the old man said kindly. "We'll travel together. My old legs vastly prefer the comfort of a seat to the uncertainty of a saddle."

Suna stepped forward, admiring the finely carved wood, the detailed decorations, and the simple yet inviting cushions lining the seats. At the back, there was enough space arranged to comfortably transport provisions, blankets, and other necessary travel equipment.

Meanwhile, the others busied themselves around them, methodically loading their baggage into the carriage. Vaelen, accustomed to leadership, rigorously supervised the process, ensuring everything was securely fastened.

"We have everything we need," he finally announced. "Water and enough provisions for several days."

Theris extended a hand to assist Aldaren onto the front seat, ensuring the elderly man was comfortably settled. Then, with equal gentleness, he turned to Suna, offering a reassuring hand to help her climb up next to the healer.

"Get comfortable," the advisor said in a soothing tone. "The stablemaster assured me this horse is gentle and obedient. You have nothing to fear, and you'll have plenty of time to learn the basics of riding if you wish."

"Thank you," she said.

Suna gratefully took his hand and climbed up to sit beside Aldaren. Once seated, she lightly brushed her fingers over the polished wood, savoring this new beginning.

Vaelen approached his own mount, a magnificent stallion with a proud and noble bearing. He glanced briefly toward Theris:

"Everything is ready."

Theris mounted his horse with ease, his posture clearly revealing his experience. Behind him, the two guards, Hestian and Korvel, followed suit, methodically adjusting their reins before positioning themselves on either side of the carriage, naturally adopting a protective stance.

"Let's move," Theris announced.

Aldaren snapped the reins to prompt the horse forward. The animal, as docile and reliable as promised, immediately began moving, pulling the carriage smoothly.

As the group set off along the road, Suna leaned back more comfortably against the seat's backrest. The rhythmic motion of the carriage, along with Aldaren's reassuring presence beside her, brought her an unexpected sense of calm. At that moment, despite her lingering doubts and questions, she felt ready to face the journey toward Balindra.

A gentle breeze blew, carrying with it the fresh scent of damp grass. Suna, seated beside Aldaren in the carriage, watched the landscape drift by.

Aldaren broke the silence.

"What's Earth like?" asked the old healer curiously.

Where to even begin? Compared to Mytherra, her own world suddenly seemed so dull, so lifeless…

"Well, it depends," she finally replied. "Our world is different. Less… magical, I suppose. We have enormous cities, buildings so tall they seem to touch the sky. Everything is built by machines run by computers rather than magic. But because of that, nature is often forgotten, even damaged."

"Computers…," repeated the old man, as if tasting the strange word. "Perhaps they've taken the place magic once held?"

Suna shrugged, a faint, sad smile briefly crossing her lips.

"That's one way to see it. But they don't replace everything. Nothing in my world resembles what I've seen here. These incredible creatures, places so full of life…"

"You seem amazed by Mytherra, but also… troubled. Is it because of the circumstances of your arrival?" he gently asked. "Tell me, how exactly did it happen? I haven't heard the details."

Suna took a deep breath, recalling that strange day which had forever changed her life.

"I was coming back from high school," she began. "It was a perfectly ordinary day, really. As usual, I took a shortcut through an old cemetery near my home."

Aldaren tilted his head slightly. He didn't fully understand all the words, but encouraged her to continue.

"That's when I saw Zayn, a boy from my class. He was standing in front of a grave. He recently lost his mother. But he wasn't alone… He was talking with a strange woman, dressed completely in black. There was something unsettling about the way she stood there—as if she was… on the prowl."

She paused, eyes gazing at the distant hills, vividly reliving the moment.

"They walked away together. Something compelled me to follow, but I kept my distance. Then they disappeared behind a large stone statue. When I reached the spot, they were gone… as if they'd simply vanished."

She took a deep breath before continuing, her voice slightly troubled.

"That's when I saw it: a circle of light floating in the air. It was filled with strange patterns. The circle itself seemed to vibrate, as if it were breathing. A peculiar breeze flowed from that portal, and beyond, I could glimpse a vast hall."

At that moment, she had never imagined that stepping through this portal would change her life so profoundly.

"I didn't know what to do," Suna resumed, shaking her head. "But curiosity overcame fear. I stepped through. When I emerged on the other side, I found myself in the temple, right behind the statue of Ætheris."

"Fascinating…" murmured the old man. "This woman in black you saw — she's the one who led this boy to the portal? And this boy, Zayn — he passed through before you?"

A feeling of guilt washed over her. Since arriving, she'd been so absorbed by events that she'd forgotten to think about Zayn again.

"Yes, I think so," Suna answered. "No one seems to have seen him here, but I completely forgot to ask!"

Aldaren remained quiet for a moment, studying her face, as though trying to unravel the mystery she had just shared. Slowly, he crossed his arms, visibly concerned.

"A woman dressed entirely in black…," he murmured thoughtfully, as if speaking to himself.

"I don't know exactly what she wanted from him, but all of it felt... strange. I haven't seen them again since stepping through the portal, but I wonder who that woman was... and what she wanted with him."

Suna watched Aldaren anxiously, suddenly realizing that this detail had taken on a far more troubling dimension than she'd imagined...

"A woman in black," he murmured again, almost to himself.

"Theris!" called Aldaren, immediately turning his head toward the front of the procession.

Theris and Vaelen exchanged intrigued glances before slowing their mounts and dropping back alongside the carriage.

"What is it?" asked the counselor, instantly noticing Aldaren's concerned expression.

"Listen carefully," Aldaren said gravely. "I'm starting to suspect it wasn't Ætheris who brought our young guest into the temple. Suna, could you please repeat your story for them?"

She took a deep breath before recounting precisely the scene she had previously described to Aldaren, trying to remain clear despite her apprehension.

When she finished, Vaelen furrowed his brow, wanting to be certain he'd understood correctly.

"You're saying another human passed through before you, accompanied by a strange woman dressed entirely in black?"

"Yes," replied Suna firmly. "I'm sure of what I saw."

The captain tightened his grip on his reins, bringing the entire group to a halt.

Vaelen drew a deep breath before speaking.

"Ereshkal was recently seen in Ætherium. You know how rarely she leaves the depths of Nekrosys. Could she possibly have used the portal herself?"

"Could she have opened the portal herself," corrected Theris.

Theris and Vaelen exchanged alarmed glances.

"That would mean," said the counselor slowly, "that she found a way to bypass Ætheris's restrictions. Worse yet, it would suggest that her power isn't fading like the others."

The captain clenched his fingers around the hilt of his sword as Theris pulled his reins again, holding the group at a standstill. Their expressions clearly reflected the seriousness of what they'd just grasped.

"If that's true…" Theris began, tension evident in his voice.

"We must inform Raenos immediately!" interrupted Vaelen with a firmness that surprised even Theris. "If Ereshkal is already making her move, she undoubtedly has precise intentions. And if another human is already under her influence, this could dramatically complicate things."

Suna suddenly realized that this woman in black—whose existence she had nearly forgotten, so absorbed had she been by Mytherra's wonders—represented a far more troubling threat than she'd ever imagined.

Without wasting another moment, Theris spurred his horse onward, prompting the group to resume their journey immediately, urgency now hanging heavily upon them all.

They soon reached Midlock. The city's liveliness was palpable, driven by the constant hustle of merchants whose calls and bargaining created a cheerful cacophony. Theris quickly guided the group to the guard post, a modest stone building located at the edge of the main square.

"I must send an urgent message to Raenos," he announced as he dismounted. "Wait for me here."

The others remained outside, attentively watching the passing crowd. Suna, sitting in the carriage, absently contemplated the market's hustle and bustle. Yet, her thoughts inevitably drifted back to Zayn and the mysterious woman whose significance had everyone so concerned. She observed the passersby, wondering what had become of Zayn, unaware that just an hour earlier, he had traveled this very same road…

Theris returned a few moments later.

"The messenger has departed," he said, remounting his horse. "Raenos will know what to do."

They moved off, taking the alley heading south. As they distanced themselves from the bustling main square, the city's sounds gradually grew muffled.

Theris guided them toward an inn located on the outskirts of town, slightly set back from the main road. The two-story building bore a delicately carved wooden sign depicting a cluster of grapes and a wine cup: *The Golden Vine*. They left the horses in the nearby stable.

As soon as they crossed the threshold, a welcoming warmth enveloped them. At the heart of the common room stood a large fireplace, the flames crackling gently. Several rustic tables were scattered around, occupied by travelers engrossed in conversation or dice games.

The innkeeper, a broad-shouldered man, immediately approached them. His thick, salt-and-pepper beard seemed to have absorbed the scents of woodsmoke and beer.

"Welcome, travelers! Looking for a hot meal and some rest, I suppose?"

"Yes," Theris confirmed. "A hot meal and a few rooms."

"Very well," the man replied. "Follow me."

They settled near the fireplace. Suna sat down, feeling her body warm and relax with relief. The dishes soon arrived: a steaming stew served with soft bread and fresh cheese.

Once finished with her meal, Suna felt the accumulated exhaustion of the day overwhelm her. She politely excused herself from her companions and rose from the table.

"Rest well, Suna," Aldaren said gently. "We have a long day ahead of us tomorrow."

She stood up and climbed the wooden staircase to the upper floor. A corridor, dimly lit by a few candles hanging on the walls, served several numbered doors. She opened the door assigned to her, discovering a modest but cozy room.

A bed covered with a thick blanket awaited her invitingly. A small, half-open window allowed the cool evening air to drift inside, bringing with it the faint, muffled murmurs of the city settling down to sleep. She took a deep breath, savoring the quiet moment.

Without further hesitation, Suna slipped off her shoes and lay down on the bed with a sigh of relief. Pulling the blanket around herself, she turned onto her side. For a moment, she felt a pang of nostalgia for her old room, wondering how long she would remain away from home.

As her eyelids grew heavy, her thoughts drifted gently, wavering between her old world and the mysteries of the one she had just entered. Soothed by the discreet creaking of wood and the faint murmurs from the common room below, she finally sank into a deep and peaceful sleep.

6 — Zayn — Northward

Zayn slowly opened his eyes as the first rays of dawn filtered through the shutters, savoring a few more moments of quiet offered by the inn.

He sat on the edge of the bed, yawning widely, then stretched his muscles, still sore from the previous day, to fully awaken. After briefly splashing his face with cold water, he joined his companions downstairs.

Thanatos and Nymeris were already waiting for him at the table, ready to resume their journey. Seeing that they had already finished their meal, Zayn quickly gulped down his breakfast. Once he was done, the three of them stepped outside into the fresh morning air. The horses awaited them, ready for departure.

At the end of the avenue stood the northern gates of the city, flanked by two imposing watchtowers. The riders passed through the gates unhindered; a single glance from Thanatos and Nymeris was enough to make the guards step aside, kept at bay by the menacing aura of Ereshkal's disciples.

Soon they were back on the dusty roads. The lively noises of the city gradually gave way to the gentle whispers of the wind over open plains.

As Midlock slowly disappeared behind them, Zayn leaned forward on his saddle.

"Where exactly are we headed?" he asked Nymeris.

The warrior slowed her mount's pace, pulling up alongside him.

"To Quarth," she replied. "We need to convince Nerath to join our cause. Afterward, we'll seek support from Thalessa and Ignara."

"Nerath and… They're great magicians, right?"

"Yes."

Curiosity piqued, and momentarily forgetting his discomfort, Zayn asked:

"Could you tell me a bit more about them?"

Nymeris looked toward the horizon, carefully choosing her words.

"As you might already know," she began with a hint of irony, "Ætheris created Raenos. Together, they shaped eight magicians in their image, supposedly representing the essential aspects of this world."

"I was told Ætheris was the source of all magic," Zayn recalled.

"That's what they'd have us all believe, yes. In truth, Ætheris designed Mytherra according to her own vision of harmony. Her idea of peace is closer to a dictatorship."

"And Raenos, what about him?"

"Raenos enjoys playing the role of leader. But don't be fooled—he only intervenes when it suits him. He claims to defend balance, but in reality, all he wants is to maintain the world exactly as he and Ætheris shaped it. They've already shown they're willing to sacrifice those who oppose them."

Zayn felt troubled by these revelations. Nymeris seemed entirely convinced, yet deep down, he remained cautious. Everything he learned about Mytherra seemed tinged with subjective truths he would need to carefully untangle.

"I see," he finally said. "And what about the others? Nerath, Thalessa, Ignara… Who exactly are they?"

"Nerath is the one we're heading to first. He'll be our greatest ally."

"Why him specifically?"

She smiled slightly, almost admiringly, eyes fixed on the horizon.

"Because he's the magician of war, the embodiment of brute strength. But he's not merely a soldier. Nerath is the greatest strategist Mytherra has ever known."

Her voice vibrated with admiration.

"But make no mistake, Zayn—Nerath isn't just a man of battle. He has something precious, something even his enemies acknowledge: an unshakeable sense of honor. He always keeps his word. Once gained, his loyalty is unbreakable."

"If he's so important, why isn't he already on your side?"

"Because Nerath accepts no master, no restraint. Raenos dominated him, subdued him, and he still harbors deep resentment. Yet, his ambition remains intact: he still dreams of conquest and glory. His kingdom, Quarth, is built entirely upon this aspiration—a fortress impossible to breach, where absolute discipline reigns."

The image of an ideal warrior slowly faded, replaced by that of a formidable and surely dangerous conqueror.

"In that case, how can we be certain he'll agree to help us? He could just as easily turn against us, couldn't he?"

"Nerath never betrays anyone. He only grants loyalty to those he deems worthy. If we prove to him that our cause can offer him what he desires, he'll follow without hesitation."

She stared at him intensely, as though to ensure her message had sunk in.

"And with Nerath by our side, we'll be invincible."

Zayn snorted softly. Having such an ally was both reassuring and unnerving.

"After Nerath," Nymeris continued, "we'll have to convince Thalessa. She's the undisputed mistress of the oceans."

"The oceans?" Zayn repeated, intrigued.

"Thalessa is as elusive as the seas she commands. She's a magician as fascinating as she is fearsome. Beneath her seductive appearance lies a power capable of sweeping away everything in mere moments."

"Another magician who sounds pretty dangerous," Zayn remarked.

"Dangerous, yes—but not in Nerath's way. Thalessa embodies a constant duality, like the tides she controls. Sometimes calm, generous, protective... she can also be violent and destructive. She's unpredictable—but that's precisely what makes her so useful."

"Does she lead an army too?"

"Not exactly," said Nymeris. "Her kingdom is a marvel—an underwater city where powerful, fearsome aquatic creatures dwell. Under her protection, her subjects represent a formidable force, always ready to surge from the depths to overwhelm her adversaries."

Zayn pressed his lips together. "Charming image," he thought.

"Thalessa will be a precious ally, but one to keep an eye on. No one ever truly knows what she's thinking."

"And if she refuses to help us?" Zayn worried.

"Thalessa always chooses the side that gives her the most power. All we have to do is show her our cause allows her greater freedom of action. That'll be enough to convince her."

Nymeris guided her horse around a stone on the path, taking advantage of the brief interruption to think before continuing.

"Then, we'll seek out Ignara," she stated, "the magician of fire and destruction."

"Another terrifying mage, I suppose," Zayn thought.

"Ignara is exactly like the fire she controls: intense, passionate, capable of consuming any obstacle in her path. Few dare approach her without fear—but those who know how to channel her destructive force wield an absolute weapon."

Zayn was seriously beginning to question what he was doing here.

"Her disciples," Nymeris continued, "are among the best craftsmen and blacksmiths in Mytherra. They work tirelessly in the blazing forges of Mount Pyros. The weapons they forge will be invaluable to us. Their reputation is unmatched, both in finesse and strength."

"Is she really a reliable ally?"

"Reliable isn't the word I'd use to describe her. Rather, let's say she's indispensable. The passion driving her is her greatest strength—once convinced, she'll stop at nothing to achieve her goals. Our challenge will simply be giving her a reason to believe in our cause."

Nymeris seemed quite comfortable with the idea of allying herself with beings so powerful—and so dangerous.

He thought about the three magicians Nymeris had just described, then his mind naturally drifted toward Ereshkal. Curiously, since their meeting, no one had clearly explained her role to him, nor the true extent of her power.

He straightened slightly in his saddle, hesitated, then finally asked cautiously, "And what about Ereshkal? What sort of magician is she?"

Nymeris took a deep breath, her expression becoming more respectful.

"She symbolizes inevitable endings. Her realm welcomes those whose journeys in this world come to an end. Often misunderstood, and feared for good reason, she nonetheless represents the essential passage to what comes after. Her presence commands respect as much as fear, for she holds an inexorable power over the fate of every being."

Zayn's eyes widened as he finally understood.

"So, that's it!" he exclaimed. "She's the magician of death. For me, death always evokes something cold and final... It's not exactly reassuring."

"What you perceive as an end is actually just a transition," Thanatos interjected. "Death isn't annihilation, it's rest. Ereshkal is not the one who causes death—she does not choose who dies; she simply gathers souls to grant them peace."

Nymeris added gently, "Think of her instead as a caring guardian, Zayn. She takes care of those who have finished their journeys in this world, gently preparing them for what comes next. Her role is essential, because without her, souls would wander endlessly, lost between worlds."

Thanatos nodded approvingly.

"Exactly," the dark angel affirmed firmly. "Ereshkal preserves the fundamental balance of our existence. What you perceive as permanent loss is merely an indispensable step in the perpetual renewal of this world. Without this crucial harmony, chaos alone would reign."

Zayn squinted skeptically, not entirely convinced.

"So, when someone dies, Ereshkal watches over them until their spirit finds peace. But then… what happens to them exactly afterward?" he asked apprehensively, his heart tightened by the lingering memory of his mother.

Nymeris exchanged a careful glance with Thanatos before replying, choosing her words cautiously.

"Some truths are not meant for mortals," she said. "There are mysteries that surpass even our understanding. The ultimate fate of souls after their rest remains knowledge reserved only for Ereshkal herself. We, her disciples, possess only a limited glimpse."

"What we can assure you," Thanatos clarified, "is that Ereshkal treats each soul with great care. In her realm, death is simply a door opening onto the next chapter. It's a necessity, a natural law that nothing can alter."

"I… I think I understand," murmured Zayn. "Even though this idea is very different from what I've always believed. Death seen from this angle seems less terrifying, though I can't say it totally reassures me. There are still many things I struggle to accept."

Thanatos turned his face toward him, showing an unusual empathy:

"The truth is rarely easy to accept, especially when it leaves so many unanswered questions," he said calmly. "But remember one essential thing, Zayn: every ending heralds a new beginning."

Still unsure whether he could fully trust them, Zayn decided to keep questioning:

"So, what exactly do Ereshkal's disciples do?"

"We're also known as the 'Watchers of Souls,'" Nymeris clarified.

"The Watchers of Souls?"

Nymeris's tone became more solemn.

"Yes, we watch over the dead. Ereshkal's disciples are present everywhere—in every city and throughout every corner of Mytherra. Our duty is to accompany those who have departed, to recover their bodies with dignity and bring them to Nekrosys, our sanctuary."

Zayn considered her words for a moment before continuing:

"And then, what exactly do you do with them?"

Nymeris replied with a note of clear respect for her role:

"We carefully prepare them for their final journey. We embalm the bodies to preserve them, gently release their souls from their earthly attachments, then open the passage to their ultimate destination."

Zayn couldn't help but draw a parallel with what he knew about ancient cultures.

"A bit like Egyptian priests when they prepared mummies?"

Nymeris briefly considered this before responding carefully:

"In a way, yes. But our role goes beyond preserving the body. We guide souls through their transition, allowing them to reach the place they're meant to go, according to a natural and immutable order."

Still uneasy, Zayn thoughtfully bit his lower lip, voicing a deep-seated concern:

"But not all civilizations have the same funeral rites. How can you be sure Ereshkal's method is the right one?"

"It's not about right or wrong, Zayn. Some peoples have their own traditions, and we don't seek to challenge them. Quite the contrary, we adapt our rituals to their customs."

"What kinds of traditions, for example?"

"Some burn their dead, others bury them deep underground, and still others send them out to sea… But regardless of the method, the principle remains unchanged: it's about closing the door between this world and the beyond, so that balance can be maintained."

Zayn opened his mouth to ask another question, clearly eager to learn more, but Thanatos cut him off sharply, his tone suddenly authoritative.

"That's enough, Zayn. We've already shared far more than necessary. Certain answers will come in time, not before."

Zayn, surprised by Thanatos's sudden firmness, chose to remain silent, understanding he had crossed some implicit boundary.

A brief silence followed, broken only by the rhythmic sound of hoofbeats.

After a moment, Zayn used a slight gap in the path to guide his horse back toward Nymeris. He waited until Thanatos had moved ahead before leaning toward her, speaking softly:

"You didn't tell me about the other magicians… There are eight, right?"

Nymeris replied quietly, not really bothering whether she was overheard:

"They're not worth discussing," she whispered coldly. "They're cowards, entirely under Raenos's orders. They have no will of their own."

Without even turning around, Thanatos let out a faint chuckle, confirming he had clearly heard their exchange.

Zayn had certainly been dropped into a complex world. The magicians seemed terrifying to him. Although he was somewhat reassured to imagine them on his side, he wasn't naïve. He could sense Nymeris had carefully chosen her words, guided by her evident loyalty to Ereshkal.

He wondered what the other magicians might have said about themselves, if given a chance to speak. Still, Nymeris's explanations offered him a clear picture of what to expect: a complicated game of alliances, where every choice could prove decisive.

Gradually, the landscape around them began to change. To their right appeared a vast stretch of water, the sunlight making its surface shimmer like a giant silver mirror. Gentle hills, lush with vegetation, framed the sea, their outlines softly fading into the mist.

The scene awoke in him the memory of a painting that hung in his living room back home. It was a simple piece depicting a sea bordered by similar landscapes. This ordinary memory suddenly felt oddly precious, belonging to a life he could no longer return to.

"That's the Sea of Ætheria," Nymeris gently explained, interrupting his reverie. "It surrounds the peninsula where Ætherium—the capital we came from—is located."

Zayn turned toward her, but his attention was immediately drawn beyond Nymeris. Vast fields stretched out like a lush carpet, softly rippling in the breeze.

He spotted scattered human figures working the land, and just beyond them rose the first trees of an immense forest, dominating the entire horizon.

Nymeris immediately noticed his interest.

"These are Sylki's lands," she continued, "the master of forests and earth. Today, we're merely skirting the edges of his territory. His realm is vast, flourishing, filled with creatures and plants you've likely never even imagined, but it's not our destination."

Zayn slowly nodded without responding, entirely captivated by the beauty before him. He allowed himself to be carried away by the tranquil images unfolding before his eyes, his mind wandering gently along with this land brimming with life.

As the sun slowly dipped behind the distant mountains, a small town revealed itself at their feet: Gildenfort, nestled comfortably within the landscape, its rooftops clad in dark slate tiles. Nearby, a river with clear waters wound through the valley, enhancing the tranquility of the scene.

They entered the town just as the first lanterns were being lit, bathing the cobbled streets in a gentle glow. Despite the apparent simplicity of the buildings, Zayn immediately noticed the care given to every detail: finely carved windows, meticulously hand-painted signs, and perfectly tended vegetable gardens. The town center was lively, animated by locals gathered around small campfires or cheerfully chatting near the taverns.

Thanatos led their small group toward a stable adjoining a two-story inn. Its wooden façade was warmly colored, and hanging lanterns cast a welcoming light. A carefully painted sign proudly announced: **Travelers' Rest**.

As they stopped, a young stable boy came running up, awkwardly wiping his hands on an apron clearly too big for him.

"Horses to stable for the night?" he asked, breathless but smiling.

"Yes," Thanatos replied, dismounting. "They've traveled well. Make sure they get fresh hay and water."

Nymeris gracefully dismounted next, handing her reins to the boy. Once again, Zayn struggled to get down. His legs, numbed by the long journey, trembled weakly beneath his weight. The stable boy quickly stepped forward, grabbing the reins and offering support.

"Thank you," Zayn murmured gratefully, rubbing his sore legs.

Once the horses were comfortably settled in clean, straw-filled stalls, the small group entered the inn.

Inside, the tavern bustled with life and high spirits. A great fire crackled in the hearth, radiating welcoming warmth after the chill of the journey. The walls echoed with laughter and lively conversation from the guests.

Near the entrance, an enthusiastic crowd gathered around a table where dice players competed eagerly. Each roll provoked cheers or disappointed groans, coins exchanging hands amidst animated excitement. At the far end, two players leaned over a game board carved directly into the table's surface, passionately debating and carefully moving their pieces with strategic intent.

Zayn and his companions found a discreet table close to the fireplace. Thanatos caught the attention of the innkeeper with a simple gesture; a robust man with a cheerful face appeared promptly before them.

"Welcome to Gildenfort, travelers!" he called out warmly. "What can I do to make your evening enjoyable?"

"A hot meal and rooms for the night," Thanatos answered.

"I'll see to it!" assured the man, hurrying off toward the kitchens.

Between mouthfuls, Zayn discreetly observed Nymeris. She seemed perpetually alert, even in such a peaceful place.

Once satisfied, Zayn sighed lightly, contentedly leaning back against his chair while savoring the pleasant warmth of the hearth.

"It feels great to eat after a day like today," he declared with satisfaction.

"And now it's time for sleep," Nymeris replied. "Tomorrow's ride will be long as well."

Zayn grimaced at the thought but stood without protest, following his companions toward the stairs where the innkeeper awaited them. The man led them to their rooms, simple yet inviting, ready to provide the rest needed before tomorrow's journey.

A few candles burned gently on the bedside tables. Zayn collapsed gratefully onto the mattress, deeply appreciating its comfort after such an exhausting day.

"Rest well," Nymeris told him from the doorway. "We leave early tomorrow morning."

Zayn slowly closed his eyes, allowing fatigue to immediately overtake him. His mind drifted toward the revelations and discoveries that had filled his first days in this unfamiliar world. Gradually, the distant murmur of voices from downstairs faded. Soon, his dreams became filled with astonishing visions: magicians of incredible power, enigmatic creatures, and wondrous landscapes that he now longed to discover more fully.

7 — Suna — Southward

Suna opened her eyes, drawn from sleep by the crowing of a rooster. She stretched, savoring the cozy warmth of the blankets a moment longer. Outside, the cheerful songs of birds heralded a new day. Sitting up at the edge of the bed, she breathed deeply, dispelling the lingering haze of sleep.

After quickly getting ready, she slipped on her clothes and made her way down to the common room. The inviting scent of freshly baked bread and fragrant herbal tea drifted through the air.

Downstairs, her companions were already seated around the table, speaking quietly among themselves. Aldaren smiled warmly as soon as he saw her.

"Did you sleep well, Suna?" the old healer asked, handing her a plate filled with fresh fruit.

"Very well," she replied, taking a seat beside him. "Thank you."

As she ate, she noticed Theris and Vaelen appeared tense, exchanging few words. Their demeanor intrigued her, but she chose not to ask questions just yet.

After breakfast, the group prepared to continue their journey.

Shortly thereafter, they left the inn, passed through the southern gates of Midlock, and resumed their travels beneath a clear sky.

The rhythmic pounding of hooves and the gentle creaking of the carriage were the only sounds disturbing the serenity of the road.

Still seated beside Aldaren, Suna observed the two riders ahead. Their serious expressions and low voices steadily fueled her anxiety. Hesitantly, she turned toward Aldaren.

"Why do Theris and Vaelen seem so worried?" she asked softly. "Who is this Ereshkal they keep talking about?"

The old man, deep in thought, took a moment before responding. Gradually emerging from his reverie, he straightened his back with noticeable solemnity, then turned toward Suna with a thoughtful expression that scarcely concealed his concern.

"Ereshkal…" he began, "is unique among the eight great magicians. Unlike the others, she represents a far darker aspect of our world's balance: death itself. She is the guardian of the inevitable end of all things."

"Death?" Suna exclaimed, stunned to learn the nature of their enemy.

"Yes, but reality is more complicated," Aldaren continued. "Ereshkal isn't simply a guardian. Her role is to guide souls of the departed into the afterlife. Her realm, Nekrosys, is both dark and sacred—a place where souls receive the honor they deserve."

He paused briefly, searching carefully for his next words before continuing in an even graver tone.

"However, though she is meant to remain neutral and impartial, she occasionally yields to less honorable ambitions. Persistent rumors even claim she can manipulate the dead for her own purposes."

"Manipulate… you mean control the dead?" Suna asked apprehensively.

"Some say so, yes," Aldaren admitted. "But it's difficult to prove. What's certain, however, is that Ereshkal remains unpredictable. And if she is truly involved with the portal matter, it means she's pursuing a specific objective. She has always desired to expand her power and influence."

Suna struggled to comprehend the complexities of this world into which she'd been unwillingly drawn.

"If she's already making her move," Aldaren added, "that explains why Theris and Vaelen are so concerned. Things could deteriorate rapidly."

Suna remained silent for a few moments, reflecting on what she'd just heard. Suddenly, she raised her eyes toward Aldaren with a hint of hesitation.

"Raenos mentioned someone important we have to see," she cautiously began. "Hugo, I think? I'm not sure I fully understood who he was exactly."

A smile brightened Aldaren's face. Clearly, he appreciated the young woman's curiosity.

"We're going to meet Enhugo," he explained, with evident respect. "He is the first of the great magicians created by Ætheris and Raenos. He's the guardian of all the knowledge Mytherra possesses and the master of creation and invention."

"You mean he's some kind of scholar?"

"Exactly," replied Aldaren. "Enhugo is a source of wisdom and inspiration. He possesses unparalleled knowledge of this world's mysteries and readily shares his expertise with those seeking to learn or create something new."

He briefly observed the young woman.

"But Enhugo is also deeply neutral. He closely observes events and advises the people but never takes sides in conflicts. His wisdom demands a certain detachment to maintain impartiality."

"Raenos spoke of Balindra as a great city of knowledge. Is it connected to Enhugo in some way?"

"Yes, directly," Aldaren replied enthusiastically. "Balindra is the very heart of knowledge in Mytherra. That's where Enhugo established his academic center, an extraordinary place where the greatest minds in our world gather."

Suna loved the intensity with which Aldaren spoke about this place. She imagined a magnificent city filled with scholars, like a grand university.

Aldaren continued:

"From scholars to artisans, inventors to sages, everyone comes to Balindra to exchange knowledge, pursue research, or perfect their creations."

He noticed her fascinated expression and concluded with a warm smile.

"It's a place of unparalleled learning and sharing, a true breeding ground for new ideas, where countless important discoveries have been made thanks to his benevolence and enlightened mind."

"Enhugo sounds like an ideal mentor," she remarked.

"That's exactly what he is," confirmed Aldaren. "His presence is truly a treasure for all Mytherra."

"Did he train you, then? I heard you were a healer."

Aldaren smiled slightly, almost amused by the question.

"No, my training didn't come from Enhugo, but from Shanur."

"Shanur?" repeated Suna. "Who is he exactly?"

Aldaren's smile deepened, infused with evident affection. He sought just the right words before responding.

"Shanur embodies light in all its forms—the one that heals, reassures, and restores hope when all seems lost."

"So, he's the source of your healing powers?" she asked gently.

"Yes," Aldaren replied, with gentle pride. "Shanur is Mytherra's greatest healer. His power can save lives, restore harmony, and heal the deepest wounds, both physical and spiritual."

He paused briefly, observing the landscapes passing around them.

"His domain, Solandar, is a peaceful place located on a vast plateau at the foot of immense mountains. Many people journey there seeking peace and healing. I myself am one of his disciples."

"A disciple? I've heard that word several times. What does it mean exactly?"

"Yes… Let me explain: long ago, when the magicians still lived on Earth, they chose certain humans to teach magic and to share part of their essence with them. These men and women then became their disciples."

He paused for a moment before continuing, a gleam of pride in his eyes.

"Through these disciples, the magicians maintained a close connection with humanity. In exchange for the power they received, the disciples took on the responsibility of preserving the balance desired by their mentors. When the magicians were exiled to Mytherra, their original disciples naturally followed, passing their magic down through generations."

"You mean you're their direct descendant?" Suna realized.

"Exactly," Aldaren confirmed. "Of course, our magic today is less intense than that of our ancestors, but it still exists. It deeply connects us to the great magicians, and it also imposes upon us a share of their responsibility towards this world."

Suna listened attentively, trying to fully grasp the deeper meaning behind his words.

"And… this magic, it's what connects you to Shanur?" she asked.

"Precisely," Aldaren replied. "But this link doesn't dictate our destiny entirely. Some deliberately choose to ignore or forget their heritage, to lead an ordinary existence, or simply follow a different path. For me, however, this connection with Shanur has always been a source of inspiration. He embodies kindness, hope, and the care of others. Following this path has always seemed natural to me."

Suna remained quiet for a short moment, feeling admiration for the elderly man.

"Being a disciple isn't just inheriting magic," he added gently. "It's also about choosing to carry within oneself a fragment of the values and ideals of the magician we're connected to."

He placed a hand on a medallion hanging around his neck.

"In my case, that means offering help and comfort, healing wounds, preserving life, and protecting the vulnerable. It's a choice as much as an inheritance. That's why I chose to join the guild of healers."

"It's fascinating," said Suna. "But I still struggle to understand… How exactly does magic work?"

Aldaren smiled, as if he'd been expecting this question.

"Every magic is different," he explained. "I only know Shanur's. It would be inappropriate for me to explain things I don't master. But I understand light."

He paused and extended his hand toward her, palm open.

"Light isn't merely brightness. It's an energy that emanates from within us, a warmth we project."

"You mean… like electricity?" she asked, searching for a comparison from her own world.

"I don't know that word," he replied. "But if you mean an invisible force manifesting through us, then yes. Watch."

His hand remained still, yet a gentle golden glow began to escape from it, spreading a soft warmth around them. Suna felt a comforting sensation filling her, as though the mere presence of this light was dispelling the fatigue and anxiety that had weighed on her.

"Amazing…" she murmured.

Aldaren guided this light from his palm to the tips of his fingers.

"This light heals," he explained. "Depending on how I shape it, it can soothe pain, warm the heart, and restore strength and hope."

Suna watched, fascinated, as the energy danced within his hand. Then, with a delicate gesture, Aldaren condensed it into a small golden sphere, hovering just above his palm.

"We can also accumulate this energy," he continued. "Give it shape. Make it tangible."

He reached out his hand toward her, and with a smooth gesture, sent the sphere floating through the air. It drifted gently, like a bubble carried on an invisible breeze. Instinctively, Suna raised her hands to touch it.

When she did, she expected an intangible sensation, like wind or diffuse heat. But no—the sphere was solid, resistant under her fingertips, like stone.

"It's solid!" she said in surprise.

"It's protection," explained the healer. "A shield against whatever threatens us."

Suna rolled the sphere between her fingers. It felt warm and smooth.

"Some can shape it differently," Aldaren explained. "Make it hotter, brighter... but I never sought to harm anyone with it."

Absorbed by the light she held, Suna suddenly raised her head.

"Could... could you teach me?"

"I doubt you can," Aldaren said gently.

Suna frowned.

"Why not?"

Aldaren hesitated, then sighed.

"Because magic flows through the veins of disciples. We're linked to our magicians from birth. We can only use one type of magic. And you..."

He gazed at her intently.

"You're different. You're not linked to any of them."

Suna pressed her lips together. It was frustrating. In stories, heroes always discovered hidden powers, exceptional destinies. But her... she was nothing more than an ordinary human, without even a trace of magic.

"Let's just try," she insisted.

"Very well. Close your eyes."

Suna complied, trying to steady her breathing.

"Focus on your palm," Aldaren continued. "Imagine warmth being born there. Something alive, a small spark ready to blossom."

She visualized a small golden flame in the darkness. She waited, expecting to feel something.

Nothing.

No heat. No shiver. Just emptiness.

She opened her eyes, clearly frustrated.

"I can't do it."

Aldaren didn't seem surprised.

"That's normal. You're not made for this."

Suna looked down, playing with a fold of her sleeve.

"So… I'll never be able to use magic?"

"That's precisely what makes you unique, Suna. You're the only one here not influenced by a magician's power. That makes you unpredictable… and precious."

Suna drew a deep breath. He was right. She was different. But was that truly an advantage?

"Can disciples… use multiple types of magic?" Suna finally asked.

Aldaren shook his head.

"No. Only one magic exists within each of us. We're the disciple of a single magician. I've never heard of an exception. Even when we live among others, even when we have children with disciples of other magicians, magics do not mix. Children inherit the magic of one parent only, never both."

"Why?"

Aldaren shrugged.

"Nobody knows. It's always been this way."

He observed Suna for a moment, then gently added:

"But you have something else. Something we don't have."

She raised her eyes toward him, perplexed.

"What's that?"

"Free choice."

Was that truly a power? Suna doubted it. Yet, deep within her, part of her mind clung to the hope that one day she would discover something uniquely hers—something that would make her more than just a simple human lost in a magical world.

But for now… she was simply Suna.

And perhaps that was enough.

She thought a moment before asking her next question.

"But… do all disciples necessarily follow the path of their magician?"

Aldaren paused. His expression grew serious, and he seemed to hesitate, as if the question was more delicate than it appeared.

"No," he finally said slowly. "Sometimes, certain individuals turn their backs on their origins. But it's rare."

Suna felt her curiosity deepen further.

"Why?"

"Because the magic that fuels us isn't merely a tool. It's an essence, an energy that shapes our very being. Following your magician's path isn't just tradition; it's harmony between what we are and what we carry within us. Shanur's magic nourishes my soul, binds me to light and compassion for others. A disciple of Thalessa feels the call of the water as something undeniable, just as a disciple of Ignara resonates with the rhythm of flames."

He paused, briefly lost in thought.

"Yet, some resist this nature. By choice, by pain, or by rebellion. But when a disciple rejects the path they were meant to follow, it creates a profound rupture, a tearing apart between who they were supposed to become and who they choose to be. Some survive this… others pay the price."

"A price?"

"The magicians' magic shapes far more than our abilities. It shapes our very essence. When we turn away, sometimes we lose part of ourselves… or transform into something else entirely—a creature that no longer fits anywhere."

He searched Suna's face, checking if she grasped the gravity of his words.

"Some manage to find a new equilibrium," he continued. "But others… fall into darkness, unable to bear the dissonance between who they are and who they should have been."

The thought of someone losing themselves by trying to escape their destiny seemed profoundly unfair, even terrifying.

"Has that ever happened?" she asked quietly.

Aldaren hesitated, then nodded slowly.

"Yes. And these lost souls often become the most dangerous among us."

Suna nodded slowly, deeply moved by these stories. This world was so complex.

She furrowed her brow as a sudden thought struck her.

"And Ereshkal… is she the only one who can manipulate those portals, like the one I saw?"

"Theoretically, no," corrected the healer. "She shouldn't even be capable of it. Ætheris alone possesses that ability—she's the sole guardian able to cross the barrier separating your world from ours."

He hesitated briefly before continuing, instinctively lowering his voice as if fearing to be overheard.

"But if Ereshkal truly managed to bypass this fundamental law, the situation is far worse than we imagined. If she's indeed convinced a human to help her reach the Pillars, it means they're more vulnerable than we thought. That's why Theris and Vaelen are so concerned."

Suna felt a rising anxiety.

"Do you think Earth could be in danger?"

"Yes, absolutely. With the power of the Pillars, nothing could stop Ereshkal. She would gain the ability to open and close portals at will. That would directly expose your world to grave danger."

An unpleasant shiver instantly ran up Suna's spine. Aldaren's words echoed relentlessly in her mind, deepening her worry and amplifying all the uncertainties she already felt.

She realized just how high the stakes were, and how their journey had taken on a far more dramatic dimension.

Her mind immediately pictured the devastating consequences if her world—fragile, and devoid of magic—were exposed to the threat of an invasion by the magicians.

The sun was sinking towards the horizon when they finally caught sight of the small town of Mulescot.

Its paved streets, illuminated by already-lit lanterns, bathed in a warm glow that pushed back the encroaching darkness. After entrusting their horses to the care of a young stableboy, they entered the local inn: the Pandokeion.

Inside, a joyful atmosphere greeted them. The tables were filled with travelers from all horizons, laughing, sharing stories as freely as drinks. At the center of the room, a satyr enthusiastically played an upbeat melody. The sound of his peculiar instrument—an aulos, consisting of two pipes joined in a V-shape—just managed to rise above the ambient clamor.

Like all satyrs, he possessed the slender torso of a youth, paired with the narrow waist and strong legs of a goat. From his thick, curly brown hair emerged two elegant horns, broad and curved gracefully backward. A soft light-brown fur covered his legs, giving him a slightly wild appearance.

In contrast, his large, hazel eyes—lively and incredibly expressive— revealed a sharp intelligence and a mischievous nature. His slightly pointed ears added a charming touch to this picture.

The group settled around a wooden table near the hearth, where a fire crackled cheerfully. They ordered food and drink, but Suna remained captivated by the satyr, whose enchanting melody seemed to tell a thousand stories.

After finishing his piece, the satyr leapt down from the central stage and approached their table with a swaying, almost dancing stride. A mischievous smile brightened his face as he addressed them.

"Well now, here's an intriguing group!" he cheerfully declared, looking them over one by one. "Allow me to welcome you warmly to the Pandokeion! I'm Pharin, storyteller and musician in my spare moments. Your journey seems promising—I sense a tale worthy of being sung!"

His sparkling eyes lingered briefly on Suna, immediately sensing her genuine interest. He then bowed, adopting a posture both theatrical and playful.

"Would you allow me to join you for a few moments? In exchange, I could enhance your meal with music or perhaps begin crafting the tale of your quest..."

Suna exchanged an amused glance with Aldaren, while Vaelen, arms crossed, eyed the satyr with evident suspicion.

"Our quest?" Theris echoed. "What makes you think we're on any such thing?"

The satyr leaned closer, tapping his nose conspiratorially.

"Oh, I can smell stories, sir! They float around you like perfume. What you carry with you distinctly speaks of adventure and mystery... You're setting off to achieve something grand, am I wrong?"

Aldaren, amused by the satyr's lively wit, smiled indulgently.

"Perhaps you're right," the old man admitted, tilting his head. "But tell me, why does it interest you so much, young musician?"

"Because I wish to bear witness firsthand!" replied Pharin. "Great stories rarely come along, and those deserving to pass through the ages must be told by someone who knows how to immortalize them."

Straightening himself proudly, despite standing barely half the height of an adult human, he declared:

"Allow me to accompany you on your quest. I promise to be as discreet as a whispering breeze… except, of course, when the time comes to celebrate your exploits with song!"

Suna was charmed by the unusual character, but the rest of the group appeared considerably less enthusiastic. Vaelen, arms still firmly crossed against his powerful chest, observed Pharin with a neutral expression bordering on boredom.

"No," the captain said bluntly. "We don't need extra company. We're already numerous enough, and this quest is not entertainment for the curious."

"No extra company, you say?" Pharin retorted cheerfully. "Are you quite certain, good sir? You look positively bursting with joy! Surely a bit more enthusiasm could only benefit you. I'll even take it upon myself to lighten your spirits!"

Vaelen said nothing, though his face clearly showed growing irritation.

The satyr, far from being discouraged, continued with disarming audacity:

"I'm certain even your mounts would appreciate a bit of music," he cheerfully proposed. "Truth be told, they seem more conversational than some among you!" he teased, throwing a mischievous wink at Hestian and Korvel, the two guards.

It was true they had been rather quiet since the start, Suna reflected.

Korvel leaned toward his comrade.

"He's mocking us, don't you think?" he muttered to Hestian.

Pharin immediately raised his instrument, playing a few airy notes as if to ease any tension, his expression falsely innocent:

"Come now, gentlemen! It's not mockery, of course. Let's call it… an observation. You do appear formidable, I'll admit that freely! But perhaps not particularly skilled at solving riddles… am I mistaken?"

Hestian emitted a low grunt, crossing his arms, visibly exasperated. Aldaren, who until then had been observing the scene with discreet interest, finally chose to intervene.

"What Vaelen means, young satyr, is that our journey is no simple stroll. Why insist so strongly on accompanying a quest you know nothing about?"

Pharin adopted a humble posture, but his bright eyes betrayed unwavering determination.

"Because I sense you're different, sir—and you as well, madam," he added, glancing at Suna. "A grand tale is unfolding, I'm certain of it, and great stories deserve to be sung and passed down! If I'm not there to do it, who else can preserve them?"

Theris sighed. Suna, however, couldn't help smiling. Pharin's liveliness brought a welcome breath of fresh air, pleasantly contrasting the seriousness of their journey.

"I fear words alone won't suffice to persuade you, will they?" asked Theris.

Pharin's eyes immediately brightened, as though this remark was precisely what he'd hoped for.

"You're absolutely right, sir! Allow me then to demonstrate exactly why you'll soon wonder how you ever managed without me!"

Pharin stepped swiftly back, gently laid down his instrument, and took a deep breath. With astonishing agility, he leaped onto a neighboring table. Without hesitation, he executed an aerial pirouette as soft as a feather, landing soundlessly on the floor, graceful as a cat. Suna gasped softly, impressed.

"You see?" he announced, raising his arms theatrically, like an artist accepting applause. "No noise, no clumsiness. I'm as light as the breeze, as discreet as a whisper in the mountains. No one would ever notice me if I chose to remain invisible."

He leaned forward, picked up his aulos, and immediately brought it to his lips. A few airy notes took flight, twirling gracefully through the inn. Several patrons turned their heads toward him, some enthusiastically applauding as the music resumed.

Suna smiled, eyes sparkling with amusement at Pharin's contagious energy. Beside her, even the guards, Hestian and Korvel, exchanged amused glances.

Pharin concluded his performance with a deep bow toward Suna.

"And you, fair lady," he said with mischievous eyes, "imagine the cheerfulness I could bring to a group so… austere," he continued, pointedly glancing at Vaelen, still impassive. "I'll be like a ray of sunlight breaking through even your darkest days. Trust me, you won't regret having me at your side!"

Suna exchanged a subtle glance with Theris, silently urging him to give in.

Theris, realizing he couldn't indefinitely ignore the satyr's infectious enthusiasm, sighed resignedly and rolled his eyes before responding calmly but firmly.

"If you're so determined to accompany us, Pharin," he began slowly, "you should understand clearly that this won't be a leisurely stroll. Our journey will offer little time for you to dance or sing at your pleasure."

Pharin immediately reacted with an exaggerated theatrical bow.

"Naturally, sir," he declared with affected solemnity, drawing another smile from Suna. "I shall be discreet as a whisper in the breeze," he continued, bending even deeper. "As useful as a sharpened blade, sir." He deepened his bow with every sentence. "You won't regret your decision, sir, you have my satyr's word, sir!"

Vaelen rolled his eyes, clearly skeptical, while Suna had to cover her mouth to suppress spontaneous laughter at Pharin's exuberance. Straightening up, the satyr made a graceful salute toward Suna, thanking her for her discreet support.

Theris shook his head, trying unsuccessfully to hide his amusement. One corner of his mouth twitched upwards involuntarily, betraying that even he wasn't immune to the satyr's jovial charm.

Vaelen finally yielded, clearly resigned.

"Fine," the angel said, looking Pharin directly in the eyes. "But at the slightest complication or if you slow us down, we'll leave you behind without hesitation. Is that clear?"

Pharin responded with a cheerful trill from his flute.

"Understood, good sir! You'll see, soon enough you won't imagine this journey without me, for I'm an utterly unforgettable companion!"

Aldaren settled further back into his chair, observing the scene with a mixture of indulgence and amusement.

"Careful, satyr," he warned softly but seriously. "The path we follow isn't intended to entertain an audience."

Pharin responded with another exaggeratedly solemn bow.

"Then I will personally ensure that music makes even the hardest paths bearable, sir!"

Then, as if definitively sealing his promise, the satyr played one final note.

He sat down nonchalantly, placing his small goat-like hooves comfortably upon the table. Casting an enthusiastic glance toward the group, still radiating a charming carefreeness, he asked cheerfully:

"Well then! Now that all that's settled, where exactly are we headed?"

8 — Zayn — Quarth

Zayn pulled up the collar of his coat and cast a final glance at the Restful Traveler inn. The establishment, modest yet welcoming, had been a true comfort after yesterday's exhausting ride. Unfortunately, climbing back into the saddle immediately reminded him of the dull ache lingering in his sore muscles.

They set out shortly after dawn under an overcast sky. The first rays of sunlight struggled to penetrate the thin veil of clouds. The journey continued at a steady pace, and it wasn't until early afternoon that their destination gradually began to take shape on the horizon.

As they advanced, the landscape around them shifted. Wild fields slowly gave way to orderly crops and lush pastures stretching as far as the eye could see. Tall grasses gently rippled under the breeze's caress, creating the illusion of a green sea. Here and there, clusters of wildflowers sprang up, splashing vibrant touches of yellow, purple, and red across the peaceful countryside.

Further along, large enclosures of sturdy wooden fences appeared, defining areas where impressive creatures with dark coats grazed peacefully. Some of the bulls, exceptionally massive, displayed thick horns gracefully curving skyward. Despite their imposing stature and bulging muscles, these creatures moved with surprising elegance, sometimes roaming alone, sometimes gathered in small groups.

Zayn momentarily forgot the discomfort of his saddle, captivated by the sight.

He had never seen such creatures before. These beasts must have stood significantly taller than his horse.

A little further on, perched proudly atop an artificial hill, the city of Quarth finally came into view. It appeared to rise directly from the rock, imposing and almost unreal in the perfection of its lines.

"It's… it's incredible," murmured Zayn, awestruck by the sight of the massive walls surrounding the city.

"Impressive, isn't it?" Nymeris confirmed. "Nerath takes great pride in his fortress."

Each stone of the ramparts had been cut with remarkable precision, fitting perfectly together without leaving the slightest gap. The high walls were punctuated at regular intervals by watchtowers, offering an unobstructed view of the surroundings. Large scarlet banners, decorated with a stylized Roman centurion helmet, fluttered lazily in the breeze, asserting the city's undeniable authority.

Encircling these immense walls stretched a wide moat filled with water. This liquid expanse, likely fed by a tributary of the vast lake located to the west, formed an additional natural defense, further enhancing the impression of an impregnable stronghold.

A massive viaduct of heavy timber and sturdy stone, securely anchored on either bank by thick pillars, spanned this watery barrier.

At the head of the group, Thanatos pointed towards the far end of the bridge.

"Remain calm," he warned. "From here on out, we'll be closely watched."

At the main entrance to Quarth stood two immense square towers, built with the same impeccable precision as the walls, closely flanking the bridge.

Two colossal bronze statues proudly crowned the towers, dominating both the entrance and the surrounding landscape. The statues wore richly decorated helmets topped with elegant crests pointing toward the sky. Their faces, sculpted with striking realism, clearly displayed a hostile expression.

"It feels like they're actually staring at us," Zayn murmured, impressed.

"That's exactly what Nerath intended," Nymeris replied. "No one enters here without feeling that way."

Each statue held a spear raised toward the heavens. In their other hand, they bore large rectangular shields, finely engraved with martial motifs that reflected sunlight. Their superbly crafted bronze breastplates displayed powerful, realistic musculature, reinforcing the impression of invincibility. From their shoulders to their ankles, finely sculpted capes appeared frozen mid-motion, immortalized by the exceptional skill of their craftsmen.

Standing beneath these gigantic sentinels, Zayn couldn't tear his eyes away from these immortal colossi, his mouth slightly agape from the combined awe and intimidation. Fascinated, he closely examined every detail of the statues, noting with astonishment the supernatural precision with which muscles, tendons, and even veins had been sculpted.

"It's like they could wake up any moment," he said. "Every detail... it's as though they're alive."

"Legend says that, in the event of an attack, they'd spring to life to defend the city."

"Do you think that's true?"

"With magic, who knows? Nerath enjoys cultivating that mystery."

These eternal sentries indeed seemed to scrutinize their approach, as if judging their worthiness to enter the warrior city. Far more than mere works of art, they embodied Quarth's power, rigor, and absolute discipline.

Before them, the city's immense gates—made of thick wood reinforced with metal plates—stood wide open, simultaneously welcoming and intimidating. Behind those massive doors stood real soldiers, wearing armor identical to that of the statues, their expressions as impassive and stern as those of the bronze warriors above.

Thanatos moved forward confidently, followed closely by Nymeris and Zayn.

"We've arrived," he said simply. "Let's not linger."

The interior of Quarth, like its walls, was a model of order and discipline. The streets, straight and perfectly aligned, formed a grid reminiscent of the meticulous designs of ancient military cities. Each cobblestone lay exactly where it belonged, and the impeccable cleanliness of the streets spoke volumes about the omnipresent rigor.

The buildings, massive and robust, were made of bare stone, utterly functional in design. Their sobriety only amplified the impression of a city wholly dedicated to efficiency.

Regular patrols of soldiers marched past, their polished armor glinting under the sunlight. Zayn watched them with fascination: each man seemed a cog in a gigantic, perfectly oiled mechanism.

"It feels like a huge military camp," he murmured, leaning toward Nymeris.

"That's exactly what it is," she replied calmly. "Nerath values order and discipline. It's only natural that his city reflects those ideals."

They soon reached a vast square surrounded by elegant arcades. Thanatos led the group to a stable where they swiftly handed over their horses. Once dismounted, he turned toward them.

"I'll go and speak to Nerath. Let's meet later at the usual inn," he stated, before disappearing into the crowd.

Zayn turned to Nymeris.

"And now, what do we do?"

"Follow me," she answered cheerfully.

They left the large square and headed toward the artisans' quarter. There, the sound of hammers striking metal and anvils echoed continuously. Shops were filled with weapons, armor, and various equipment destined for warriors. Nymeris stopped before a stall loaded with meticulously aligned swords. She picked one up, expertly weighing it in her hand before agilely spinning the blade between her fingers.

"Steel or alloy?" she asked the blacksmith—a stocky man with a soot-covered black beard—in a neutral tone.

"Tempered steel, madam," he responded proudly. "Flexible yet strong, capable of piercing through any light armor."

She narrowed her eyes, carefully examining the blade's edge.

"It seems a bit fragile. Are you sure it would hold up for more than two battles?"

The blacksmith scowled, clearly offended.

"I'd wager my forge it could split an oak shield without so much as chipping."

Nymeris gave a mocking smirk.

"Let's hope you never have to prove it," she said, placing the sword back down and moving off toward another stall.

Meanwhile, Zayn had paused in front of an array of daggers. One of them, adorned with small black gems along its handle and equipped with a thin, curved blade, particularly caught his attention. He hesitated briefly before reaching out to touch it.

"A pretty piece, isn't it?" came an amused voice from behind the counter.

Zayn looked up at the merchant, a man with a grizzled beard whose eyes glinted predatorily.

"Yes, it's beautiful," Zayn replied, immediately pulling his hand back.

"Not just that, lad," the seller countered. "This blade is perfectly balanced—just as good for slipping between an enemy's ribs as for throwing into their throat."

Zayn stepped back, uneasy at the thought. Nymeris, having watched the scene, approached, picked up the dagger, and briefly tested its balance, assessing it with an expert eye.

"How much?" she asked.

The merchant quoted a price, continuing to extol the merits of his weapon.

Without bargaining, Nymeris reached into her purse and paid instantly. Then she turned toward Zayn and placed the dagger in his hand.

"Here," she said. "This is no toy. If you carry it, I'll teach you how to use it."

Zayn blinked, surprised.

"Really? Thank you…" he murmured, gripping the weapon's handle. He was impressed by its weight and fine craftsmanship. More than that, he was intrigued by the prospect of future training with Nymeris. Even though he suspected the lessons wouldn't be easy, he felt ready to take up the challenge.

They then moved on toward other stalls. Nymeris methodically chose throwing daggers and a sturdy sheath for Zayn, before leading him toward the textile and provisions stalls to restock supplies for the journey ahead.

Meanwhile, Thanatos strode through Quarth's immaculate streets, his dark coat billowing behind him. He finally reached the central fort, an imposing square structure proudly dominating the heart of the city. The inner walls, smaller yet equally sturdy, displayed the red banners boldly emblazoned with Nerath's warrior helm.

Thanatos entered the vast courtyard where soldiers trained rhythmically, their shouts punctuating each sword strike in perfect martial choreography. Recognizing him, the guards at the entrance promptly stepped aside. He ascended the stone stairs leading to a massive door and stepped inside. He stopped before another door guarded by a centurion.

"I wish to see Nerath," Thanatos announced in a glacial voice.

The centurion gave a brief, impassive nod and knocked twice sharply on the door.

"My lord, Ereshkal's right-hand wishes to see you," he announced loudly.

A terse command echoed from within, and the guard immediately pushed open the heavy door. Thanatos entered, discovering an immense room whose walls were covered with detailed maps of the continent, every point of interest meticulously annotated. At its center stood a massive, carved wooden table, on which Mytherra was depicted in a remarkably realistic relief.

Behind a large desk cluttered with parchments sat Nerath, the magician of war. His imposing frame was accentuated by armor richly engraved with golden motifs. He greeted Thanatos with a stern gaze, displaying only mild interest.

"To what do I owe the honor of your visit, Thanatos?" he asked, his powerful voice echoing throughout the room.

Thanatos stepped forward.

"Ereshkal is hunting the Pillars."

"The Pillars of Creation?" Nerath repeated. "And how do you intend to achieve this? Did you find a human wandering about?"

"Precisely," Thanatos confirmed. "She managed to open a portal to Earth, and now she has the power to do so at will. She found a human there and… convinced him to join our cause."

"She's achieved a remarkable feat," Nerath admitted, leaning forward, now fully attentive. "Her power is even greater than I imagined."

"Ereshkal wants to restore the magicians' greatness," Thanatos continued. "Imagine, Nerath… the old world ripe for conquest, within our grasp."

Nerath's expression brightened with a greedy glint.

"Interesting…" he said. "And how can I assist you?"

Thanatos flashed a predatory smile.

"Give me your finest soldier to accompany us. And prepare yourself."

Nerath settled deeply into his chair, sorting through his thoughts, immersed in contemplation.

"But first, I want to see this human," he declared, turning toward Thanatos. "I want to know what this boy looks like, upon whose shoulders so much now rests."

"We are doing our best to keep him under control," Thanatos replied. "Currently, he's accompanied by one of our disciples, probably busy resupplying."

Nerath understood immediately. He signaled to the centurion standing by the door.

"Fetch me this human. He should be with Ereshkal's disciple. Bring him here immediately."

The guard promptly bowed and left without a word.

Meanwhile, in the artisans' district, Zayn followed Nymeris, curiously observing the different stalls when two guards suddenly approached them.

"Lord Nerath wishes to see the human," one of them announced bluntly.

Zayn shot a questioning look at Nymeris, but she gently encouraged him to follow.

"It'll be fine," she murmured calmly. "Go with them. Be respectful, but reveal nothing."

Zayn tried to mask his nervousness and trailed behind the two soldiers. They quickly crossed the city toward the central fortress, where training exercises had momentarily ceased. The soldiers' curious gazes followed him, intensifying his discomfort.

The guards led him into the grand hall where Nerath and Thanatos awaited. The magician of war rose slowly as Zayn entered, imposing in both size and natural charisma.

"Come closer, young man," he commanded in a deep, yet surprisingly warm voice.

Zayn stepped forward hesitantly, impressed by Nerath's stature and aura of authority. Nerath circled him slowly, examining him intently.

"So, you're the human from Earth," Nerath resumed, folding his arms, studying him closely as one might inspect livestock. "You don't seem particularly sturdy."

Zayn swallowed hard but lifted his chin, attempting to conceal his anxiety.

"I… I'm stronger than I look," he replied.

Nerath burst into hearty, genuine laughter that echoed throughout the hall.

"I like that!" he declared, clapping him firmly on the shoulder and causing him to stumble. "But you'll need to learn real strength to survive what's ahead."

Zayn regained his balance, his heart racing from the surprise.

"You see," the magician continued, "I respect courage. Thanatos and Ereshkal think you're special, and I trust their judgment. Do not disappoint them."

Thanatos observed the scene, a satisfied gleam crossing his features. The magician had played his role perfectly.

Nerath stepped back and signaled to the guard at the door.

"Bring Garnius," he commanded briskly. "He will accompany our friend."

The centurion immediately obeyed, exiting with rapid strides.

Nerath refocused his attention on Zayn, examining him one last time. He stepped forward, his imposing figure casting a shadow over the young man. With an almost protective gesture, he placed his hand on the boy's still-sore shoulder, commanding his complete attention.

"Listen carefully, young human," he began in a deep voice. "True strength, the kind that topples empires and overcomes trials, does not come from muscles or weapons alone. It lies here," he said, touching his own temple. "In willpower. In the determination to keep going when everyone else gives up."

He released his grip, but his penetrating gaze remained fixed on Zayn's.

"Never forget that," he insisted firmly. "That kind of willpower—and nothing else—is what tips the scales between victory and defeat."

"I… I'll remember," Zayn promised earnestly.

He bowed awkwardly, intimidated yet strangely encouraged.

Thanatos then stepped forward, discreetly but firmly placing a hand on the young man's back to guide him toward the door. The two soldiers stationed near the entrance waited, faces impassive.

"Escort him back to the disciple," Nerath commanded authoritatively but calmly, not taking his eyes off Zayn.

The guards briefly bowed before gesturing for the young man to follow. As Zayn passed through the door, he still felt the warmth from Nerath's vigorous pat.

Once the doors closed behind him, Thanatos waited a moment, allowing Nerath to remain lost in thought. Eventually, the warlord turned back to his ally, immediately regaining his usual firmness and authority.

"Garnius will accompany you," Nerath continued. "He's my best man, leader of my praetorians. A true war machine, formidable in battle, and absolutely loyal. I would entrust him to Ereshkal without hesitation, knowing he will not fail. As for being prepared… I always am."

"I never doubted it, Nerath," Thanatos replied.

Nerath's gaze drifted toward an ancient map hanging on the wall, his eyes filled with nostalgia and hunger. In red, it outlined the Roman Empire at its peak. Each line, each frontier represented the promise of a glory he had dreamed of for far too long.

"Imagine it, Thanatos," he murmured, almost to himself. "Imagine what we could build together once the barriers fall."

Thanatos watched the magician, his own secret thoughts resonating with Nerath's. A new age was dawning, and they both knew their alliance held the key to dominating both worlds.

Later that evening, Zayn and Nymeris sat at a secluded table in a corner of Quarth's tavern, *The Popina*.

The establishment was bustling and lively: soldiers laughed heartily, pounding tables with their fists, while others exchanged playful insults over games of dice. Servers hurried back and forth, balancing trays laden with steaming dishes and overflowing mugs of beer. Occasionally, women with sensual strides approached discreetly, whispered a few words into the ears of select patrons, then quietly disappeared with them upstairs. Zayn, uncomfortable at this unfamiliar scene, modestly averted his gaze.

Nymeris sat upright, quietly observing the crowd as she slowly rotated her cup between slender fingers. Her cold, watchful eyes methodically swept from one table to another.

"You think Thanatos will be here soon?" Zayn asked awkwardly, trying to break the heavy silence between them.

Nymeris replied calmly, "Don't worry. They had much to discuss with Nerath. Be patient; he'll be here shortly."

As if to confirm her words, the tavern door suddenly swung open. A gust of cold air rushed inside, causing the candle flames to flicker. Thanatos stepped in, followed by a man so massive that silence fell over the room, all eyes converging upon the new arrival.

The man was colossal. His powerful stature was accentuated by armor intricately etched with martial symbols. A deep crimson cape fell down to his sturdy boots, fastened at his broad shoulders by two metallic eagle-claw clasps. The warrior's face, scarred from countless battles, hinted at a life spent fighting. But it was his eyes that immediately captivated Zayn—icy blue, almost metallic, they assessed every person present as a predator would size up prey. Most soldiers straightened or inclined their heads respectfully.

Thanatos crossed the room with determined steps, leading the giant to their table.

"This is Garnius, commander of Nerath's praetorians," he announced succinctly.

Nymeris trusted Thanatos implicitly, thus refraining from unnecessary questions. Garnius seated himself heavily opposite them, his armor creaking slightly. Crossing his muscular arms over his chest, he appeared even more imposing.

He scrutinized Nymeris, then Zayn, a smirk pulling at the corner of his mouth.

"So, this is your elite squad?" he remarked with provocative amusement. "A woman… and a kid?"

Nymeris instantly replied in a firm tone, "A woman who's never lost a fight. You'd do well not to underestimate us."

Garnius burst into rough, genuine laughter, clearly pleased with her retort.

"Ha! I like your spirit," he said, holding her gaze. His attention shifted to Zayn, who was struggling to maintain composure. "And you, boy, can you even use that blade you carry?"

He nodded towards the dagger hanging from the young man's belt.

Stung, Zayn straightened and shot back dryly, attempting to imitate Nymeris's cold confidence, though clumsily.

"Not yet… but I'm training, all right?"

There was a hint of defiance in his voice, just enough to provoke a mocking smirk from Garnius. Before the praetorian could continue, Thanatos interrupted, his voice sharp and authoritative.

"Enough, Garnius."

The berserker shrugged.

Nymeris subtly nodded—almost imperceptibly—indicating approval, and Zayn realized he'd passed a test he hadn't even known he was taking.

The lively tavern atmosphere resumed, fueled by bursts of laughter from other patrons and mugs banging against wooden tables. Thanatos swiftly ordered a meal, and the group ate while discussing the road ahead. Garnius, despite his crude and provocative manner, revealed surprising knowledge of the regions and potential dangers along their route. Nymeris occasionally nodded, clearly attentive to each useful detail. Zayn, unfamiliar with the places mentioned, soon lost track of the conversation.

At the end of the meal, Thanatos rose fluidly.

"We depart before noon tomorrow," he announced. "Enjoy your evening."

Garnius chuckled, eyeing a passing serving girl.

"Oh, trust me, I intend to."

Thanatos made no reply and moved away without a word. Nymeris immediately stood, gracefully following her leader. Zayn hesitated, feeling the praetorian warrior's penetrating gaze on him. Finally, he too stood, but before leaving the table, he glanced back.

Garnius raised his cup toward him.

His expression was unreadable: provocative, amused, yet strangely threatening.

Something about the man unsettled Zayn, like a game whose rules he didn't understand—one in which he was undoubtedly just a pawn. He lowered his gaze, as if breaking an invisible connection, then stood uneasily and hurried to join Thanatos and Nymeris on the stairs.

Now alone, the praetorian watched him leave.

His smile faded, replaced by a more serious expression. He knew exactly what was at stake in this mission.

After a brief moment of reflection, Garnius drained his cup in one gulp. He sat still for a moment, fingers resting on the rim of the empty cup, before straightening. He signaled to the innkeeper for another drink. Tonight, he'd savor one last respite; tomorrow, fresh battles awaited.

# 9 — Suna — Unexpected

Suna and her companions left the inn at first light. The horses stood ready, the cart securely loaded. Pharin, perched atop a mule, waited with evident impatience.

At a signal from Theris, they set out once more. The rising sun painted the sky in hues of pink and orange, the peacefulness of the streets strongly contrasting with the joyful bustle of the previous night.

After a few moments, unable to tolerate the morning silence any longer, the satyr addressed Theris with a mischievous voice:

"So, dear Counselor," he began, tilting his head to one side, "what exactly are you searching for in Balindra?"

"You recognized me, then."

"Of course," Pharin confirmed. "You're famous, even in Velissia. The real question is: what brings a counselor of Raenos so far from the capital, accompanied by such an odd company?"

Theris cleared his throat, answering carefully.

"We're merely seeking ancient artifacts. We want to prevent them from falling into the wrong hands."

Pharin laughed openly.

"Oh, naturally!" he exclaimed theatrically. "And it's for these trivial baubles that the Captain of Ætherium's guard himself is escorting you?

Of course!" he emphasized. "And I suppose Kraken and Sardine over there are just innocent tourists in armor?"

He gestured toward Hestian and Korvel, whose faces turned bright red.

Suna let out a small laugh, attempting unsuccessfully to hide her amusement behind her hand, while Hestian and Korvel struggled to maintain their dignity, their cheeks burning with embarrassment.

Vaelen, who had been checking the strap of his sword, rolled his eyes with a sigh.

"You're already making me regret allowing you to come along, satyr."

Pharin instantly feigned a wounded look, placing one hand dramatically on his chest.

"Very well, my sweet chickadee, I shall hold my tongue," he purred, dripping with irony.

But Pharin, unable to contain his curiosity, immediately continued:

"And the elderly gentleman there, bearing the medallion of the healers' guild—I suppose he's a disciple of Shanur?"

Aldaren politely inclined his head.

"Indeed."

The satyr regarded Suna with a perplexed eye.

"The young lady here doesn't seem at all familiar to me. Have I missed something?"

"She's my daughter," Aldaren replied calmly. "Nothing teaches better than experience in the field."

Suna turned sharply toward him, eyes widened in surprise, but managed quickly to mask her confusion.

Pharin scrutinized Aldaren with a dubious pout, before carefully examining Suna.

"Really? A disciple of Shanur looking like this? Have customs changed recently?"

Theris decided then to redirect the conversation.

"And you, satyr, who seem so well-informed, who exactly are you to ask so many questions?"

Pharin immediately straightened, striking a majestic pose while swaying atop his mule.

"Me? I am Pharin, personal tibicen to the great Lady Elvira. Weaver of divine melodies, charmer of dragons, prince of feasts! In Velissia, it's my aulos that makes hearts beat faster, souls swoon, and... wakes up drunks snoring under tables after midnight."

Theris stared at him a moment before an amused smile lit up his face:

"Wait a second, now I remember you! But then… what are you doing so far from Velissia's splendors?"

Pharin immediately straightened, striking a theatrical pose despite the comic swaying imposed by his mule.

"Ah, Counselor! For the first time in my life, I have left Velissia. I even turned my back on Elvira herself!"

"You?" exclaimed Theris. "Leaving Elvira? I thought nothing could tear you away from her endless festivities and pleasures."

"Imagine the scene," Pharin narrated, employing dramatic gestures and sound effects. "A sumptuous banquet: the highest dignitaries draped in flawless togas; the ladies sporting hairstyles so elaborate they defied gravity itself. And myself, naturally at the center of attention—as the renowned artist and indisputable virtuoso that I am."

Pharin let a theatrical silence linger before continuing:

"There, carelessly placed on a table, I spot this marvelous instrument: magnificent bronze crotala glittering under the torchlight. My artistic heart immediately falters, overwhelmed by the beauty of these modest yet undeniably worthy instruments! 'Pharin,' I said to myself, 'these noble guests deserve better. It's time to show them your talents extend beyond ordinary boundaries!' So, I slip the crotala onto my fingers and begin a marvelous series of rhythmic acrobatics. My first spirited tac-tac is met with exclamations from the audience. One lady even choked with admiration—or at least, that's what I thought at the time. With hindsight, perhaps she merely swallowed the wrong way. Anyway, it hardly matters: the mood was at its peak!"

He paused dramatically, savoring the suspense he had built. Suna leaned forward eagerly to hear what followed, while Aldaren already anticipated the inevitable disaster.

"It was then that I decided to do something even more daring, more magnificent! I leaped onto a table—because every self-respecting artist climbs onto tables—and there, mid-spectacular somersault, one of the crotala suddenly decided to claim its independence. It flew through the air with the precision of a hungry bird of prey, and—bam!—landed directly into a giant amphora of wine!"

Suna covered her mouth, eyes wide. Even Vaelen had to turn away to hide his amusement.

"That amphora, I swear to you, toppled with tragic elegance, like a dancer who had awaited for centuries the perfect occasion to perform her act. A cascade of red wine—of the finest vintage, naturally—poured forth majestically, and with remarkable artistic flair… directly onto the pristine toga of a prominent senator, whose expression transformed instantly from dignified composure to absolute horror."

Pharin raised his eyes to the sky, a comical expression of ecstasy on his face:

"And I, attempting to salvage this catastrophic moment, cried out with all the passion of desperation: 'Senator! What sumptuous crimson! Now you're dressed like Bacchus himself, the true prince of the harvest!'

But apparently, senators have little appreciation for the subtle humor of Velissia's satyrs, especially when they are literally swimming in wine."

Suna burst out laughing openly, quickly joined by Aldaren and Theris.

"In short," sighed the satyr with melancholy, "that is how I was… politely escorted to Velissia's gates with very relative politeness."

Pharin concluded his tale by placing a hand over his heart:

"Since that day, I have sworn to devote myself solely to my aulos. After all, at least it only flies into hearts… and never spills wine onto grumpy senators."

"Ultimately," Suna laughed, "bringing him along was the right choice."

"Yes," Aldaren replied, "as long as he stays far away from amphorae, of course."

The group burst into laughter; indeed, this satyr was truly one of a kind. Pharin's teasing accompanied them as they continued along a road bordered by woods, where the shadows of trees gently stretched beneath the golden morning light.

But the relaxed atmosphere was abruptly shattered by a piercing whistle.

An arrow suddenly thudded into the ground in front of Vaelen's horse, causing the entire group to startle.

Around twenty men burst from the undergrowth, quickly encircling the convoy in a practiced maneuver. Their worn weapons—rusted swords and crude bows—contrasted with their hardened faces, their eyes glinting with a troubling greed.

Their leader, a mountain of muscle whose scarred face spoke volumes about past battles, strode forward slowly, carelessly twirling a chipped sword that had obviously seen too many fights. His gaze methodically assessed each traveler, searching for their weaknesses.

"Lay down all your belongings, and maybe I'll consider letting you leave with something other than a blade in your gut," he growled harshly.

Vaelen unfurled his golden wings with a deep whoosh, briefly silencing the murmurs of the brigands and casting a menacing shadow before them. His voice rose, calm and authoritative:

"You'd better retreat now, before it's too late."

The leader burst out laughing mockingly, clearly unimpressed by the angel.

"You think your pretty feathers scare us, bird-man?" he sneered, waving his sword towards his men. "Get them!"

Everything happened at once.

Theris was the first to react: his hand flashed to his belt, and his dagger flew from his fingers so swiftly that the brigands had no time to respond. The blade lodged neatly in the leader's chest, whose shout turned into a muffled gasp.

"Protect Suna!" Vaelen shouted as he sprang into action.

The angel surged powerfully upward before diving violently down upon the brigands, his luminous sword tracing blazing lines through the air, taking out two adversaries before they even realized the attack had begun. With each strike, a dazzling flash erupted from his blade, blinding his enemies. He spun gracefully, a whirlwind of wings and steel, scattering panic among their foes. The brigands struggled to raise their weapons, but Vaelen was too swift.

Amid the chaos, Pharin suddenly jumped up from his mule, brandishing a small sling with an almost childlike glee:

"At last, an audience worthy of my talent!"

With startling accuracy, he spun his projectile and sent it directly into the forehead of one brigand, instantly knocking him unconscious.

An attacker tried to approach Theris from behind, but the counselor spun around, a dagger materializing in his hand as if by magic. The attacker jolted, then collapsed to the ground.

Aldaren, noticing several brigands trying to flank the melee, shouted urgently to his escorts:

"Hestian, Korvel! Don't let anyone get near Suna!"

The two guards swiftly dismounted and moved to position themselves on either side of the cart, blocking the attackers. Korvel slammed his shoulder forcefully into a bandit, knocking him back. He deflected an axe blow with a powerful parry before smashing the pommel of his sword into the temple of his adversary. Hestian, more agile, rolled smoothly on the ground, avoiding a blade, before quickly disarming his opponent. Rising swiftly, he kicked out sharply at another attacker's knee, sending him tumbling into the dirt.

But the brigands were numerous, and several broke off from the main group, circling around the battle to charge directly at the cart.

Suna felt her heart tighten painfully as the attackers rushed toward her. Panic surged through her. Instinctively, she stood, intending to retreat deeper into the cart, but fear rooted her in place, paralyzed as the brigands bore down on her.

Aldaren, immediately perceiving the danger, stepped protectively in front of her, spreading his arms wide in a shielding gesture.

"It's all right, don't move," he murmured gently. "I won't let anyone touch you."

Golden light poured from his hands, weaving swiftly around them into an impenetrable barrier. The brigands' blows bounced harmlessly off the magical shield, their weapons sliding uselessly over its shimmering surface.

From the woods, an arrow whistled through the air, aimed directly at Aldaren. It struck the magical barrier with a muffled thud before falling broken to the ground. Vaelen instantly spotted the hidden archer behind a tree trunk. Swiftly extending his hand, he unleashed a bolt of blazing light that struck the archer squarely in the chest, hurling him violently against a distant tree.

Taking advantage of the chaos, Korvel charged forward with a fierce battle cry. His blade flashed with deadly precision, cleanly breaking an enemy's spear. With a swift reversal, he cut down another assailant before he even had a chance to react.

The tide of battle quickly turned in favor of Vaelen's group. Disorganized and panicked by this unexpected resistance, the brigands began retreating, leaving behind weapons and wounded comrades.

Vaelen, still airborne, dove after the fleeing bandits like a hunting eagle, his glowing blade slicing mercilessly through their disorganized ranks.

Suna noticed something strange at the edge of the woods. A dark figure, hooded and unsettling, was observing the battle. She immediately wanted to alert the others, but as soon as she blinked, the figure had melted into the darkness, as if swallowed by the shadows themselves.

"Someone was there…" she whispered, troubled, almost to herself.

Aldaren lowered his magical barrier. Vaelen landed gracefully beside them, folding his great wings. Pharin, evidently unfazed by the gravity of the moment, played a few teasing notes on his flute.

"Really? Now?" the angel groaned.

Pharin responded with a sweetly innocent smile. "A little music after a fight does wonders for the nerves!"

Theris hurried to Suna, concern etched deeply on his features. "Suna, are you alright? Nothing injured?"

She slowly shook her head, but her gaze remained fixed on the edge of the woods. "I saw someone in the shadows. They were watching us."

"Probably their true leader," the counselor speculated. "We should put some distance between ourselves and this place. He might return with more men."

Aldaren turned to Korvel, whose arm bore a deep, bleeding gash. Without a word, the disciple of Shanur stretched out his hands, and an amber glow enveloped the wound, sealing it shut in mere moments. Suna watched the phenomenon with wonder.

"Incredible…" she murmured, impressed by this demonstration of magic.

Theris, after ensuring everyone was safe and no further threats lurked nearby, signaled for departure.

"We shouldn't linger," he declared firmly.

The group set off again, moving at a brisker pace. Once they had put sufficient distance behind them, the tension began to fade.

Pharin, unable to tolerate silence for too long, decided it was time to definitively lighten the mood.

"Did you see their faces when Vaelen dove at them? I think they forgot to mention 'no warrior angels' in their battle plans!"

He continued by exaggeratingly mimicking the brigands' general panic, waving his arms around so wildly that even Vaelen chuckled.

"And Hestian," he went on, "your expression when that giant came charging at you… You turned so pale, I thought you'd been replaced by a wax statue! Unforgettable! I swear even the trees laughed!" He recounted the afternoon's skirmish with overly dramatic mimicry, emphasizing Korvel's expression when a sword wounded him.

Suna couldn't help but smile at the satyr's antics and exaggerations. The fear she'd felt moments before had vanished, replaced by genuine amusement. Aldaren and Theris laughed heartily as well, while Korvel turned slightly red.

"You truly have an innate talent for brightening even the worst situations, satyr," Aldaren chuckled.

Pharin responded with an exaggerated bow from atop his mule.

"Delighted to finally be recognized for my true worth, Master Healer! Know that my genius is at your service under any circumstance… even death itself won't stop me from laughing."

With the tension fully lifted, the small group continued their journey, feeling more united than ever after this first ordeal.

The surrounding woods were peaceful again, filled only with birdsong and the gentle rustle of leaves. Suna, sitting comfortably in the cart beside Aldaren, admired the scenery as it rolled by.

The group passed through a quiet hamlet set at a crossroads. A few whitewashed houses bordered the single intersection. At the center of the hamlet, a fountain topped by a majestic stag served as a landmark for travelers. As they passed, villagers busy with their harvesting briefly raised their heads, offering discreet greetings before returning to their tasks.

The local inn, *The White Stag*, stood just behind the fountain.

It was still relatively early, but the altercation had delayed them. Catching sight of *The White Stag*, they decided to stop there for the evening and night.

As soon as they pushed open the door of the inn, a gentle tranquility enveloped them—the kind typical of late afternoons when the inn prepared for the evening rush. A lovely serving girl with a radiant face framed by silky curls invited them to sit down.

Barely settled at a table, Suna felt an unexpected weight land on her lap. Surprised, she looked down to discover an enormous gray-striped cat, who had just settled onto her with the nonchalance of a king. He gazed up at her through half-closed eyes, clearly implying that Suna's lap was his natural birthright.

"Ah, I see you've been adopted by Calius," said a cheerful serving girl, setting down their order.

"My dear Suna," proclaimed Pharin dramatically, "it seems your irresistible charm affects even the most discerning creatures… unless, of course, Calius has definitively forsaken all feline dignity to plunge into the deepest, most comfortable obesity. Honestly, hard to tell which…"

Suna narrowed her eyes at the satyr, feigning indignation but unable to conceal her amusement. Calius, indifferent to the critique of his generous proportions, began purring insistently, comfortably nestled on her lap. Visibly pleased with his conquest, he occasionally rewarded her with a lazy flick of his tail.

After a while, Suna attempted to shift positions, but the cat immediately fixed her with such a reproachful stare that she quickly abandoned any resistance, resigning herself to her new role as a cushion.

As the inn began to fill, Pharin, in an especially jovial mood, declared with his customary theatrical flair:

"Well, my friends, I shall liven this evening with some of my finest melodies!"

Without waiting for a reply, he drew out his flute and bounded toward the center of the room. Carried away by his enthusiasm, he accidentally bumped into the serving girl. She stumbled, performing an impressive acrobatic feat to keep her glasses balanced.

Pharin, utterly unfazed, immediately flashed her a disarmingly innocent smile:

"A thousand apologies, lovely maiden! To celebrate your heroism and your unmatched grace, I shall dedicate a ballad to your extraordinary skills of balance!"

The serving girl, cheeks slightly flushed but clearly amused, shook her head, smiling.

Pharin then launched into an energetic tune. His music instantly captivated the audience, encouraging several patrons to venture onto the floor for a few improvised dance steps.

Theris, watching the scene with indulgent amusement, turned to his companions:

"Enjoy yourselves thoroughly tonight, friends. Tomorrow's journey will be short."

Hestian and Korvel raised their hands simultaneously, as though having read each other's minds. Clearly, they intended to order several additional rounds in a determined effort to methodically test every cask the inn had to offer.

Soon, the cozy atmosphere of the inn was infused with the comforting scent of burning logs, the joyful melodies from Pharin's flute, and the lively chatter of the guests. At their table, Suna absently stroked Calius, who purred in her lap with the lazy satisfaction of a king.

Noticing Korvel repeatedly sneaking furtive glances toward the pretty serving girl, Hestian clicked his tongue, popping his companion's dreamy reverie like a soap bubble. Korvel jumped in surprise.

"Come on, old friend," teased Hestian. "You've glanced at her at least ten times already. Muster some courage!"

Korvel shot him a silent glare, sharp as a reprimand. But when the serving girl approached to collect their empty tankards, he immediately straightened, flashing what he hoped was a charming smile.

"Tell me, miss, I couldn't help noticing how well the cats are treated here," he began, nodding toward Calius. "Do all your guests receive such lavish privileges?"

Her eyes widened briefly in surprise. She was about to reply when a smooth, almost musical voice rose from the stage where Pharin was playing.

"You know, Korvel, if you're going to advertise your sitting skills, you might just offer your lap directly. But honestly, she'll find the cat far more comfortable."

"I'll stay standing, actually," the young woman quickly interjected. "I'd hate to subject the poor cat to unfair competition."

"A wise choice, my dear," Pharin added cheerfully. "Besides, Korvel purrs significantly less pleasantly and has a troubling tendency to drool."

The inn erupted into unified laughter, spontaneous applause even bursting forth from some patrons. Korvel turned beet-red, opening his mouth desperately seeking a retort, before muttering unintelligible curses under his breath instead.

Suna, shoulders still shaking, affectionately patted Calius's plump flank, grateful to both cat and satyr for making this evening far more entertaining than she could ever have imagined.

A few moments later, a young village girl approached timidly, inviting Vaelen to join her for a dance. He politely attempted to decline, but Pharin interrupted mid-note:

"Come now, Captain! You wouldn't dream of breaking this young lady's heart. You certainly don't want to tarnish your heroic reputation!"

Vaelen eventually conceded and rose reluctantly. The villagers warmly applauded as he awkwardly joined the dance. The young woman confidently took his hand, guiding him into a joyful circle.

Suna laughed softly at the improbable scene, immediately drawing Hestian's attention.

"What about you, Suna?" he teased with a playful smile. "Don't you want to join them?"

"Me? Dancing? I'm already clumsy enough on horseback. On two feet…"

Hestian stood and extended a hand.

"Come on, you can't possibly be worse than Vaelen!"

Suna blushed, hesitating, then shyly took his hand.

They joined Vaelen and the village girl in the middle of the room, accompanied by the lively notes of Pharin's flute. To her own surprise, Suna soon found herself laughing freely, her usual worries evaporating to the cheerful rhythm of the music. Hestian showed infinite patience, gently and humorously guiding her to keep pace.

When the music finally ended, Suna realized everyone's eyes were upon them. She let out a spontaneous, clear laugh—almost childlike— the echo of a joy she hadn't expected.

Pharin applauded enthusiastically:

"My friends, that was a performance for the ages! Rest assured, your dance will be forever remembered in the chronicles of Mytherra!"

The evening stretched late into the night, filled with spirited discussions, dancing, and lively melodies. Eventually, fatigue claimed the group's energy, and each retired to their beds for some well-deserved rest.

As Suna lay down, her heart still light, the muffled sounds from downstairs gently lulled her into a peaceful sleep.

It was already late the next morning when Suna awoke to the neighing of a horse. She prepared herself leisurely before heading downstairs to join her companions, already seated around an appetizing breakfast.

"Good morning, Suna," Aldaren greeted warmly. "Sleep well?"

"Yes, very well," she replied, taking a seat beside him.

The meal was delicious and invigorating, filled with local flavors.

After warmly thanking the innkeeper, they stepped outside to resume their journey.

Outdoors, they noticed some commotion near the fountain. Several villagers had gathered around a clearly recent wooden notice board. Curious, the group approached to investigate.

"What's going on here?" Theris asked an elderly man standing near the board.

The old man pointed to a poster pinned to the board.

"A reward's just been offered for capturing a gang of bandits. Apparently, they've been active farther north, near the woods."

Vaelen and Theris immediately recognized the description. Pharin opened his mouth, clearly preparing to boast:

"But that's exactly the group of —"

Theris placed a firm hand on the back of the satyr's neck, silencing him.

"Yes," Theris interrupted smoothly. "We've heard about them. Let's hope someone catches them soon."

"We'll be careful not to draw attention," Vaelen added, giving the satyr a pointed look.

Pharin sighed, frustrated at being denied the chance to recount their exploits.

"Yes, and… if we run into them," he awkwardly ventured, "I'll play them a tune so dreadful they'll flee immediately."

The villager merely shrugged and walked away.

It was clearly not the satyr's finest comeback, and realizing this, he mounted his mule with a sheepish grimace.

They had barely set off when their progress was abruptly halted by a surreal scene. Calius, the large cat from the night before, as panic-stricken as a Roman senator caught in a clandestine brothel, sprinted across the path right under their noses, running for his life. Behind him, half a dozen particularly vindictive hens charged forward, beaks first, wings fully spread.

Pharin immediately pulled back his mule's reins, eyes widening at this improbable spectacle. He burst into laughter so loud it startled his mule.

"By all the golden curls of Elvira, would you look at that! Wouldn't want to be in his paws!"

"What could he possibly have done to deserve this?" Suna wondered from the cart.

Delighted to have an audience receptive to his ramblings, the satyr adopted a dramatic posture, proclaiming in the grave tones of a storyteller:

"Let me tell you the tragic tale of the legendary Calius, also known as 'The Coop-Ripper,' eternally hunted by the merciless squadron led by the fierce Bellica and her savage laying commandos. Legend has it that Calius stole a sacred egg—or perhaps simply bit into a chicken that was a bit too tough; sources vary. Either way, he's doomed to run forever, chased by vengeful poultry!"

"I wonder if your Calius simply took his chances with one of their chicks..." Theris interrupted.

Pharin blinked, looking deeply betrayed. He clutched his chest as if struck to the heart.

"And here I was, believing you capable of a little imagination!"

"It does seem more plausible," Aldaren chimed in. "That would explain why these hens look so determined to teach him to leave feathers alone!"

Pharin widened his eyes, feigning shock, then threw his arms up with a tragic sigh.

"Wonderful. I'm surrounded by pragmatists without poetry, skeptics without heart!"

He turned his back on the group, like an actor delivering a tragic monologue.

"I offered you an epic—and you reduce it to a mere poultry squabble."

Vaelen, who hadn't slept much, irritably snapped at the satyr:

"All right, Pharin, you realize we're all waiting on you and your little performance?"

Pharin immediately raised his hands in appeasement, suddenly serious:

"Come now, Captain, a little respect! What we're witnessing here is true drama: predator becoming prey, the weak exacting revenge on the powerful! Honestly, what happened to your sense of tragedy?"

"I think it's thoroughly exhausted since you've joined us," Vaelen growled, crossing his arms.

Meanwhile, Calius, cornered near a fence, let out a plaintive meow in the face of his aggressors.

Aldaren, touched by the cat's pitiful plea, calmly raised his hand. Immediately, a protective sphere enveloped the poor animal.

The hens, caught mid-charge, skidded abruptly before the sudden barrier of light, awkwardly tumbling into a dusty pile. They stared at each other in confusion, pecking and tapping their beaks uselessly against the magical shield. One hen, clearly the bravest—or perhaps the least clever—even took a run-up, bouncing comically off the protective magic with a ridiculous-sounding *pok*. Defeated, they eventually dispersed, clucking indignantly at this blatant injustice.

Taking advantage of the distraction, Calius fled to the safety of a nearby bush, hissing indignantly at the flock of hens as he vanished.

Pharin sighed with mock disappointment, casting a dramatic pout toward Vaelen:

"There, Captain, the path is clear."

The group finally resumed their journey, leaving behind a hamlet whose inhabitants appeared accustomed to small animal dramas.

The monotony of the scenery, similar to the previous day's, encouraged everyone to chat quietly with their neighbor to alleviate the boredom of travel. Frequently, Suna's eyes drifted toward the riders accompanying them, notably Korvel, whose ease on horseback inspired admiration mixed with envy.

Quickly noticing her furtive glances, Korvel slowed his mount to ride alongside the cart, an impish smile on his lips.

"You've never ridden a horse, have you?" he asked gently, without mockery.

"Never," she confessed. "Where I come from, horses were something we only saw on TV… or in history books."

"Well, it's about time you learned!" he announced cheerfully, extending an inviting hand toward her.

Suna widened her eyes, caught off guard. "Now? Here, on the road? But… what if I fall?"

Pharin, who immediately sensed a promising spectacle brewing, moved his mule closer.

"If you fall, we laugh, help you up, and repeat!" declared the satyr enthusiastically. "Frankly, the worst that can happen is bruised dignity and a memorable story to your credit!"

Suna turned to him. "Thanks, Pharin, you're very comforting…"

"Ignore him," Hestian interjected reassuringly. "Korvel's a great teacher. And anyway, in the worst case, Aldaren can patch you back up."

The old healer smiled gently, nodding in reassurance.

Encouraged by the silent support of her companions, she eventually relented. Once on the ground, facing the horse, Suna paused, impressed by the animal's imposing size as it calmly regarded her, seemingly evaluating its new rider.

"You sure this is a good idea?" she asked uncertainly, eyeing the horse's powerful muscles.

Korvel chuckled, gently stroking the horse's neck. "You have nothing to fear—he's the gentlest horse in the world. Come closer."

The soldier dismounted with practiced ease, firmly holding the bridle to steady the animal, then guided Suna.

"Place your foot here," he instructed, indicating the stirrup, "and hold onto the saddle firmly."

Suna inhaled deeply to calm her nerves, hesitantly placing her foot in the stirrup and awkwardly hoisting herself up, supported by Korvel. The horse snorted gently but stayed perfectly still.

"There you go!" Korvel exclaimed proudly when she was finally in the saddle. "You see? Already a victory."

Suna, stiff as a board, clutched the saddle as if her life depended on it.

"It's a lot higher than I imagined," she murmured nervously.

"Relax," Aldaren advised kindly. "Horses sense your stress. Just breathe, it'll be fine."

Pharin, having drawn close so as not to miss any potential entertainment, began bouncing atop his own mount.

"You know what would be hilarious, Suna?" Pharin called joyfully. "If he suddenly decided to break into a gallop!"

"Pharin…" Vaelen growled warningly.

Suna shot the satyr a glare, lips pressed together in a silent promise of retribution.

Korvel began patiently instructing her. "Take the reins, but don't pull too hard. Guide him gently. That's right, perfect. Now squeeze your legs lightly against his sides to move forward."

Suna obeyed timidly and jolted when the animal took a calm step forward, letting out a small squeal of surprise.

"It works!" she exclaimed, almost amazed by her own success.

Theris observed from behind with amusement. "Very good, Suna," the counselor praised her. "You're a quick learner."

"Thank you…" she replied, a hesitant smile revealing quiet pride.

Seeing her gaining confidence, Korvel decided to push her slightly further.

"And now, move to a trot," he said, feigning innocence.

"Wait, trot—that's—"

But before she could finish, Korvel gave the horse a gentle tap, prompting it forward. Suna jumped, desperately clutching the saddle, shaken about like a ragdoll.

"Eee-aaah! Gen-tle!" she cried.

Pharin burst into booming laughter. "Behold, friends, our intrepid heroine, tamer of mighty steeds!"

"I—am—going—to—strangle—you—Pharin!" she shouted between jolts, as the satyr trotted alongside, exaggeratedly mimicking her jerky movements.

Korvel quickly reassured her, jogging alongside. "Relax, go with the rhythm. Breathe calmly. That's it, perfect. Use the stirrups to support yourself."

Gradually, Suna's movements grew more confident. Her body began adjusting to the horse's steady pace, and the tension in her shoulders dissipated.

"I—I'm starting—to get it!" she exclaimed breathlessly.

Vaelen nodded approvingly. "Well done, Suna. A good start."

Pharin, ever himself, joyfully commented: "What talent! What a show! I already feel an epic poem coming on in honor of this feat!"

Then, with exaggerated theatricality, the satyr proclaimed loudly:

"Atop her mount, uncertain yet so proud,

Suna tames her fear, brave and unbowed.

The gentle horse moves so patient and slow,

Guided by Korvel, kind teacher below!"

The group burst into laughter. Korvel offered a simple remark, but the intent behind it was clear: he was proud of her.

"I knew you could do it. Soon enough, you'll gallop alongside us."

Suna, her cheeks flushed with effort and emotion, let her eyes express what words could not—a silent but radiant thanks. Despite her initial embarrassment, this moment of camaraderie made her realize she was beginning to find her place among her companions, in this strange yet captivating world of Mytherra.

The day passed without incident beneath clear skies dotted with wispy clouds, bringing welcome warmth to their journey.

Encouraged by her earlier successes, Suna readily accepted Korvel's invitation to try riding again. After ensuring she was comfortably settled in the saddle, the young guard went to sit beside Aldaren in the cart. While keeping an attentive eye on Suna, they chatted quietly about the passing landscape.

Initially nervous, Suna quickly began to relax, lulled by her horse's steady gait. Gradually, she found reassuring stability, her shoulders easing and her posture becoming more confident. Every time she glanced discreetly toward the cart, Korvel offered a silent nod, a reassuring expression that gave her comfort.

As the hours passed, she even found herself genuinely enjoying this newfound sense of freedom, discovering unexpected joy in this day of travel.

Taking advantage of a broader stretch of road, she guided her horse toward Pharin and his mule.

"Everything going well on your new mount?" the satyr asked playfully.

"Surprisingly well," she replied. "I never imagined riding a horse could be so pleasant."

She hesitated a moment before continuing.

"Actually, there was something else I wanted to ask you… Earlier, I heard you say you'd been… a tibialist, was it?"

Pharin laughed, amused by her confusion.

"Close enough! It's 'tibicen.' An elite musician, a player of the aulos, a double flute like this," he said, brandishing his instrument. "That was indeed my role at Elvira's court, in Velissia."

"Sorry," she said with an embarrassed smile. "But actually… I wanted to ask you more about Elvira."

"Elvira..." he sighed. "She's difficult to describe. She's the magician of art, beauty, and seduction."

"You mean she's especially beautiful?" she asked.

Pharin nodded, his gaze drifting somewhere far away.

"Yes, but it isn't just her looks," he explained. "Elvira possesses a unique kind of magic, capable of inspiring absolute admiration in anyone who encounters her. She inspires artists, draws crowds, fascinates effortlessly..."

"What was it like there?"

Pharin's expression softened.

"Velissia..." he murmured nostalgically. "It's undoubtedly the most marvelous city in all Mytherra. Imagine a place entirely dedicated to beauty in all its forms. Every building is a work of art, every street an open gallery overflowing with music, dance, and poetry. Delicacy and elegance reign supreme there, and you could easily spend a lifetime just admiring this endless spectacle."

"You truly loved it," she observed.

"Deeply," he admitted without hesitation. "Life there was a constant celebration. There was always a feast somewhere, banquets, concerts... An endless whirlwind of color, sound, and sensation."

Suna felt her imagination stirred by the idyllic scene Pharin painted.

"Of course," he continued more soberly, "such a place has its excesses. When every pleasure becomes easily accessible, some people inevitably abuse them..."

He paused, his expression growing strained, as though reluctant to continue.

"And?" she encouraged gently, sensing he was holding back.

Pharin took a breath and continued cautiously.

"And what Elvira embodies can sometimes be dangerous. Beauty and love, pushed to extremes, can easily become obsessions. Many who encounter her lose all sense of moderation and eventually lose themselves, consumed by desires that can never truly be satisfied."

The satyr gave her a sad smile.

"I've seen too many people lose their way chasing after what she represents. Even I nearly lost myself…"

Suna remained quiet for a moment, reflecting on the musician's words. She clearly sensed that Pharin's relationship with Elvira was complex, marked by deep, painful feelings.

"She sounds fascinating," she murmured finally.

Pharin shrugged lightly.

"Fascinating, certainly. But if you want my advice, it's best to admire her from afar. Too close, and you risk getting burned."

As the sky gradually turned shades of orange and pink, signaling the end of the day, they finally spotted their stop for the evening.

It was a small village with a few thatched-roof houses lined along the main road. They halted in front of the only inn, a welcoming building with a carved wooden sign: "The Sleeping Fox."

Inside, a few travelers had already settled in, engaged in a lively dice game punctuated by bursts of laughter, or chatting quietly over drinks. A comforting warmth filled the room, accompanied by the mouthwatering aroma of a golden pie fresh from the oven.

While Aldaren and Theris spoke with the innkeeper, Suna noticed a man seated near the fireplace with an unusual creature perched on his shoulder.

It was a fire salamander. Suna had briefly glimpsed one before in a forge at Ætherium, but never this close. Its deep black skin was speckled with tiny glowing red scales.

Intrigued, Suna timidly approached the man, a sturdy traveler with a short beard, dressed in a thick traveling coat.

"That's incredible," she murmured, keeping a cautious distance. "Is it... dangerous?"

The traveler smiled, amused by her caution.

"Only if you make her angry," he replied with a reassuring wink. "But Cinder is a gentle salamander. Come closer—she won't harm you."

Encouraged by his reassuring tone, Suna stepped forward. The salamander tilted its head, bright orange eyes fixed on her. The creature climbed down its master's arm, approaching the edge of the table.

"You can stroke her back," the man kindly suggested, noticing Suna's hesitation.

She slowly reached out her hand, gently brushing Cinder's smooth back with her fingertips. An astonishing sensation of warmth, pleasant and soft, radiated across her palm. The salamander let out a contented hiss, tilting its head appreciatively.

"She likes you," observed the traveler. "She doesn't do that with just anyone."

"Really?" Suna murmured, flattered. "Thank you."

She looked down at Cinder, who vibrated gently beneath her hand.

"I... I never imagined a creature like this could be so gentle."

Returning to her group, her eyes sparkled with wonder. Aldaren greeted her with an amused expression.

"So, it's official—you're making friends everywhere you go now?"

"What a tragedy," Pharin remarked to Korvel. "Even a salamander has more success with girls than you. Perhaps you should invest in some scales yourself..."

The soldier turned to him with a look that clearly said: you're going to regret that.

The innkeeper soon returned, placing a large pot in the center of the table, followed by a basket of fresh bread. The savory aroma of stew immediately filled their noses.

"Enjoy, my friends!" he called out cheerfully, before hurrying off to another table of guests.

Theris generously filled the bowls while Suna handed out bread to everyone. The initial silence of the meal, where each person enjoyed this simple moment of comfort, was quickly interrupted by Pharin.

"I remember a similar evening," he began. "It was a long time ago, when I was desperately trying to escape from a band of raving madmen."

"Another one of your fantastic tales?" Korvel mocked. "What did you do to them?"

The satyr, adopting an indignant expression, placed a hand on his heart.

"Me, an innocent, misunderstood musician! I'd done nothing more than charm the daughter of a Velissian merchant a bit too much. You understand—sometimes my talent gets away from me," he explained, dramatically batting his eyelashes.

Hestian rolled his eyes, but the corner of his mouth betrayed his amusement.

"And then, what happened next?"

Pharin sat up straight, his face lighting up with mischief.

"Well, you see, these fine people weren't exactly art lovers… in fact, they had a pronounced preference for pitchforks. So I thought, 'Pharin, it's time to show some subtlety!' I came up with the brilliant idea to disguise myself as a human to pass unnoticed!"

Vaelen, his face filled with skepticism, slowly crossed his arms.

"You, disguised as a human? With your horns, furry legs, and hooves?"

Pharin raised a triumphant finger.

"Exactly! I found some old pants, a shirt, even a ridiculous hat to hide my horns. I was unrecognizable! Well, almost…"

"So, what gave you away?" Suna asked.

"My hooves! Believe it or not, finding shoes my size is nothing short of a miracle. I tried all sorts of sandals or boots, but nothing worked—either my hooves stuck out or I couldn't even walk. So there I was, disguised from head to toe… well, except for the toes, actually! Quite a notable detail, wouldn't you think?"

Aldaren burst into laughter, easily imagining the scene. Theris shook his head at such absurdity.

"And how did this brilliant escape attempt end?" the counselor inquired.

"I was confidently strolling through the market when suddenly an old man with a messy beard pointed at me and shouted: 'By my beard, look at that! A man with hooves!'"

"And how did you ultimately escape?" asked Korvel, amused.

Pharin displayed a triumphant grin.

"Thanks to my genius! I shouted, 'Oh, haven't you heard? It's the latest trend in Velissia! Human hooves, a fashion started by Elvira herself!' Then I had to run for dear life, chased by the furious father while the whole village mocked me!"

Suna couldn't contain her laughter, quickly joined by the rest of the group. Several patrons turned, intrigued by the contagious good humor.

"Truly, Pharin, I'll never get bored with you around!"

The satyr winked playfully at her.

"It's my sacred duty, dear lady! To transform this journey into an unending series of delightful moments!"

"In any case," Aldaren declared, "you've made us forget today's fatigue. Thanks for that, Pharin."

"Always at your service, my friends," Pharin replied with a theatrical bow.

The rest of the meal unfolded in a relaxed atmosphere, each in turn sharing amusing memories and more personal anecdotes. Suna, who had started this journey as a stranger, now felt fully integrated into this eclectic group.

At the end of the meal, as the innkeeper cleared the table, Pharin addressed him with feigned seriousness:

"Good sir, would you perhaps have a comfortable stable to accommodate a man with delicate hooves?"

The innkeeper frowned, perplexed.

"What's that?"

"Pay him no mind," Theris intervened. "Just a joke from our friend here."

The innkeeper walked away, shrugging.

"Strange travelers," he muttered under his breath, returning to his tasks.

The group burst out laughing.

"Truly, Pharin," Aldaren remarked, "you never cease to amaze me."

"I make a point of it, my dear friend! After all, routine is the sworn enemy of heroes."

Gradually, the conversation naturally faded. The first signs of fatigue appeared, and they rose to retire to their quarters.

Upon reaching the upper floor, they exchanged a few warm words of goodnight in the corridor illuminated by flickering lantern light. Watching them disappear one by one behind closed doors, their voices gradually turning into whispers before fading away, Suna felt a comforting warmth spread through her chest.

Lying in bed, Suna closed her eyes serenely, mentally reliving the pleasant moments of the day. She realized how privileged she was to discover this fascinating universe, where each encounter seemed more extraordinary than the last. This world, she was convinced, still held countless secrets to explore and wonders yet to discover.

10 — Zayn — Atlantide

Thanatos and his group left Quarth in mid-morning. Garnius, whom Thanatos had not spared a sharp remark, wore deep shadows beneath his blue eyes. The warrior responded with a gruff grunt, clearly disinclined to discuss his short night.

"Restless night, Garnius?" Nymeris asked sweetly.

"Very funny," retorted the warrior, adjusting his cloak. "Some of us know how to make the most of our free time."

Nymeris added nothing, but a telling smirk crossed her face. Zayn, who had followed their exchange closely, was amused by their almost childish rivalry.

Taking advantage of the calm during their lunch break, Zayn approached Nymeris to inquire about their next destination.

"Where are we heading now?" he asked.

"We're going to see Thalessa, in Atlantis," Nymeris replied.

Zayn straightened on his mount, nearly losing his balance:

"Atlantis?" he echoed immediately. "There's a similar legend in my world—a sunken city, lost for millennia…"

"Interesting indeed. Thalessa feels a particular nostalgia for Earth. Perhaps she drew inspiration from your Atlantis to create her own… or maybe she once actually lived there—who knows? Her connection to your world remains very mysterious."

"People spend their entire lives trying to unravel that mystery," Zayn pointed out.

"Amusing," Nymeris noted. "Atlantis is a semi-submerged city. Its port, the most important maritime trading hub in Mytherra, extends into a complex network of canals. Some buildings only emerge at low tide. Be careful not to fall into the water. The creatures living there aren't all friendly."

"Of course," Zayn thought, longing briefly for the comforting simplicity of his former life.

Garnius, who had lumbered closer, intervened with a gruff voice:

"Don't worry, kid. If you fall in, I'm sure the fish will find you tasty."

"Charming as always, Garnius," Nymeris sighed.

The warrior broke into guttural laughter before dropping heavily to the ground, attacking his meal voraciously.

"You've never seen the sea, have you?" Garnius said to Zayn, biting into a piece of stale bread.

Zayn hesitated, surprised by the colossus's sudden interest.

"I have, but… back home, it was different. Calmer, safer."

"The sea's never safe, even for a warrior. It always hides something: deceitful creatures or dangerous secrets. If you're not ready to face it, eventually it swallows you whole."

Zayn shivered at the warrior's unexpected seriousness. Thanatos straightened in turn, reluctantly approving:

"For once, Garnius isn't wrong. Thalessa and her kingdom must never be underestimated. We'll have to be extremely cautious."

Zayn felt his heartbeat quicken, intrigued and eager at the prospect of exploring this legendary city. He had always dreamed of marine mysteries and forgotten stories. Now, he was about to walk into a myth.

After finishing their meal in silence, the group quickly packed their belongings and resumed their journey beneath a sky that had turned gray and threatening.

The relative calm of their journey was shattered when around twenty men sprang out from behind a large, moss-covered boulder, blocking the road ahead. They were poorly dressed brigands, their hardened, filthy faces brandishing rusty weapons or hastily crafted bows.

Their leader, a corpulent man whose face was flushed red from alcohol and a harsh life, stepped forward arrogantly, sword drawn.

"Choose: your gold or your life!" he roared in a gravelly, threatening voice, his decaying teeth adding further ugliness to his greasy visage.

A chilling silence followed. Thanatos, at the head of the group, regarded coldly the man who dared block his path. The emptiness in his eyes spoke louder than any words, piercing the brigand as if his gaze alone could extinguish even the smallest spark of life within anyone bold enough to stand against him.

A cruel smile stretched across Thanatos's pale lips as, with a fluid and menacing gesture accompanied by a sinister rustle, he unfurled his immense black wings. The terrifying shadow forming behind him swallowed even the daylight, casting a sinister aura over the brigands. Even the wind seemed to freeze, gripped by this nightmarish presence.

"With pleasure," Thanatos whispered softly, menace dripping from his voice.

The brigand leader attempted to mask his fear with a nervous, obviously forced laugh.

"It'll take more than a few feathers to—"

But his words died in his throat.

In Thanatos's hand appeared an enormous scythe, straight from the depths of the underworld. A disturbing aura emanated from the weapon, its darkness so intense it warped the space around it, bending and drawing in the light like a black hole. The curved blade, massive and merciless, was surrounded by violet mists, as if imbued with a sinister energy.

A lethal cold overtook the scene, palpable and paralyzing. The brigand leader stood frozen, eyes wide, mouth agape, utterly incapable of movement. Behind him, his men reacted far more quickly than their leader. Screaming in panic, they threw down their weapons and scattered in every direction, some stumbling over their own feet in their desperate haste to flee the horror confronting them.

"Come back here, you cowards!" the chief shouted, his voice trembling, instantly stripped of its earlier arrogance.

But already the hooves of Thanatos's mount pounded the earth, drawing inexorably closer. The man spun around, gathering his last shred of courage, only for it to evaporate immediately upon seeing the terrifying vision awaiting him. Thanatos loomed above, astride his pitch-black steed, immense wings unfurled and scythe raised high, ready to reap the souls of any who dared obstruct him.

"Mercy…" squeaked the chief pathetically. Dropping his rusty sword, he stumbled away, fleeing into the underbrush.

Garnius, who had drawn his sword, sighed in deep frustration and slowly sheathed his weapon.

"Pity," he grumbled with a disappointed frown. "I would've enjoyed stretching my muscles a bit."

Nymeris, who hadn't even bothered to unsheathe her blade, rolled her eyes in exasperation.

"Yes, it's always the same with him…"

Thanatos slowly lowered his scythe, silent and emotionless. The terrifying weapon dispersed into the air, dissolving into dark smoke, taking with it the freezing aura that had filled the scene.

The three warriors resumed their journey.

Zayn had remained rooted in place, his hands gripping the reins tightly. His heart hammered violently, and a primal fear still constricted his throat. The vision of the weapon and the terrifying ease with which Thanatos had scattered the brigands without even fighting had profoundly shaken him.

He swallowed painfully, suddenly realizing the true menace Thanatos represented. He felt horribly vulnerable, trapped among forces he couldn't comprehend. Shaking his head to chase away these disturbing thoughts, he pressed his horse's sides and quickly rejoined the group, vainly attempting to ignore the threatening figure of Thanatos moving ahead of him.

They arrived at the inn, *The Traveler's Rest*, toward the end of the day, greeted by the comforting scent of wood smoke mingled with that of simmering stew. The common room was already bustling: exhausted soldiers had started a noisy game of dice, while a lone musician listlessly plucked the strings of an old lute.

As they settled at their table, a man staggered toward them, obviously drunk. He halted before Nymeris, his foolish grin and lingering stare sticking to her like a wine stain on a tablecloth.

"Hey there, gorgeous," he slurred clumsily, "what's a woman like you doing with guys like them?"

Nymeris pointedly ignored him, but the man persisted, awkwardly reaching out to touch her face.

Without even looking up from his plate, Garnius roughly grabbed the intruder's wrist, stopping his hand in midair.

"She's busy. Get lost."

The drunkard spun around to protest, only then noticing the warrior's imposing stature. He froze, paled visibly, and hurried away, muttering confused apologies. Nymeris glanced up at Garnius, almost amused:

"At least you're useful for something."

Garnius shrugged, finishing his meal with a satisfied grunt.

Exhausted from the long day, the colossus soon excused himself and headed upstairs, citing temporary fatigue. Zayn and Nymeris exchanged mocking glances but said nothing.

When bedtime came, Zayn slowly climbed the creaking wooden stairs, his mind weighed down by all the unanswered questions now troubling him. Garnius, in the adjacent room, was already snoring loudly. As he lay down on the narrow bed, Zayn thought again about Nymeris—so cold yet strangely reassuring—and Thanatos, terrifying yet undeniably effective. He no longer knew what to think about these bewildering allies.

The next morning, Zayn was abruptly awakened by the piercing cries of a terrified chicken being chased through the corridors by the inn's cat. After this strange awakening and a hearty breakfast, they set off once more toward Atlantis.

To their right, mountains rose majestically, their peaks vanishing into the clouds. Zayn admired the silvery waterfalls cascading down steep slopes before merging into numerous rivers. The murmuring water blended softly with the rustling leaves.

To their left, the landscape gradually transformed into a broad, damp valley invaded by lazy sheets of mist. A winding river cut through the plain, marking the boundary where solid earth merged into water and signaling the beginning of an expansive marshland. Here, massive trees with moss-covered trunks plunged their roots into dark, stagnant waters.

Zayn slowed his horse to take a closer look.

"Impressive, isn't it?" Nymeris remarked, noticing his fascination. "These swamps mean we're getting close to Atlantis."

"I never thought I'd ever see such a place," Zayn replied, captivated by the mysterious reflections on the dark water.

"You haven't seen anything yet, kid," Garnius added. "Just wait until we reach Atlantis."

As they advanced, the valley broadened, and the river spread generously, flooding the plain and forming a labyrinth of silvery canals. The water, intermittently reflecting the sunlight, resembled a mosaic of shattered silver. In the distance, a few stilted houses emerged, fragile islands lost amidst stagnant waters.

Approaching the sea, the first houses of Atlantis began to appear. Some buildings were half-submerged, their walls marked by different water levels. The facades displayed colors faded by the tides, ranging from off-white to dark grey, covered with deep-green mosses and algae. The lower floors vanished underwater, occasionally revealing windows behind oxidized bronze grills, hinting at interiors adapted to aquatic life.

Above, aged wooden pontoons connected buildings, creating an intricate maze across which the residents moved with ease.

"Fascinating," Zayn murmured with awe, observing the tangled pontoons and the disconcerting ease with which the inhabitants navigated them.

His attention was drawn to a group of children running along the narrow walkways with surprising agility.

"How do they not fall?" he wondered aloud.

"It's just habit," Garnius answered. "You'll get used to it soon enough—provided you don't fall in on your first day."

Zayn peered anxiously at the opaque surface of the water, trying to guess what might lurk beneath.

"Why? What's in there?"

"Oh, just a few grumpy aquatic residents," Nymeris replied lightly. "Usually harmless… but you'd still do well to stay cautious."

Garnius burst into laughter at Zayn's worried expression.

"You should see your face, kid! Don't worry, I'm sure Nymeris will fish you out."

Thanatos, leading the group, remained silent, clearly indifferent to his companions' mundane chatter. He scanned their surroundings, his gaze pausing briefly on the sleek boats gliding through tranquil waters, guided by fishermen with weathered faces.

They continued along the broad road into the city's heart. As they ventured deeper into the town, buildings crowded closer together, still connected by the dizzying tangle of pontoons.

Garnius and Nymeris, unmoved by the wonders around them, were already engrossed in discussing combat techniques they planned to practice later. Zayn, meanwhile, gazed around in fascination, absorbing every detail of this extraordinary landscape.

Atlantis itself gradually unfolded before them, majestic and imposing. The city sprawled across a complex delta where rivers and canals merged into a vast aquatic mosaic.

At its heart rose an immense palace, a half-submerged monument whose foundations disappeared beneath shimmering waters. Marble columns, dulled by humidity, supported graceful suspended bridges. These harmonious walkways connected the city's various levels, forming a complex network resembling the arteries of a living organism, all converging toward the central palace.

The paved streets, polished by the constant passage of inhabitants, were interconnected by numerous wooden pontoons, slippery from the perpetual dampness.

Closer to the shores, rooftops barely emerged from the waves, like artificial islands floating on the surface. These dwellings gave the impression of a city perpetually suspended between land and sea.

Next came the grand port of Atlantis, vibrant with incessant activity. Elegant gondolas glided gracefully among ships laden with varied goods. The sea air was heavy with mingled aromas: the salty tang, the scent of freshly caught fish, and the damp wood of vessels.

Added to these scents were the lively shouts of sailors and melodious songs of gondoliers, creating an atmosphere as lively as it was picturesque.

The docks were bustling with maritime activity: carefully coiled ropes here, nets laid out to dry in the sun there, and a little further on, stacked barrels ready to be loaded. People constantly moved between boats and market stalls, breathing life into this part of the city, evoking the perpetual motion of waves.

"Incredible…" Zayn murmured. "It's like the city lives as much in the water as it does on land."

Nymeris scanned the lively canals. Even she had to acknowledge Atlantis's unique beauty. She briefly smiled before resuming her usual impassive expression. Garnius, meanwhile, observed the scene with detached interest, enjoying the spectacle without giving it much importance.

They soon arrived at a small stable near the docks. A stocky man emerged immediately, his skin bronzed by years spent beneath the marine sun. His boots, still caked with mud, and his clothing permeated with salt and spray, betrayed a life governed by the fickle rhythm of the tides.

After entrusting their horses to the man, Thanatos stepped forward, briefly turning to his companions.

"I'm heading to the palace," he announced. "I'll meet you later."

He quickly disappeared into the crowd.

"Well, might as well explore," Garnius declared. "Atlantis is full of good deals—and probably one or two good taverns, too."

Zayn, excited by the prospect of discovering the city, quickly followed the two warriors.

They walked along a wide avenue flanked by narrow canals, bustling with floating markets. Vendors perched skillfully on their boats called out to passers-by, offering pearly shells, exotic fish, or fabrics as vivid as coral reefs.

Suddenly, a loud splash rang out. A barge laden with crates and barrels had overturned, scattering its cargo across the canal. A commotion quickly swept through both passers-by and nearby sailors.

"Well, there's some excitement for the day!" Garnius said with amusement, folding his arms to watch the spectacle.

Zayn had stopped, captivated by the strange ballet unfolding before his eyes. While boatmen struggled to retrieve floating crates, several figures swiftly emerged from the water, hauling up submerged goods. Glistening reflections of fins flashed above the surface as these mysterious divers slipped back into the depths.

"Mermaids!" he blurted out spontaneously, forgetting he was in a dense crowd.

A few curious onlookers immediately turned toward him, intrigued by his outburst. Zayn felt heat rush to his cheeks, realizing his mistake:

"Um, mermaids," he repeated quietly to Nymeris. "I didn't realize those shapes beneath the surface were... well, you know."

"Mermaids and Tritons," Nymeris corrected. "Trust me, they're quite sensitive about the distinction."

"It's incredible..." he whispered, unable to tear his eyes away.

The mermaids were beautiful: their scales shimmering in blues and greens, catching the daylight with every movement. Their hair flowed around them like living halos, and their graceful gestures displayed complete mastery of their aquatic world.

Garnius gave Zayn a playful nudge with his foot, urging him forward.

"Come on, kid, don't just stand there! We've still got plenty to do."

"Alright, but... it's fascinating," Zayn marveled, enchanted. "I never imagined seeing anything like this."

Nymeris studied him briefly, showing a rare indulgence, before speaking again.

"Keep your eyes open—but stay cautious. In Atlantis, things aren't always what they seem."

As he turned to leave, Zayn's gaze met that of a mermaid who had paused at the surface. A silent tension passed between them—fragile and mysterious—lasting only a heartbeat. Then, without a sound, she disappeared into the depths. Reluctantly, Zayn turned away and jogged to catch up with his companions through the maze of narrow streets and bridges.

Garnius and Nymeris, both connoisseurs of practical equipment, stopped at a stall where a suit of scale armor hung prominently above a counter filled with assorted marine objects. The merchant, a Triton with blue-tinged skin and elegant fins, perked up upon seeing them pause.

"Come, warriors! Come admire a wonder like none you've ever seen!" he called, gesturing toward the cuirass.

Nymeris stopped abruptly, her eyes locked onto the armor. Its bluish scales shimmered subtly, shifting from turquoise to deep marine blue depending on the angle of the light. Each piece was linked by elegant translucent membranes, providing a striking contrast to the obvious solidity of the breastplate.

"Take a closer look!" the merchant continued enthusiastically. "Leviathan scales—stronger than steel and lighter than a feather! Perfect protection for a refined warrior like yourself."

Almost hypnotized, Nymeris stepped forward and brushed her fingertips across its scaly surface. Her face lit up.

"Garnius, it's absolutely stunning," she murmured in awe. "And this texture! It feels so smooth."

The berserker observed the scene skeptically.

"Maybe it's beautiful," he conceded, "but armor shouldn't be that shiny... or that lightweight. Looks like you're headed to a ball, not a battlefield."

He folded his arms, glancing skeptically between Nymeris and the armor.

"You can't seriously be thinking of—" he started.

Nymeris interrupted him eagerly. "I must try it on!"

"I knew it..." Garnius groaned.

With remarkable agility, the Triton merchant helped Nymeris adjust the armor, while Garnius watched with visible exasperation. Nymeris twirled with nearly childlike excitement, savoring the lightness and fluidity of her movements.

Yet the armor, though splendidly and delicately crafted, clearly seemed designed more to distract than protect. Broad pauldrons adorned with menacing fangs gave it a fierce appearance, but her abdomen remained surprisingly exposed, leaving most of her body vulnerable. The artfully sculpted scale plates covered only strategic areas, leaving a considerable amount of skin uncovered. Ultimately, the armor accentuated her curves far more elegantly than it provided genuine protection against combat dangers.

"So, what do you think now?" she asked proudly, turning before Garnius.

Zayn nodded approvingly, his cheeks flushed. Garnius stood momentarily speechless before finally regaining composure.

"Honestly? I think we're seeing far more than we should," he declared. "Are you planning to fight, or distract the enemy?"

"You're just jealous you couldn't pull off something this refined," she replied with a teasing smile. "If we must fight the enemy, we may as well do it in style."

The Triton applauded, delighted by the outcome.

"It suits you marvelously! A warrior such as yourself deserves the finest."

Garnius sighed dramatically, rolling his eyes.

"If we stay much longer, you'll end up buying his entire stall."

Nymeris laughed, placing a hand on her hip and striking a theatrical pose.

After a brief negotiation—during which Garnius grumbled repeatedly—Nymeris bought the armor, a radiant smile on her face.

"I bet you already have dozens of armors," the warrior muttered as he dragged his feet along behind her.

"Exactly," she rejoiced. "But none quite like this."

As they moved on, Zayn, captivated by the bustling surroundings, tripped over a heap of ropes lying on the dock. Without any chance to react, he tumbled into the water with a loud, splashing "SPLASH!" Garnius planted his hands firmly on his hips while Nymeris rushed to the edge of the pier.

"You sure he even knows how to swim?" the berserker called out, amused.

Disoriented but unharmed, Zayn opened his eyes beneath the surface. What he saw froze him instantly, pushing every other thought from his mind. Beneath the water stretched an entirely different Atlantide, a magnificent underwater city.

Submerged buildings cascaded down along a massive rocky cliff, covered in brilliantly colored corals. Each façade, shaped by the currents, was illuminated by countless bioluminescent organisms covering walls and windows alike.

Within this enchanting world, he clearly saw figures gracefully swimming between submerged structures. Sirens and Tritons moved elegantly, their bodies undulating naturally with the currents. In the distance, the titanic shadow of Thalessa's palace loomed over everything—vast and impressive, a mysterious fortress rising from the abyss.

Zayn floated open-mouthed, mesmerized to the point of forgetting to breathe.

On the surface, Garnius finally lost patience and leaned over the water.

"That's enough now! I'm not waiting until he grows gills!"

Without further hesitation, the warrior plunged his powerful arm into the water and grabbed Zayn firmly by the collar, pulling him back to the surface like a fisherman hauling in his catch.

Zayn emerged coughing, hair dripping and plastered to his face, looking completely dazed.

"I… I've never seen anything so…" he murmured, shivering from both cold and excitement. "You have no idea! Underwater, it's vast, magnificent!"

Garnius stared at him, unimpressed.

"You saw fish—congratulations. Now get back on your feet; you're embarrassing us."

Nymeris, suppressing a smile, handed him a towel taken from a nearby stall.

"We figured it must be grandiose," she gently added. "Now at least try to dry yourself off."

Zayn, still overwhelmed, wiped himself mechanically, his eyes still sparkling with amazement.

Garnius heaved an audible sigh, shaking his head, and eyed a nearby tavern.

"I can't handle this without a drink. Meet me inside," he called, walking away.

After taking a moment to regain his composure, Zayn followed Nymeris as they continued their exploration along the bustling pontoons. The warrior, ever on the lookout for new treasures, was already passionately negotiating prices with stubborn merchants attempting to stand their ground.

After a few purchases and with Zayn finally dry, they rejoined Garnius, already comfortably seated in the crowded tavern among a group of laughing sailors.

"Ah, here comes our underwater explorer!" Garnius called out, raising his tankard high. "Let's hope our fish stays on dry land for the rest of the journey!"

The sailors burst into hearty laughter, some enthusiastically pounding their rough hands on the table. Zayn immediately felt his cheeks flush.

Garnius gestured for them to join, patting the boy's back with a force that nearly toppled him over.

Zayn sat down, eventually enjoying the warm atmosphere despite his initial embarrassment. Nymeris rolled her eyes before taking a seat next to him. Surrounded by the still-laughing sailors, they settled in together, waiting for Thanatos to return.

"To your next dive!" Garnius toasted mockingly, sparking another round of laughter in the lively tavern.

"To Atlantide," Zayn murmured in reply, his thoughts drifting back to the underwater spectacle.

On the opposite side of the city, Thanatos advanced with assured steps. His boots skimmed the damp stone of the narrow alleys with steady rhythm. The dense crowd that filled the pontoons and narrow streets instinctively parted as he approached, conversations ceasing abruptly into whispers. Even the air seemed to grow heavier, charged with the icy, unsettling energy Thanatos radiated. His large black wings, slightly spread behind him, accentuated the imposing menace of his presence.

The main walkway, wide and adorned with carved wooden arches, led directly to Thalessa's palace. Today, however, it was obstructed by an unusual disturbance: two merchants argued loudly in the middle of the path, their faces flushed with indignation. Scattered goods lay overturned on the ground, obstructing the usual flow of pedestrians. A circle of curious onlookers had gathered, animatedly commenting on the spectacle, while two guards struggled to push through the crowd and restore order, their efforts hampered by the dense throng.

Thanatos paused, visibly annoyed by the congestion before him. With a quiet sigh, he stepped away from the center of the bridge to find an open space. He climbed onto the parapet and unfurled his wings in one fluid motion. The vast span of his dark wings cast an intimidating shadow over the petrified crowd. Thanatos gracefully lifted off, leaving the ground with a single powerful beat.

"By the abyss..." murmured one of the merchants, eyes fixed skyward, his quarrel instantly forgotten.

A ripple of awe swept through the crowd as Thanatos glided over the turmoil, leaving behind impressed murmurs and astonished exclamations. Below, pedestrians stared in astonishment at the figure silhouetted against Atlantide's bright sky.

Thanatos crossed the distance to the palace in mere wingbeats, soaring above the city like a dark omen.

Before him now stood the majestic façade of Thalessa's palace, shimmering in the sunlight. The structure was an architectural marvel; walls of bluish marble intertwined with vivid red coral and colored gemstones evoked a reef risen from an imaginary sea.

With one final beat of his wings, he descended toward the palace entrance, landing silently on the steps. Facing him loomed ornate doors, intricately carved with complex reliefs depicting marine scenes entwined in an eternal, frozen ballet. Delicately embedded luminous gems brought these aquatic dances to perpetual life.

Two guards clad in shimmering scale armor nervously straightened, gripping their spears tightly.

Without offering them the slightest attention, Thanatos raised a gloved hand, grasped the heavy trident-shaped handle, and pushed the doors open. A deep groan accompanied their motion, unveiling the sumptuous interior of Thalessa's palace.

Thanatos crossed the threshold confidently, leaving the two guards frozen behind him.

After crossing a vast corridor, Thanatos entered a room of vertiginous proportions. Everything appeared to have been designed to mesmerize visitors and intimidate potential adversaries.

To the right, the floor of polished chrysocolla sharply contrasted with the immense pool occupying the entire left side of the chamber, fed by several underwater tunnels. The water rippled gently, animated by an invisible current, creating an atmosphere both serene and mysterious. Tall fluorescent algae rose slowly from the depths, spreading an ethereal glow throughout the hall.

At the far end of this majestic chamber, upon a throne fashioned from iridescent coral, sat Thalessa.

Two waterfalls flowed gracefully on either side of her seat, and a shaft of sunlight illuminated her directly, creating an imposing aura around her slender figure. Her silhouette was draped in a silvery gown that shimmered like the sea beneath moonlight. Long hair of brilliant blue-green, streaked with silver highlights, cascaded freely over her shoulders. Her deep blue eyes fixed Thanatos with an intensity capable of unsettling any visitor less determined.

"Thanatos," she said, her voice clear and composed, "what brings you to my palace?"

Ereshkal's right hand stopped a few paces before her, inclining his head respectfully without breaking eye contact.

"I bring greetings from Ereshkal," he began in a measured tone. "My mistress wishes for us to speak… privately."

Without shifting her gaze, Thalessa slowly raised a hand in an elegant yet authoritative gesture. Immediately, the guards positioned near coral columns bowed briefly and left the hall. In the water, ripples indicated other aquatic creatures discreetly retreating into the depths.

Once certain the room was empty, Thalessa crossed her arms, her posture becoming firmer.

"You have my full attention, Thanatos," she declared, impatience subtly threading through her apparent calm. "Speak."

"Ereshkal has succeeded in opening a portal to Earth," he announced. "She has brought back a human, capable of helping us retrieve the Pillars of Creation. Her aim is clear: restoring the magicians' full power, particularly for those who support her."

Thalessa imperceptibly furrowed her brow, a flicker of interest crossing her face. Thanatos continued immediately, aware he now held her attention:

"She desires your support in this quest and the trials to come."

Thanatos took another step forward, unfurling his wings to emphasize his argument. His voice was calm, almost seductive.

"She believes your strength would make all the difference. She considers your potential far greater than the world imagines."

He held her gaze directly and delivered his final argument, knowing it would inevitably draw her into his net.

"Imagine a power you never dared dream of… and that we could help you attain."

Silence settled once more over the immense hall, broken only by the soft murmur of waterfalls. Thalessa did not respond immediately. Her slender fingers played thoughtfully with the shell pendant around her neck. She remained motionless, focusing intently on Thanatos' words, weighing every syllable.

At last, she straightened slightly on her throne, her expression hardening imperceptibly, the emotional barrier reinstated.

"Your words are intriguing," she finally conceded, her tone carefully guarded. "But I do not make decisions lightly."

She accompanied her words with a fluid wave of the hand, signaling the conversation was concluded.

"Our time is limited, Thalessa," Thanatos emphasized. "Waiting might jeopardize our mutual interests."

"I know," she retorted sharply. "You will have my answer in due time."

Thanatos moved forward slightly, ready to insist. Thalessa clicked her tongue irritably.

"Do not test your luck, Thanatos," she warned, her voice sharp. "My patience has limits."

She fixed her gaze on his, as if in challenge. Thanatos maintained eye contact briefly. Finally, he inclined his head in acceptance.

"As you wish," he replied before turning on his heel, his dark wings folding behind him.

The angel left the hall with the same confident stride as when he entered. Thalessa remained immobile upon her throne, staring thoughtfully into the tranquil ripples of the pool. The messenger's words echoed persistently in her mind, urging her to consider every opportunity… and every risk.

She knew all too well that Ereshkal's promises often concealed carefully laid traps.

Thanatos rejoined the others at the tavern. The atmosphere had grown calm once more, sharply contrasting with the turmoil still lingering in his mind after his conversation with Thalessa. The gentle hum of casual chatter, the occasional laughter from nearby tables, and the rhythmic lapping of water beneath the floorboards created a soothing ambiance.

As he settled at their table, all eyes immediately turned toward him, awaiting instructions.

"We'll stay here for a while," he announced in his deep voice. "Thalessa will take her time before giving us an answer."

Nymeris, surprised by the magician's apparent indecision, knew Thanatos well enough not to press further. Garnius, on the other hand, reacted with open indifference:

"Good," he grumbled, draining his cup in one gulp. "I was just looking forward to some rest. That ride made me thirsty—and not just for water."

He accompanied his comment with a meaningful wink at the waitress, who returned his smile before stepping away to fetch another pitcher of wine.

Zayn sat uncomfortably, glancing nervously toward Thanatos in a futile attempt to read his expression. He hesitated, anxiously tugging at his sleeve, but curiosity finally overcame him. Gathering his courage, he asked:

"Do you think Thalessa will agree?"

Thanatos slowly turned his head to face him, his black eyes as impenetrable as ocean depths.

"She will agree," he replied, leaving no room for doubt.

Zayn felt heat rise to his cheeks under Thanatos's sharp tone. He quickly lowered his gaze, distracting himself with the breadcrumbs scattered across the tabletop. The dark angel was clearly annoyed. It was best not to push him.

Sensing the growing tension, Nymeris attempted to lighten the mood:

"By the way, I found new armor at the market," she announced with forced enthusiasm. "Leviathan scales! I never thought I'd find something like that."

Thanatos barely listened, clearly distracted. Garnius emitted a grunt, rolling his eyes in protest.

Nymeris merely shrugged and briefly turned her attention to Zayn. The young man quickly looked away, feeling awkward and uncertain about what to say.

After a brief silence, Thanatos released a barely audible sigh.

"You should all go rest," he stated curtly. "We'll discuss our next move tomorrow."

Nymeris complied and headed toward the rooms. Zayn hastily stood to follow, relieved to escape Thanatos's oppressive presence. Just before exiting the room, he risked a discreet glance back at the dark angel. Thanatos had not moved; his back remained straight, fingers absently tracing the rim of his cup, lost in deep thought.

Garnius, unimpressed by his companion's somber mood, gestured for the waitress to approach.

"Finally, a bit of peace, sweetheart," murmured the warrior as she generously refilled his cup. "Sometimes you'd think that angel carries all the world's hate on his shoulders."

The waitress smiled awkwardly before moving away. Thanatos gave no indication of having heard him, remaining thoughtful, his gaze fixed upon the dark contents of his cup. Garnius, realizing conversation was pointless, chose instead to savor his wine in silence.

Thus, each remained alone with their thoughts, waiting for Thalessa to finally reach her decision.

11 — Suna — Balindra

The morning light filtered through the inn's ill-fitting shutters, casting golden beams directly onto her bed.

Suna stepped out of her room and headed down the stairs to the common room, the wooden steps creaking softly beneath her feet.

The tempting aroma of breakfast immediately stirred her appetite. Around the tables, other guests had already begun their day, exchanging quiet conversation punctuated by the occasional clink of cutlery.

She quickly spotted her companions, seated in a secluded corner, clearly absorbed in an important discussion. Vaelen, his wings neatly folded, spoke softly with Theris. Aldaren, lost in thought, absently turned a slice of fruit between his fingers. Korvel and Hestian appeared far more interested in their plates than in any ongoing conversation.

Suna crossed the room and took the empty chair beside Aldaren.

Moments later, Pharin appeared, barely awake, clumsily adjusting his tunic as though he'd just waged a fierce battle against it.

"Don't tell me you're all already up!" he protested, stifling a yawn worthy of a bear emerging from hibernation. "It's unnatural to rise this early!"

Vaelen rolled his eyes. "Odd, I thought you were half goat. But apparently, your other half is clearly sloth."

Pharin sat down, adopting an exaggeratedly sulky expression under his companions' amused gazes. But his face instantly brightened when the innkeeper placed a heaping plate of food before him.

"So?" asked Suna. "Where do we go from here?"

Theris set his cup down on the table.

"We're at the gates of Arachnea," the counselor replied calmly. "We need to cross the city to reach Enhugo's island, which we'll traverse before reaching Balindra later this afternoon."

Suna felt anxiety rising within her. She sincerely hoped that the name "Arachnea" had nothing to do with the creatures that disgusted her so much.

"Arachnea?" she echoed nervously. "It doesn't have anything to do with… spiders, right?"

Her voice betrayed her unease. Aldaren responded with an apologetic smile.

"Almost," the old man replied. "It's the city of Ariane and her spider hybrids."

"Spider hybrids?!" she choked.

"Yes, but don't worry, the inhabitants are perfectly civilized."

"Civilized or not," she exclaimed, "they're still… spiders."

"Yes," Pharin added helpfully, "big… very big spiders."

Korvel and Hestian exchanged amused glances, clearly entertained by the young woman's obvious discomfort. Theris tried to reassure her.

"They aren't just ordinary spiders," Theris explained gently. "They're intelligent beings, perfectly capable of polite conversation. They're very welcoming to travelers."

"They also weave marvelous fabrics and produce incomparable silks," Aldaren added warmly, attempting to distract her fears by piquing her curiosity.

"And don't worry," Pharin quipped, "if one scares you too much, I'll be there to lull it to sleep with an improvised lullaby on my aulos."

Suna was not reassured at all.

"Well, fine… I suppose we don't really have a choice," she sighed in resignation.

Once they had finished breakfast, they prepared swiftly to resume their journey. Suna felt her heart quicken as she left the comforting safety of the inn behind. No matter how supposedly civilized these creatures were, she had absolutely no desire to test their hospitality too closely.

The road ahead gradually dipped into a deep natural furrow, carved directly into the rock, while the terrain rose on either side.

"Come," Theris suggested. "Let's take a slight detour—the view from above is breathtaking."

They left the main road, following a narrower path, evidently less traveled. The trail rose gradually toward the edge of the cliffs, where the sea breeze swept across sparse, low vegetation.

Reaching the summit, Suna remained speechless at the sight unfolding before their eyes.

Arachnea lay just below, nestled between two sheer cliff faces. It connected the cliffs at the heart of the mainland with those, farther out, on Enhugo's island. The city was a marvel of engineering. An immense aerial network sprawled around a large central bridge, wide enough to allow two carts to pass comfortably.

Stone pillars rose dramatically from the sea below, each crowned by slender towers interconnected by a sophisticated maze of walkways.

The spectacular bridge wound gracefully among the most imposing towers, lending the city a dizzying, aerial feel. Silken threads, gleaming silvery-white, shimmered in the sunlight like a glittering web—a vast jewel suspended above the abyss. These threads appeared delicate yet were sturdy enough to support entire dwellings.

Arachnea's buildings were equally remarkable. Their walls were strengthened by silk threads skillfully woven with plant fibers and wood. Suspended walkways linked the various structures, reinforcing the impression of a city hanging entirely over empty space.

The inhabitants moved gracefully along these walkways or glided effortlessly along threads stretched between towers. The spider hybrids navigated as easily on solid ground as in the heights, their slender limbs effortlessly grasping every available support. Their arachnid bodies were covered by a fine, iridescent carapace.

Suna felt a complex emotion rise within her, torn between admiration and instinctive revulsion. She stood motionless, transfixed by the view.

"It's… impressive," she admitted reluctantly.

Vaelen smiled, appreciating the unique spectacle before them.

"Magnificent, isn't it?" the counselor murmured.

"I… I'm not sure yet whether I find it magnificent or terrifying."

Pharin, perched beside her, couldn't resist adding:

"If that bridge breaks, we'll all end up neatly wrapped like pretty little flies…"

"Thank you so much for that charming image, Pharin! Exactly what I needed…"

The satyr burst out laughing. "Always happy to help, my dear!"

"Don't worry," Aldaren reassured her. "Their silk is strong. The only one likely to fall through is a clumsy satyr with hooves and a tongue that's far too loose," he added, winking at Pharin.

This playful jab slightly eased the young woman's worry.

"You'll see, Suna," Theris added. "The people of Arachnea are particularly welcoming. They're very proud of their city and jealously ensure the safety of their network of walkways."

She nodded slowly, somewhat reassured but still mesmerized by the dance of the arachnids along their silk threads.

"Let's go," Theris announced confidently, stepping forward toward the entrance of the dizzying bridge.

When they finally set foot upon the main bridge, Suna felt her heartbeat quicken. For her, this crossing promised to be a genuine challenge.

Their mounts' hooves landed upon the web's surface, both supple and incredibly strong. The ground barely rippled beneath their steps.

All around them, life bustled with restless activity that made Suna uncomfortable.

The magically reinforced threads bore witness to Arachnid ingenuity. Gradually, Suna felt her worries dissipating. Every detail of the city, from its dizzying network of walkways to its towering spires, formed a magnificent spectacle.

"It's incredible," Suna admitted, looking upward. "I don't even know where to look—it's so beautiful!"

Behind her, a quiet, plaintive squeak emerged:

"Personally, I suggest especially not thinking about what's below...," Pharin squeaked, his voice strangled.

Suna turned around and discovered the satyr in a pitiful state. Sitting stiffly atop his mule, eyes fixed straight ahead, gripping the reins with all his strength. His face, usually so mischievous, was pale as a sheet.

"Well now, my dear friend," teased Hestian, "could it be that your hooves miss solid ground that much?"

Pharin attempted to protest, turning to reply—but the instant he moved, his precarious balance was immediately compromised. His eyes widened, his arms flailed frantically. In a desperate reflex, he grabbed hold of his mule's mane, letting out a shrill cry.

The animal, startled by this sudden movement, stopped dead, ignoring the satyr's panicked kicks.

"No, you demon donkey, move! Don't just stand there!" the musician whined.

Pharin then closed his eyes, letting out a long moan, frozen atop his motionless mount.

"Come on, move, you infernal beast!" he hissed through clenched teeth.

Hestian passed beside the paralyzed satyr, giving the mule a gentle slap on its hindquarters. The animal immediately broke into a trot, eliciting a terrified scream from Pharin. His little goat legs, stretched out to the sides, bounced uncontrollably with the rhythm of his mount.

"Stop, you diabolical mule!" he shouted. "I command you to stop! I didn't sign up for this!"

His companions burst into laughter; even Vaelen and Theris, usually more reserved, couldn't hold back. Korvel and Hestian laughed openly, slapping their thighs.

"Hang in there, Pharin!" shouted Suna.

"Try playing her a tune to calm her down," Vaelen added. "I'm sure your talent alone will be enough to tame that wild beast!"

Still jostled by his mule, the satyr managed to turn around with a furious grimace and shouted back, his voice broken by the bouncing:

"I warn you... if I survive... you'll get a satirical ballad about your wickedness... that'll be remembered for posterity!"

"I can't wait to hear it!" retorted Korvel, laughing even louder.

The promise, far from having the threatening effect intended, doubled the group's hilarity, as they joyfully continued their crossing of Arachnea, accompanied by the desperate protests of their unfortunate rider.

Yielding to temptation, Suna leaned out of the cart to peer at what lay below. Immediately, a powerful dizziness seized her. Her heart seemed to leap within her chest, and she instinctively tightened her fingers on the edge. The pillars of the bridge appeared endless, plunging into a dizzying abyss. For a fraction of a second, she felt as though she were falling, swept away by the disorienting sensation of being drawn into the void. She took a deep breath, trying to calm the frantic beating of her heart.

Then, as the dizziness gave way to fascination, she dared to gaze again at the extraordinary landscape beneath her feet. Her eyes widened at the immense expanse stretching beneath her. The ocean extended far below, much farther than she'd imagined. Distant waves crashed against rocks in explosions of white foam.

Huge square nets, woven from thick silk, descended into the sea, guided by sturdy cables. Once submerged, they disappeared for a moment, then resurfaced, filled with an abundance of wriggling, trapped fish.

These catches were skillfully hauled up by Arachnid inhabitants, whose limbs drew up the nets with remarkable precision. They perched on rocky walls or clung to other vertical webs. The sun's rays danced on the water, reflecting off the wet threads, creating a mesmerizing ballet of light and movement.

Captivated, Suna felt her apprehension fade away, replaced by a sense of pure wonder. This city, which she'd initially feared, was revealing a hidden beauty—utterly fascinating.

When they finally reached the outskirts of Arachnea, Suna noticed a strikingly beautiful woman standing before what appeared to be a sewing workshop. She stood behind a stack of fabric rolls, her long hair cascading like silk around her delicate face, hazel eyes observing passersby with curiosity. Although the woman appeared slender, she towered nearly a head above those around her. As they drew closer, Suna couldn't stop her jaw from dropping slightly in astonishment. Beneath the woman's elegant dress extended a large spider abdomen, supported by six slender legs.

"Welcome to Arachnea," she said melodiously, clearly amused by Suna's reaction. "May I help you find something to your liking?"

Suna swallowed, unable to tear her gaze away.

Upon seeing the rest of the group, the spider-woman's face lit up radiantly.

"Counselor Theris! It's been far too long since you've walked upon our webs," she said in a gentle voice, tinged with mild reproach.

"My duties often take me far away," the counselor apologized. "But I never forget the exceptional quality of your silk. I must congratulate you, by the way—the last delivery exceeded our expectations."

Ariane straightened her delicate torso, evidently pleased.

"I'm delighted to hear it," she replied gratefully.

"Arachnea's workshops produce absolutely extraordinary silk," Aldaren explained softly to Suna. "It's fine and soft to the touch, yet incredibly durable. Some fabrics are even imbued with protective enchantments taught at the Academy of Weaving. Ætherium's guards all wear garments crafted from this silk. No ordinary blade can tear it."

Theris cast a sidelong glance at Suna, whose unusual clothing was drawing many curious stares from passersby.

"Suna," he began cautiously, "I believe it would be wise to find attire that's more… appropriate. Your current outfit draws a bit too much attention."

Surprised by his remark, she immediately glanced down at her faded jeans and oversized sweater.

"You really think so?" she asked with mock innocence.

"I'd say it's a necessity," he replied firmly.

Suna's eyes instantly brightened, a wide, enthusiastic smile lighting up her face. Without the slightest hesitation, she jumped out of the cart with almost childlike excitement, causing Aldaren to startle.

"That's an excellent idea!" she cried, already rushing toward Ariane's workshop. "I'll finally have something proper to wear!"

Theris remained motionless for a moment, blinking at this unexpected reaction. He let out a gentle sigh before dismounting and following after the exuberant girl.

Quickly, Suna stopped in front of a clothing rack. Her fingers eagerly browsed through the garments, enjoying their texture and elegant cut.

"Theris, come look at this!" she exclaimed, holding up a fabric whose colors shifted with every change in angle. "It's so soft!"

Ariane approached, clasping her hands together, sensing an easy sale.

"Ah, you have very refined taste, young lady," Ariane remarked gently. "It changes color according to your mood."

Suna's eyes widened even more. She grabbed Theris's arm, pulling him quickly to her side to show him.

"According to my mood? Oh, Theris, it's exactly what I need!"

"I was thinking of something more discreet..." the counselor ventured cautiously.

Suna energetically shook her head, already clutching the fabric tightly against herself, as if afraid it might suddenly disappear.

"No, no, it's perfect!" she declared eagerly before grabbing another dress, then another, and another.

Soon, a small mountain of clothes formed in her arms, threatening to topple at any moment. Ariane, delighted by this unexpected windfall, followed closely behind, praising each item.

"This is enchanted silk, able to keep you warm or cool you down depending on circumstances. Perfect for evening wear."

"And this?" asked Suna, pointing to a tunic embroidered with golden thread.

"Perfect for festivities—it's stain-proof," replied Ariane, visibly delighted by the young woman's clear interest.

Suna sometimes rejected an item with a small pout before adding two more to her initial selection.

Suna rushed toward a small changing booth behind a canvas curtain.

"Wait here, Theris! I'll be right back!"

Theris crossed his arms patiently in front of the booth, exchanging a resigned glance with Aldaren, who seemed visibly amused by the scene.

A few seconds later, Suna reappeared in a flowing dress shimmering with violet reflections. She spun around with charming awkwardness, the fabric swirling around her like a small tornado.

"Well? What do you think?"

"Magnificent," Theris conceded, "but perhaps not ideal for traveling?"

She thought for a second before disappearing again behind the curtain. A series of muffled noises and indistinct mutterings followed.

When she reappeared, she was wearing a more practical outfit with carefully crafted details.

"That's better..." Theris commented.

"Better?" she repeated, feigning indignation. "I look absolutely incredible in this!"

Ariane immediately nodded with clear enthusiasm.

"You look utterly ravishing," she confirmed, exchanging a discreet wink with Theris.

Without further ado, Suna piled up more dresses, cloaks, and scarves, each new item triggering fresh exclamations of delight. At one point, poor Ariane had to free herself from beneath an avalanche of clothing Suna had inadvertently heaped into her arms.

"Suna," Theris interjected, "you realize we must continue our journey? You've picked out enough clothes for ten trips!"

She turned toward him with absolute seriousness.

"Theris, you don't understand," she replied earnestly. "What if we're invited to a banquet? I simply can't wear the same dress twice!"

Aldaren, amused by the situation, added mischievously, "She has a point, Theris! You never know what might happen!"

Theris sighed, surrendering to Suna's irrational argument. He reached for his pouch to pay Ariane, who was already jubilant at this profitable sale.

Ecstatic, Suna seized his arm gratefully.

"Thank you, thank you, a thousand times thank you!" she cried, practically bouncing with excitement.

Burdened like never before, they returned to the cart, Suna holding her packages protectively against her chest. She meticulously arranged them in the back of the cart, double-checking repeatedly to ensure nothing could fall out.

"It appears you've discovered one of the greatest dangers of our journey," Aldaren whispered discreetly to Theris.

Theris rolled his eyes.

Suna, entirely absorbed by her new acquisitions, inspected her purchases one last time, her face radiant with happiness. The journey could wait a little longer, as long as they could admire the joyful sparkle in the young girl's eyes.

Pharin was the first to cross onto solid ground, releasing a particularly loud sigh of relief.

"Solid earth at last!" he cried, exaggerating his joy.

The rest of the group quickly joined him. Now on the island of Enhugo, they soon saw the cliffs giving way to gentle green hills dotted with groves.

These lovely expanses were interspersed with tiny hamlets surrounded by impeccably maintained gardens. Small wooden bridges spanned canals lined with rushes and wildflowers. Along the banks, white ibises stood motionless, lending an elegant note to this bucolic landscape.

They ventured onto a lane bordered by blooming magnolias. Delicate white and pastel-pink petals drifted to the ground, carpeting the path. Here and there, tall clusters of hollyhocks and geraniums dotted the landscape with vibrant color.

Suna inhaled deeply, closing her eyes for a moment to savor the floral fragrance floating in the air. When she opened them again, her eyes sparkled with wonder.

"All these colors… it's enchanting," she murmured, captivated.

Pharin, unable to resist the occasion, improvised a melody on his favorite instrument:

"Beneath magnolias' tender shade,

A rain of petals softly laid.

Pink petals blaze in vivid glow,

Suna breathes deep, peace starts to flow..."

"Oh, put that flute away!" giggled Suna.

The satyr jumped upright, adopting an exaggerated, offended posture.

"My flute? It's an *aulos*, you young barbarian!"

His mock indignation was so comical that Suna burst out laughing, quickly infecting the entire group.

Satisfied at having brightened the mood, Pharin trotted merrily ahead of them, continuing his melody in a cheerful whistle.

Before them stretched a vast plain. Balindra revealed itself, bathed in the glow of the setting sun.

They passed through Balindra's open gates, where a lone guard stood, seemingly unconcerned about security. He stepped forward and greeted them with a friendly wave.

"You can't enter with your horses," he explained kindly. "Large animals aren't permitted inside the city, to preserve its cleanliness and tranquility. The streets are narrow, filled with stairways and footbridges—your mounts wouldn't be comfortable."

He pointed toward a building nearby.

"There's a travelers' stable just over there," he added.

They thanked him with a nod, followed his directions, and entrusted their horses to the stablehands before continuing on foot.

Upon entering the city, Suna felt her muscles instinctively relax, overtaken by the serene atmosphere. Everything radiated harmony, inviting profound peace. Graceful columns decorated with plant motifs supported finely carved pediments. The last rays of sunlight caressed pastel-colored façades, revealing subtle hues of ivory, pale pink, and soft green.

Buildings were arranged around large courtyards lined with lush, carefully maintained gardens. The air was fragrant with medicinal herbs, mint, and jasmine. Here and there, fountains murmured softly, their sparkling jets catching the fading daylight.

The inhabitants, dressed in long, sober yet elegant tunics, calmly went about their tasks, greeting the newcomers with nods or warm smiles. Some remained absorbed in daily chores: pruning geometric hedges, watering aromatic herbs, or copying ancient texts while seated on stone benches.

"This city breathes peace," Suna observed admiringly.

"There are few places in Mytherra as peaceful as Balindra," Aldaren replied softly.

As they moved forward, Suna's attention was irresistibly drawn to imposing monitor lizards. Crocodile-like, they strolled leisurely through the streets.

At their approach, one stopped beside a small clear-water pool to drink, its forked tongue delicately brushing the surface. Slowly, it raised its head toward them, its golden eyes attentive yet surprisingly gentle, scrutinizing the visitors.

"They're… huge," exclaimed Suna. "Yet they seem so calm."

"They are," Theris reassured her. "Balindra's monitors are completely harmless and have lived harmoniously alongside the inhabitants for generations."

Indeed, several townspeople walked casually alongside these gigantic reptiles, as if they were mere household pets. One laughing young boy even affectionately clung to the neck of one, riding the animal as it ambled placidly forward.

At the back of the group, Pharin emitted an admiring whistle:

"Now, there's a creature worthy of respect! It would make a splendid mount for a satyr like myself."

Vaelen, at his side, rolled his eyes.

"I fear even a creature that calm would struggle to endure your incessant chatter."

The satyr feigned a look of indignation.

Suna, absorbed by the tranquil surroundings, observed further along an elderly man seated on a bench surrounded by bamboo, carefully engraving a clay tablet. Beside him, a monitor calmly watched his work.

They continued their journey, wrapped in the calm radiating from every corner, plant, and inhabitant of the city.

The winding waterways that ran through the town had been crafted to enhance this sensation of tranquility. Canals blended harmoniously into their surroundings, gliding gently between pavilions with delicate façades. The water flowed softly, murmuring gently, its surface reflecting the soft glow of lanterns gradually coming to life.

Suna admired these canals bordered by broad slabs of carefully polished white stone. At each intersection, small wooden bridges lacquered in bright red connected the buildings to the paths. Here and there, wisteria and climbing ivy adorned the railings, cascading blossoms brushing lightly against the calm surface of the water.

The squares were magnificent, built around expansive pools adorned with intricate mosaics. At their center stood statues quietly watching over the scene. Beneath their reflections, koi fish with scales of gold and crimson glided smoothly between lily pads.

"It's splendid," Suna breathed.

Nearby, a group of children gathered around a smaller pond. Laughing, they lightly prodded small, colorful creatures resembling starfish with translucent bodies that responded with a gentle blue glow.

"What are those?" Suna asked.

"They're called asterids," Theris answered. "They're native to the island of Enhugo. It's said their glow calms the mind."

"I can confirm that," Pharin interjected enthusiastically. "I already feel incredibly calm!"

"It'll take more than asterids to quiet your mind, satyr," teased Hestian.

His comment drew muffled laughter from the group.

Suna's attention turned to a small adjacent park. There, cherry trees were in full bloom, branches heavy with pink petals gently drifting down like a fragrant, light snowfall. The ground beneath was entirely carpeted, forming a soft, colorful blanket underfoot. A scattering of stone lanterns tastefully punctuated the setting.

A slight breeze rose, causing the petals to dance gracefully in the air like rosy snowflakes. Some inhabitants had settled on carved benches beneath the shaded canopy of crimson maples, peacefully enjoying the spectacle.

Water, flowers, creatures, and even the residents themselves all contributed to Balindra's unique atmosphere. In this idyllic setting, every element seemed perfectly synchronized, creating a place where nature was carefully preserved and respected.

This natural coexistence, this evident harmony between humans and animals, made Suna realize the wisdom Enhugo had instilled in this city.

"This place is unlike anything I've ever seen," she murmured. "They've figured it all out."

"And that," Aldaren replied softly, "is precisely why we're here. To find the answers we seek, in this sanctuary devoted to knowledge."

The group reached a sprawling estate devoted to study and contemplation, the true heart of knowledge, maintained by the Guild of Scholars.

The buildings of the estate were arranged in a circle around an immense central structure.

Expansive gardens stretched in all directions, meticulously cultivated natural sanctuaries. White gravel pathways wound their way through thick rows of azaleas, their colors vibrant, ranging from soft pink to deep purple. Trees with wide, spreading branches provided shade beneath which numerous students sat in semicircles, absorbed in lessons taught by their professors.

A gray-haired teacher passionately explained an ancient text to students seated on the grass. They listened with almost religious attention, meticulously taking notes. A little further away, two young scholars were engaged in an animated debate, gesticulating energetically as they discussed a historical or philosophical disagreement.

"Look," Suna whispered to Aldaren, amused by their dramatic gestures.

Aldaren smiled gently. It reminded him of his own days as a student.

They continued down the path, passing a pavilion that immediately drew Suna's attention. Its walls were inlaid with mosaics arranged in geometric patterns. Through partially opened windows, she glimpsed delicate glass instruments and vessels containing brightly colored fluids bubbling over flickering flames, occasionally emitting small sparks or faint plumes of vapor. The walls were covered with panels depicting elemental symbols.

Above the pavilion, a dome with narrow openings released gently curling fumes tinted sapphire blue, emerald, or vivid crimson.

Suna paused, fascinated by a nearby basin whose water slowly changed color from turquoise to deep mauve.

She hesitantly reached her hand toward the water, intrigued, but Aldaren stopped her.

"It might be best not to touch," he said, amused. "One never quite knows what might happen here."

"True," she laughed softly, withdrawing her hand. "I'm not particularly eager to turn purple."

They continued on their way to the next pavilion, even more imposing than the last. Constructed of black marble, inlaid with golden flecks reminiscent of a starry vault, it clearly belonged to the realm of astronomy. Graceful arches supported a vast circular terrace topped by an impressive astronomical telescope of polished bronze, aimed toward the heavens. Students wearing midnight-blue tunics moved calmly about the platform, which was entirely covered with meticulously engraved star charts. Some adjusted their instruments; others spoke in hushed voices, occasionally pointing toward a constellation currently invisible.

"They can study stars during the day?" Suna asked in surprise.

"Knowledge never sleeps," Aldaren replied, amused by her enthusiasm. "But for now, they're just preparing for their nightly observations."

A little farther along, the group passed a rectangular building pierced by large, intricately carved windows. Inside, Suna glimpsed broad tables covered with detailed maps and terrestrial globes. A young scholar glanced up briefly upon noticing their presence, his face smudged with ink, his brush frozen in mid-stroke. He gave them a quick nod before immediately immersing himself again in his work.

The pavilion's exterior walls were adorned with extensive frescoes depicting lands unknown to Suna, painted with remarkable precision.

Suna couldn't help marveling at each detail; she wished she had more time to soak up the scholarly atmosphere and the beauty of these surroundings.

Suddenly, a shadow passed over her, causing her to look upward. Entranced, she discovered about a dozen small winged creatures, graceful as flying serpents. As she observed one more closely, she realized they were crafted entirely of paper, like delicate origami figures.

"Pharin, look!" she whispered excitedly, pointing up at the creatures in the sky.

The satyr nearly lost his balance as he craned his neck upward. Suna watched the creatures for another moment, captivated by their graceful flight.

The central library of Balindra, an undisputed jewel of knowledge, rose majestically in a gravity-defying spiral. Constructed in harmonious balance between pale marble and finely carved wood, its presence was gracefully imposing.

Each floor was encircled by a stone balcony edged with elegant balustrades, upon which small lanterns gently swayed. A broad, square roof inspired by pagodas sheltered every level, yet unlike the temples of the Orient, each story turned slightly, creating a frozen spiral of stone and wood. Scholars, robes billowing gently in the breeze, strolled leisurely along these balconies, deeply immersed in books or speaking in hushed whispers.

Some scholars lingered quietly on the balconies, leaning against the railings, absorbed in their reading or exchanging low conversations.

The topmost roof, shimmering with pearlescent reflections, redirected each ray of sunlight like a beacon of wisdom. Above it, a glass dome crowned the tower, capturing daylight to flood the spacious reading halls beneath with clarity.

Around the library's perimeter, elegant lanterns hung at regular intervals, naturally guiding visitors toward the main entrance. At their feet, the scholars' emblem was intricately engraved: a hand grasping an open book covered in countless runes, promising infinite knowledge to those who crossed the threshold.

The entrance itself, consisting of double doors of solid wood, was decorated with carvings depicting the various disciplines taught within the campus.

Inside opened a vast hall where students and professors mingled freely. A few scholars delicately handled scrolls, occasionally exchanging discreet whispers or nods of approval.

As the group approached the porch, a graceful silhouette emerged. A young woman awaited them, her mid-length brown hair framing a delicate, expressive face. Her large brown eyes scrutinized each member of the party with evident curiosity.

She stepped forward and stopped before them, fine hands stained with ink clasped gently in front of her.

"Welcome to Balindra," she greeted them, her voice soft and melodic. "I am Liore, a disciple of Enhugo. I've been expecting you."

Vaelen stepped forward, a concerned crease forming on his brow.

"How do you know who we are?" he asked.

Liore, entirely unperturbed, replied calmly, "I was informed of your arrival. Let's just say it wasn't particularly difficult to recognize a group so… distinctive." Then, eyeing Pharin pointedly, she added, "Your furry friend, however, is a surprise."

Hestian and Korvel burst into laughter.

Pharin, startled by the sudden attention, puffed out his chest and spoke up with exaggerated indignation.

"Furry? That's hardly fair! I prefer the term 'fluffy.' I'll have you know I'm their artistic guide, epic storyteller, virtuoso musician, and chronicler extraordinaire. Without me, this group would be as tedious as a dissertation on the life cycle of mushrooms!"

With his usual diplomacy, Theris smoothly intervened.

"I am Theris, counselor to Raenos. This colorful individual," he stressed each word carefully, "is a guest whom we tolerate… at least for now."

"Tolerate?" Pharin choked dramatically, clutching at his chest as if struck by an arrow. Turning to the young scholar, he continued, "I am the very soul of this group of ingrates, entrusted with the noble mission of immortalizing their deeds throughout the ages!"

"I'm certain your contribution is utterly invaluable," she replied, a hint of irony in her voice.

Then, adopting a more serious tone, she addressed the entire group.

"If you'll kindly follow me, I'll show you to your quarters. You must be tired after your long journey, and Enhugo is eager to meet with you."

She turned gracefully and, with an elegant gesture, invited them to follow her deeper into the heart of the university grounds.

The group followed her along paths lined with blooming magnolias. Liore guided them toward a large building, set apart from the pavilions. The structure, which the scholars called an "insula," reminded Suna of university dormitories from her own world. The beige stone building, simple yet inviting, displayed understated frescoes.

The insula was arranged around a charming interior courtyard, bordered by galleries draped with climbing plants. From the balconies surrounding this courtyard, one could admire a central fountain whose gentle murmur contributed to the prevailing serenity.

"Here are your rooms," Liore announced as she led them down a long corridor. "Each room is modest but comfortable. I'll leave you to settle in. Take your time. When you're ready, I'll guide you to the main building—Enhugo awaits us there for dinner."

Suna entered the room designated for her. It was a space both simple and elegant. She approached the balcony overlooking the courtyard, inhaling deeply to savor the fresh air infused with evening fragrances.

After a brief pause, she carefully freshened up, enjoying the pleasant sensation of water against her skin.

She selected one of the dresses she'd purchased in Arachnea and slipped it on carefully. The fabric, incredibly soft, flowed down her arms and moved fluidly with every gesture. She couldn't hold back a satisfied smile when she saw herself in the mirror.

When she rejoined her companions, Suna caused a brief stir: everyone stopped their conversations to look at her. Even Pharin, usually quick with a joke, found himself momentarily speechless. He let out a low whistle, a mix of surprise and admiration.

"Well now, Suna," he said theatrically, "you're literally lighting up the evening! Be careful, Enhugo might mistake you for one of his precious stars."

"I must admit," Theris complimented her warmly, "that outfit suits you perfectly. You're radiant."

Suna felt warmth rise to her cheeks. She stood there, lips parted as if to reply, but couldn't find the words. This unusual attention moved her more than she cared to admit.

Liore, with that gentle expression seemingly fixed on her face, invited the group to follow:

"Are you ready? Let's join the Grand Master," she said calmly, though a subtle eagerness was evident in her voice.

They returned to the central building. The rear section of the edifice, reserved for Enhugo's private quarters, distinguished itself with a more austere architecture, yet without sacrificing any of its elegance.

Once past the threshold, the atmosphere grew quieter. The main room was dominated by bookshelves filled with carefully arranged manuscripts and enigmatic artifacts. A scent of old paper, mingled with polished wood, hung gently in the air.

At the heart of this domain stood the master himself, his presence imbued with natural authority. Enhugo, temples whitened by the passing years, carried in his gaze that solemnity unique to those who had spent a lifetime exploring the depths of knowledge. Each wrinkle on his face marked decades of reading, writing, and reflection. Tall and slender, the magician wore an elegant robe interwoven with shades of deep blue and gold. His hazel eyes, lively yet serene, regarded the group with infinite patience.

Liore stepped forward respectfully and introduced the guests.

"Grand Magician Enhugo," she declared, "here are the travelers sent by Raenos."

"Welcome to Balindra," he said in a deep, calm voice. "Please, follow me. Your journey must have been long and tiring. We shall speak quietly over a good meal."

He invited them, with a graceful gesture, into an adjoining room, where an elegantly prepared table awaited. On the finely embroidered tablecloth, numerous aromatic dishes had already been arranged.

Candles cast dancing shadows upon the walls, enhancing the intimacy of the setting.

As the group took their seats, Suna caught sight of a discreet silhouette slipping into the doorway. A creature of rare elegance confidently entered the room. It was a nine-tailed fox, its silky, russet fur gleaming in the golden candlelight. On the animal's forehead and upper paws, silver inscriptions shimmered, adding to its enigmatic aura. Its bright yellow eyes sparkled with all the mischief characteristic of its kind.

The fox approached Enhugo slowly, raising its head gently to receive a caress. The magician's fingers lightly ran through its flaming coat, eliciting a barely audible sigh.

Then, with evident curiosity, the animal moved toward the visitors, passing close by Hestian and Korvel. It emitted a low, raspy growl toward them. Hestian jumped slightly, while Korvel furrowed his brows.

Pharin, always quick to seize an opportunity for teasing, couldn't suppress a small chuckle.

"Ah! Seems he knows exactly who the real troublemakers among us are."

The satyr earned himself a murderous glance from Hestian, but the fox, indifferent to their exchange, continued advancing toward Suna. Intimidated, she remained still as the creature approached, its golden eyes locked onto hers, strangely mesmerizing.

The fox tilted its head, seemingly assessing her, then stepped closer. Suna cautiously extended her hand toward it. Her fingers brushed against the thick, silky fur. The fox closed its eyes for a moment, then comfortably settled itself next to her.

Liore knelt down as well, affectionately stroking its coat.

"This is Kitsune," she introduced. "Enhugo's faithful companion for more lifetimes than I could count. Very little escapes him, believe me."

Suna, captivated, continued gently stroking Kitsune's fur, enchanted by this unexpected closeness to such a mysterious being.

Enhugo watched this interaction fondly, then resumed the conversation.

"Tell me everything," he said, gazing intently at Theris. "Raenos's message was brief, and I would prefer to hear the details directly from you."

Theris then meticulously recounted Suna's mysterious arrival in Mytherra and the hope she represented. He also explained their certainty: valuable clues about the Pillars lay hidden somewhere in Balindra's library. Enhugo listened carefully.

The meal continued quietly, punctuated by muted conversations. As dinner drew to a close, Suna felt fatigue weighing heavily on her eyelids. Noticing her exhaustion, Enhugo rose gently to conclude the evening.

"You must be exhausted after such a long journey," he said softly. "Go and rest. We will continue our conversation tomorrow, and I shall personally accompany you to begin your research."

Gratefully, they all stood to take their leave, departing the warmth and tranquility of Enhugo's sanctuary. Before closing the door behind her, Suna cast one final glance back and glimpsed Kitsune curled at Enhugo's feet. His golden eyes faintly glowed in the shadows, like a sentinel watching over his master's rest.

12 — Zayn — Unexpected encounter

A messenger arrived at the door of Thanatos's chamber. He raised his hand to knock, but the door abruptly swung open, revealing the dark and imposing figure of the winged man. Caught off guard, the messenger instinctively stepped back from the black-winged angel.

"What do you want?" Thanatos asked, his voice low and sharp.

The messenger swallowed hard, gathering his courage.

"Thalessa has sent me to fetch you," he declared nervously. "She requests your immediate presence at the palace."

Thanatos regarded him coldly, scrutinizing every detail of his face as though assessing the truth of his words.

"Lead me," he commanded simply.

The messenger immediately turned on his heels, eager to put distance between himself and Thanatos's intimidating aura. The dark angel followed him, his wings brushing against the narrow walls of the corridor.

Outside, the first rays of a pale sun cast a weak glow over silent alleys. The wooden walkways stood empty, covered by a thin morning mist floating gently above the canals. The messenger quickened his pace, frequently glancing anxiously over his shoulder.

When they reached the massive gates of the palace, the guards instantly straightened at the duo's approach. No words were exchanged; they simply stepped aside, letting them pass.

The messenger guided Thanatos through vast corridors, eventually stopping before a finely carved door. With a mechanical gesture, he gave a brief bow before swiftly disappearing down an adjacent hallway, visibly relieved.

Thanatos opened the door without hesitation, stepping into a spacious, elegant room. Thalessa sat behind a desk of mother-of-pearl and coral, radiating natural authority. Her eyes, as cold as a winter sea, scrutinized her guest without blinking.

"Thanatos," she said, "I thank you for accepting my invitation."

He inclined his head slightly, eyes remaining fixed upon hers.

"I am merely carrying out Ereshkal's wishes. Your decision?"

A joyless smile stretched Thalessa's lips.

"You have my support," she promised. "But under one condition: one of my daughters will accompany you."

Thanatos showed no emotion. He simply tilted his head, accepting without hesitation.

"As you wish," he said. "Is she ready to leave immediately?"

"She will reveal herself to you in due course."

Thanatos clenched his jaw, impatience simmering beneath his customary calm.

"If your decision is made, why play these little games?" he finally retorted, his voice charged with restrained anger.

Thalessa rose slowly from her seat, circling the desk with leisurely grace. Her footsteps echoed in the room, amplifying the already palpable tension.

"Because here, Thanatos, no one dictates my rules," she replied, meeting his eyes directly. "Not even Ereshkal."

Thanatos stared at her for a long moment, every fiber of his being fighting to contain his growing irritation. Finally, he bowed his head slightly, swallowing his pride with difficulty.

"Very well. In due course," he repeated icily.

Satisfied by this small victory, Thalessa turned and took a few steps away, clasping her hands behind her back.

"You may leave, Thanatos."

Thanatos struggled to control the irritation rising within him. His black wings shuddered, betraying his mood, before he spun around abruptly. He crossed the room and exited without a sound.

Left alone, Thalessa returned to her seat with a discreet sigh. Her fingers gently brushed the pearly surface of the desk.

She had won this round.

While Thanatos was being received at the palace, and his two acolytes were quietly enjoying their breakfast, Zayn had decided to slip away. He exited through the inn's back door, seeking a moment alone to clear his thoughts. Atlantide's morning atmosphere was strange yet soothing. Around him, winding alleyways and peaceful canals reflected the first rays of sunlight, creating hypnotic patterns on the water.

Absorbed by his thoughts, he jumped slightly when a soft, melodic voice called out to him:

"You're Zayn, aren't you?"

Turning quickly, he froze.

Before him stood a breathtakingly beautiful young woman. Her moon-pale skin shimmered gently with delicate, pearly scales reflecting subtle blue hues. In her long, wavy hair, tiny seashells and bits of seaweed jingled softly with each movement. Her clear blue eyes, as deep as the ocean, had an intriguing, almost hypnotic quality. And her ears — elegantly curved, subtly reminiscent of fish fins.

"Yes…" he replied cautiously. "But… who are you?"

The woman smiled, her thin lips gracefully curling upward.

"My name is Fynna," the stunning young woman replied. "Thanatos sent me to guide you."

Zayn stepped back, instinctively defensive. Something in the way she had spoken Thanatos's name felt wrong, yet her beauty and kind expression gradually disarmed his mistrust.

Fynna reached out her hand, her eyes shining with unsettling gentleness.

"Come," she whispered. "Follow me."

Zayn hesitated briefly, then took the offered hand. He followed her through the winding streets, gradually leaving behind the inn's district to reach the bustling heart of the harbor. As they walked, Zayn noticed Fynna's movements were nearly weightless. She appeared to glide rather than walk, and the morning sunlight danced along her skin and hair, giving her astonishing radiance.

"Tell me, Zayn, why are you traveling with a man like Thanatos?" she asked softly.

Caught off guard, Zayn looked away uncomfortably. A lump formed in his throat as thoughts of his mother, his promise, and the doubts that continually haunted him resurfaced.

"I… have my reasons," he finally replied.

Fynna did not press further. She continued guiding him until they reached a tiny shop at the edge of a canal. Behind a rickety counter, an elderly man with human features — though his arms resembled octopus tentacles — was mixing peculiar ingredients. Fynna approached him, exchanged a few whispered words, and the old man nodded knowingly, casting a quick glance toward Zayn. She returned holding a bowl filled with a thick green liquid streaked with iridescent reflections.

"Here, drink this," she said, offering him the concoction.

Zayn took a step back, put off by the brew's unpleasant appearance.

"What exactly is that?"

She smiled, almost teasingly.

"Trust me. Just drink."

Zayn hesitated, eyeing the viscous liquid apprehensively. Yet Fynna's gaze disarmed him. Her beautiful eyes weakened his resolve. Reluctantly, but never breaking eye contact, he lifted the bowl to his lips. The cold, slimy substance slid into his mouth, leaving behind a salty, bitter taste. He tried swallowing, but the substance stuck in his throat, instantly triggering a choking sensation. His heart raced.

Panicked, he tried speaking, but no sound came. His hands flew to his throat, eyes widening, as an odd heat filled his lungs. Struggling for breath, he opened his mouth repeatedly, gasping desperately like a fish suffocating out of water.

Fynna quickly stepped closer, her reassuring smile now tinged with mischief. Without giving him time to react, she embraced him tightly, pulling him into a firm, unexpected embrace.

Before he could protest, she fell backward with him into the canal's waters.

The inn door swung open abruptly, revealing Thanatos, his expression grim and even darker than usual. Several patrons looked up, swiftly averting their gazes, chilled by the intimidating aura surrounding the winged figure. He crossed the room with swift, purposeful strides. Regulars instinctively shrank away as he passed.

Nymeris and Garnius, sitting at a table near the fireplace, simultaneously raised their heads as he halted abruptly in front of them.

"Where's Zayn?" Thanatos snapped sharply, his features tense with irritation. "I don't see him anywhere."

"He was here moments ago," Nymeris replied, caught off guard. The behavior of her leader worried her.

Garnius, visibly annoyed, slammed his cup down on the table, splashing wine onto his hand.

"That kid is really starting to get on my nerves," he grumbled. "Always doing whatever he pleases."

Before Thanatos could respond, an icy gust flooded the room, momentarily extinguishing half the candles in the common area. The murmur of conversations abruptly ceased.

All heads turned toward the fireplace, where a specter had appeared, rising from the shadows cast by the flames. A banshee materialized before them. Her ethereal form was shrouded in dark veils, floating around her as though possessed of their own will. Her long black hair obscured her face, revealing only a pair of milky-white eyes.

Several patrons shot to their feet, chairs tipping over behind them. Garnius swore under his breath, fingers tightening around his sword's hilt. Nymeris, however, remained perfectly still, watching the apparition impassively.

The banshee slowly opened her mouth, releasing a horrifying sound—a chilling blend of metallic screeches and shrill whistles. Thanatos stepped forward, his face as cold and expressionless as that of the apparition. He responded in a dark, guttural language. Each word resonated against the walls, like a sinister echo.

The banshee listened motionlessly, then emitted one final hiss, a sound that dissipated into an icy breath. Just as suddenly as she had appeared, she dissolved into the shadows. Gradually, the room's warmth and light returned.

Thanatos remained frozen, features contorted by a barely restrained rage.

"What's going on?" Nymeris asked.

Thanatos was silent for a moment, eyes fixed on the glowing embers. Then he turned sharply toward them, his voice sharp as ice:

"Raenos knows. He knows everything about Zayn. Worse, he's not alone. He has a human with him."

Garnius shot upright, fists clenched.

"How is that possible?" he hissed through clenched teeth. "Have they reopened the portal as well?"

But Thanatos cut him off abruptly with a swift gesture.

"It doesn't matter how. We must find Zayn before things spiral completely out of our control."

He stared hard at each of them before decisively ordering:

"Split up. Search every street. We must find him—now."

Thanatos slipped deeper into Atlantis's shadowy alleys, moving like a ghost across the moisture-slick planks of the pontoon.

He advanced silently, his boots barely brushing the uneven boards beneath. With each step, his senses captured every subtle shift in the surrounding air. As he rounded a corner, he caught sight of a figure quietly trailing him—too stealthy to be a casual passerby.

Without hesitation or betraying the slightest unease, Thanatos turned into an even narrower alleyway, guiding his mysterious pursuer toward a darkened dead end. He stopped abruptly, his back facing the path from which he'd come, and waited.

Behind him, an almost inaudible shuffle. His keen hearing recognized the hesitant tread of his follower. The hooded figure froze, startled by Thanatos's sudden halt.

"Who are you?" Thanatos asked without turning around, his voice echoing against the crumbling walls.

The man said nothing. Instead, he drew a dagger hidden beneath his cloak.

"Speak," Thanatos growled, the command dripping with threat.

The intruder, breathing raggedly, took a step forward, gathering his courage to complete the mission he'd been given. Wordlessly, he raised his weapon—but in the blink of an eye, Thanatos vanished into the shadows.

The hooded man froze, eyes darting frantically around the alley, searching desperately for any trace of his quarry.

"Where are you?" he shouted, his voice betraying his mounting panic.

The only reply was the faint murmur of waves lapping against the pilings below. Suddenly, the temperature plummeted, amplifying the intruder's fear. Whirling around, he felt cold sweat trickle down his spine. He sensed his target nearby yet saw nothing. A feeling of being hunted tightened around him like a vise.

From behind, a voice whispered almost gently:

"Here."

The man spun around, and his face went pale. Thanatos stood before him, wings spread wide, blocking any possible escape.

Panicking, the man brandished his dagger.

"Do you truly believe that blade can harm me?" Thanatos asked softly, with a touch of amusement.

The spy attempted to speak, but only terrified stammering escaped his lips.

Thanatos raised one hand. Out of darkness itself appeared his immense scythe, materializing instantly in his grasp. The blade, black as night, devoured the surrounding light.

"Wait…" the man stammered, taking a shaky step back. "I—I didn't mean…"

Thanatos smiled coldly, eyes as dark as the abyss.

"Too late."

With a fluid motion, he swung the scythe. The blade fell silently, slicing effortlessly through the spy's body, encountering no resistance, as though the man were merely a shadow. The unfortunate intruder's eyes widened in horror. He felt nothing—not even pain—only the chilling shadow of death seizing him. He swayed, then collapsed lifelessly onto the rain-slicked boards with a dull thud.

Thanatos lingered briefly, staring down emotionlessly at the lifeless body before him.

With a thought, his weapon faded back into shadow. Around him, the alley gradually regained its warmth and usual calm, as if nothing had happened at all.

"Amateur…" he muttered contemptuously over the corpse.

Before anyone could notice, he had already melted back into darkness.

Nymeris moved leisurely through the depths of Atlantis.

Her fluid, almost feline gait drew glances that quickly turned away. There was something about her—too perfect, too sharp—to be simply beautiful. A certain tension in the way she held her head, a coldness in her eyes. Her sharp gaze brushed past strangers like the edge of a blade.

Something subtly disturbed her heightened senses.

An intruder, awkwardly attempting stealth, appeared at regular intervals in her peripheral vision—like an inexperienced predator following prey far beyond his reach. Nymeris allowed herself a cruel smile. She had noticed her pursuer long ago.

She subtly quickened her pace, deliberately weaving through narrow, darkened alleys. The man, believing he held the advantage, followed blindly—unaware she was leading him exactly where she intended. Soon she reached an isolated spot: a narrow canal, dimly illuminated by a solitary lantern.

Nymeris halted abruptly, feigning interest in the murky waters. Behind her, the man's footsteps slowed. She felt him approach, his rapid breathing betraying his nervousness.

"You can come out now," she said calmly, her voice as cold as ice, without even bothering to turn around.

Caught off guard, the man froze. He swallowed audibly, steadying his breath. Finally, he emerged cautiously from the shadows, gripping a crude crossbow with both hands.

"I wouldn't move if I were you," he said, aiming the weapon at her.

Nymeris released an almost amused sigh and finally turned around. Her voice grew soft, almost musical, yet chillingly threatening:

"Oh, I think you have no idea what you've just gotten yourself into, poor thing."

She raised a hand, fingers elegantly spread in a gesture both graceful and deadly. Instantly, the surrounding shadows seemed to awaken, detaching from walls, floors, even the water's surface, slithering toward the man like serpents.

The intruder panicked. In desperation, he pulled the crossbow's trigger. The bolt flew straight at her face. Nymeris moved just enough.

The projectile grazed her cheek, slicing off a strand of black hair that drifted slowly to the ground.

She didn't flinch, her eyes locked onto his, lips curling into an icy smile.

"Poor choice," she whispered, almost disappointed by how easily she controlled the situation.

The shadows lunged at him, wrapping him in their cold, dark embrace. He released a muffled scream, dropping his weapon, struggling uselessly against their hold. The darkness engulfed him entirely, solidifying, suffocating his breath and cries.

Nymeris approached, each step echoing like the toll of an inevitable verdict. She watched him suffocate, fascinated—not by him, but by the effects of her own magic.

"Fear," she murmured softly, almost tenderly, "is a tool you should never underestimate."

With her hand still raised, Nymeris elegantly tightened her fist. The shadows instantly obeyed, constricting their victim even further.

The man tried to speak, but his lungs were starved of air. His face grew pale, eyes wide with terror. He struggled briefly, movements growing weaker until his body collapsed onto the paving stones.

The darkness released its hold, gliding across the ground back to their original positions, seamlessly merging into the surrounding gloom. Nymeris gazed briefly at the lifeless body at her feet.

She tucked the severed strand of hair casually behind her ear, as if the incident had been merely a minor distraction.

She turned lightly on her heel, stepping gracefully from the alleyway.

Garnius strode through the winding alleys of Atlantis in great, purposeful strides.

His heavy boots slammed loudly onto the damp pavement. He paid no attention to the wary glances of passersby. The idea of having lost track of Zayn irritated him deeply.

Soon, he sensed a familiar presence: a subtle weight pressing upon the back of his neck.

He spun around just in time to glimpse a silhouette disappearing into a narrow passage. Garnius's smile widened, revealing his teeth in a predatory grin.

"Wrong target, my friend," he murmured to himself.

Without hesitation, he entered the secluded alleyway. Midway down, he abruptly halted, pretending to adjust a loose strap on his boot. His steady, controlled breathing betrayed his vast experience in handling confrontations like this one.

Behind him, a blade scraped quietly from its sheath. Hurried footsteps approached.

Garnius didn't turn immediately, deliberately allowing his adversary to close the distance, giving him false hope that he had an opening.

Then, with astonishing speed unexpected from his massive frame, Garnius spun around and clamped his hand around the attacker's forearm before he could complete his strike.

The assassin cried out in shock and pain, eyes widening in terror as he faced the towering giant before him.

"I gave you a chance to run," Garnius growled. "But clearly, you're the stubborn type..."

Garnius let out a harsh, savage laugh, then hurled the intruder violently against the nearby wall. The impact echoed throughout the narrow passageway. The man crumpled heavily to the ground.

He struggled weakly to rise, gasping for breath. But before he could react further, Garnius was already upon him. In one fluid motion, he seized him by the throat, his merciless grip crushing the man's windpipe.

Effortlessly, Garnius lifted him from the ground, holding him at arm's length. The spy flailed helplessly, feet kicking uselessly in empty air, desperately trying to reach his tormentor.

"Weak," Garnius sneered contemptuously.

He tightened his grip until the man's eyes rolled back and his limbs went limp. Once the spy ceased to move, Garnius dropped the body unceremoniously onto the wooden planks.

Whistling softly, he strode away from the alley without a backward glance.

The biting chill of the ocean enveloped him instantly.

Zayn struggled, trying to swim back to the surface, but Fynna dragged him ever deeper.

Within moments, his lungs burned. Every fiber of his being screamed for air. Unable to resist any longer, he opened his mouth, ready to feel icy water flood his throat.

Yet instead of choking, an unexpected freshness filled his chest. He felt the water flowing freely into his lungs, as easily as air. His eyes widened as panic dissolved into wonder.

He stopped struggling and turned toward Fynna, astonished. She was watching him with an amused smile, her delicate face illuminated by the shimmering reflections dancing around her. She released her embrace, holding only his hand in hers.

"I told you," she whispered gently. "Trust me."

Zayn responded with an incredulous, blissful smile. He opened his mouth to speak, but instead of words, only bubbles escaped his lips, drifting lazily upward.

Fynna laughed softly, placing a finger over her lips to show him speaking was pointless.

"The hydronis potion only allows you to breathe," she explained. "Speaking underwater is a bit more complicated."

Surprised, he could only nod.

Gently, Fynna guided him deeper into the underwater heart of Atlantis, gliding effortlessly through the water. She swam with astonishing ease, far faster than her slender legs should have allowed, as if the currents themselves were aiding her movements.

Atlantis unfurled before his eyes, revealing a fantastical world far more vast than what he'd glimpsed on the surface. The city was vibrant, glowing with gentle, enchanting bioluminescence.

Buildings with delicate curves were covered in coral ranging from deep blue to soft pink, emerald, and pale gold. The structures seemed an extension of nature itself, blending seamlessly with coral and mother-of-pearl, as if grown rather than built.

They passed beneath massive natural arches of coral, draped with aquatic plants. These formations created passageways through which merfolk and sirens gracefully swam.

Luminescent fish slipped between the arches, their unpredictable trajectories tracing hypnotic patterns in the water. Majestic rays drifted elegantly, their wide wings casting shifting shadows over the seabed.

Fynna slowed, pointing to an amphitheater carved directly into the reef, protected by a colossal dome of glass. Sea turtles lazily circled above, while crustaceans climbed along the dome's surface, adding life to the imposing structure. Softly glowing anemones illuminated the interior, where young sirens and tritons listened attentively to a white-haired mermaid. Her melodic singing rippled through the water, reaching even them.

"She's a storyteller," Fynna explained. "She preserves our people's history. Here, collective memory is passed on through song, dance, and communion with the water."

They glided above a large underwater square adorned with an elaborate mosaic. Each fragment of shell and mother-of-pearl caught the ambient light, forming a shimmering fresco. At the edges, tritons patiently carved new details with delicate precision.

Fynna guided Zayn through a dense forest of seaweed, tall as trees, whose leaves swayed gently with the currents. Seahorses drifted peacefully between stalks, anchoring themselves with their curled tails, their tranquil movements accentuating the serenity of the place.

Further ahead, they moved through a vast cluster of small jellyfish. The creatures glowed, bathing the water in soft hues of mauve and turquoise. Zayn reached out cautiously, his hand brushing gently against their gelatinous bodies, surprisingly soft and harmless.

She paused briefly, indicating a group of young sirens playing a game, tossing and catching flat stones like underwater frisbees.

Zayn widened his eyes, captivated by every detail, every subtle hue. The current brushed against his face, enveloping him in profound calm.

"Here, everything is in harmony," she explained, seeing the wonder in his eyes. "It's not just a city, it's an ecosystem. Every coral, every creature has its role."

As she spoke, Zayn began to understand: everything seemed interconnected, alive, in perfect unity. Atlantis was a delicate balance where magic and nature coexisted as one.

He recognized the imposing structure toward which they were swimming. The palace of Thalessa rose majestically from the depths of the underwater cliff. Its massive walls, covered with countless vibrant corals blending shades of scarlet, deep azure, and gold, faded into the surrounding darkness. Oblique rays of sunlight filtered down from above, sliding gracefully along the walls, highlighting every detail and causing the palace to shimmer.

Surrounding the palace, imposing triton guards slowly patrolled. Armed with tridents and lanterns, they calmly watched the area. Upon noticing Fynna, they greeted her warmly or offered wide smiles. She replied with the same ease, hinting at her importance within the community.

They reached an entrance concealed behind an immense giant clam. The shell slowly opened at Fynna's approach, allowing them to pass. They glided through an area of semi-darkness, emerging into a vast cavern as sumptuous as it was unexpected.

Gigantic coral pillars supported the ceiling like the columns of a temple. Their delicate pale pink structures pulsed gently, radiating a soft, rhythmic glow. Waves of gentle light rippled across the walls hypnotically, reminiscent of a heartbeat deep within the ocean.

Zayn froze, overwhelmed by the beauty of the place. Fynna, attentive to his reactions, turned toward him, eyes sparkling with delight at his wonder.

"This is one of my favorite places," she whispered reverently. "These pillars are much more than natural formations. They are the true heart of Atlantis, guarding secrets known only to a privileged few."

Zayn opened his mouth to reply, but managed only a few clumsy bubbles that slipped along his face. Amused by his attempt, Fynna let out a crystalline laugh, echoing throughout the cavern.

"You're an exemplary listener, Zayn," she murmured.

Zayn merely smiled back, unable to express his awe otherwise. Everything around him evoked deep respect, an almost sacred reverence. He allowed himself to be guided without resistance, eager to discover the secrets Fynna was about to reveal.

A guard suddenly appeared in front of them, blocking their path. The triton had a powerful build, and his voice was deep, respectful yet authoritative.

"Fynna," he declared solemnly, "your mother is waiting. She grows impatient."

Fynna thanked him gracefully before turning toward Zayn, an expression of regret crossing her face.

"It seems our walk must end here," she apologized.

She led him by the hand toward a passage lined with seaweed. After passing through several tunnels, they emerged into a large cavity. Above them, the ceiling undulated like a liquid mirror: it was the water's surface. They climbed a staircase carved from rock, emerging into the great throne room where Thalessa waited.

Her presence, both gentle and imposing, immediately filled the room. Her deep blue eyes settled directly upon Zayn.

"So, here is the famous human," she said softly. "Come closer, young man."

Fynna respectfully stepped aside, encouraging Zayn forward. He approached on trembling legs, awkwardly bowing before her.

"Your Majesty," he managed to say, shaken by the piercing way she studied him, as if seeing through to his soul.

Thalessa rose slowly, moving with natural grace. Her flowing gown, shifting colors like the reflections on a calm sea, slid across the floor with every step. She descended the stairs separating them, stopping just before him.

"I know who you are and why you have come," she said clearly. "Your quest holds far greater significance than you realize, young Zayn."

Startled, he lifted his eyes toward her.

"You... you know?" he asked, voice tight with anxiety.

"The ocean whispers to those who know how to listen," Thalessa revealed. "The ripples of your footsteps reached me. You bear a heavy destiny, and the path before you is filled with trials and dangers. Tell me, Zayn, do you truly understand what you seek?"

He hesitated, breath shallow. He couldn't grasp the hidden meaning behind her words.

"I... I just want to see my mother again," he whispered.

Thalessa studied him intently, reaching out a delicate hand to gently grasp his wrist.

"So, it's desire that guides you... but beware: it may also blind you."

Her grip tightened slightly—a subtle warning—before releasing him.

"Fynna, accompany Zayn. Watch over him. Return to Thanatos," she instructed firmly. "You know your mission."

The young ondine bowed respectfully.

"Of course, Mother."

Zayn followed Fynna, deeply shaken. As they moved away from the throne, his thoughts raced, overwhelmed by Thalessa's cryptic warnings.

One thing was certain: this encounter had left him with far more questions than answers.

Fynna and Zayn pushed open the tavern door, finding the room strangely empty. The abandoned tables and overturned chairs revealed a commotion that had just subsided. A heavy silence lingered, scarcely disturbed by the gentle lapping of water beneath the floorboards.

In the center of the room stood Thanatos and Garnius, their faces darkened by barely-contained anger. Thanatos, motionless, exuded an icy aura. His deep black eyes locked onto Zayn, pinning him to the threshold.

"There you are, finally!" Garnius growled. "We were beginning to think you'd been kidnapped."

Zayn opened his mouth to reply, but a shadow surged behind them. With terrifying swiftness and precision, Nymeris slipped behind Fynna, pressing a thin blade against the ondine's throat.

"Who are you?" she hissed in her ear, her voice as cold and sharp as the steel of her dagger.

Fynna remained still. Only the subtle quickening of her breath betrayed any tension. With surprising calmness, she fixed her gaze directly on Thanatos.

"I am Fynna, daughter of Thalessa," she declared, her voice clear and steady. "My mother sent me to assist you."

Nymeris waited, her blade still pressed firmly against Fynna's delicate skin. Thanatos approached slowly, scrutinizing the young woman as though reading into her very soul.

The seconds stretched into eternity. Zayn, palms sweating, sought Fynna's reassuring gaze, but she remained wholly focused on Thanatos, her expression serene.

At last, Thanatos's cold voice sliced through the air:

"She's clear."

Nymeris lowered her blade wordlessly and stepped back. Fynna raised a hand to her throat, where a thin drop of blood glistened from the blade's touch.

Thanatos turned from her, eyeing Garnius and Nymeris with unquestionable authority.

"She stays," he announced.

Garnius merely nodded. Nymeris, however, continued to watch Fynna warily, her cold eyes assessing the ondine's every movement.

Thanatos slowly turned toward Zayn.

"As for you, you will not wander off again without my permission. We have spotted spies sent by Raenos. We must remain cautious."

Zayn felt his stomach tighten. He knew nothing about these enemies—but if they were as dangerous as Thanatos himself, it was indeed wise never to cross their path.

"But…" Zayn began.

"Zayn."

His voice cracked like a whip.

"Outside. Now."

Garnius and Nymeris were already moving toward the exit, followed by Fynna. Zayn timidly stepped toward the door, eyes lowered, desperate to escape the angel's oppressive presence. But as he passed by Thanatos, he felt the full weight of his cold, unyielding aura pressing down on him.

Instinctively, Zayn lowered his head, shoulders hunched beneath an invisible pressure, hastening his pace to reach the open air. Once outside, he released a trembling breath, realizing he'd been holding it the entire time.

"Move," commanded the leader.

Without waiting, Thanatos took the lead once again.

The sun hung high in the sky, bathing Atlantis in dazzling light, intensifying the humid air that enveloped the city.

Thanatos led the way firmly, indifferent to the bustling streets around them. Garnius and Nymeris followed closely behind, their eyes scanning every corner, alert and watchful.

Trailing at the back, Zayn deliberately slowed his pace, savoring each moment before their departure. Once more, he admired the reflections of rippling canal waters dancing upon the facades of buildings. Beside him, Fynna seemed radiant.

"There's something magical about Atlantis," she said softly, almost dreamily. "Sometimes, it feels like living in the heart of a dream."

"Yes," Zayn murmured, almost to himself. "A dream... but one that's very real."

They soon arrived at the stables near the docks. The stablemaster, a sturdy triton, gave them a respectful nod before returning to his tasks. Garnius, pleased to reunite with his horse, ran a rough hand along the animal's neck. The horse snorted softly, compliant.

"At least here, they know how to treat animals," he grumbled.

Nymeris meticulously inspected her saddle, double-checking every strap and buckle.

Once mounted, Thanatos directed his horse toward the docks, moving in the opposite direction from the city's exit. Confused, Zayn tugged gently at his reins, hesitating.

"Wait," he stammered, "aren't we leaving the city?"

Thanatos whipped around. His glare alone froze Zayn in place, his heart tightening instantly. He lowered his gaze, immediately regretting his question.

"We'll explain when it's time, Zayn," Nymeris warned softly. "We're being followed. We must remain cautious."

Zayn nodded silently. He hadn't realized they were being pursued, and he still didn't know who these people were—nor did he particularly wish to find out. Resigned, he quietly followed the group, plunging once more into the unknown.

The port buzzed with activity.

The docks swarmed with perfectly orchestrated chaos: shouts of sailors, snapping ropes, creaking hulls.

The group stopped before an imposing ship moored at the end of a long pier, its planks bleached by salt and weathered by time. The hull, dark blue accented with subtle gold detailing, proudly bore the name Crown of the Waves, engraved in large, elegant letters. Two masts rose skyward: a large rectangular sail, and a smaller, triangular one at the ship's bow. They rippled gently in the breeze, ready to carry them toward the open sea.

At the foot of the gangplank stood a stocky man awaiting their arrival, arms crossed over his chest. His brown beard cascaded down his torso, and his salt- and sun-weathered skin spoke of a lifetime at sea. His long coat fluttered in the wind. Upon spotting Thanatos, he stepped forward.

"You must be the passengers I was told about," he called out in a deep, gravelly voice. "I'm Captain Roark. Come aboard—everything's ready to set sail."

Thanatos replied with a brief nod and boarded confidently. Garnius and Nymeris followed without hesitation, while Fynna, visibly pleased to return to the sea, wore a delighted expression.

Zayn, however, paused briefly before stepping onto the gangplank. He felt his heartbeat quicken as the boards creaked under his weight. Captain Roark noticed his hesitation and clapped him heartily on the back as he reached the deck.

"First time at sea, young man?" he asked.

Zayn nodded shyly.

"Don't worry," Roark reassured him with a wink. "The Crown of the Waves has weathered worse than this. You're in good hands."

Zayn quickly hurried to rejoin the others.

Two experienced sailors led the horses down into the hold. The captain moved to the helm, barking orders to his crew.

The sails snapped taut, the moorings were cast off, and slowly, the Crown of the Waves slipped away from the dock, gliding gracefully into the vast expanse of the ocean.

Once out at sea, Thanatos gave a few instructions to the captain before moving to stand at the prow, his gaze lost on the distant horizon. Nymeris and Garnius quickly settled, savoring the tranquility of the open water.

Zayn found a wooden bench away from the others, quietly watching the gentle waves. Gradually, the tension left him, as though an invisible knot had loosened. He constantly felt observed, and the oppressive atmosphere weighed heavily upon him.

Fynna soon broke his solitude, discreetly approaching to sit beside him.

"I know it's not easy," she said gently, sensing his discomfort. "Try to enjoy the view—it'll help clear your mind."

Zayn timidly nodded. He didn't know what to say, but her presence brought him comfort.

A short while later, as the ship glided smoothly across calm waters, Fynna pointed toward the distant shoreline.

"Look over there."

Zayn followed her gesture: small houses on stilts emerged from the dark marshes, suspended precariously above the water.

"These marshes are tied to my mother," Fynna explained. "The people there learned to live in harmony with the creatures that dwell within—even though those creatures aren't always welcoming."

Zayn squinted, fascinated by the tiny wooden walkways connecting the homes. Children played on the platforms, their laughter mingling with birdsong and the whisper of the wind through the reeds.

"Aren't they afraid the water might carry everything away?" he asked.

Fynna shook her head.

"They built those homes to last. The pillars are coated with natural oils, protecting them from moisture and algae."

Zayn quietly admired the structures, impressed by their simple ingenuity.

"It's... peaceful," he murmured.

Fynna nodded.

"The people know life here is fragile. The marshes shift with the tides and seasons, but they adapt. They don't fight against the water—they learn to live with it. Sometimes strength isn't just about confrontation, but knowing how to adapt."

Zayn felt the weight of her words. He thought about everything he'd witnessed since arriving in this world—the struggles of others, his own inner conflict.

Perhaps survival wasn't always about fighting. Maybe it also meant knowing when to bend without breaking.

Zayn nodded slowly, his thoughts drifting with the shifting reflections of the marsh. The scene contrasted so sharply with the chaos and anxiety of his own existence. Part of him envied this calm. Perhaps I could learn to live again, he thought, not daring to speak the words aloud.

"So, Zayn," she asked curiously, "if you could go anywhere in this world, where would it be?"

Caught off guard, Zayn struggled to find an answer.

"I... I don't know. Just somewhere far away from all this."

Fynna studied him closely, her smile losing some of its lightness.

"Sometimes running away seems easier," she said gently. "But it isn't the answer. You're stronger than you realize."

The connection between them was unmistakable. They continued talking, Fynna's laughter blending naturally with Zayn's hesitant replies.

Thanatos, meanwhile, kept himself apart from the rest of the crew.

Standing in the shadow of the railing, he stared out over the ocean. The breeze stirred the black feathers of his wings.

Fynna observed him for a moment, noting his motionless form wrapped in darkness. Then she approached, resting her elbows beside him, eyes fixed—like his—on the distant horizon.

"You should talk to him," she murmured quietly. "He's not your enemy, you know."

Thanatos remained silent for a brief moment before turning his face toward her. His black eyes regarded her, cold and impenetrable.

"I speak when necessary," he replied sharply. "You mortals always speak too freely. You waste words and time as if their true cost eludes you."

Fynna sighed softly, straightening without pressing further. She returned to Zayn, who had closely observed the exchange.

Thanatos resumed his contemplation of the ocean, sealing himself again within his solitude like armor.

Yet something flickered briefly in his eyes. A fleeting spark. A doubt? A distant memory? Only he knew its true nature.

The sailors prepared a simple but comforting meal: wheat bread, a few slices of salted, hardened cheese, and a generous serving of fish seasoned with a drizzle of garum. They shared it all around small earthenware plates.

They readily shared stories of their adventures, punctuating the meal with laughter and colorful anecdotes. One sailor recounted how, during a particularly fierce storm, mermaids had guided their ship safely into port. Another, older sailor swore he had once seen a sea serpent longer than their vessel.

Their tales, both unbelievable and captivating, eased the lingering tension.

Zayn found a certain comfort in this modest meal, reminding him that, even in this strange world, moments of simplicity still existed—and perhaps even a semblance of peace.

After the meal, they returned to enjoy the sunset on deck.

The ship sailed southward, gently rocked by the calming sway of the waves. Gradually, the sun dipped toward the horizon, flooding the sky with a symphony of golden, pink, and purple hues. The ocean, calm as a mirror, reflected this spectacle, doubling its beauty.

To port, an immense forest stretched as far as the eye could see. Evening light slipped through it, igniting the foliage. Zayn gazed, fascinated, at the scene. His attention was captivated by an extraordinary tree. It soared high above the others, dominating the forest like a sentinel. Its branches extended like protective arms, a presence both comforting and mystical.

Unable to contain his curiosity, Zayn pointed toward it.

"Look at that tree! It's gigantic! What is it?" he asked Fynna.

"That's Sylvaris," she answered. "It towers at the heart of Sylki's forest. It shelters the city of the same name, where Sylki and his people live in symbiosis with nature."

"Sylki?" Zayn repeated. "Yes, I think Nymeris mentioned him to me."

"Sylki is one of the great magicians," she explained. "Guardian of the forests, protector of animals... He ensures the preservation of natural harmony in Mytherra. He advocates respect for every living being—plants and animals alike. His domain covers vast, lush lands inhabited by fantastical creatures, such as dryads, fairies, and even some giants."

Zayn listened attentively, his gaze still fixed on the majestic Sylvaris. He tried to imagine an entire city concealed in a magical forest, filled with wondrous creatures.

"It would be incredible to see it one day," he murmured.

Fynna smiled, charmed by his innocent enthusiasm.

"Who knows?" she said softly. "Perhaps you will, one day."

"On Earth, humans can't respect nature. They constantly destroy it to enrich themselves, without thinking about the consequences..."

"In that case, you'd better be careful. Sylki is deeply devoted to the harmony he fiercely protects. Anyone attempting to exploit or plunder his lands quickly discovers how severe he can be. He can trigger earthquakes and cataclysms when his balance is disturbed."

"So, he's dangerous?"

"Not dangerous, exactly," she corrected gently. "More like uncompromising. He doesn't tolerate threats against nature. Those who respect his domain see him as a wise and benevolent protector. But those who dare push too far quickly learn how determined he is to preserve his world."

The ship continued its journey, peacefully following the coastline. Fynna and Zayn resumed their conversation, bound by a growing complicity. She spoke to him of Atlantis, its legends and peculiar customs, with the enthusiasm of someone who loved her world.

Zayn shared memories from his own world, made of asphalt, rain, and solitude. Fynna's light, crystalline laughter often punctuated their discussion, enveloping the deck in warmth and ease.

As night settled in, the temperature dropped, prompting Zayn to retreat toward the common cabin.

Inside, several hammocks swayed gently with the rhythm of the waves. Tired from the day and soothed by this regular motion, he slipped into one of them.

His thoughts gradually quieted, replaced by the boat's slow rocking and the distant whisper of waves. Without even realizing it, Zayn drifted into a deep, dreamless sleep, far removed from the day's tensions.

Meanwhile, the white sails of the *Crown of the Waves* billowed gracefully, carrying the ship onward into the silence of the night.

13 — Suna — Clues

The sun rose over Balindra, draping the city in a golden veil. Through the open window, a fragrance of flowers mingled with the morning dampness drifted into the room, gently pulling Suna from her dreams. Still wrapped in the lingering haze of sleep, she opened her eyes, silently contemplating the floral carvings on the ceiling.

She stretched, savoring these quiet moments before leaving the warmth of her blankets. Slipping into one of her new outfits, she carefully tied back her hair, then quietly left the room, the atmosphere still softened by the morning calm.

In the inner courtyard of the residence, the other members of the group already awaited her, exchanging a few quiet words. Liore greeted them, her large brown eyes sparkling with infectious energy. Lying atop a low wall, Kitsune allowed his nine tails to catch the morning sunlight like lazy flames.

"Good morning, everyone," Liore said cheerfully. "I'm glad to see you're all well-rested. Enhugo is already expecting us. Follow me."

The group fell into step behind her, walking through Balindra's gardens, still wrapped in the early morning calm. At this hour, the city was immersed in gentle lethargy. Only a few early-rising scholars strolled along the pathways, scrolls tucked under their arms.

Entering Enhugo's sanctuary, they passed by the great hall where they had shared their meal the night before. Liore guided them down a long corridor adorned with tapestries.

Finally, she opened a large carved wooden door. Inside, a study bathed in soft light filtered through sheer curtains awaited them. The walls, lined with shelves heavy with knowledge, displayed precious artifacts: intricately decorated globes, engraved tablets, and polished metallic instruments.

At the center of the room stood an imposing table of solid wood, finely carved with complex patterns. Around it, several chairs with plush cushions invited thoughtful dialogue and reflection.

Standing near an open window overlooking the garden, Enhugo awaited them, serene and still. Slender and dignified, his figure blended into the azure tones of his robe.

"Good morning, my friends," he finally spoke, his deep voice gently filling the room. "Please, sit. We have much to discuss and many mysteries to unravel together."

They took their seats around the table.

Enhugo remained standing, his fingers gently brushing the polished surface of the table. He looked at each of them in turn before speaking again.

"Let's start from the beginning," he said. "You already know that the Pillars are the very heart of Mytherra. But few truly grasp their essence. They don't just contain a fragment of our power—they hold the key to our world's very existence."

He let his words settle into the silence before continuing in his deep, resonant voice:

"The Pillar of Knowledge is unique. It holds all the knowledge accumulated through history—all the ideas and concepts that shaped Mytherra."

He paused briefly, allowing each of them to imagine the immensity of what he described.

"But this knowledge, precious as it is, would remain lifeless without two fundamental forces to animate it: creation and destruction. The Pillar draws its power from my own magic, bound to knowledge and creation, and from Ignara's, mistress of fire and destruction. Together, these forces breathe life into what would otherwise remain fleeting thoughts."

Suna opened her mouth, perplexed. This pairing confused her.

"So," the magician continued, "the Pillar of Knowledge isn't simply the sum of wisdom—it's the balance of these two forces, without which nothing can be born or endure."

"But..." Suna interrupted, hesitant. "How can destruction lead to creation? Aren't they opposites?"

Enhugo smiled understandingly, picking up a small spoon from the table, spinning it gently between his slender fingers.

"Not necessarily," he explained. "Think of the artisan who created this spoon. He broke down the ore, heated it until it was malleable, and then shaped it. The original form was destroyed, making way for something new, something useful. Without this destructive step, the final object would never exist. Without prior destruction, creation itself is impossible. Similarly, you cannot create something from nothing."

He placed the spoon back down carefully.

"But remember: destruction does not mean senseless annihilation. It's a necessary step, measured and deliberate. The Pillar of Knowledge symbolizes this fragile equilibrium—destroying only what must be destroyed, just enough to let something better emerge."

Suna considered this, slowly grasping the artisan metaphor. What had initially seemed contradictory now made perfect sense.

Enhugo circled the table, silence following him as he moved. He spoke again, placing a hand gently on a nearby shelf.

"The Pillar of Matter is different," he continued. "It embodies the balance of the physical world, the perfect union of the solid power of Sylki, master of earth, and the fluid energy of Thalessa, guardian of the oceans."

Suna recalled tales about the world's creation, where earth and water emerged together from primordial chaos, forming the essential foundation for all life.

"This Pillar is the steady strength of the ground beneath your feet, as well as the ceaseless motion of waves. Through it, mountains, forests, and oceans find their rightful place in the world."

He paused, studying Suna's reactions to ensure she understood. She remained captivated, hanging on every word.

"As for the Pillar of Life," he continued, "it unites two completely opposite yet inseparable forces: Vital Light and the Darkness of Death. It is the joint work of Shanur, guardian of light and healing, and Ereshkal, mistress of endings and eternal rest."

Aldaren leaned forward slightly at the mention of his master.

"This Pillar maintains the balance between beginning and end, life's eternal cycle. Returning to our artisan metaphor—imagine this time a forest: when a tree dies, it falls and decomposes. That might seem negative at first. Yet, this death nourishes the soil, allowing new growth. Without this natural ending, the forest would suffocate beneath its own abundance, unable to regenerate."

Suna nodded, familiar with the necessity of nature's cycle.

Enhugo came to stand behind her chair, placing his hands on its back. As he drew near, her heart quickened, caught between nervousness and anticipation at the magician's closeness.

"Finally," Enhugo continued, "there's the Pillar of Emotions—perhaps the most complex, as it encompasses all the nuances of living beings' feelings: love, hatred, joy, sorrow, anger…"

He looked down at Suna, whose cheeks warmed under the intensity of his gaze.

"At this very moment, our friend here is experiencing a whirlwind of emotions she struggles to unravel," he explained gently, as if reading her thoughts. "That's precisely the magic of this Pillar: making life intense, unpredictable, deeply authentic."

He released the chair, stepping back to return to his place before them, allowing Suna a chance to regain her composure.

"This Pillar arises from the encounter of two utterly opposing forces: Elvira, embodiment of love and beauty, and Nerath, lord of war and hatred. It's the synthesis of everything that makes our existence worth living."

They sat silently for a moment, contemplating Enhugo's words. Suna now understood much more clearly what true balance meant.

Theris leaned forward.

"These Pillars… do you know where they are? Or how to find them?"

A shadow briefly crossed Enhugo's face.

"Unfortunately, their exact locations are unknown, even to me," he responded quietly.

Suna took a deep breath, and after a moment of reflection, found the courage to speak, her voice slightly hesitant yet determined:

"When I touched the stone slab beneath Ætheris's statue, it activated. A text appeared, stating that only a human without magic could touch the Pillars."

"That indeed confirms the ancient legends," the magician replied slowly. "We've long known that only a being devoid of magic could hope to reach the Pillars. This requirement discouraged many seekers, and gradually, the quest faded into obscurity."

"The slab instructed to bring the Pillars back to the statue," Suna recalled. "Why is that?"

"What you saw that day, near the slab, wasn't merely a statue," Enhugo explained. "It was Ætheris herself, frozen in her purest form. Few still know this, as she has remained motionless since Mytherra's creation."

"But…" stammered Suna.

Seeing her surprise, a breath from the past seemed to pass over Enhugo's face, softening his features with a gentle melancholy.

"Ætheris is fading," he said. "And her current appearance is nothing like she once was. She was pure light—a gentle mother, radiant with kindness. I cherished being at her side. Together, we taught humans to cultivate the land, build cities, and lay the foundations of their civilizations. Her patience was boundless, her heart inexhaustible."

Suna opened her mouth, frozen in astonishment, eventually managing to ask:

"But… how old are you exactly?"

At this question, Theris coughed discreetly, looking away in embarrassment. Enhugo, however, burst into a soft, warm laugh.

"I witnessed the first civilizations of your ancestors," he replied, eyes fixed intently on hers. "I've seen kingdoms rise, flourish, then vanish. We, the Great Magicians, are immortal… at least, in theory. If Ætheris were to disappear, Mytherra would crumble with her, dragging us down as well."

Suna remained speechless, suddenly realizing the dizzying magnitude of what they truly were.

She had always considered Raenos and Enhugo respectable authority figures, bearers of rank or status. Never had she imagined they could be so much more powerful, so much older than she'd believed. This new understanding made her head spin.

She turned toward Theris.

"And you… are you also…?" she stammered.

Vaelen chuckled. Theris immediately raised his hands, shaking his head.

"No, no!" he quickly clarified. "Only the Great Magicians carry this burden. Their disciples and descendants—meaning almost everyone here—are mortal."

"Precisely," Enhugo confirmed. "Although the magic permeating this world grants its inhabitants increased longevity, their origins remain human."

Until then silent, Pharin straightened up, eyes sparkling mischievously, ready to release one of his trademark remarks:

"Though, I've always had my doubts about Aldaren. Are you sure he isn't hiding a few extra centuries?"

The satyr's comment drew discreet laughter from the group, immediately lightening the atmosphere.

Enhugo resumed gently:

"In truth, our earliest disciples were different. The magic they embodied protected them completely from time's ravages. Yet that didn't make them immortal. Most have vanished over centuries, claimed by wars or tragedies. Mytherra has known dark periods whose marks remain even today."

Vaelen and Theris exchanged a glance, discreetly confirming the old magician's words.

At that moment, Liore reappeared, gracefully balancing a tray filled with fragrant drinks and dried fruits. She approached and began serving each guest.

Enhugo discreetly nodded his thanks to Liore, waiting for everyone to savor this brief respite before continuing:

"Regarding the Pillars," he calmly resumed, "I spent my earliest centuries searching for answers, trying to unravel their mysteries. But something—perhaps crucial—eluded me. I was never able to determine their exact locations. I abandoned these searches long ago, and now my memory sometimes falters."

He let out a melancholic sigh before adding, his voice regaining vigor:

"However, certain ancient legends, preserved within our library, might aid you. I encourage you to consult them as often as necessary. Liore, whom you've already met, is my most gifted disciple. I trust her implicitly to guide you effectively."

Liore humbly inclined her head at these words.

"It would be my pleasure to assist you. I've spent my life exploring the library, and the Pillars remain one of its most fascinating mysteries."

Enhugo gestured towards his apprentice.

"Liore knows every corner of this place. If anyone can unlock the secrets of these archives, it's her."

"With your permission, Grand Master, we should begin our research immediately," Liore added.

Enhugo elegantly waved his hand in approval.

"You're right. Go ahead—time is now more precious than ever."

Aldaren rose gently.

"I fear I won't be of much help among the books," he said simply. "I'll join the hospice, lend my assistance to the healers, and perhaps forge stronger bonds with the locals."

Vaelen nodded approvingly; he, too, had little place among the library shelves.

"Very well. As for us," he continued, gesturing towards Hestian and Korvel, "we'll head to the guards' training grounds."

At these words, Hestian and Korvel stood up, clearly enthusiastic at the prospect of stretching their legs after several days of travel.

Enhugo, meanwhile, approached Suna with evident curiosity.

"Suna," he gently said, "might you spare me a few moments? I'd be delighted to learn more about your world. Its civilizations, its knowledge—all of it fascinates me greatly."

Initially intimidated, the young woman hesitated. But faced with the magician's sincere interest, she soon became animated. She spoke about Earth: its immense, noisy cities, its technologies, the diversity of its people. She shared anecdotes from her daily life, evoking memories with a touch of nostalgia, now seeing her old teenage problems from a fresh perspective.

Enhugo listened intently, eyes gleaming with curiosity. Occasionally, he interrupted to jot down notes in a small notebook, muttering reflections that he promised to explore later. After a long exchange, he closed his notebook.

"You've given me a precious window into a world that had grown distant," he said with emotion. "I will reflect upon all of this. But now, it's time for you to visit the library. I'm certain you'll find answers there."

Liore, who had been waiting discreetly, stepped forward.

"If you would kindly follow me," she invited, gracefully indicating the way.

Accompanied by Theris and Pharin, Suna followed Liore through the corridors. The hallway leading to the library was lined with captivating frescoes, depicting the great turning points of human history. Suna slowed momentarily to better examine certain scenes: ancient wars, the rise of the first kingdoms, and great civilizations... Everywhere, she was convinced now, were the silhouettes of the great magicians.

"It seems these walls are preparing us for what we're about to discover," Theris murmured.

"Or warning us!" Pharin joked, pointing to a panel illustrating a particularly chaotic battle.

They stopped in front of an immense dark wooden door. Liore placed her hands gently on it, and the door opened effortlessly beneath her touch.

As it swung open, revealing the magnificent interior of the library, Suna froze, captivated by the grandeur and beauty of the place. Beside her, Liore smiled.

"Welcome to the very heart of Mytherra's knowledge," she announced, inviting them to enter.

The interior of the library was breathtaking.

The central hall opened into a vast, circular chamber. Far above, a wide oculus allowed a shaft of natural light to fall directly into the heart of the building.

At the center of this column of light, an immense fire crackled—the living heart of the library. Tall, fluid flames danced elegantly, illuminating the entire room without producing the slightest trace of smoke. The blaze was sheltered beneath a graceful kiosk, supported by slender columns, open on all four sides and raised on a platform of pristine white marble.

Surrounding this, the floor was paved with mosaics of polished tiles, capturing and dispersing the warmth of the fire. Tables were arranged around it, inviting visitors to sit and study.

Pharin, craning his neck to admire the dizzying height of the upper levels, tipped backwards. He stumbled awkwardly before steadying himself against Theris's arm.

"Careful, my friend," Theris remarked dryly. "We're not here for acrobatics."

Liore stifled a laugh behind her hand before reassuring the satyr:

"Don't worry; it happens frequently to newcomers. This architecture can be dizzying even to the steadiest minds."

From below, the library rose in an ascending spiral: each level was divided into two opposing quarter-circles, revolving around the central fire. Wide staircases connected the floors, offering a graceful ascent towards the summit. Smaller, discreet spiral staircases provided a quicker climb for the scholars.

On each level, spacious balconies edged with finely carved, dark wooden balustrades overlooked the central shaft. Numerous scholars sat at tables, immersed in their research. Some scribbled on yellowed parchment; others were absorbed by ancient grimoires and codices. Small hanging lamps bathed every corner in a subdued glow.

Theris's gaze swept across the room, noting each detail: the richness of the engravings, the subtle harmony of the sculptures, and the impeccable arrangement of the shelves. Suna, meanwhile, moved slowly forward, her fingers almost reverently brushing the delicate spines of the lined volumes. She paused at each shelf, captivated by the breadth of knowledge gathered here.

"This is incredible," she marveled. "It's like the entire history of the world is here. Perhaps even more."

"It truly is," Liore confirmed. "But it isn't merely a sanctuary of the past. It's a living place, where we enrich our understanding of the world every day. It holds many secrets and just as many mysteries, patiently awaiting discovery."

She stepped forward, inviting her companions to follow.

"Come," she added, "I'll take you to the oldest archives. That's where we'll begin our research."

Suna cast a final glance toward the fire in the hall's center, hypnotized by the timeless beauty of the place. Then, with determination, she followed Liore, feeling a newfound conviction: the answers they needed were here. They had to be.

Liore guided them from one floor to another until they reached an archway covered with runes. When she placed her hand on the engraved stone, the symbols illuminated. The door opened with a gentle whisper.

The top floor formed a series of concentric circles beneath the vast glass dome. At its center, a column of light descended straight from the sky, traversing the building from top to bottom. Around it, the brightness softened, filtered through tinted panes at the dome's edge. Bookshelves were bathed in a warm, almost velvety glow. A peaceful atmosphere reigned here, as if time itself was holding its breath.

Suna timidly approached one of the tables. Open books floated just above it, suspended motionless in mid-air. She reached towards one, then paused hesitantly.

"May I...?" she murmured softly.

"Of course," Liore replied. "Each volume is here to be consulted. Just handle them with respect, given their age. Some of these writings have survived thousands of years."

She took a thick grimoire, its pages yellowed and edged with gold. As she leafed through it, she found herself lost in complex diagrams and runes that seemed to shiver beneath her fingertips.

"These writings... they look alive," she remarked.

"In a sense, some of them are," the scholar confirmed. "They're dormant spells, inscribed here long ago. They remain inactive until someone recites the formula, sometimes noted on the first page. But don't worry, they're not dangerous. Their purpose is to preserve the content."

Theris was impressed. He had traveled to many places throughout the world for his duties, yet never before had he set foot here.

Meanwhile, Pharin, resistant to scholarly stillness, began examining the carved decorations of shelves and columns. By accident, he bumped into a bookshelf. A stack of precious manuscripts swayed dangerously, ready to topple.

"No, no, no!" Liore cried, rushing toward the manuscripts.

With a swift gesture, she caught the stack, putting the books back in place, before casting Pharin a falsely stern look.

"Please be careful," she urged. "Everything here is priceless."

Pharin, somewhat sheepishly, straightened up with dignity and raised a theatrical hand:

"You misunderstood! It was intentional, obviously. An experiment on the gravity affecting ancient parchments. I've confirmed my hypothesis: they do indeed fall downward. A major scientific advancement!"

"Sorry," he added more quietly.

This welcome levity broke the solemnity of the place.

Returning to seriousness, Suna opened an ancient codex laid before her. A faint scent of parchment rose to her nostrils. The paper barely crackled beneath her fingertips. The pages, thin and fragile, revealed fascinating illustrations: legendary creatures, mystical landscapes, and representations of Mytherra's elemental forces. Each page blended images and delicate script, almost calligraphic, whispering mysteries worn thin by time.

Soft footsteps drew their attention. A figure approached: an elderly man clad in a gray robe embroidered with esoteric motifs, copper glasses patinated by age resting upon his nose. Behind the tarnished lenses, two brown eyes sparkled vividly, illuminating a face marked by both time and a joyful spirit.

"This is Myrmes," Liore introduced him respectfully. "He's the guardian of the library. He'll help us find what we're looking for."

Myrmes bowed in greeting.

"How may I assist you, Liore?" asked the guardian in a high, quivering voice.

Liore stepped forward, hands clasped, and explained their quest for the Pillars—and how essential this knowledge was to their mission. At the mention of the Pillars, the librarian's eyes brightened. He thoughtfully stroked his carefully trimmed beard.

"I believe I have something for you," he murmured dreamily. "Wait here for a moment."

With surprising grace for his age, Myrmes moved toward a small wooden cart leaning against a shelf. Then, without hurry, he slipped between the rows packed with ancient volumes. The wheels of his cart creaked on the floor.

Suna, Theris, and Pharin watched the old man with curiosity. Myrmes seemed to engage in a silent dialogue with the books: occasionally, he would brush the spines with his fingertips, muttering softly to himself.

From time to time, he stopped, tugging thoughtfully at his beard. He would read a title or skim the first pages of a manuscript. Then, with a sure gesture, he replaced the book… or carefully added it to his cart. Each movement was precise, yet filled with infinite tenderness.

After a considerable while, Myrmes returned, pushing a cart overflowing with books, scrolls, rolls, and ancient tablets. Everything was piled with meticulous care.

He stopped before a large table. Suna, stunned, stared at the mountain of documents.

"This should put us on the right track," Liore declared. "Thank you so much, truly."

"I didn't know exactly what to expect… but this will take us months," Suna groaned, burying her face in her hands.

Liore laughed softly, touched by Suna's spontaneity. She slipped a hand into her pocket and took out a small ring engraved with delicate runes.

"Don't worry," she said with a wink. "We have some tools to speed things up. This ring can identify relevant passages… and save us precious time."

Liore approached the first volume and placed the ring in the center of its cover. She closed her eyes, concentrating, her lips moving almost imperceptibly. A faint glow flickered across the metallic surface of the ring, but nothing else happened. Undeterred, she shook her head, replaced the book carefully, then took another.

Again, nothing occurred.

Pharin crossed his arms, a sly smile playing on his lips as he observed the scene with amusement.

"The ring might be defective," he suggested. "Or perhaps… the user?"

Theris shot him a sharp glance, accompanied by a dry cough. Pharin lifted his gaze to the ceiling, suddenly fascinated by the beams.

Liore, unruffled, continued her methodical search, calmly opening the next volume. When she placed the ring upon the tenth book, a bright light burst forth, illuminating her face with a bluish halo. Liore lifted her eyes to Pharin.

"It appears both the ring—and its user—are working just fine."

Pharin stuck out his tongue.

Liore placed the leather-bound volume carefully before Suna.

"Here's your first clue," she said, clearly pleased.

She continued her meticulous process. With each sparkle of the ring, another book revealed its worth. Liore set aside each valuable find. Beneath his casual demeanor, Pharin watched with growing fascination. Beside him, Suna and Theris closely followed Liore's every move.

Finally, only four documents remained, neatly aligned on the large table. Liore let out a long sigh of satisfaction.

"There," she said, relieved. "Now, it's our eyes' turn to work."

Suna gazed at the books lined up before her, a restless anticipation rising in her chest. For the first time, she felt genuinely close to advancing their quest.

"Let's get to work," she declared with determination.

Each chose a document. Liore picked up a thick grimoire with yellowed pages; Theris, a volume bound in leather worn by centuries; Pharin grabbed a crumpled scroll. Suna, meanwhile, immediately leaned over the book in front of her, scanning the fine script and illustrations.

True to form, Theris quickly began taking precise, neat notes on a blank page. Silence gradually settled, interrupted only by the rustling of pages and thoughtful murmurs from the absorbed researchers.

After some time, Pharin raised his head.

"This scroll vaguely mentions the creation of the Pillars… It speaks of ancient temples where they might be hidden, but it's frustratingly unclear," he said, grimacing.

Theris gave a quiet sigh.

"Nothing helpful on my side, unfortunately."

Suna stretched, yawning. The fatigue from concentrated reading was starting to take its toll. She closed her book and tapped its cover lightly, disappointed.

"Mine only describes the temples, but there's no precise indication of their location…"

"What about you, Liore?" she asked. "Did you find anything interesting?"

"Nothing useful either," Liore answered, closing her grimoire. "Plenty of allegorical accounts, but no clear leads."

Pharin sighed loudly, slumping against the back of his chair.

"It looks like these Pillars really do want to stay hidden," he grumbled.

Myrmes the librarian reappeared, carrying a tray of refreshments. He set fresh fruit, pastries, and nuts on a side table designated for breaks. The group thanked him, taking a well-deserved moment of rest.

They were chatting softly, sharing their modest meal, when Theris sprang to his feet, instantly alert, cutting off the conversation. A rustle, muffled footsteps behind the shelves—too discreet to be innocent.

"Wait here," he whispered. His voice was tense.

Without waiting for a reply, he disappeared behind a row of shelves.

A few moments later, Theris reappeared, face hardened, grasping by the collar a young man with messy brown hair and a pale, terrified face. The intruder clutched a book tightly to his chest, fingers trembling.

"This one," Theris declared coldly, "tried to steal one of our books." He pointed to the volume in the thief's hands.

Liore's eyes widened, while Suna stood up, bewildered.

"That's… impossible!" Liore exclaimed. "Who are you, and why?"

The young man, a student barely out of adolescence, stammered:

"I… I'm sorry! It's just… someone promised me a big reward if I brought back what you were studying!"

Theris tightened his grip, his voice sharpening.

"Who asked you to do this?"

The boy shrank under the counselor's authority, swallowing with difficulty.

"A man… dressed all in black. I don't know who he is. He wore a cloak—just told me to take a book. He was in the main hall."

Theris cursed under his breath and approached the balcony. Down below, leaning against one of the columns of the central kiosk, a figure dressed in black observed the hall casually. The stranger raised his head, as if sensing Theris's presence. For a brief instant, his face was visible.

Their eyes met. Then the figure pulled up his hood and disappeared into the crowd of students.

Theris turned back, fists clenched, expression tight. He fixed his eyes on the boy, then said icily:

"Get out, before I change my mind."

The boy didn't need further prompting. Muttering apologies, he fled the library, his face red with shame and fear.

Theris stood motionless for a moment, staring toward the archway where the young spy had vanished. When he returned to the others, his face carried a new worry.

"That was one of Ereshkal's disciples," he stated gravely. "Our suspicions were correct. She knows we're searching for the Pillars and will do anything to get ahead of us."

At these words, Liore paled, fingers tightening on the edge of the table. Ereshkal was not known for gentleness. Suna hugged herself tightly. A heavy silence fell, broken only when Pharin attempted to lighten the mood.

"If all Ereshkal's minions are like that one," Pharin joked, "we can sleep soundly."

Theris shot him a dark glance, clearly unamused. Pharin instantly fell silent.

"Go fetch Vaelen," the counselor ordered him. "Right away. We must prepare—we're no longer alone on this trail."

Pharin was about to leave, but Liore's clear voice stopped him:

"Wait, Pharin!" she called, hastily grabbing her notebook.

The satyr halted.

"What, are you planning to write him a novel? I'm perfectly effective verbally, you know," he joked, folding his arms.

Liore rolled her eyes as she took out a fine pencil. Quickly, she jotted a few lines, then traced four complex runes at the top of the page.

"Watch and learn," she said to Pharin.

She placed the sheet in front of her, laying her fingertips on the runes. Closing her eyes, she concentrated. A soft bluish glow escaped the symbols, casting a faint halo under her hand. Under Suna's and Pharin's wide eyes, the paper began to move of its own accord. Corners folded first, followed by other sections, creating intricate geometric patterns.

"It's... a magical origami?" murmured Suna.

Within seconds, the paper assumed the shape of a winged serpent. Its wings trembled slightly, as though uncertain before flight. Its triangular head and eyes, delicately formed by the folds, gave it an almost lifelike appearance.

Liore took the paper serpent gently between her fingers and placed it on her open palm.

"Go, deliver this message to Vaelen," she ordered calmly but firmly.

The serpent spread its wings and soared into the air. It spiraled silently upward, just a whisper of paper accompanying its flight, then passed through the open window. The daylight illuminated its wings, translucent like bat membranes.

Suna stood speechless, eyes locked on the paper serpent as it flew away.

"But... these are the same as those we saw flying around the pavilions!" she exclaimed.

"They're called Amaru—magical messengers. The Scholars' Guild uses them for swift and secure communication."

Theris straightened up, arms crossed, thoughtfully watching the horizon.

"Convenient," Theris admitted. "But nothing beats a messenger who can improvise."

Pharin couldn't resist chiming in:

"At least an Amaru won't stop along the way to flirt or have a drink!"

Liore rolled her eyes again, then laughed softly. Suna continued to gaze through the window, watching the Amaru soar into a world where everything seemed possible.

Theris returned his attention to the scattered books, worry etched on his features. He ran a hand across his forehead, then sighed deeply.

"All right… what now?" he asked, looking from one open book to another.

Liore shrugged slightly, her eyes scanning the countless rows of bookshelves. The answer had to be here, somewhere. She had always considered these shelves as a boundless well of knowledge. She pursed her lips thoughtfully… then a triumphant gleam lit her face.

"I have an idea!" she exclaimed enthusiastically.

Theris straightened up, intrigued. Liore pulled the rune-engraved ring from her pocket and turned it gently between her fingers.

"So far," she explained, "I've only concentrated on the location of the Pillars. But maybe we've been too restrictive. What if instead, I targeted hidden or protected places without explicitly mentioning the Pillars? These books already reference them… Perhaps we'd find indirect clues."

"That's an interesting lead," the counselor agreed. "Let's try it."

Encouraged, Liore placed the ring on the first book. She closed her eyes briefly, focused. Nothing happened. Undiscouraged, she moved on to the next volume, repeating the motion carefully. Still nothing.

"Patience," she murmured, more to herself than to anyone else.

Liore's gestures were precise and delicate, quickly moving from one book to another.

Hurried footsteps echoed behind them. Vaelen appeared, followed closely by Korvel, holding the unfolded Amaru, still bearing Liore's runes.

"We received your message," Vaelen said, catching his breath. "What happened here?"

Theris raised a finger to his lips, imposing silence. He drew both men aside, safely away from Liore's concentration, and quietly explained the situation: the spy, his likely connection to a disciple of Ereshkal, and their newfound urgency.

Vaelen listened, expression grim. Korvel stood close by, visibly anxious.

"Did you get a clear look at this disciple?" Korvel asked.

"Yes… but he vanished into the crowd. I'd never seen him before, but I'd recognize him again," Theris answered.

"Good. We'll need to be even more careful now."

Meanwhile, Liore continued her tireless search, sliding the ring from one book to another. Suna, staying by her side, watched in silence, torn between fascination and anxiety. She hoped one of these books would finally provide them with a lead.

When Liore placed the ring on a particularly hefty volume, a bright light surged forth, illuminating the room. Liore straightened up.

"At last…" she breathed, relieved, setting the book down beside her.

She finished sorting without any further reaction from the ring. Once completed, everyone gathered around Liore and the thick remaining tome.

"Finally, a ray of hope," Vaelen murmured gravely.

The scholar, holding her breath, slowly opened the book. Inside, dense, almost illegible handwriting covered pages yellowed by age. She squinted carefully at the characters.

"It looks like Sumerian… but different. Much more intricate."

She returned to the first page. Her finger froze mid-motion. Her breath hitched, and she paled.

"Well…" she whispered, straightening up. "Theris, remember those dormant spells? This might be the most dangerous one I've encountered. To open the book, I must utter a formula… which will trigger a truth spell. If I lie—even unintentionally—it could kill me."

A frozen silence fell. Suna stepped forward, her face strained.

"Liore," she said, "are you sure this is a good idea?"

Liore remained bent over the page a moment. When she rose again, determination filled her expression.

"Yes," she replied firmly. "This is our best clue, perhaps the only one left. I must try."

She read the spell's formula once more. Closing her eyes, she drew a deep breath and pronounced in a clear voice:

"I swear upon my life that I act solely for the good of Mytherra and Ætheris."

The runes glowed fiercely, casting shifting shadows upon the walls. Liore opened the book randomly, watched by everyone in fascination.

The mysterious symbols came to life, rearranging into new, readable text.

The room gradually returned to calm.

"It worked!" Liore exclaimed, breathing quickly but unharmed.

Pharin applauded enthusiastically, bowing theatrically before Liore.

"My dear, you truly have an unrivaled talent for dramatic moments!"

Liore leaned over the book, quickly scanning the now-readable pages. But as she read, her expression fell apart.

"It's impossible…" she murmured, crestfallen.

"What is it?" Theris asked, peering over her shoulder.

Liore lifted her gaze toward him.

"It's… a cookbook."

An awkward silence filled the room. Pharin burst into nervous laughter.

"Oh, wonderful!" he exclaimed. "Here lies the legendary secret of the Pillars: an ancient stew recipe!"

"I'm sorry… I don't understand. This book should never have reacted…"

"It's all right, Liore," the counselor soothed. "We'll keep searching. The real clue must be here somewhere."

Suna gently took the volume from Liore's hands. As soon as she touched the book, an icy sensation traveled up her fingers—the same feeling she'd experienced upon touching the stele beneath the statue of Ætheris. A chill ran up her arms. And before she could even react, the book stirred.

Under everyone's astonished gaze, the pages began turning, slowly at first, then faster and faster… until abruptly stopping at the book's center. Symbols tore free of the pages, floating into the air. A text formed, shimmering in silver light.

She leaned forward and read aloud clearly:

> *"If the Pillar of Knowledge you would seek,*
>
> *Read carefully these words, your path they speak.*
>
> *In a hidden place, concealed from sight,*
>
> *Lie eternal secrets, cloaked by the night.*
>
> *Where knowledge and destruction intertwine,*

One must fade away for the next to shine.

To cross this threshold, let your heart be clear,

Pronounce now the oath that binds you sincere."

Vaelen regarded Suna with clear admiration.

"What does it mean?" Pharin asked, searching the faces around him for answers.

Liore took a few thoughtful steps, eyeing the shelves as if waiting for one of them to whisper the solution.

"No idea," she finally admitted. "It's all so cryptic... 'Where knowledge and destruction intertwine'... Perhaps we're taking it too literally?"

"Not necessarily," Theris reasoned. "'In a hidden place, concealed from sight' seems quite literal to me. Perhaps a restricted section? A sealed area holding dangerous—or forbidden—texts."

Liore narrowed her eyes skeptically.

"A restricted area, here? I know this library inside out; I've never seen any hidden rooms."

"Precisely because it would be hidden," Pharin countered mockingly.

Suna raised a hand, calling for quiet as she thought aloud.

"What if it's symbolic instead? The balance between knowledge and destruction... Maybe it refers to ancient manuscripts being gradually erased when recopied?"

Liore immediately dismissed the idea.

"No. Here, it speaks of deliberate destruction. Not gradual fading. And here, manuscripts are preserved, never sacrificed."

Korvel abruptly straightened, struck by an idea.

"Wait! What if the poem refers to a forge? Like Enhugo's example: melting things down to create something new."

"Interesting," Liore considered thoughtfully. "But a forge in a library? That seems unlikely. It would require a furnace, a hidden workshop… and this place contains mostly books and scrolls."

"I suppose you're right," the soldier admitted.

"Perhaps it refers to an altar," Theris suggested. "Something where scrolls might be burned ritually to release magical power. A form of ritual destruction."

Liore shivered slightly, disturbed by the thought alone.

"Burning books? Even ritually, that goes entirely against the spirit of this place. This is a library, not a sacrificial temple. Knowledge here is never destroyed. Even mistakes are preserved."

Theris sighed, conceding her point.

"You're right."

"Maybe the place is hidden behind a specific book?" Suna hesitantly suggested. "If we pulled out one particular book, perhaps it would open a secret passage."

Liore folded her arms skeptically.

"Can you imagine pulling out every book? We'd be here for years. And someone would surely have tried it by now."

"True enough," Theris admitted. "There must be a more logical solution."

"What if it's a metaphor for the mind?" Liore ventured. "Forgetting as a form of destruction… necessary to make room for new ideas."

"That's profound," Vaelen said, impressed. "But unfortunately, not very practical for finding the actual location of the Pillar."

Liore sat back down, acknowledging the limits of her reasoning.

"Yes… I'm afraid so."

"Perhaps," Pharin interjected, "we should focus on the phrase, 'One must fade away for the next to shine.' What if plunging a certain spot into darkness reveals an inscription, a door, something?"

"The entire library is bathed in natural light," Liore pointed out, gesturing toward the dome. "We can't extinguish it."

"I suppose that was too simple," Pharin muttered.

They all mulled over the poem's verses, hoping inspiration would strike from nowhere. Suna felt frustration rising. They'd offered so many ideas, all plausible, yet nothing quite fit.

"At this rate," Pharin lamented, "we'll spend the night here going in circles."

"That's always the way with riddles," Liore remarked. "Once solved, they seem simple—but before that, they drive us mad."

Suna gazed around at the library, intuitively sensing the answer was there, just within reach. They simply needed to see things differently— but how?

Footsteps echoed in the room. Enhugo appeared, slightly breathless from climbing the stairs. He paused briefly to catch his breath.

"What's happened?" he finally asked. "Myrmes mentioned a thief…?"

Liore quickly recounted the incident with the young spy, followed by their discovery of the poem. Enhugo listened closely, stroking his beard thoughtfully.

"If this text references Knowledge," he murmured, "it can only mean the library itself. This is where my power is rooted."

He paused briefly, eyes drifting unfocused across the book-filled shelves.

"But destruction..." he continued thoughtfully. "That's Ignara, the Magician of Fire. Logical, since the Pillars combine our essences. We must find a place where fire and knowledge coexist..."

He looked up sharply, eyes brightening.

"Of course! Fire and knowledge combined...!"

Suna's face lit up, completing Enhugo's thought:

"The great fireplace at the heart of the library! That's where they meet!"

A stunned silence followed her words. Enhugo nodded approvingly. Suna wore a triumphant smile.

"Well then," Theris said decisively, "we now know exactly where to go. Let's not waste another moment."

The group rushed down the stairs toward the vestibule, drawing curious looks from students who paused their work as they passed. Upon reaching the great central fireplace, Liore stepped forward without hesitation.

She recited the oath inscribed in the book clearly and confidently.

Nothing happened.

In a burst of frustration, Theris threw his notes into the fire.

Liore and Enhugo froze, wide-eyed in horror. Destroying a written page. Even a novice student would never have dared—especially not in the central hearth.

As murmurs of protest began to rise, Suna noticed something strange.

"Look! The pages aren't burning!" she exclaimed.

The group moved closer immediately, captivated by this unexpected phenomenon. Flames danced around the paper without consuming or even charring it. Intrigued, Suna approached the fire. The heat rose gently—but never became painful.

She extended her hand toward the flames. Warmth enveloped her, almost pleasantly.

"It tickles!" she cried out. "It's warm, but it doesn't burn at all."

Without further hesitation, she crossed the threshold into the fireplace, moving into the heart of the fire. Vaelen reached out to hold her back.

"Suna, be careful!" he shouted, anxiety clear in his voice.

But she was no longer listening. Arms outstretched, she stepped further into the flames. They rippled around her, gently brushing against her skin without biting.

At the center of the blaze, Suna raised her head and declared in a strong, clear voice:

"I swear on my life that I act for the good of Mytherra and Ætheris!"

A powerful crack echoed throughout the library.

A shockwave rippled outward like an invisible tide, vibrating the walls and shaking the bookshelves. Absolute silence fell across the room. Suna, standing in a halo of light, became the focal point of everyone's attention.

Suddenly, the metallic mosaics beneath her feet began glowing and then shifted apart. The tiles sank away one by one, revealing a staircase descending into the depths beneath the library.

Enhugo approached, his eyes wide with awe.

"All these years… it was right here, beneath our feet," the magician whispered.

Suna stepped aside, letting him descend first. Liore followed closely. Suna went after her, her heart racing. Theris and Pharin cautiously brought up the rear, both alert and watchful.

Korvel moved to follow, but stopped abruptly before the fireplace.

"I'll stay here and keep watch," he said firmly, stepping back toward the entrance.

Vaelen briefly considered the situation before nodding in agreement.

"I'll stay as well. If anything happens, call out—we'll be ready."

The rest of the group disappeared into the newly opened passage.

The staircase was carved from dark stone, glowing faintly with runic patterns that illuminated the steps.

At the bottom, they emerged into a circular chamber. Shelves carved directly into the rock circled the room, overflowing with cracked bindings, sealed scrolls, stone tablets, and clay fragments. Intricate designs etched deeply into the walls glowed softly, casting pale, silvery light.

At the chamber's center stood a pedestal, upon which rested a fragile, yellowed parchment, seemingly suspended in time. The group stood motionless, feeling the weight of this moment. This parchment had clearly been waiting for centuries.

Enhugo slowly approached the pedestal, his movements reverent. He carefully lifted the parchment, gently unrolling it to reveal its long-guarded secrets.

"It's... a fragment of a map," he murmured, eyes gleaming. "It depicts the southern part of Mytherra."

His finger traced the lines until stopping at a carefully marked cross.

It indicated an isolated mountain rising from the sea, between Enhugo's island... and Ignara's volcano.

"At last, we have a precise location," Liore breathed.

"Yes, but it's not enough," Theris remarked thoughtfully. "There must be something more—another clue or clearer instructions."

Liore nodded, producing her rune-inscribed ring. She moved toward the shelves and slowly passed the ring over the ancient books, working meticulously, attentive to any reaction. After a few minutes, four volumes had begun glowing, activated by the runes.

"Here. These four should fill in the blanks. One each."

They sat down on the floor in a circle, reading by the silvery glow. Each took a volume, becoming silent and intent on their research.

Enhugo meanwhile eagerly scanned the shelves, drawn by the wealth of new knowledge.

Suna leafed through the pages of a richly illustrated book. Beside her, Theris studied an intricate grimoire, absorbed by every word. Even Pharin, normally easily distracted, was quickly engrossed in his reading. Liore read with fervent concentration. The scale of what they were uncovering had clearly grown beyond anything she had imagined.

After a lengthy silence spent reading, the first clues began to emerge.

"'The temples of the Pillars lie scattered across Mytherra,'" Liore read aloud. "'And each one is protected... by a guardian.'"

Enhugo raised his head from a manuscript, his brow furrowed.

"Of course... And I know who guards this one," he said, pointing to the cross on the map. "This stretch of sea is off-limits. It's the domain... of a Kraken."

Suna's face drained of color.

"A Kraken?" she squeaked.

Pharin chuckled at her high-pitched tone.

Enhugo explained calmly:

"Imagine a gigantic octopus, with tentacles large enough to drag an entire ship under the waves..."

"Great, yes, an actual Kraken... fantastic," muttered Suna.

Theris read aloud from his book:

"'The temple doors will open only when two incompatible halves are reunited.'"

He looked up, puzzled.

"That's certainly a cryptic clue…"

"Two incompatible halves?" Liore mused. "I have no idea what that could mean yet. We'll need to dig deeper."

Suna continued reading aloud:

"'Each temple holds a trial, with the Pillar as the ultimate reward.'"

"'And these trials are always overseen by a dragon,'" added Pharin. "'They explain the rules and ensure they're followed.'"

Suna blinked in disbelief, looking from one companion to another.

"Wait just a minute… Are you telling me we have to survive an encounter with a giant Kraken… and then pass a test supervised by a dragon? Do you honestly think this quest is even possible? I'm not sure I'm up for all of that."

"You're the only one who can touch the Pillars, Suna," Theris reminded her gently. "Which means you must accompany us for these trials. All of them."

Every gaze settled upon her.

Suna froze, weighing his words. She chose to respond with humor. Throwing her arms out dramatically, she struck a mock-heroic pose.

"Tadaa!" she proclaimed grandly.

Laughter burst forth, finally easing the built-up tension.

Liore regained her composure and continued reading, her fingers tracing the handwritten lines.

"'The missing fragments of the map will only reveal themselves once the Pillars have been recovered.'"

She closed the book slowly.

Enhugo stood straighter, the map still in his hand.

"Then it's settled," he declared firmly. "You now have all the information you need."

"There's just one small detail remaining," Theris mused aloud. "How exactly does one fight a Kraken?"

"Let's return upstairs," said Enhugo. "It's time we discussed how to deal with such a creature."

They climbed the stairs back to the main hall.

There, Aldaren and Hestian had joined Vaelen and Korvel by the large hearth. Everyone waited impatiently, eager to hear what the secret room had revealed.

They all took seats around a wide table, their expressions serious and focused. After a brief summary by Enhugo, Theris spoke up, his fingers tapping nervously on the worn surface.

"All right," said the counselor. "The Kraken is our main obstacle. Does anyone have an idea how to defeat it… or at least get around it?"

Vaelen shook his head, arms crossed, wings neatly folded behind him.

"I doubt we can directly defeat a creature of that size; it would be suicidal. We need another approach."

Hestian, perched nervously on the edge of his chair, tapped the hilt of his sword.

"Maybe… poison? A toxin or something venomous?"

Theris regarded him dubiously.

"And where exactly do you plan to find enough poison to take down such a monster? We don't even know if it would affect it."

"What if we tried to trap it?" Suna suggested. "A cage, or some strong nets might at least hold it off for a while."

"Suna, we're not talking about some oversized shrimp here," countered Vaelen. "This is a legendary beast capable of swallowing an entire ship."

"Why don't we just lure it away from the entrance?" offered Hestian. "A clever distraction could cause it to leave its post."

Pharin chuckled mockingly.

"And exactly how do you plan to lure a giant Kraken away? By floating a 'free meal' sign in the water?"

Vaelen leaned forward, serious.

"What if we created an underwater illusion? A gigantic prey, large enough to attract its attention elsewhere, even for a short while."

Theris shook his head, skeptical.

"Unfortunately, none of us controls the aquatic element. We need something else."

Korvel revisited his comrade's idea:

"Then perhaps we could provoke it. If it senses a threat, it might emerge from the water. On land, it might be more vulnerable."

"Oh, brilliant," mocked Pharin. "Let's lure a massive sea monster onto the beach. Want to offer it legs while you're at it?"

Korvel rolled his eyes.

"It's not that foolish," Liore interjected. "What if we used a decoy? Something to attract the Kraken's attention without it noticing us?"

Aldaren nodded thoughtfully.

"Yes," he murmured. "If we can make it focus on something other than us…"

"Or maybe," Korvel suggested, "we look for the Kraken's natural predator. Something to make it flee."

Hestian rolled his eyes dramatically.

"A predator of a Kraken? You want to attract something even worse? I'm not sure that's the smartest idea."

Korvel crossed his arms, visibly annoyed, but said nothing. Hestian had a point.

"Listen," Enhugo said decisively, regaining control. "Let's go back to basics. Several ideas have merit: a decoy, a distraction… What we need now is to choose something we can realistically implement."

Theris nodded sharply.

"He's right. Let's combine what we've got. Not every idea was worthless."

Suna stared at the map, desperately searching for a more logical solution. Nothing came immediately to mind.

It was Enhugo who, after a long moment of contemplation, tapped the parchment with his finger.

"Here!" he exclaimed, pointing to a precise spot on the map.

Intrigued, everyone leaned in to see what Enhugo was indicating.

"Right here, at the foot of these cliffs, there's a natural platform. It starts above water and gradually slopes downward over a considerable distance. If we lure the Kraken there, a rockslide might be enough to trap it."

"A rockslide?" repeated Hestian. "Seriously? We're talking about tons of stone. Planning to push all that by hand?"

Enhugo met the warrior's disbelief with indulgence.

"Not by hand, no. But with the right spell, it's doable. We simply need to find a weak spot—and exploit it."

Liore straightened up, her eyes shining with enthusiasm and determination.

"That's within our abilities, Master Enhugo. With your help, we can devise an explosive spell strong enough to trigger a rockslide… at just the right moment. But the timing will need to be perfect."

Enhugo nodded, pleased by his apprentice's methodical thinking.

"We'll have to prepare the trap at the cliff, then lure the creature beneath it."

"It's a good idea, but risky," Theris pointed out. "If the Kraken senses the trap before it triggers, it'll react violently. It's no dumb beast, far from it."

"And we'll have to keep it in place," Pharin chimed in. "Any volunteers to play the bait?"

Several eyes rolled upward, but Liore, already inspired, quickly interrupted before anyone could comment further.

"No, we need something that can keep it occupied long enough," she explained thoughtfully. "Something like… food that's difficult to consume quickly."

Suna's eyebrows shot upward, her face suddenly lighting with excitement.

"I know!" she cried out. "Back home, my cat is a bit plump…"

"Wait—are you planning to sacrifice your cat to the Kraken?" Pharin protested with mock outrage.

"No, silly!" she replied, laughing. "He has a toy that slowly releases food—but only if he plays with it."

"Interesting," Theris agreed. "If we could replicate that mechanism…"

"We could create an effective lure," Suna finished. "Something the Kraken has to manipulate and unravel slowly to consume. That could buy us time. Does anyone know what a Kraken eats?"

"I doubt it feeds on seaweed," Liore guessed. "If I had to bet, I'd say large fish—other marine creatures, anyway…"

"There's a fishing village to the south," Enhugo offered. "They'll certainly have something to attract this creature."

Liore beamed, delighted at Enhugo's approval.

Aldaren spoke up:

"I can place a protective barrier on a net. With enough fish inside, the Kraken would take time to break through it. That would buy us the time we need."

"Wait—do we throw this net from the cliff?" asked Korvel.

"No, too complicated," Theris countered. "We'll need a ship to reach the temple anyway. We could place the lure at the right spot first… and only then attract the Kraken."

"Let's just hope its hearing isn't too sharp," Pharin quipped. "…Or its gills? Honestly, I don't even know how you'd say it with a Kraken. Fine… my joke's sunk."

Suna and Liore burst into laughter anyway.

Theris, however, remained focused on the real issue.

"What bothers me is how we're going to draw it into the trap. It won't simply go there willingly. We need to provoke it, force it to follow us."

Vaelen straightened, his wings shifting behind him.

"I might be able to lure it out. If we know what could genuinely irritate it, I could provoke it… And if things go wrong, I could always escape by air."

"Oh sure," Pharin mocked. "If you insist on risking your life, don't let us stop you."

"Why don't we try attracting it another way?" proposed Suna, uncomfortable with the idea of putting the angel in danger. "A loud sound. Vibrations. It works well on marine creatures, right?"

"That's true," Enhugo confirmed. "I remember sailors mentioning Krakens being sensitive to simple movements of ships. If we make enough disturbance, it will come."

"That makes sense," Theris agreed.

"And… how exactly do we do that?" Suna asked uncertainly. "Do you have bombs? Gunpowder?"

"Gun-what?" Enhugo inquired with interest.

Suna blushed, aware she'd slipped.

"No, never mind," she stammered, shaking her head. "Nothing important."

Enhugo fixed her a moment, intrigued by this stranger and her knowledge from another world. This world didn't need to learn of such things. Suna quickly changed the subject.

"What I meant was… Vaelen could drag something heavy across the surface. If he strikes the water near the temple entrance, the Kraken would eventually take interest, wouldn't it?"

"That's a clever idea," Vaelen confirmed. "Give me a sturdy barrel, and I'll drag it right under that beast's nose to the perfect spot."

Enhugo nodded in approval.

"Very well, Vaelen. But we'll need an escape route. A good plan always includes a retreat."

"We could secure ropes along the cliff," Hestian suggested, "to facilitate access… and an escape, if necessary."

Theris silently agreed. After a few seconds of thought, he concluded:

"And we'll stay aboard the ship, nearby. Ready to intervene or retrieve Vaelen if things go wrong."

A brief silence fell as everyone weighed the risks.

"If… anything happens," Suna said softly, "I want to help. I refuse to just stand by and do nothing."

Theris, surprised by her determination, softened his expression.

"Suna… you're already doing so much for us. If all goes according to plan, you won't have to intervene."

Suna met his gaze, hesitated, but chose not to protest further.

Enhugo brought the conversation to a close.

"It's decided. We depart at dawn. Rendezvous at Port Waste: prepare the ship and the bait. Be ready for anything. By tomorrow, this Kraken will no longer be a problem."

They all nodded silently. Excitement mingled with apprehension. The trial was drawing near.

14 — Zayn — Full sail

Zayn opened his eyes, awakened by the noises of the sailors bustling about on deck. Around him, the cabin was empty; the other hammocks swayed gently. He stretched, his body stiff from the night spent rocked by the ship's movements.

He stepped out of the cabin and climbed onto the deck. The fresh morning air struck him, filled with spray and an invigorating salty scent.

The sea was calm, smooth as glass.

To the east, the horizon was tinged with pink and gold, gradually dissolving the night's mist. A few seagulls circled near the ship, their sharp cries echoing as they hunted for fish.

On deck, a few sailors were already busy, checking ropes and adjusting sails with calm precision. At the helm, the captain held the wheel firmly.

Zayn approached the rail, resting his arms on the salt-worn wood. The shoreline drifted slowly by to port. The land, still veiled in morning mist, revealed towering rocky cliffs. Occasionally, he glimpsed secluded coves nestled between rocks, or wild beaches slapped by the waves.

He soon sensed Fynna stepping up beside him. The ondine gazed at the horizon alongside him.

"Tell me, Zayn… do you have any brothers or sisters?" she asked.

"No," he replied, surprised. "I've always lived alone with my mother. My father… I never knew him."

He fell silent for a moment, then asked:

"And you? Do you have brothers or sisters?"

Fynna burst into laughter—a clear, musical sound that echoed across the deck, catching Zayn off guard.

"What? I don't see what's so funny…"

Her shoulders shook.

"There are hundreds of us!" she said, laughing. "Everyone knows that."

Zayn stared at her, incredulous. He scratched his head, confused.

"Wait… What?"

"Thalessa isn't like human women, Zayn. She never had a faithful or exclusive partner. The ocean is vast… she's always refused to be bound to one soul."

Seeing Zayn's raised eyebrow, she continued, a playful smile forming at the corner of her lips.

"Yes, exactly what you're thinking. Thalessa chooses her lovers as she chooses the currents: freely, according to her mood. Warriors, sailors, scholars… sometimes human, sometimes Atlantean. Even, they say, marine beings of… varying intelligence. And from these unions come children. Many, many children."

Zayn stared at her, speechless. He barely grasped what she had just told him.

"So… you actually have hundreds of brothers and sisters?" he murmured.

"Oh yes," she said, laughing again. "Thalessa has had… a wide variety of children. Some are almost human. Others… let's just say they take after sea creatures. Fins, gills, skin colored like the depths… You'd be amazed how varied we look."

She raised her arm, letting sunlight dance across her pale skin. Tiny scales shimmered faintly, nearly invisible.

"For instance, I inherited slightly iridescent skin, almost like the sheen of mother-of-pearl."

He couldn't help staring. The shimmering reflections on her skin, the shifting shades in her eyes, the fluidity of her hair—all of this gave the young woman a charm impossible to ignore.

He realized, a bit too late, that he was staring at her.

"I… I never really noticed before," he murmured, lowering his eyes.

"I'm caught between two worlds," she said simply. "I can't stay underwater indefinitely. Or on land, for that matter… but I manipulate water better than most."

"And your brothers and sisters?" Zayn asked.

"Well… I have a sister with skin dark as the abyss. And a brother with eyes white as mother-of-pearl. You'd swear he was blind… but underwater, he sees better than all of us."

"Some can stay underwater for days. Others speak the language of the seas. Some control the currents. You see… we're all very different."

She rested her elbows on the rail, gazing at the dark water beneath the ship.

"They call us Children of the Tides because, like the tides, we're all different, unpredictable… and untamable."

"Untamable, huh? And yet, you obey a dark angel," Zayn teased gently.

Fynna's expression darkened.

"Yes," she murmured.

Embarrassed by his lack of tact, Zayn changed the subject.

"But… if there are hundreds of you, she can't possibly raise you all."

"No. She doesn't even try."

She pursed her lips.

"We're her children, yes, but not as you imagine. She doesn't tuck us in, or teach us to walk, or speak. She brings us into the world… and entrusts us to those she chooses to shape us."

Zayn was troubled by this cold conception of parenthood.

"Some are given to disciples, scholars, weapon masters…" the ondine continued. "Our upbringing depends on our father, on his rank, and on the role chosen for us."

"That seems… so distant," he murmured.

"That's just how it is," said Fynna. "You might call it 'cold'. But for us, it's like the ocean: unpredictable, powerful, unforgiving."

"And you? How was it for you?"

"Me? My father was a respected Atlantean, a strategist known throughout Atlantis. From childhood, I was destined… to be more than just another daughter."

Bitterness seeped into her voice.

"Not all of Thalessa's children are equal. Some inherit rare gifts. A glorious future. Others… are expendable. Too weak. They're sent away. Sometimes discreetly. Sometimes permanently. Very early on, we were taught one thing: only those capable of adapting deserve to survive."

"That's… cruel."

"It's the law of the ocean. No mercy. No weakness. Thalessa instills it in us from childhood."

Fynna took a deep breath.

"I wasn't taught to be a princess. I was taught to survive."

Zayn observed her silently.

"First, there was hunting. We had to learn to catch our own food: fish, crustaceans… sometimes worse. No nets. No harpoons. We had to sense our prey, anticipate, strike fast."

"We also learned to speak. Negotiation is worth a blade, Thalessa would say. And a well-placed wave can crush an army before it ever draws a sword."

Fynna straightened up.

"To prove our worth, we had to bring back the heart of a lanternfish."

Zayn blinked.

"That's all?"

She gave him a crooked smile, like one would to a child asking if fire was hot.

"It's not like diving into a pool, Zayn. A lanternfish is bigger than a horse, and lives… in the abyss."

"I should've guessed."

"At some point, the water turns black. No more light. No more landmarks. Just pressure that crushes you, unpredictable currents… and creatures living where nobody should go."

Zayn swallowed hard.

"You know you've found it when a little glow appears in the darkness, like a lost star underwater. But it's not an invitation. It's a trap. That light is its lure."

She paused, her gaze darkening.

"It doesn't hunt, Zayn. It waits. It senses you before you ever see it."

Zayn cleared his throat.

"So, you fight blind," she said softly, "to the rhythm of your heartbeat, with fear sticking to your skin like a second layer. And if you survive…"

She slowly raised her hand, closing her fingers in a gentle, almost ceremonial gesture.

"…you take its still-warm heart. And you swim up, hoping it was the only creature down there that sensed you."

"And you did it?"

"Obviously. You only had one chance. If you failed… you didn't come back. I was sixteen."

"What was it like down there?" asked Zayn.

"The water rips the breath from your lungs, the darkness erases you, and the silence… screams at you. It's cold, silent, and terrifying."

Fynna turned her eyes toward the sea. Her expression grew distant.

"But I came back up. With its heart. And I was alive."

Zayn remained silent. His childhood no longer seemed so tough. And sharing this moment with Fynna… felt good.

"All right," said Fynna, "enough about dark stuff. Want to know what we did for fun?"

Zayn was curious to discover this world. Everything about it was incredible. So what could ondines and sirens possibly do for fun?

"When we were kids, we raced dolphins."

"Seriously?"

"Yep, and let me tell you, they never let us win. If you managed to grab onto a fin… and hold on for a few seconds… you were king—or queen—for the day."

"And it wasn't just dolphins. Stingrays joined in too."

"Stingrays?" he repeated, squinting skeptically.

Fynna nodded.

"Yeah, calmer than dolphins… but they had an advantage: they could carry you around on their backs."

She crossed her arms.

"We also messed around with sharks. A bunch of us kids would group together and provoke them a little. Like, scare away their prey, swim circles around them. Obviously, that annoyed them, so they chased us."

She chuckled at Zayn's stunned expression.

"Well… there were a few accidents, sure. But it was rare."

Zayn was astonished.

"And you did this… often?"

"A bit too often," she replied, laughing.

"You had strange games."

"When you live underwater, you use what you have."

She leaned toward him.

"But if you want, we could see if we can find a dolphin to race."

Zayn raised his hands in surrender.

"No, thanks! I'll stick to dry land… for a very long time."

"As you wish, land-dweller."

They laughed wholeheartedly.

"And… what about Thalessa's mother? What was she like? Did you know her?"

Fynna spun toward him abruptly, her mouth hanging open. Her eyes widened… then a sudden burst of laughter shook her shoulders, betraying uncontrollable amusement.

"What? What did I say that's funny?" he asked, feeling awkward.

She shook her head, quickly regaining her composure, though a playful sparkle lingered at the corner of her lips.

"Sorry, Zayn… It's just that Thalessa has no mother. None of the great magicians do. They're… well, they're immortal. Didn't you know that?"

Zayn was speechless. A chill seemed to pierce through his chest.

That meant Ereshkal wasn't merely a magician as he'd naively believed…

She had existed forever. Death itself.

All their interactions suddenly took on a much more daunting dimension. He was nothing but a breath, a blink of an eye in the eternity she embodied.

"And… are there other immortals besides them?"

"Not that I know of. There are very ancient creatures, of course… but truly immortal? I don't think so."

Zayn remained thoughtful for a moment.

"So, your mother has ruled Atlantis forever?"

"Oh, she's the queen, without question. No one can challenge her. And no one will ever succeed her. But that doesn't mean everyone accepts it."

"She has rivals?"

"Not directly, no. Let's just say beneath the surface, things aren't as peaceful as they seem."

"There's a Senate, with representatives from various factions: sirens, tritons, ondines… even a few human families who've long been tied to the city. Each one seeks more influence. More power."

Zayn narrowed his eyes.

"But if Thalessa is so powerful, why doesn't she just sweep them aside?"

"Because the sea is ever-changing. She knows no storm lasts forever. She listens. She manipulates. She makes promises… that she can choose to keep—or not. She loves playing that game."

"So, it's a real shark tank down there?" Zayn quipped.

Fynna laughed.

"Exactly. A nest of vipers… in a palace of coral."

"And you, in all this?"

"I keep my distance as much as possible."

Fynna fell silent. She gazed out toward the horizon, where sea and sky blurred into one. A shadow had crept into her eyes.

Meanwhile, Nymeris and Garnius had claimed a clear section of the deck, turning it into their training ground.

The sea breeze swept Nymeris's dark locks about her face. A few sailors paused their tasks nearby, watching the duel unfold with keen interest.

They began. Garnius swung his two-handed axe with confidence, surprising agility evident despite his massive build. Nymeris, light-footed, danced around him, evading each strike with graceful ease, anticipating his every move.

"Is that all you've got?" she taunted, effortlessly dodging a frontal assault.

Garnius feinted cleverly, immediately following with a sideways blow. Nymeris barely avoided it… laughing.

"You talk a lot for someone who keeps running away," he growled.

She spun on her heel, leaping backward out of reach of another strike.

"I'm going easy on you—just prolonging the fun," he retorted with a smirk.

Their pace quickened. Garnius's blows grew more rapid and precise, yet Nymeris flowed around him like water, never striking back.

"You hit hard, but so slowly I could take a nap between swings," she mocked lightly.

"Don't push me, little witch," he snarled. "I might just stop holding back."

"That sounds like a good idea," she replied smoothly, ducking beneath a sweeping attack. "We might finally have some fun."

Garnius growled, though a smile twitched at the corners of his lips. He relished the challenge.

The sailors, intrigued, gathered into a loose circle around the fighters. Bets quickly started flying, adding to the cheerful uproar.

"Ten coins on the brute!" shouted a red-haired sailor, grinning.

"Twenty says she'll dodge three in a row!" cried another.

Excitement rippled through the crowd, fueling Garnius's determination.

"So, showing off for your fans?" he growled, eyes blazing. "Let's see if you're still smiling after this!"

Garnius charged, unleashing rapid, powerful blows. Sailors stepped back, startled by his sudden fury.

Nymeris, far from rattled, responded calmly. Eyes narrowed, she danced gracefully around his strikes, using barrels and ropes as obstacles to her advantage.

"She moves like an eel," murmured an admiring sailor.

"More like a serpent ready to strike," laughed another.

"She'll take him down," whispered a third, mesmerized.

"I wouldn't want her as an enemy," said another, tightening a rope nervously.

Garnius cursed through gritted teeth, torn between frustration and grudging admiration at her infuriating agility. Nymeris vanished in a blink… reappearing behind him, her blades just grazing his back.

The warrior turned swiftly.

"Finally showing your true colors, little trickster. Fight fair!"

Garnius lifted his axe, bringing it crashing down. Nymeris leaned back gracefully, barely evading the strike.

"Too slow!" she mocked.

Furious, Garnius followed up with a rapid side blow, but again she leaped backward effortlessly.

Captain Roark, watching from the helm, observed with fascination, arms folded.

"Impressive…" he murmured, enjoying the spectacle.

Thanatos remained silent. He knew Garnius stood no chance. Watching Nymeris toy with her prey sparked an idea in his mind.

As Garnius prepared another strike, Nymeris vaulted off the rail into a graceful backflip. Her blade brushed Garnius's cheek, leaving a thin, clean cut. Before he could react, she slipped behind him, pressing the cool tip of her dagger to his throat.

The berserker froze. His breath came in heavy rasps, contrasting sharply with her icy calm.

"Better now?" she whispered into his ear.

Garnius stood motionless, then burst into booming laughter, his broad shoulders shaking.

"You got me good," he roared, raising his hands.

Nymeris withdrew her blade, letting him breathe, and tapped his shoulder in mock tenderness.

"Nicely done. But be careful next time—an enemy won't be so generous."

Cheers erupted from the sailors. Coins changed hands amid laughter and congratulations. Garnius chuckled, wiping blood from his cheek, then approached a barrel of fresh water near the mast.

"Not bad," he admitted grudgingly, splashing water on his face. "But that was just a warm-up. Next time, I promise a real fight. Watch that pretty face of yours."

Nymeris crossed her arms, eyes sparkling with challenge.

"I hope so. It'd be a shame if you bored me too soon."

Garnius raised his tankard to her with a wide grin, downing it in hearty gulps as the crew watched, amused.

Zayn and Fynna observed from afar.

"Those two really will kill each other someday," Zayn remarked.

"I doubt it," replied Fynna softly. "They respect each other too much."

Zayn, having watched from the other side of the ship, felt impressed.

Thanatos appeared on deck, and as always, silence followed him. Unexpectedly, he came to stand beside Zayn. Zayn tensed, but Fynna's reassuring gaze soothed him. She recalled suggesting to Thanatos the night before that he should speak to the young human.

"Getting used to the sea?" Thanatos asked softly.

Zayn glanced timidly upward. "Yeah… well, trying."

"Your Earth must be very different from here," Thanatos remarked. "Do you miss it?"

Zayn hesitated, surprised by the question. "Of course," he answered honestly. "Even if Mytherra's incredible."

Thanatos paused, seemingly choosing his words.

"Tell me… what's your world like?"

Zayn turned in surprise. He never imagined Thanatos curious about Earth.

"Very different," he said. "Everything runs on technology there."

Thanatos's brow furrowed slightly. "Technology? I don't understand."

"Well… at home, there's no magic. So, we invented machines. To travel, communicate, protect ourselves… everything."

"What exactly are these 'machines'?"

Zayn hesitated. How could he describe the obvious?

"They're man-made objects," he explained. "For instance, to communicate, we have 'telephones'—small devices sending your voice to someone anywhere in the world."

"Interesting… How does it work without magic?"

Zayn shrugged, smiling uncertainly.

"I don't know exactly," he admitted. "It involves signals sent through the air."

"And your transport?" Thanatos asked, tone neutral.

"We have fast vehicles," Zayn answered eagerly. "Cars and even airplanes—flying machines crossing entire continents above the clouds."

"Flying machines?" Thanatos repeated, genuinely surprised. "Like… birds?"

Zayn smiled.

"Almost. They have fixed, metallic wings. No flapping—engines push them through the air."

"And how do you defend yourselves without magic?"

Zayn hesitated, but Fynna's quiet support encouraged him.

"We have different weapons. Firearms. They shoot projectiles quickly, precisely, from afar."

"Like bows?" Thanatos asked.

"No. Far more powerful. Fast enough to pierce nearly anything."

"That sounds… dangerous," Fynna murmured.

"Yes," Zayn admitted sadly. "Too often…"

Silence settled, broken only by gentle waves against the hull.

"And who makes these wonders?" Thanatos continued quietly. "Smiths?"

Zayn smiled at the comparison's simplicity.

"Not exactly. We have factories—large buildings where machines produce thousands of items daily."

"Fascinating…" Thanatos murmured. "Your leaders… do they rule alone? An emperor?"

"No, not exactly. In my country, it's a democracy. Citizens choose leaders."

Thanatos had heard the term before but doubted its promise.

"Does it work?" he asked.

Zayn shrugged ironically.

"Not always. But it's better than nothing."

Thanatos remained thoughtful, nodding slowly.

"Your world is… interesting," he murmured at last.

He turned abruptly, heading toward his cabin. Zayn watched silently.

"That was… strange," he whispered to Fynna. "I've never heard him speak so much."

Fynna leaned against the rail, smiling gently.

"Yes. It was his attempt at being polite. And for that, you've got to give him credit."

In late morning, as the sun warmed the deck, Nymeris motioned for Zayn to follow her aside.

He joined her, curious, and saw she was holding a dagger—similar to the one she'd given him in Quarth.

"I promised you a first lesson," she reminded him. "Now's the perfect time."

Zayn, surprised but eager, drew his dagger—and nearly dropped it onto the deck.

"First, try not to injure yourself before we even start," Nymeris teased, rolling her eyes. "Come here, show me your grip."

Zayn grabbed the handle so tightly his knuckles turned white.

"Too tense. Relax a little," she corrected, adjusting his grip gently. "The dagger should feel like an extension of your arm, not some foreign object."

Zayn attempted to loosen his fingers, breathing deeply.

"Like this?"

"Better. But never drop your guard. Your blade must be ready to counter at any moment. Keep your wrist flexible."

She demonstrated with a fluid arm movement, her dagger glinting in the sunlight.

"See the difference between this…and this?" she said, repeating the gesture stiffly, comically imitating Zayn's overly rigid stance.

"Yeah, but…it looks so much easier when you do it."

"It's all about fluidity," she explained patiently. "Now, the basics: a direct attack. Blade pointed at your opponent, weight on your supporting leg, always ready to spring forward."

She took position, standing still like a warrior statue. Zayn tried to copy her stance, somewhat awkwardly. Nymeris nodded briefly in approval.

"Not bad. Now, a simple strike: Step forward, thrust straight ahead. Your movement should be swift, sharp, precise."

Nymeris demonstrated an attack so rapid Zayn saw only a silver flash.

"Your turn," she ordered, stepping back.

Zayn executed the move clumsily.

"You're attacking a target, not an imaginary fly!" she corrected sharply. "Again, with confidence this time."

Zayn repeated the movement, more decisively.

"Better," she approved. "Now, dodging. It'll save you far more surely than any armor."

Without warning, Nymeris feinted. Zayn jumped, stepping back too hastily—and nearly tripped over a bucket behind him.

"Hey!" he protested, flailing to regain his balance.

"Rule number one: Always be ready. If I step forward, don't retreat. Move sideways. Like this."

She demonstrated a few graceful steps, pivoting fluidly around an invisible opponent.

"Try it."

Zayn practiced repeatedly, until Nymeris nodded with approval.

"Good. Now, let's combine it all. I'll attack slowly; you dodge and counter. Ready?"

Zayn got into position.

Nymeris launched a slow, deliberate strike. Zayn dodged, pivoted…and attempted a clumsy counterattack, missing by a wide margin.

"Faster," Nymeris encouraged. "Strike immediately after dodging."

They repeated the drill several times. With each attempt, Zayn felt the rhythm better—but his breathing grew heavier.

"It's…harder than I expected," he gasped, breathless.

Nymeris smiled.

"Nobody said it would be easy. Combat demands breath and stamina. Fatigue is just another obstacle. Stay focused."

She sped up slightly, increasing the pressure. Under stress, Zayn's precision suffered—but he managed to hold his own. Gradually, his reflexes improved.

"Now, a feint," Nymeris announced. "Pay close attention."

She feinted left, then swiftly struck right. Zayn, confused, felt the flat of her blade tap his shoulder.

"Ouch!" he exclaimed, retreating quickly.

"In a real fight, you'd be dead," she said bluntly. "Watch your opponent's body, not just their blade. Their posture always betrays intention."

She continued feinting until Zayn finally started recognizing the subtle cues in her movements.

With perseverance, he managed to evade several attacks.

"There!" Nymeris exclaimed, satisfied. "Exactly like that. Combat isn't about strength. It's about reading your opponent and anticipating them."

"Got it," Zayn panted, arms shaking. "I didn't think…it'd be so physical."

"It's because you're overthinking your movements. Don't think—feel. Trust your body; it's smarter than you realize."

Fynna, watching their practice from nearby, coughed discreetly at that remark. Neither Nymeris nor Zayn reacted.

They continued training, with Nymeris showing him parries, rapid counters, and techniques to conserve energy.

"Alright, that's enough for today," she said, noticing his exhaustion. "Stretch a bit, it'll spare you some soreness tomorrow."

He obediently complied, relieved—but with an unfamiliar sense of pride deep within.

"So, how was it?" asked Fynna, watching him stretch.

"Really instructive," he answered. "But I'll definitely suffer tomorrow."

"That's a good sign," Nymeris commented. "Means you worked hard."

"Thanks, Nymeris. Honestly, I didn't expect you to be…such a good teacher."

"Don't get used to thanking me too quickly," she teased. "Today was easy. Next time, we'll get serious."

She winked playfully before walking away. Zayn, exhausted yet pleased, regained his breath facing the ocean.

He carefully sheathed his dagger. For the first time, it no longer felt foreign. It was beginning to become a part of him.

The ship continued slowly on its course, skirting the cliffs of Enhugo's island to the west. Birds circled above the rocks, their sharp cries mingling with gusts of wind.

On deck, Nymeris and Garnius had resumed their training. They opted for a more constructive approach this time, exchanging tips like comrades sharing the same passion.

"You're exposing your side too much," Nymeris remarked, dodging a wide strike. "A quick opponent would finish you off."

"Maybe," the berserker replied. "But if they take the bait… they're the one who won't get back up."

He punctuated this with a provocative grin, then returned to his stance, weapon raised.

Nymeris shook her head, half amused, half exasperated.

"You won't always be the strongest," she murmured, taking her position.

From the quarterdeck, Captain Roark shifted his gaze between the landscape and the duel. He seemed to savor both the view and the skills of his passengers, a delighted expression lighting up his weathered face.

The combat intensified. Sailors shouted the names of their favorites, heightening the tension on deck. The two fighters were sizing each other up, but more than anything, they enjoyed this exchange.

Spotting an opening, Nymeris struck at Garnius's left side. But the berserker reacted swiftly, pivoting and easily blocking her attack. A satisfied grunt escaped him.

"See, sweetheart? I'm a quick learner," he boasted, pushing away her blade.

Nymeris nodded calmly.

"Perhaps, but you're still predictable."

Garnius glanced downward. Nymeris's second dagger was pointed firmly at his groin.

He immediately raised his hands, hissing through his teeth:

"Alright, lesson learned," he laughed. "I yield. No sense killing each other over practice."

"Wise decision," she approved, catching her breath.

Garnius handed Nymeris a water flask, a knowing smile on his face. She took a quick drink before pressing it back against his chest, a direct gesture betraying her eagerness to resume their fight.

Absorbed by their training, neither paid attention to the spectacular scenery unfolding behind them.

Along the shore, a natural arch stretched out over the sea, forming a majestic bridge above the restless waves. Scattered here and there were small secluded coves accessible only by water. Black sand beaches punctuated the cliffs, sharply contrasting with the vivid green moss that carpeted the rock.

In the late afternoon, they reached a place where nature had carved its own whims.

Around them rose islands of stone, standing like sentinels guarding the bay. High limestone cliffs erupted from the turquoise waters, forming a mineral maze through which the ship carefully made its way.

Each rocky peak had been sculpted by time and the elements, creating strange, almost dreamlike shapes. Some resembled immense towers reaching skyward; others, broader, were hollowed by caves from which seabirds burst forth. On the damp walls, lush vegetation had taken root, cascading in verdant waterfalls down the cliff faces.

In places, streams of clear water flowed from the heights, shattering into fine droplets. When sunlight struck them, shimmering rainbows formed, enhancing the magic of the surroundings.

"It's… magnificent," whispered Zayn, admiring the crystal-clear water where schools of fish swam gracefully.

Fynna, standing beside him, nodded silently, equally captivated by the beauty.

The *Crown of the Waves* glided carefully between these natural stone columns, navigating a narrow, winding channel. At times, the hull passed so close to the rocks that they could hear the echo of water lapping gently against the cliffs.

At last, they emerged from this fantastical stone labyrinth. In the distance, the first outlines of Port Waste appeared.

As they sailed around the town, a ship caught Zayn's eye. A large fishing vessel, bigger than the others, with a black sail adorned with a white feather, and its prow sculpted into the shape of an octopus.

"Very pretty," murmured Nymeris, who had joined the group on deck after her latest duel.

The *Crown of the Waves* continued its slow course without stopping, quietly passing Port Waste by.

When Sulfurhurst finally came into view, the crew bustled across the deck, preparing for docking.

Twilight descended upon the ocean, painting the landscape in warm hues ranging from deep orange to purple.

Sulfurhurst was a peculiar coastal village, vastly different from the majestic Atlantis they had left behind the previous day. Here, there were no coral palaces or graceful buildings—just rows of dark wooden structures, blackened by salt and smoke.

Tall cranes mounted on sturdy beams slowly hoisted heavy crates from ships. Soot-covered saccarii, their faces weary, labored beneath the pale glow of lanterns. They loaded and unloaded cargo amid curses and shouts, their coarse voices blending with the barked orders of foremen.

Everywhere, work set its relentless rhythm: hammers against wood, ropes creaking... and black smoke rising steadily from chimneys. The harbor exuded sweat, the heat of furnaces, and the scent of fresh fish—creating a gritty yet intensely lively atmosphere.

The horses, eager to leave the ship, were carefully disembarked. They seemed as relieved as their riders to feel firm ground beneath their hooves once more.

Thanatos guided the group through the streets. The men and women they passed had rough skin, their features etched deeply by hard labor and the passage of time. Their coarse canvas clothing was often stained with soot, and their calloused hands spoke of countless hours spent working.

The narrow, muddy alleyways were lined with noisy taverns and open-fronted workshops, revealing forges and warehouses in full swing. The relentless clang of metal never ceased—anchors, hooks, chains corroded by salt—all were being repaired or reforged.

Zayn watched as a long line of miners returned from the hills, picks resting on their shoulders. Their faces, blackened with soot, made the tired whiteness of their eyes stand out starkly. The lanterns they carried cast shifting shadows, turning the street into a strange nocturnal procession.

They found an inn nestled between two large warehouses with dark red roofs. The building, constructed from aged timber and sturdy beams, bore a sign half-erased by the salty spray of the sea.

Pushing open the heavy door, they were greeted by a reassuring warmth. The rich scent of grilled fish and craft beer filled the room. At large wooden tables, workers laughed heartily, toasting the end of their day's toil.

"Let's rest," Thanatos ordered. "Tomorrow we set out again at dawn."

He approached the counter, exchanging a few brief words with the innkeeper—a stocky man whose sparse hair was slicked back across his scalp.

As soon as the meal was finished, Zayn headed upstairs without delay, collapsing onto a narrow but comfortable bed.

15 — Suna — The Temple of Knowledge

At dawn, the group gathered, ready to face the Kraken—and uncover the secret of the Pillar of Knowledge. A quiet tension hung over them as they set off toward Port Waste and the treacherous cliffs of the inland sea.

The road wound its way between rolling hills. A gentle breeze lifted swirls of dust, making the tall grasses dance. Seated at the front of the wagon next to Aldaren, Suna watched the horses, her mind wandering. At the head of the convoy, Vaelen and Theris led confidently, while Hestian and Korvel flanked the cart.

Driven by curiosity, Suna felt it was time to learn a bit more about them. After all, they shared both the road and its dangers.

"Where do you two come from?"

Korvel glanced at Hestian, who answered first, holding the reins loosely.

"We're from Quarth. Ever heard of it?"

Suna narrowed her eyes, searching her memories.

"Quarth... it's Nerath's city, isn't it?"

Hestian nodded, absently adjusting his gauntlet.

"Yeah, north of the plains. A fortified city—not as big as Ætherium, but lively enough. The kind of place where everyone knows everyone else... and where rumors travel fast."

"Especially when it's bad news," Korvel added.

"So, you left Quarth to become soldiers?"

"To find work, mostly," said Hestian. "Ætherium's guard was recruiting, good pay and all. It was either that or end up as a merchant or laborer. Honestly, spending my life counting copper coins? Not my thing."

Korvel snorted, amused.

"I wouldn't have minded becoming a merchant. Traveling, meeting people, selling rare items... That had its charm."

"Oh really?" Hestian intervened. "Are you saying you never dreamed of becoming a mercenary?"

Korvel hid his embarrassment behind a cough.

"It was an idea, not a dream. I just figured if I'm going to wield a sword, I might as well do it for gold."

Hestian shook his head, entertained.

"Nobility, adventure, risk-taking... clearly far behind your thirst for gold."

"But then, why didn't you stay there?" Aldaren asked curiously. "Quarth's a military city, isn't it? Ideal for a warrior."

"That's what we thought at first," Hestian shrugged. "But things didn't go as planned."

"Let's just say we had a... disagreement... with an officer," Korvel added.

"A disagreement?" Aldaren asked.

"Yeah," Korvel muttered. "One of those guys who thinks he knows everything. Thinks honor matters more than sense. We refused to follow an absurd order. He made us pay for it. After that, we had no chance of advancement."

"So," Hestian continued, "we decided to leave. Why stay somewhere you're stuck?"

"And you chose Ætherium? Why?"

"Why not? The capital's always bustling, and the Guard was recruiting. We thought, why not start fresh?"

Hestian's tone grew serious.

"And sometimes..." He paused. "Death shows us another path."

"What do you mean?" Suna asked.

"Oh, just that sometimes, one event can change everything. A battle, a loss..." He shrugged again. "You think your path is set, then suddenly, it breaks. And you have to start again, somewhere else."

Korvel sniffed mockingly.

"He's turning philosophical now."

"Just thoughtful," Hestian replied. "You should try it sometime."

Their banter remained light, but beneath their teasing was a genuine bond.

"So... how did you end up on this mission?" Suna asked.

Korvel and Hestian exchanged a quick glance. Hestian answered first.

"Mostly chance. We joined Ætherium's guard a few months ago. Patrols, rounds... nothing exciting."

"And one morning, Vaelen showed up. He needed volunteers for a special mission. We had no clue what it was, or how long it'd take—just that it involved escort and protection."

"So we raised our hands," Hestian concluded.

"Just like that?" Suna asked, intrigued.

"Why not? We weren't going to turn down a chance to get out of Ætherium. Honestly… I'd rather be moving than guarding gates."

"Besides, it was Vaelen. The Guard captain himself? It promised to be interesting."

"And now that you know what you've gotten yourselves into?" asked Suna.

Korvel laughed quietly.

"Oh, we're definitely getting a clearer idea of what's coming, that's for sure."

Hestian shrugged mischievously.

"Too late to turn back now, right?"

As the journey continued, Pharin joined the conversation, steering the discussion toward the warriors of Quarth—and their escapades in Velissia.

After half a day's journey through the lush hills of the island, the group halted at a narrow crossroads. It was here they had to part ways.

Enhugo studied the winding trail leading upward toward the cliffs.

"We'll set the trap here," Enhugo said, indicating the distant cliff. "We must be precise. At that height, the slightest mistake could ruin everything."

"How much time will you need to get it ready?" Theris asked.

"Not long," Enhugo replied. "The spot is difficult to access, but the spell itself is simple. Everything will be ready before you arrive."

Suna listened closely, anxious. Everything depended on perfect timing.

"Don't worry," Aldaren murmured gently. "Everything will go smoothly. Enhugo and Liore know what they're doing."

She smiled at him, comforted by his reassuring presence. Yet the unease nestled deep in her stomach remained unmoved.

Enhugo regarded the group, appreciating the bond they had forged beneath the shadow of their mission.

"Very well," said the mage. "Liore, it's time for us to go. Be careful, my friends."

"You too," Vaelen replied.

Enhugo gave Suna one last reassuring smile, conveying confidence and encouragement. Beside him, Liore waved discreetly before following her master toward the heights.

The others watched as they disappeared into the rocky ascent. A bird's cry broke the silence.

"Let's move," Theris said. "We still have a ways to go."

They resumed their journey toward Port Waste, guided by Theris.

As they walked, Suna allowed her mind to wander. She thought about the trials ahead… but above all, about the newfound trust she had in her companions.

Yes, she was afraid—but she was not alone. And that simple thought calmed some of the turmoil inside her.

On the docks, the air was thick with sea spray and the pungent smell of freshly caught fish. The harbor bustled with relentless noise: ropes creaked, and merchants called out hoarsely, praising their catches. In the distance, masts rose like a forest, their furled sails snapping in the gusts of wind.

The group struggled through the crowd, eventually making their way to the packed wharves. Theris, walking confidently, stopped before a group of sailors unloading their cargo. They were sturdy men, their skin weathered by salt and sun.

"We need a full net of fresh fish," he announced calmly, "and a large barrel to carry them."

The sailors paused momentarily in their work. One of them, a burly man with hair tied by a rough cord, stepped forward, eyeing Theris carefully.

"It can be done," he grunted, scratching his beard. "But it'll cost you plenty, stranger. Fish ain't free—especially not in those quantities."

Theris nodded and discreetly revealed a hefty purse. The sailors exchanged knowing looks.

A few gritty jokes, a couple of brief exchanges… and the deal was struck, though Theris couldn't hide a slight grimace at the agreed price. Still, what mattered was that they had what they needed.

But when Theris brought up their final request, the atmosphere shifted dramatically.

"We also need a ship. To reach the solitary mountain, out there in the middle of the sea," he said, gesturing vaguely in that direction.

Silence fell. The smiles vanished, replaced by tense, almost hostile expressions. Several men even took a step backward.

An old sailor with weathered skin, perched on a barrel, froze mid-motion. He slowly rose, a charred pipe clamped between his teeth.

"You won't find anyone here willing to take you there," he murmured hoarsely, exhaling a slow puff of smoke. "No man in his right mind would risk his ship, let alone his life. That's where the Kraken dwells. Those who venture there never return."

His tone allowed neither doubt nor debate. Several sailors nodded grimly in agreement. Judging by their faces, one might think the group insane for even suggesting such a voyage.

Vaelen stepped forward, his wings spreading slightly behind him. Silence instantly fell again. His voice carried a calm but undeniable authority.

"We know the risks. We ask nothing more than a ship to get close. The rest is our concern."

His gaze swept the crowd, hard and piercing.

Beside him, Theris opened his purse wider. The gold inside could sustain a family for a long time. Several sailors hesitated, clearly tempted by this rare opportunity.

But even gold wasn't heavy enough to outweigh their fear of the Kraken.

No one moved. Some withdrew even further, distancing themselves from the group.

"So be it…" Vaelen murmured, unable to entirely conceal his disappointment.

A heavy silence settled once more, broken only by the creaking of hulls rubbing against the docks.

Just as they were about to give up, a voice stopped them:

"You speak of this Kraken as if it were just some oversized catfish."

Surprised, Theris and Vaelen turned simultaneously.

A man leaning against a post watched them. He was broader than the others, his face partially concealed under a wide-brimmed leather hat, weathered by the sun.

In the shadows behind him lay a ship with black sails, adorned with a white feather rippling gently in the breeze. At its prow, the carved figure of an octopus wrapped its tentacles around the hull in a frozen gesture.

The man stood upright, unfolded his arms, and approached with heavy steps. He scanned each member of the group as if assessing their worth and courage.

"I can take you there," he said, stopping a few paces from Theris. "I can tell you're itching to tackle the big squid."

"Very well, captain," Theris replied. "What do you want in return?"

A crooked smile spread across his lips, revealing worn teeth.

"Let's just say I like a challenge. These waters have haunted me far too long. I've dreamed for years of treasures hidden beneath the waves, but no sailor in his right mind would venture there without proper escort. Perhaps with warriors like yourselves aboard, things might finally change..."

His gaze slid to the open purse in Theris's hands.

"That," he added, "along with that very fine purse you seem eager to offer, of course."

The message was clear.

Theris exchanged a brief glance with Vaelen. The man was seizing an opportunity, but they had nothing better.

"Of course," Theris answered.

He extended his hand, which the sailor grasped with his large, calloused palm.

The deal was sealed.

"You've made the right choice," declared the captain, releasing Theris's hand. "I'm Captain Arlan, and that's my ship: the *Black Ink*. You won't find a better crew to face the Kraken."

"You've faced a Kraken before?" asked Suna, her eyes fixed on the ship's prow.

"Not directly, young lady. But close enough never to forget. Few ships can say the same—and live to tell the tale."

Vaelen looked surprised.

"And yet you're willing to go back?"

Captain Arlan rubbed his hands together eagerly.

"Nothing motivates a sailor more than the promise of treasure. And besides… it's about time this beast stopped ruling our seas."

The captain turned to his crew—solid men awaiting his command.

"Ready the *Black Ink*!" he shouted firmly. "We have guests aboard—and a monster to challenge!"

An approving cheer rose from the deck. The sailors sprang into action, raising sails, checking ropes and blades with practiced efficiency.

"We sail immediately," Arlan announced, gesturing them aboard.

The ship swayed beneath their feet, impatient to set off across the sea. The captain grasped the helm, and the *Black Ink* eased away from the docks, gliding toward the dark waters and the secrets hidden below.

Suna felt her heart quicken. Everything was falling into place. And strangely, she found herself trusting this rugged captain.

The group set course toward the north. Soon, the island appeared, rising majestically from the waves. Its sheer cliffs stood sharply against the deep blue of the sea.

Following Theris's instructions, the ship cautiously ventured along the western cliffside. The captain had ordered them to keep their distance. From atop the precipice, Enhugo activated a smoke signal. Colored swirls rose into the sky: the spell was ready.

"The signal is given!" Theris announced gravely.

The ship maneuvered toward the half-submerged promontory, grazing the cliff's base. It took position beneath the rock face. Meanwhile, Aldaren leaned over the net filled with fish placed nearby. He reinforced the mesh with a protective enchantment, preparing the trap to withstand the assault.

"May the light guide us," he murmured.

Pharin, seated nearby, commented with irony, "Let's especially hope the light guides that monster far away from us…"

A few nervous sighs echoed his remark.

Suna moved closer to Vaelen, seeking reassurance. She crossed her arms tightly, anxious despite her outward composure.

"Everything will be fine," Vaelen told her gently. "We have a good plan."

In the distance, beneath the surface, a shadow passed by. No one saw it. Not yet.

Hestian and Korvel cautiously approached the edge, gripping tightly the net heavy with fish. They tipped the bait overboard, and it hit the water with a slick, wet noise. Some of the fish were still wriggling.

Carefully, they dragged the net onto the rocky platform barely visible above the surface. Their boots slid on the slick stone, but they kept their balance, carefully advancing toward the spot Enhugo had indicated.

Once they reached the location, Hestian quickly unfolded the ropes. Korvel knelt down, methodically tying the net to heavy stones to ensure it remained firmly in place. He double-checked every knot, pulling hard on the cords. They had to hold.

Satisfied, they returned to the deck. Their expressions betrayed the tension of the moment. As they climbed back aboard, Pharin, leaning casually against the mast, said in a relaxed tone:

"Well, I don't know about you, but I smell victory—or maybe fish, who knows?"

Out of breath, Korvel shot Pharin a furious glare as he passed by. Now was not the time. Pharin raised his hands in mock innocence, delighted by their reactions.

"Oh, don't give me that look, Korvel. A bit of humor never hurt anyone!"

The warrior simply sighed in reply.

Turning toward Arlan, he watched as the captain immediately took control, expertly repositioning the ship with the precision of a craftsman. He guided the helm with a sure hand, slipping the vessel into a safer area, hidden within the shadow of the cliffs. From this concealment, they could observe unseen.

Meanwhile, Theris lifted the empty barrel—the decoy designed for the Kraken. He attached it securely to a thick rope, checked the knot, and handed the other end to Vaelen. The angel grasped it firmly, his wings already trembling with anticipation.

"Make sure everything's ready," Vaelen murmured.

He raised his eyes toward the cliffs, searching for Enhugo and Liore. High above, the spell awaited only their signal to unleash its power.

Theris nodded in Vaelen's direction. Suna moved closer to Aldaren.

"Do you think it'll work?" she whispered, her voice sounding more fragile than usual.

The older man remained silent for a moment, then gave a reassuring nod.

"We've done everything we could. Now we wait...and remain vigilant."

Pharin, unusually quiet for once, clenched his fists tightly, staring out at the sea.

With a powerful beat of his wings, Vaelen rose, the barrel swinging behind him at the end of the rope. The barrel skipped across the water, spraying silver droplets with each impact.

From the deck, Suna held her breath, fingers clenched tightly on the railing. Silence had fallen over the bay, broken only by the gentle lapping of waves against the hull. Even the wind seemed to have fallen still.

All eyes were fixed on Vaelen. His winged figure skimmed just above the surface of the water. The echoes of the bouncing barrel drifted among the cliffs, like a call.

Calm still reigned—but it was the calm that precedes storms.

Then something moved. A shadow. Fleeting, immense, rippling beneath the surface, just below Vaelen.

Suna narrowed her eyes.

"There..." breathed Theris, frozen.

A sailor cursed softly.

No one dared move.

Ripples appeared on the water's surface, subtle at first, almost gentle, as if an enormous fish were brushing it lightly with its back. They drew nearer, slowly converging on the barrel.

A deep rumbling, rising from the depths, made the deck vibrate beneath their feet.

The silence turned into raw tension.

Then everything erupted.

The sea exploded with deafening violence. A fountain of foam shot skyward, driven by an inhuman force, and from the heart of that eruption emerged the unspeakable.

Massive tentacles burst forth, streaming seawater, covered with suckers the size of shields. One of them slammed against the surface in a thunderous crack.

Suna took a step back, her heart hammering wildly.

The Kraken was here. It had answered the call.

Vaelen's face hardened. He pivoted sharply, beating his wings faster, struggling against the weight of the barrel as he headed for the trap. Every muscle was stretched to its limit, teeth clenched in exertion. He knew that the slightest delay would be fatal.

The Kraken's body surged upward, a dark mass tearing through the spray of foam. It charged at the decoy, its enormous tentacles thrashing the sea into towering waves.

"Faster, Vaelen!" Theris growled.

With every beat of his wings, the massive creature closed the distance to the bait.

"It's gaining on him!" Suna shouted, eyes fixed on the monstrous silhouette bearing down on Vaelen.

The angel doubled his efforts, wings slicing furiously through the air, wind roaring past his ears. He couldn't see the beast—but he could feel it, mere wingbeats away. A tentacle shot from the waves, skimming just past the barrel, barely missing its target.

"He needs to drop the rope!" Hestian shouted.

"Not yet!" Theris countered. "He needs to get closer to the cliff or it's all over!"

A colossal tentacle erupted from the dark waters and slammed down with cataclysmic force, sending an explosion of foam into the sky.

Vaelen veered sharply, wings churning desperately. But the rope was slowing him down. Behind him, the barrel skipped wildly over the water, like wounded prey enticing the creature's hunger.

The Kraken lashed out with terrifying precision, its massive limbs like giant whips. Vaelen twisted through the air, dodging each strike in a tense aerial ballet. With each daring maneuver, he swung the barrel just out of reach, the Kraken's arms repeatedly crashing into the sea, whipping it into a storm of foam.

Suddenly, an enormous shadow erupted from below with blinding speed. This time, the tentacle struck directly at Vaelen—no more diversions. The attack shot toward him, lightning-fast. Vaelen twisted away at the last possible second, feeling the monstrous limb graze his calf. Suna let out a muffled cry, clasping her hands over her mouth.

"It changed targets," Aldaren murmured.

"It's smarter than we thought," Theris replied, eyes wide with mingled fear and awe.

Vaelen surged forward, eyes locked on the cliffs ahead. Tentacles brushed past his wings, his legs. Yet he persevered, dodging at the very last moment. On deck, no one spoke, their eyes fixed, fascinated yet terrified.

But Vaelen couldn't keep up this pace. He veered left sharply. Too late. A tentacle curled around the barrel, squeezing with devastating strength.

Wood splintered violently, shards exploding into the air. The rope yanked the angel downward, dragging him toward the waves.

Her heart clutched by terror, Suna screamed as Vaelen plunged toward the dark water:

"Vaelen!"

Yet Aldaren had already stretched out his arms toward the angel.

A sphere of pure energy enveloped Vaelen just before he hit the surface. The bubble, a cocoon of radiant light, cushioned the waves and kept him afloat.

It pulsed brightly as a tentacle crashed down onto it—a dull, reverberating blow. The monstrous appendage slid harmlessly off the smooth, glowing surface, unable to grasp it.

Suna let out a breath of relief. But another blow came, then another, each smashing into the bubble, pushing it underwater before it surged back to the surface like a balloon under intense pressure. With every impact, the light dimmed. The shield trembled.

"He won't last long!" Korvel shouted, fists clenched.

"Vaelen, get out of there!" Theris cried.

Blows rang through the sphere, each strike rattling Vaelen, disorienting him. He clenched his teeth, waiting for the right moment.

As the Kraken struck again, Vaelen timed it so that when the magic bubble bounced upward, reaching its highest point above the waves, he thrust his wings with all his strength, launching himself clear of its protection.

He soared into the turmoil once more.

Behind him, the Kraken flailed at empty air, unable to seize its prey. Vaelen wove frantically between tentacles, each escape narrower than the last. He flew breathlessly, muscles burning, eyes locked on the cliffs.

"Come on, Vaelen, you can make it!" Suna shouted.

Vaelen landed heavily on the rocky platform, gasping, heart hammering wildly in his chest. He was now safely out of the monster's reach.

But the Kraken, enraged, had no intention of letting its prey escape.

The beast erupted from the waves, its tentacles gripping the rock with terrifying strength. The sight was awe-inspiring: each tentacle, thick as a tree trunk and streaked with dark veins, bore deep scars from ancient battles. Its eyes, black as the abyss, locked onto Vaelen. They glittered with equal parts intelligence and cruelty.

Suna felt a shiver crawl up her spine. She couldn't tear her gaze away from the abomination rising before them. The sinuous movements of its tentacles held an almost hypnotic quality.

"Vaelen, move!" she shouted.

But on the platform, Vaelen was calm. He had caught his breath. He was ready.

He crouched low, fluid as a predator, his majestic wings spread wide above him. His gaze met the Kraken's directly, unflinching in challenge. Around them, the world seemed to freeze.

And just as the Kraken lunged toward him, Vaelen leapt.

He launched himself from the ground in an explosion of pure strength. The jump was astounding, powerful, defying gravity with unsettling ease. He rocketed skyward, evading the deadly tentacles snapping at his heels.

When he reached the height of the cliffs, he spread his golden wings triumphantly. The sun burst forth behind him, bathing the angel in brilliant radiance. His feathers shimmered with reflections of gold, amber, and fire. Vaelen cast one final look down at the monster far below.

On the ship, sailors and companions stood motionless, dazzled by the sight. Nobody moved. A few mouths hung open.

"Wow, impressive," Pharin murmured. "I'm definitely turning that into a song."

From deep within the Kraken rose a roar of pure fury, vibrating with frustration. The dreadful sound echoed across the bay, ricocheting off the cliffs, sending chills through the bones of the crew.

Then, as if guided by its own intelligence, one massive tentacle slithered toward the net. With precision, it coiled around a fish protruding from the opening, lifted it… and casually tossed it into its gaping maw lined with razor-sharp teeth.

With a sickening snap, the Kraken's jaws slammed shut upon its prey. Slowly, ominously, the creature turned away from Vaelen.

Unleashing its wrath upon the net, the Kraken's tentacles smashed down with brutal force. Yet, against all odds, the magical mesh reinforced by Aldaren withstood the initial assault.

Far from giving up, the beast adapted. Methodically, its tentacles wormed through the gaps, each movement displaying terrifying patience and cunning.

Then, with devastating strength, the Kraken wrenched upward. The net burst apart, scattering fish in every direction. A chaotic ballet unfolded, tentacles darting like serpents to snatch up the fleeing prey.

It was a chilling sight. Each tentacle moved independently, meticulously retrieving fish and feeding them into the creature's monstrous mouth.

On deck, all watched breathlessly, equally fascinated and horrified.

"It's smarter than we expected," Theris murmured. "Far more dangerous, too."

From high above, Enhugo and Liore stood frozen, unable to tear their eyes away. The chaos below—the Kraken's raw power, its movements both graceful and savage—held them hypnotized.

A cry from above snapped them out of their trance:

"The trap! Trigger it now!" Vaelen shouted.

Enhugo and Liore blinked, urgency seizing them once more. Sharing a swift glance, they turned back toward the engraved runes awaiting activation.

"Ready?" Enhugo asked his apprentice.

Liore inhaled deeply, steadying herself.

"Yes, Master."

They closed their eyes, placing their hands upon the glowing symbols. The runes flared brightly, shifting from pale blue to fiery red, pulsing in rhythm with their magic. The air around them hummed, charged with tangible power.

A low rumble echoed from within the stone. Light surged from cracks along the cliff edge.

Liore and Enhugo opened their eyes simultaneously.

With a thunderous explosion, a massive section of cliff broke away. Colossal boulders plummeted directly onto the Kraken below. Too consumed by its prey, it never saw the threat approaching. The stones crashed mercilessly into it, unleashing a storm of foam and dust that engulfed the area.

A stunned silence followed the violent impact.

Breathless, Enhugo and Liore moved carefully to the edge.

On the ship, all eyes were fixed on the enormous rocks. Slowly, the tentacles ceased their thrashing, dropping lifelessly beneath the rubble. On deck, the companions erupted in celebration. Pharin jumped about like an exuberant child.

"We did it!" Korvel shouted, fist raised triumphantly.

Vaelen descended gracefully, wings spread wide, landing beside Enhugo and Liore.

"Coming?" he asked. "The temple awaits."

"No, Vaelen," Enhugo replied gently. "I'm not made for this kind of action anymore. I could have put everyone in danger. I'll return to Balindra. My place is among books, not on a battlefield."

Liore nodded, moved by the old man's humility.

Vaelen stepped close, embracing her briefly before extending his wings. Liore's heart raced as they rose together into the air. The cool wind brushed her face. Glancing down one last time, she caught Enhugo's gaze. He was smiling warmly. And she knew, in that moment, that he was proud.

A few moments later, Vaelen gently landed with Liore on the ship's deck. The others welcomed them with relieved smiles. Pharin, ever theatrical, bowed like a court troubadour.

"What a flight! Such a lovely couple," he announced, punctuating his words with a playful wink.

Liore felt her cheeks flush, and quickly hid her smile.

On the cliff above, Enhugo observed the scene silently. He raised a hand in farewell, then turned toward Balindra, disappearing slowly behind the rocks. The group stood together, eyes now turned toward their future.

"Korvel, be careful!" Aldaren shouted as the soldier excitedly leaped onto the rocks.

Caught up in the thrill of victory, Korvel was already posing triumphantly atop an inert tentacle.

Suna, amused, stepped closer to Theris.

"That was a close call," she whispered. "I hope the other Pillars won't be as difficult to reach."

"Each trial will bring its own challenges," Theris replied gently. "But today we've proven we can overcome them—together."

Suna smiled. The words were simple, yet comforting.

Gradually, calm settled over the deck again. Hestian climbed down to join Korvel, who was already examining the enormous tentacle protruding from beneath the fallen rocks.

But the victory was short-lived.

A massive block of stone shifted with an ominous crack, revealing the Kraken's head. Amid the rubble, the monster's eye snapped open. Its gaze, black as obsidian, locked onto Korvel, and its pupil narrowed sharply.

"It's still alive!" Theris shouted.

No sooner had he spoken than the tentacles stirred again, rocks sliding off the creature's slick body. Freed, the beast rose to its full height, towering over the two soldiers.

Hestian and Korvel scrambled back toward the ship, but the Kraken was faster. It slammed a tentacle onto the rocky platform. Korvel rolled aside, narrowly escaping a deadly blow, the stone vibrating under the impact. Hestian threw himself flat as another tentacle sliced through the air, pulverizing the ground where he'd stood moments before.

"Get back here, quickly!" Theris cried.

The Kraken pursued them relentlessly, its tentacles striking in a macabre dance.

Vaelen launched himself skyward with a powerful beat of his wings, his blade flaring with light. He sliced through the first tentacle within reach. The sudden pain immediately drew the Kraken's attention.

Roaring, the monster focused on this new threat, lashing several tentacles toward the angel. Vaelen weaved through them, evading blow after blow, each wingbeat lifting him higher, drawing the beast's attention upward.

Theris drew his daggers and leaped onto the platform, carefully observing the monster's movements, searching desperately for a weak point.

"We need to immobilize it!" he shouted. "If it reaches the sea, it's over!"

Vaelen nodded sharply.

Korvel and Hestian stood side by side, ready to face the monster again.

Frustrated by its inability to catch Vaelen, the Kraken turned back to the platform. Its tentacles hammered the rock with renewed fury, shattering stone around them.

Korvel ducked beneath a tentacle, swift and precise. He plunged his sword deep into the creature's flesh. A deafening cry shook the air. The tentacle jerked back sharply, knocking Korvel to the ground. Another arm lunged toward him.

Aldaren intervened instantly. A golden dome burst forth, enveloping Korvel. The barrier deflected the Kraken's massive limb, sending it recoiling violently.

"I can't hold it for long!" Aldaren shouted, his face twisted with effort. "Find a solution—fast!"

"We need a weakness!" Theris shouted back. "A vulnerable spot—anything we can exploit!"

Liore stared at the scene, brow furrowed, her mind racing. She mentally sifted through everything she knew about such creatures. There had to be a weakness.

"It's not immortal," she said suddenly. "It has to have a vulnerable spot!"

"Then find it quickly!" Theris shouted back, barely dodging a thrashing tentacle.

Liore briefly closed her eyes. An image flashed clearly in her mind.

"Its eyes!" she called out urgently. "Their skin is tough, but their eyes are always fragile. If we could just strike its eye…"

"Give me some time!" she yelled. "Distract it while I prepare… something."

She shot a pointed glance toward Pharin.

"You're not seriously thinking of using me as bait, are you?" the satyr protested.

Despite the situation, Liore managed a faint smile.

"No, Pharin—but feel free to volunteer if you're eager to help!"

The satyr muttered something incomprehensible.

Without hesitation, everyone jumped back into action.

Theris leaped around wildly, daggers slashing at the slimy tentacles. Beside him, Hestian and Korvel hacked relentlessly at the monster's flesh, their blades biting deep yet barely slowing its relentless attacks. But against such colossal power, their efforts seemed almost futile.

"This isn't working!" Korvel yelled, leaping aside just in time to avoid being crushed. "It barely feels our attacks!"

"It's too fast!" shouted Hestian. "We'll never reach its body without getting crushed!"

The trio retreated steadily, while the Kraken pressed its advantage, striking harder with every blow.

Aldaren summoned another protective shield just in time, intercepting a vicious strike from the monster. The old man strengthened the barrier despite clear exhaustion etched across his face.

Above, Vaelen soared and dove like a hawk, constantly harassing the Kraken from the air. His evasive maneuvers were as spectacular as they were dangerous. He drew the creature's attention, but each move had to be flawless—or it would cost him dearly.

On deck, Liore knelt near a suspended fishing net. She ripped off one of the metal weights.

She placed it on the planks, drew her knife, and swiftly carved runes onto its surface, jaw clenched in concentration. She pressed her hands against it and closed her eyes. The metal vibrated softly, glowing faintly blue beneath her fingertips.

The object flared brightly with intense blue light. She sprang upright.

"Pharin! Catch!" she shouted, tossing the object toward him.

Pharin jumped, barely catching it, and stared down in confusion.

"Uh... What exactly am I supposed to do with this? Is this really our secret weapon?"

"Use your sling!" Suna understood immediately.

"And aim straight for its mouth!" Liore finished.

Pharin approached the railing. The Kraken battered Aldaren's barrier relentlessly, each blow cracking its glowing surface.

"Vaelen!" Suna shouted. "Make it raise its head!"

Vaelen understood immediately. He raised his sword skyward, flooding it with magic until it shone like a second sun.

The monster froze, its tentacles motionless. Its black eyes rose to the blazing light.

Theris hurled both daggers straight into the Kraken's eye. They whistled through the air and buried themselves deep in its pupil.

The Kraken unleashed a deafening roar of pain. The scream shook the air and water, causing small rocks to crumble from nearby cliffs. Hestian and Korvel stumbled backward, stunned.

Pharin drew a deep breath... and spun his sling swiftly.

"Come on, little guy... don't fail me now," he muttered, targeting the monster's gaping mouth.

The enchanted metal weight whistled through the air, narrowly missing the Kraken's flailing tentacles, slipping straight into its open mouth.

Time slowed, seeming almost to halt as the glowing object disappeared down the creature's throat, illuminating its gaping maw briefly from within. The guardian snapped its jaws shut, swallowing the object whole.

A tense silence fell. The waters barely stirred. Suna glanced at Liore, who murmured incomprehensible words, eyes ablaze with intense concentration.

Ignoring the fighters, the Kraken lunged straight for the ship. Just as it opened its mouth wide, ready to strike, Liore suddenly thrust her hands forward, unleashing the stored lightning energy. A brilliant blue light exploded from the Kraken's maw, washing over the crew and sails with otherworldly radiance.

The Kraken froze, its enormous body wracked with violent spasms. Electric arcs coursed across its tentacles.

Then, with an earth-shattering crash, the creature collapsed into the sea, triggering a huge wave that rocked the ship violently.

On deck, a stunned silence reigned. Everyone held their breath, watching the turbulent waters intently.

Slowly, the Kraken's tentacles sank, trailing limply behind its massive body, vanishing beneath the waves.

Only then did the unbearable tension break. A victorious cheer erupted into the air. Liore, exhausted, staggered, leaning heavily against the railing, breathing hard. A weary but triumphant smile stretched across her pale lips.

"Aquatic creatures," she whispered breathlessly, "never did like lightning."

Suna stood frozen, staring at the dark waters where the monster had disappeared. She could hardly believe they'd actually done it.

The ship moved away from the dark waters where the Kraken had disappeared, leaving behind a now silent sea. Ahead, the sun cast golden reflections upon the solitary mountain. Leaning on the railing, Suna watched the rocky peak rising imposingly from the ocean.

"A mountain in the middle of nowhere," she murmured. "As if guarding a secret."

Theris, standing beside her, simply nodded.

Vaelen took flight. All eyes followed the angel as he vanished behind the massive rock formation.

He soon reappeared, gently landing back on deck.

"The cliffs hide an inlet large enough to dock," he announced. "I noticed a cave set back from the shore. That's probably the place."

The ship followed Vaelen, skirting the rugged coastline until reaching the secret cove. Amidst the shadows of the cliffs, a discreet opening was barely visible from the sea. They moored the ship and disembarked. The air was fresh, carrying the scent of salt and damp stone.

The cave stretched before them, dark and cold, like the mouth of a sleeping beast. Its walls, naturally carved by water and time, felt rough beneath their fingers. Their footsteps echoed softly, each sound amplified by the oppressive silence.

Suna felt her heart beating faster. Their goal had never felt so close. Yet their hope quickly faded: the cave ended abruptly in a wall of rock. No door. No crack. A dead end.

"It's impossible," Theris murmured, leaning against the cavern's far wall, hand resting on his dagger.

They examined every surface, scrutinizing each crevice. Liore concentrated, running her hands along the stone, murmuring barely audible incantations.

"No illusions," she concluded. "It's just a wall."

"I'll fly around again," Vaelen announced, ascending with a flutter of feathers.

"Sure, go ahead," Pharin called after him, voice dripping with sarcasm. "Maybe there's a secret-entry button on the roof. If you meet some wise old man up there, don't forget to ask for a map."

Suna smiled despite herself.

"We faced the Kraken," Liore reminded them. "Everything suggests we're in the right place."

She crossed her arms, deep in thought.

Pharin raised his arms theatrically, ever the showman.

"I swear on my life that I act for the good of Ætheris and Mytherra," he declared dramatically.

Nothing happened.

"Well, at least I tried," he said, turning away with exaggerated indifference.

Liore's eyes suddenly widened with realization.

"The two incompatible halves!" she exclaimed. "'The temple doors only appear when the two incompatible halves are reunited.'"

"We focused too much on the Kraken," Aldaren admitted. "We overlooked the rest."

"'Two incompatible halves,'" Theris repeated thoughtfully. "Is it a riddle or an instruction?"

"We know each temple is linked to two magicians," Liore continued. "Perhaps we need an element from each of them to activate it."

"You think we have to use paper and fire again?" asked Suna.

"It's worth trying," Theris agreed. "Anyone have something suitable?"

Liore pulled out her personal notebook.

"Do you think a blank page will suffice?" the scholar asked hopefully.

"I doubt it," Aldaren replied. "It's knowledge, not the medium, that counts."

Reluctantly, she tore a page from the book and handed it to the disciple of Shanur. Aldaren delicately took the torn sheet.

Light emanated from his hand, condensing into a thin, brilliant beam. The paper instantly ignited upon contact, a gentle flame illuminating the cave. Korvel gave an impressed whistle.

Without a sound, a crack appeared at the cave's end. The walls parted, revealing an opening wide enough for two people.

Vaelen returned at that exact moment.

"Nothing," he began as he landed. "I couldn't—"

He halted, spotting the group gathered, laughing before the now-open doors.

"While you were out frolicking, we were busy working!" Pharin teased. "Birdbrain, remember those incompatible halves? We burned a page, and poof, the wall opened."

Vaelen, exasperated, rolled his eyes—but the laughter of the others eventually drew a smile from him. He even playfully stuck his tongue out at the satyr, prompting an astonished exclamation from Suna. The mood had relaxed, and, for a rare moment, even Ætheris's Captain of the Guard appeared at ease. Pharin delighted in this and beckoned him to rejoin the group.

The new passage led them into a chamber of titanic proportions.

An orange glow bathed the place in an almost supernatural brilliance. At the center, a broad river of lava flowed slowly, an incandescent serpent crossing the cave, emitting a deep, continuous rumble.

The heat was overwhelming. Immediately, Suna felt beads of sweat forming on her forehead and trickling down the back of her neck. The scorching, sulfur-filled air bit her lungs with every breath.

All around them, the atmosphere shimmered, distorting the underground landscape. The steady murmur of the lava, strangely calming, contrasted sharply with the burning threat it represented.

Two identical bridges stretched over the molten river, leading toward deep darkness engulfing the far shore. At the entrance to each bridge, a colossal creature waited silently, coiled like serpents.

They were dragons. But nothing like Suna had imagined. These delicate creatures seemed sculpted from finely folded paper, their elegant, sinuous bodies reminiscent of Eastern dragons from human legends. Complex folds covered their surfaces, over which flames danced without ever consuming them. They were perfectly identical.

Suna's jaw dropped slightly at this surreal sight.

"Origami dragons…" she murmured, eyes wide.

Then she added under her breath, almost to herself:

"…on fire. Of course."

The dragons turned their heads, incandescent eyes locking onto them.

There was no doubt: they were alive. And they guarded this place.

The group advanced, each step becoming increasingly difficult in the oppressive heat. As they approached, the two dragons rose slowly, their entire attention fixed upon them. Burning eyes pierced the intruders, scrutinizing their every movement.

A silence filled the cavern, broken only by the dull murmur of flowing lava below. The two creatures emitted an intimidating aura, as suffocating as the heat surrounding them. Their sinuous bodies undulated gently, casting dancing patterns of shadow and light on the rocky walls.

Instinctively, Suna slowed down, feeling her heart quicken under the intensity of those gazes. The group drew closer together, unconsciously seeking collective protection against a presence that seemed to penetrate the very depths of their souls.

The dragon on the left extended its head toward them, the folds of its neck unfurling fluidly. Its delicate jaws, bristling with barbed-paper edges, opened slightly. When it spoke, its deep, powerful voice filled the space, resonating within their chests.

"Two paths appear beneath your tread.

One bears your weight, one falls instead."

The other dragon bowed in turn, speaking in a voice perfectly identical.

"To find the way your steps should take,

One question only may you make.

The first dragon continued, unperturbed.

"Beware, young mortals, one alone.

One question asked, your path is shown."

Finally, the second concluded, rising to its full height.

"Weigh your next words with utmost care.

This choice will shape the fate you bear."

Silence fell again, broken only by the rumbling of the lava. Then their mouths stretched into mocking smiles, and they spoke again.

"Ask your question," said the dragon on the right. "But remember: I always tell the truth."

"Do not listen to him," replied the dragon on the left. "I speak only truth. He always lies."

Theris clenched his jaw, eyes darting back and forth between the two guardians.

"What a liar," murmured one of the dragons.

"It matters not," said the other. "Make a mistake, and you'll plunge into the lava."

Their voices joined together, relentless:

"But if you cheat, fear our wrath."

They straightened silently, awaiting the fateful question.

The heat radiating from the lava river made the air thick, almost unbreathable. The group stood motionless, frozen in place, paralyzed by what was at stake.

Pharin stepped forward, a mischievous curl to his lips.

"Why not just ask them which bridge to take?" he said as though the answer was obvious.

The dragons turned simultaneously, eyes fixed upon Pharin as if urging him on.

"Absolutely not!" Liore interrupted. "It doesn't work like that."

"They'd give two answers. It's useless," Theris said. "These creatures thrive on ambiguity. Every word counts."

"So we must find the liar first?" ventured Hestian.

"No," said Aldaren. "One question only. That's all we have."

Liore knelt, short of breath, looking from the dragons to the two bridges. Everything was perfectly symmetrical.

"The key is logic," she murmured. "A single question can reveal the truth... provided it's properly phrased. How can we formulate it to circumvent both lies and truths?"

Her fingers absentmindedly brushed the dusty ground as she thought.

Beside her, Suna briefly closed her eyes. Then she fixed the dragons with a determined stare.

"There must be a way to ask," she said softly. "A formulation that traps them both, regardless of which one lies."

The air trembled around them, saturated with heat. Breathing became an effort: each inhalation scorched their lungs. Sweat streamed down their temples, stinging their eyes, clouding minds already strained by pressure.

The rumbling lava ceased to be a sound; it was a pulse, a dull throbbing at the back of their skulls, suffocating any thought. Cool air had vanished. No retreat possible now. Nothing but acidic heat, sulfuric breath pressing against their throats.

Suna struggled to think, but ideas slipped away, elusive, swallowed by the heat. Even the ground vibrated beneath their feet, as if it could collapse at any moment.

She took a deep breath, trying to impose order on her inner chaos. Her heart hammered in her ears, nearly as loud as the lava itself. Suddenly, she raised her head. Her expression had shifted. She stepped forward decisively.

"If I asked the other dragon which bridge he would advise me to take, what would he say?" she asked the dragon on the right.

Everyone froze. The question had been asked. There was no turning back now.

Silence stretched out. The dragon narrowed its eyes, as though savoring the wording. Then he spoke—a deep, rumbling voice.

"He would tell you to choose this bridge," he said, indicating the one he guarded.

Suna turned back to her companions. Confusion marked their faces. She took a deep breath and began explaining.

"All right, listen closely. I asked the dragon on the right what the other one would answer. Whether he lies or tells the truth, he inevitably points to the wrong bridge."

"Yes, of course!" Liore exclaimed.

"Wait… what?" said Theris.

Liore crouched down and picked up a stone. With it, she drew a circle, then a cross—the two dragons.

"Imagine I'm questioning the lying dragon," she began, placing the stone on the cross.

"He knows the other one—the truthful dragon—would have indicated the safe bridge," she explained, tracing an arrow passing through the circle. "But since he lies, he reverses that answer. Result: he points to the dangerous bridge." She stopped her arrow, marking a bridge and crossing it out.

She paused briefly, letting everyone catch up, then continued.

"Now, let's try again, questioning the truthful dragon." She repositioned the stone on the circle. "He knows the other—the lying dragon—would point to the wrong bridge," she said, tracing another arrow from the circle toward the cross. "So, faithfully repeating that answer, he also indicates the wrong bridge." She stopped her arrow on the same crossed-out bridge.

"So, either way, the bridge indicated is always the dangerous one," Liore summarized.

"You mean they've given themselves away?" Pharin chuckled, scratching his head.

"Exactly. Without realizing it, they both provided the wrong answer and betrayed themselves."

Suna stood, radiant, and stepped confidently toward the dragons.

"The correct bridge is the one you didn't indicate. We take the left one."

The dragons watched them silently for a moment, their glowing eyes vibrating with barely concealed frustration. The dragon on the right straightened, and a deep growl escaped from its throat, shaking the surrounding stone. It opened its jaws and spewed a blast of fire toward the ceiling. The cavern ignited in a burst of red—a silent cry, burning with wounded pride.

One by one, the two guardians withdrew without another word, their sleek, scaled forms sliding into the lava, leaving the path across the bridge open.

In the distance, two lines of braziers ignited, tracing a luminous path toward a pedestal emerging from the shadows.

Suna took a step forward, paused, and turned toward her companions. Her smile said everything: confidence mixed with restrained impatience.

"Let's go," she said firmly.

They crossed the left bridge in silence. Beneath their feet, the heated stone vibrated, a stark reminder of the fragility of this path above the molten river.

The magma's breath rose around them, enveloping them in suffocating heat. Suna squinted and lifted a hand before her face, trying to dispel the fumes rising from below.

Behind them, the dragons watched intently. The rumbling lava intensified, echoing their barely contained fury.

"Whew," Pharin exhaled as soon as they reached the other side. "I trust you, Suna, but for a second, I really thought we were goners."

Liore laughed openly, one hand still pressed to her chest.

"You see?" she said. "There's always a solution. Even for the toughest riddles."

Suna stepped carefully forward. The pedestal grew larger, emerging from the gloom. The air turned cooler but felt heavy, saturated by some invisible force.

Behind her, the others followed, their expressions tense.

The pedestal, carved from black stone veined with silver, commanded respect. Its polished surface absorbed the light, making the engraved runes shimmer faintly.

Suna held her breath. The Pillar hovered there, suspended above the pedestal.

The Pillar of Knowledge.

She stood frozen, mesmerized.

The necklace, crafted from pure gold, was of exquisite delicacy. A gem pulsed at its center, glowing red like the heart of a volcano. Scarlet reflections danced across Suna's face. Around the gemstone, the two temple guardians curled in a spiral. Their bodies, covered in tiny runes, seemed to breathe in harmony with the gem, each engraved mark glowing in sync with its pulse.

She reached out. A gentle warmth already brushed her skin.

"So this is it…" she murmured. "It's… beautiful."

A soft, playful melody rose lightly into the air, dreamlike, accompanying the scene.

"Pharin…" Liore groaned. "Not now."

"Did you really think this was the right time?" Theris said irritably.

"Seriously?" sighed Vaelen.

Suna half-turned.

"Save it for later. Promise."

Pharin raised his hands in surrender, stowing the flute behind his back.

"Honestly, it's not easy being an artist around here…"

Suna turned back, taking a deep breath, fully aware of the significance of this moment. Her fingers brushed the warm metal, a comforting heat spreading through her. Carefully, she closed her hand around the necklace and placed it in her palm. Its glow intensified, as if acknowledging its true bearer.

A soft breeze passed through the cavern. The runes on the pedestal faded, then vanished entirely. Silence filled the space.

"Put it on," said Theris.

Suna hesitated. Her gaze traveled across the faces of her companions, searching for their approval. Everyone watched her closely. No doubt in their eyes.

She placed the necklace around her neck.

The gold felt warm against her skin. Softer than she expected. Immediately, the gemstone flared brightly. The runes ignited briefly, then settled into a subtle glow.

"Are you alright?" Aldaren asked.

"Yes… It's warm."

Suna stood motionless. She hoped for… some sensation. An echo. An image. A sign.

But nothing came.

Intrigued, she touched the still-warm gemstone, hoping to sense some hidden energy or shiver.

"Is that all?" she whispered. "I thought… something would happen. Magic, a power…"

Aldaren approached gently, almost tenderly.

"Precisely. It's because you're human, without magic, that the necklace doesn't overwhelm you. It recognizes the one who can wear it without being consumed."

Suna looked up at him uncertainly.

"So… I won't feel anything?"

"No powers, no. But that's fortunate. For an ordinary person, this energy would be overwhelming, possibly even fatal. You bear the Pillar precisely because you can contain it. And that is what makes you special. You're not here to control it, Suna. Your role is to protect it. Believe me, that's already a tremendous burden."

Aldaren's words resonated within her, more deeply than she anticipated.

She lowered her eyes to the glowing gemstone.

She understood now the importance of what she had just accomplished.

The necklace carried a weight she finally recognized.

Not from its magic.

But from responsibility.

Barely had they crossed back over the bridge when a deep rumble shook the cavern. They spun around in unison toward the two dragons.

The dragons stirred, their sinuous bodies undulating through the dust.

Theris brushed his dagger. Aldaren grasped his arm lightly. The dragons displayed no hostility. Suna watched the guardians approach, their serpentine forms appearing endless.

They bowed their heads toward Suna.

"You have passed the trial, human," said the first dragon. "Knowledge grants no power. Bear it wisely."

"Your courage has been acknowledged," continued the second. "Take this. You will need it."

The immense creature opened its jaws, revealing a fragment of finely rolled parchment nestled between its fangs. Then, surprisingly delicately for such a massive being, the dragon placed it gently before them.

"So…" Pharin began casually, "you breathe fire, speak in verse, guard ancient secrets… but you can't deliver a parchment without slobbering all over it?"

Stunned silence fell. Everyone froze.

The dragon inhaled deeply. A heavy, burning breath kicked up a swirling cloud of dust.

Theris stepped back. Suna clenched her jaw. Even Vaelen tensed his wings.

Then a rumbling sound rose from deep within the dragon's throat… but instead of flame, a gravelly laugh filled the cavern.

"Your bravery borders on insolence, little satyr," he said calmly again. "But hold onto it. You will need it."

Pharin, unfazed, sketched a mock salute and opened his mouth to respond. Theris gripped his shoulder firmly, cutting him off before he could push his luck further.

The counselor knelt and gently took the parchment.

"This fragment reveals the West of Mytherra," he said thoughtfully.

Theris traced the lines on the map until his finger rested on a cross-shaped mark.

"Look here," he announced. "A landmark, halfway between Sylvaris and Thalessa's domain."

"Before you reach it, travel first to Sylvaris. What you uncover there will clear the path toward the next Pillar," the dragon instructed.

Without another word, the dragons withdrew, coiling their bodies back into their original posture, becoming impassive guardians once more. Silence returned, as though nothing had ever disturbed it.

Theris carefully tucked the map fragment away.

A single exchange of glances was enough. They knew exactly where to go—and that they would go there together.

They turned toward the exit. Mytherra awaited.

Suna clutched the necklace tightly in her hand.

When they emerged from the cavern, daylight momentarily blinded them.

Suna closed her eyes briefly. The salty breeze brushed gently against her face, fresh and invigorating. She took a deep breath, savoring the open air once more. She felt different now. Stronger. And already focused on what lay ahead.

"Next stop, Balindra," Theris announced, stepping aboard. "Enhugo needs to know what we found."

"What a day…" Suna whispered. "And yet all of this… it's just the beginning."

"We'll be by your side," Aldaren reassured her gently. "All the way."

Suna looked up at him, touched by his simple, sincere promise. A smile lit up her face.

"I know. Without you… I wouldn't have made it."

"You're stronger than you realize," Vaelen added. "And I don't say that lightly."

The crew bustled around them, and soon the ship set course for Port Waste.

Suna enjoyed the calm journey alongside Vaelen. His folded wings caught the fading sunlight. The sky was shifting from orange to purple, the last rays of sun dancing upon the waves. In the distance, she noticed a large two-masted merchant ship. Its midnight-blue hull, subtly trimmed in gold, sailed southward. She briefly wondered what cargo it might carry.

After heartfelt farewells with the captain and his crew, they headed into the bustling streets of Port Waste.

Liore took the lead, guiding them confidently to an inn she knew well, tucked within lively alleyways. Above the doorway, a wooden sign engraved with a seahorse swung gently on two small chains, promising warmth and rest.

Dinner reflected their group perfectly: animated, boisterous, and cheerful.

Pharin improvised a ballad, staying true to his sense of irony. He exaggerated his own feats while downplaying those of his companions. Even Vaelen laughed as the satyr mimed his "heroic" flight from the grasping tentacles.

"If I hadn't seen it myself," Theris remarked, "I might have almost believed you."

"That's the bard's talent," Pharin replied with a wink.

Liore and Suna exchanged amused smiles, enjoying this rare moment of peace.

Gradually, the conversations grew quieter. Fatigue weighed on their eyelids. One by one, they retired to their rooms.

Suna sat down on the bed. The sudden silence contrasted sharply with the tavern's earlier noise. She stared at the necklace. In the dimness, its gem pulsed softly and regularly. She brushed it lightly with her fingertips.

She knew this was only the beginning. But tonight, surrounded by friends, she could rest. Just for a while.

She inhaled deeply. Closed her eyes.

Every victory brings me closer to home. As long as I hold on… it'll be alright. It has to be.

She gripped the necklace, allowing its warmth to replenish her strength.

What lay ahead would be tougher. Less clear. Perhaps even crueler.

But tonight, she felt proud. And nothing, no one, could take that away from her.

On the docks, one of the sailors from the *Black Ink* stepped off the ship.

He slipped away quietly, heading up the narrow alley at the end of the pier.

A quick glance over his shoulder. No one.

He ducked into a low house, unmarked, hidden between two warehouses.

Inside, the air was colder. Darker.

Behind a desk, a man dressed in black looked up.

"I have an important message," said the sailor.

Final

Suna had just taken a decisive step: the Pillar of Knowledge now rested in her hands.

This first victory had strengthened the bonds between her and her companions. It had given them more than a common goal: trust.

She no longer felt alone. Her courage now drew strength from their presence.

Yet, despite this unity, despite the pride in what she'd achieved, another feeling never left her: longing.

For Earth.

Her daily life, family, friends, all her familiar landmarks—everything she'd been forced to leave behind. Those memories haunted her constantly.

Each victory brought her closer to home, but she held no illusions: the journey ahead would be long.

And nothing would come easily.

Zayn, meanwhile, moves in shadow.

With each passing day, his uncertainty grows. This world still escapes him: shifting, foreign, dangerous.

Around him, faces blur.

Thanatos unsettles him. He senses there's something hidden.

Nymeris and Garnius each unsettle him in their own ways—her cold indifference, his brute force. Only Fynna offers him some stability.

He still doesn't fully grasp what this quest involves. He doesn't understand its rules or its stakes.

Yet he moves forward, because every step brings him closer to his mother.

This promise is all he has left.

Even though deep down, he knows the price he must pay may be higher than he imagines.

Two teenagers from Earth, separated by circumstances and by their choices.

Yet they move toward a shared destiny—a destiny that will inevitably bring them together.

In the shadows, the magicians of Mytherra pull the strings of a story that surpasses both their dreams and nightmares.

Soon, their paths will cross. And what they discover will change everything: alliances, conflicts, and truths that may be hard to accept.

This first Pillar, as crucial as it is, was only the beginning.

The true battle has just begun.

Acknowledgments

To Benoît and Simon:

My brothers, attentive readers with precious advice.

Thank you for your support throughout this adventure.

To my mother:

Whose encouragement has always meant so much to me.

Thank you for everything.

Finally, and above all, to Fanny:

My friend and most faithful reader.

Thank you for carefully going through every line,

For being a meticulous proofreader,

And an exceptional assistant.

Without you, this book would never have seen the light of day.

Thank you all for standing by my side.

Lastly, to my readers:

I hope you enjoyed reading this adventure as much as I enjoyed writing it.

Character Glossary

Ætheris

Primordial entity at the very origin of Mytherra. Embodying both light and shadow, she is the source of all magic. Her gradual disappearance threatens the balance of the entire world. She sleeps in Ætherium, the capital city.

Raenos

Supreme guardian of cosmic balance. Wise and fair, he watches over the harmony established by Ætheris. He rules Mytherra from the capital.

The 8 magicians:

Enhugo   (Balindra)

Magician of knowledge, wisdom, and creation. Keeper of ancient lore, he leads Balindra's great library, a center of learning and reflection where scholars and seekers converge.

Ignara   (Pyros)

Mistress of fire and destruction, impulsive and passionate. She reigns over Pyros, an active volcano, and inspires artisans capable of creating objects of exceptional beauty and power.

Sylki   (Sylvaris)

Guardian of earth and forests. Protector of nature and its balance, he watches over Sylvaris, a lush land inhabited by extraordinary creatures.

Thalessa   (Atlantide)

Mistress of seas and oceans, as beautiful as she is unpredictable. She rules the aquatic peoples from Atlantide. Her tumultuous character mirrors the waters she commands—sometimes calm, sometimes merciless.

Shanur   (Solandar)

Bearer of light and hope. Kind-hearted and generous, he trains the finest healers in Solandar. His disciples traverse Mytherra, soothing suffering and inspiring hope.

Ereshkal   (Nekrosys)

Guardian of inevitable ends. She receives the souls of the departed in Nekrosys. She is feared as much as respected, as her domain embodies death and passage to the afterlife, but also promises renewal. Behind her apparent neutrality, she harbors dark ambitions.

Elvira   (Velissia)

Incarnation of arts, beauty, and seduction. As fascinating as elusive, she founded Velissia, a city where artists and dreamers gather to seek inspiration and celebrate aesthetics in all forms. Her captivating aura inspires both genuine admiration and envy.

Nerath   (Quarth)

Lord of war, drawn to strength and glory. He rules Quarth, a warrior city where discipline and courage are the sole recognized values. As brave as he is ruthless, Nerath respects only power proven in battle. His loyalty can only be earned through indisputable strength.

<u>Suna's companions:</u>

Theris

Pragmatic and discreet advisor to Raenos. He prioritizes efficiency over displays of strength. Calm and thoughtful, his advice is precious and often decisive for the group.

Vaelen

Captain of the guard, upright and loyal. This angel with golden wings masters aerial combat and wields a luminous sword capable of generating blinding light. Protective of Suna, he embodies justice and discipline.

Aldaren

Disciple of the Light, deeply benevolent and reassuring. His magic allows him to heal wounds and create protective barriers. His warm presence provides essential comfort to the entire group.

Hestian

Guard of Ætherium, discreet and conscientious. A skilled swordsman who follows orders without question and integrates smoothly into the group. His discretion makes him a quiet yet dependable companion.

Korvel

Guard of Ætherium, robust and determined. Not particularly thoughtful but sincere in his actions, he compensates for his lack of subtlety with loyalty and courage in the face of danger.

Pharin

Joyful satyr and talented musician. Equipped with mischievous humor, he brings levity and optimism to the group. His loyalty to Suna and his companions is unquestionable, although he often enjoys teasing them.

Liore

Disciple of Enhugo, scholar passionate about runes. Curious and occasionally absent-minded, she assists the group with her deep knowledge and analytical mind.

<u>Zayn's companions</u>

Thanatos

The only known dark angel, he is Ereshkal's right-hand man—silent, cold, and intimidating. His menacing appearance and ability to meld into the shadows make him both a feared and respected figure.

Nymeris

A faithful disciple of Ereshkal, cold and distant, she skillfully manipulates shadows. Wary and observant, she impresses Zayn as much as she unsettles him.

Garnius

An impulsive and brutal warrior, devoted to raw strength. Preferring immediate action over intricate plans, he is often loud and unpredictable. His blunt demeanor and exceptional strength make him a formidable fighter.

Volkran

An exceptional craftsman, he is immune to fire and can control it at will. He is the creator of Ignarion, a powerful automaton that accompanies him in battle.

Fynna

An undine sent by Thalessa, empathetic and warm toward Zayn. She regularly attempts to ease tensions within the group and reassure the young boy. Her water-based magic and keen intuition make her a discreet yet invaluable ally.

www.ingramcontent.com/pod-product-compliance
Lightning Source LLC
Chambersburg PA
CBHW071728150726
47998CB00005B/1551